Brendan Cowell is an Aust

born in Cronulla, New South Wales, and completed a Bachelor of Arts in Theatre/Media at Charles Sturt University, Bathurst.

Brendan's plays have been produced by prominent theatre companies in Australia and internationally, and he has received the Patrick White Playwrights' Award, the Griffin Award and the Philip Parsons Young Playwright's Award. Brendan played the popular character Tom in *Love My Way* and wrote many episodes of the critically acclaimed television drama series which won the AFI Award for Best Television Drama Series for each of its three seasons (2005–2007). He has played the lead role in feature films, including the 2007 crime drama *Noise* for which he was awarded a Film Critics Circle Award and nominated for an AFI Award; the World War I drama *Beneath Hill 60* and the rom-com *I Love You Too.* He played *Hamlet* in a 2009 Bell Shakespeare production.

Brendan lives in Newtown, Sydney, and is a committed supporter of the Cronulla Sharks rugby league team.

You can follow Brendan at twitter.com/brendancowell.

[illegible] Australian actor, writer and director. He was [illegible]

HOW IT FEELS

BRENDAN COWELL

PICADOR
Pan Macmillan Australia

First published 2010 in Picador by Pan Macmillan Australia Pty Limited
1 Market Street, Sydney

Reprinted 2011

A CIP catalogue record for this book is available from
the National Library of Australia

9781405039291 (pbk.)

A823.4

Typeset in 11.5/16 pt Golden Cockerel by Midland Typesetters, Australia
Printed in Australia by McPherson's Printing Group

For Bart

Either you turn your back forever on those who have seen your youth, or else you will admit its nakedness, and even shame has some sweet melancholy.

– Patrick White

Part 1

1

This was not how I dreamt it.

Clutching the frame of the too-high bed with my left hand, trying to unlock a Target sports bra with the other, erection blasting out of my groin like one of the pylons that held up my school, I now knew why virginity was referred to as a 'loss.'

I mean, all the crap my two best friends had taught me about 'doing it' was doing my head in. This was Stuart, my six-foot-two Ken doll rooting expert whom I had known since the first day of Kindergarten:

'Here's the maths: If she lets you touch her tits for ten seconds that means you can suck on them, if she lets you suck on them for fifteen seconds that means you can finger her gash. If she lets you finger her gash for thirty seconds that means you can give her the stick. Give her the stick, Nelly!'

And Gordon, my best mate in the world, five foot seven inches and stocky from the United Kingdom:

'Chicks want it, that's the look they're giving you. Even if they say they want to wait, they don't. It's up to you Cronk, cos chicks want a bloke to take the steering wheel.'

We had started kissing in the computer room where Courtney was showing me brochures of the two universities she was pumped about, when I dunked my mouth into the ramp of her neck–shoulder connection, letting my tongue and lips dot the tarmac of her milk-dipped skin, luring alto gasps and moans from her encouragement place. She was seemingly stoked by all this, as instigating wasn't what I was known for and Courtney was tiring of this – she had wanted to have sex since we first got together over a year ago and we saw each other every day, which made the past twelve and a half months pretty strained and weird. Just a week ago she said I may as well have gone to war.

Down the beige carpeted take-off strip we moved into her bedroom like Torville and Dean, so eager. She pushed my left hand up and through her summer dress, where I found her leg, I found her inner leg, I found wetness and the heat. Poised, I looked down into her eyes and like every other time my dick connected with my soul and the world went static and floppy.

We were the wrong age for love and yet it was all we could think about. Who were we to pretend we were capable of such sophistication? Pubic hair was only just arriving in patches – we had no idea how to relate to the other sex, and yet we were insane with perversion. Erections launching their campaign out of nowhere and often too; I had planned to wait until I was at least forty till I got a girlfriend, if at all.

Not to say I hadn't noticed Courtney before. Of course I had, she was my style after all, a style I liked to call 'bookish and smart' and Gordon liked to re-label 'weird and sad with father issues.' I often wanked off to invented scenarios of her playing tennis or reading poetry naked, but I never ever imagined we would actually *date each other in real life.* She was too beautiful for me, too exotic and otherworldly with her big green eyes and sharp facial bones. Her brown hair was long and thick and she was really polite and curious, always reading at lunch, or lifting up her glasses to peer out at the ocean which set off from the base of our little school. I did catch her looking at me in 3 unit English a couple of times, and we did have a laugh that time we were asked to co-narrate the story of *The Taming of the Shrew* in less than a minute in front of everyone, but still, no way! I was the quiet theatre boy with the satchel and the cigarettes and she was really something. I tell you, a genuinely unique person who wasn't afraid to use her brain. This was not so common at De La Salle High School, where ninety-six percent of students prided themselves on 'bludging'; if you were seen to be trying too hard you copped it large. The enigma of Courtney deepened when her younger brother suicided. Tommy was a real popular kid, and no one saw it coming. After the funeral, *which it seemed the whole fucking Shire attended,* I spotted her in the corner drinking Fanta on her own. I don't know what came over me – I'm such a loser I never talk to chicks, or people for that matter – but seriously, one second I am looking at her through an archway, the next thing I know I'm sitting next to her, sitting *with* her, staring at her tiny knees through the lace of her black funeral leggings. We sat there for a minute or two, breathing in and not doing much, when she took my hand and said, with a million cracks in her voice: 'Will you walk with me?'

By the end of Year 11 we had conveniently altered our trails and started walking home by the same route, passing each other and nodding, then 'hello.' A month or two of waves and small chats then like *whoosh,* ritual had us in a spirited, almost gay canter come bell time. Every afternoon at 3.15 pm we would flee the school grounds to the manicured lawns of Woolooware Road to buy pine-lime Splices at the brick-brown strip mall Gumnut Village like there was a show tune behind us. Then out past the eyes of the main street we'd scale the tall snaky track of Burraneer Reserve, smoke Drum by the boat ramp and drift by the gully where the yabbies breed. We'd hold hands and swing our arms all the way home, talking about school, about the people at school, about life after school, about our fucking families and the meaning of life, loping at that gorgeous three-quarter pace reserved for turtles, old people and seventeen-year-old lovers who in their hormone circus feel every drop of rain, every car that passes and every shift of thumb in the hand that holds theirs. And this suited me; it was playful, innocent, and still miles away from things I had seen in some of Stuart's VHS like 'fingering Asians', 'fucking hard' and 'sluts that squirt'.

I loved Courtney and it wasn't long before I told her. She needed to know there was love in this world for her and I wasn't one of those dickheads who couldn't express such stuff. Yeah, I was quiet, but I wasn't a moron, if something needed to be said, I said it. But like my mum told me: 'If nothing needs to be said, then don't say anything.' And I didn't. Until I met her, and all of a sudden I couldn't shut up about things. It was like we had both been half-asleep for ages, then woken up by the other and those magical little hummingbirds of love. I loved everything about her, and I didn't care how dark she got. If anything it was what I loved most, the veil of pain that fell across her face most of the day, and all of the night. My life was pretty drama-less, whereas hers was riddled with hell, and for some reason I couldn't wait to get over there, where the clouds hung low in the living room and her grieving, torn-apart mother Nina made fruit whips in the kitchen like a mad woman. Death crippled the big old house, and it felt real. I liked it.

My house was boring in comparison to hers, so I just hung out there all the time; with Mum always at the hospital working shifts and my sister Agatha asleep or baking cakes, no one seemed to notice I was gone. Whenever I felt like I had overstayed my welcome I would say to Courtney 'I'll go' and she would say 'You don't have to' and I would say 'Ok, I won't.'

Jill, Tamsin, Fiona, Shauna, Caroline, Bryony, Siobhann, Daniela, Faye, Leisa, Maria, Emma, Wong-Shu and most of the Year 12 girls had lost their peach in back seats, basements, friends' houses, classrooms and even toilet cubicles over the last five years, but not Courtney Gonzales, who time and again resisted the advances of wogs and surfers and even one teacher. She swam against the currents of her 'easy' time, instead waiting in the wings to find a guy who she believed was worthy of what my mother called 'the great intrusion.'

Stalling, I cupped Courtney's breasts, recalling the advice Stuart had offered me so freely. As I started counting to ten I realised how stupid this was – I had permission! I had more than permission; Courtney was gagging for it . . . I just hadn't told the boys that. I mean, I'd vaguely told them of long heated sessions of '69' and explained that she was 'almost ready', but I hadn't told them the exact truth. *I* was the reason why Courtney and I were still in *Adrian Mole* world not *Debbie Does Dallas*.

Gasps of hot air jetted out of Courtney's mouth as I teased the edges of her southern place. She liked this, how I'd duck and dive, threatening to finger her deep, then not. I was a performer, using performance to hide the frightening monster that sex was to me. It was now, I thought, in this golden afternoon on results day, that I would finally 'get there' and be able to call my two friends and say 'It's done, ok?' But those eyes, those big green eyes of hers, they bore right into me with crippling force. She wanted it too much; the space Tommy left in her, she wanted me to fill it. And I couldn't. She looked too young and too scared, almost like she didn't really want it either, she just needed it. I couldn't stick it in and fuck her pain away. I did not know how to fuck at all, let alone as therapy. Those eyes, pleading dumbly at me from below, saying 'just do this thing so it is done', they were too loud. She didn't want me, she didn't even want this, she just wanted it over. My dick went soft and my girlfriend knew it was gone again.

Courtney and I had met at the corner of Burraneer Bay and Gannons roads at 8 am that morning, kissed by the swings, bought two takeaway cappuccinos and made our way down to the post office to open our HSC results. To open up the rest of our lives with a rip. Courtney, being a complete brainiac, had nailed 4 unit maths, French, legal studies and 3 unit English, scoring a blazing 99.1 Tertiary Entrance Rank, whereas I, spending most of Years 11 and 12 smoking and reading Metaphysical Poetry, scored a modest 74.45. Courtney and I had discussed it and set our plans in stone. I would apply to do a Bachelor of Arts at Sydney Uni, or UNSW, or even Macquarie out in Ryde, and she would go for law at one of the same. We would live together in Glebe and cook and fuck and make interesting friends on campus. Planning my future with her was the most fun I had ever had. Courtney was incredible, and her future would be the same. Given what she had *been through* I imagined her as some sort of legal counsellor, helping those in need. Her mind was brilliant but her heart was the true phenomenon.

The only thing was, I hadn't discussed it with Gordon yet, and I still had no idea how to. We hadn't been apart for more than a day since we'd met five years earlier in Year 8, and the idea of going our separate ways dropped so hard neither of us could even speak of it. So we didn't.

I rolled off Courtney and she pulled up her undies. 'What is so wrong with me that you do this? Am I that ugly?'

'No! We'll do it tonight!' I said. 'Tonight at the party . . . your mum's just outside.'

Courtney did her bra back up. 'I can't believe this!' she fumed.

'I want it to be special,' I said.

'It feels really fucking special now!'

'I'm sorry, Courtney. I just want to make it something we'll never forget,' I said, kissing the dent her glasses had left. She smiled and nodded. God knows how much more she could put up with.

'Look at your funny penis.' Courtney flicked my cock, the culprit. She'd forgiven me, again, but I could see in her eyes that she was getting pretty bored of the prevarication and I felt for her. I wanted it bad too, but the weight of it always won out. The vagina, to me, was like one of those national parks the teachers led you into on orienteering day. They give you a compass and a hat and you're on your own. I had no sense of direction and the woods went deep and curved endlessly into themselves.

Courtney kissed me full and open on the mouth, swirling her tongue around the back of my teeth as she gripped the middle of my chest with a threat and promise. 'Tonight . . . or else . . .'

She disappeared into the bathroom with the flash of a sky-blue Cronulla Sharks towel, leaving me squashed against the corner of her bedhead where I met with the fifteen ceramic elephants that stood on her bedside table. The elephants were from all sorts of places and people; whenever it was time to give Courtney something everyone thought 'elephant.' Courtney loved elephants;

she said they had a 'quiet grace' about them, and that if she was an animal she would want to be an elephant. I adored this in her, but today they were no longer my friends, today they were judging me, having witnessed my failure at the edge of the river bank. So I rolled over and away, where I was met with a blu-tacked bit of poem I had written her a week after Tommy's funeral.

I am this thing
I am this thing that needs to go
I love my sister and my sport
Love the way the water feels
But I am this thing
I am this thing that needs to go
From the darkness
Beneath the surface
From the spaces
You don't swim in
It's not your thing, sister
Your thing is living
You glorious thing

Two things struck me as I read the poem: (1) I had stolen the style and structure from one of Leonard Cohen's *Book of Mercy* poems, and (2) I had arrogantly assumed the position of first-person narrator – ie Courtney's dead brother. Artists can be such cockheads.

The smell of chopped fruit flowed from the kitchen where Courtney's mum would be hacking into pineapple and kiwi with a cleaver. I knew Courtney would be more than five minutes in the bathroom so I started to wank, thinking in montage about Courtney in the shower and Nina in the kitchen. It was always better this way and not like orienteering at all.

2

Since the sudden and theatrical suicide of her fifteen-year-old son Tommy, Nina Gonzales had got way into making fruit whips. Something about the whirling mess of colour, the slutty integration of flavour, or perhaps the dull, thudding vibration of the blender made her stand there for hours on end pushing orange, pineapple, kiwi and mint deep down into the tall glass cylinder, then flicking up the metal lever to violently whip fruit into beverage. We all knew how weird it was, but no one dared stop her; hell hath no fury like a woman blending.

Tommy was a super-bright kid who had been named Student Leader in Year 7, 8, 9 and, finally, 10. He was loved by every teacher and student who came into contact with him, and his English essays were always so opinionated and cool that kids would talk about them in the playground. Tommy also volunteered at Special Education twice a week, reading Roald Dahl novels out loud with such warmth and diction.

But outside school was where he really came alive; Tommy could surf big waves, kick a conversion from the sideline (in the rain), and when he'd cleaned up a six-pack or two of cold tins he could do a reckless, gravelly cover of The Offspring's 'Come Out and Play'. He was famous for it.

Fourteen weeks, four days and eight hours before Tommy died he met a girl named Bianca. Tommy had already lost his virginity to Year 10 Captain Angela Chapman, but everything from before disappeared when Bianca took position.

Courtney hated Bianca from the outset. She knew she was trouble and she was right. 'Something rotted inside her,' Courtney told me, on our first walk after the funeral. Bianca had such a strong effect on Tommy that he no longer surfed, his grades plummeted and the Special Ed kids were left to read *The BFG* on their own.

Then one overcast Friday close to school break, Bianca met Tommy at 'their spot' by Lilli Pilli Baths and broke up with him. She had 'found someone else' or said something about 'the wrong head space right now'. Tommy was never fully capable of explaining it, apparently. Then he was gone.

The following Saturday Tommy hanged himself from a tree in Lilli Pilli Park. He called Nina from the phone booth half an hour before, telling her what he was about to do and how it wasn't her fault, or Courtney's, or their dad Eric's; he just couldn't go on without Bianca. As soon as Nina realised the finality of the phone call, she wrote on a bit of calendar with texta and Eric read it and jumped in the Subaru with Courtney beside him screaming to go, and go faster. But they arrived too late, Tommy's brilliant frame already swinging in the morning air.

Making my way into the kitchen I was struck by the way Nina's buttocks shook in her black leggings as she gripped the thick glass of the Breville blender.

Nina was way fit for her age, a taller, yet almost identical, 'vintage' version of Courtney, her skin slightly darker from the weekly home-tanning sessions (another thing she'd picked up since the death of her son) and her eyes, though slightly smaller than Courtney's, were the same deep green. Her good breasts pointed out and up from within whatever they were within, and her voice was low and husky. Stuart would often smack me in the neck, jibing that I had chosen the *second*-hottest chick in the Gonzales family, and he wasn't far wrong.

'Hi, Mrs Gonzales.' I moved through the tall foyer, skimming my fingers on the exposed-brick wall. Nina instantly buttoned off the blender and turned to greet me, wet-eyed and frantically still.

'Neil, hello, would you like a fruit whip?'

'I'd love one!' I am not a massive fan of fruit-driven drinks, but I'd happily guzzle a gallon a day if it made Nina happy.

'Congratulations on your results, Courtney told me you got enough for arts or communications. You and Courtney can get the train in from Sutherland station – big uni students travelling together!'

I leant on the marble counter. I felt strangely comfortable in Nina's presence, sometimes even more comfortable with her than her daughter. Relating to Nina came without all the expectation and fear that were so abundantly present with every look, word or touch involving Courtney. With Nina everything was just so cool.

'Yeah, not a bad result, I guess, Mrs G.'

'Not bad? You topped drama and 3 unit English! Your mother must be over the moon.'

'I haven't told her yet. She's still sleeping off the night shift.'

Nina poured the smoothie into two tall metal milkshake cups she kept cool in the fridge. 'How is your mother?'

'Oh yeah, she's ok, thanks. Still working graveyard at the hospital.'

Nina popped a sprig of mint on the top of my orange-pink drink and handed it over.

'You're ok though, aren't you, Neil?' Nina took some of the counter herself, her eyes cracked and meaningful.

'Yeah, generally I'm pretty ok. Glad school is over. Is that what you mean, Mrs Gonzales?'

'Yes. No. I guess. With your parents being apart. Not being together.'

'Um . . .'

'It's ok. You don't have to say anything. I just wonder how you go . . . how kids go . . . in that situation.'

Well aware of the strain Eric and Nina's marriage had been under since Tommy's death, I did my best to stay cool and play naive. This kind of real-life performance was something I really enjoyed. I was good at it. She went on.

'Eric doesn't talk to us anymore. He just waters the garden or sits on his chair in the garage listening to the horse races on the radio.'

'I'm not that into horse races.'

'I just worry about my daughter.'

I had several speeches in mind, all of which would work in this situation, so I chose the simplest and most positive. 'At first I was pretty devastated when Dad left, but then after a while I realised it was kind of cool.'

Nina snapped, 'How can it be *cool* for a teenage girl *not* to have her father around when she needs him the most?'

Man, did I wanna reach out and kiss Nina, hug the fuck out of her with my whole body, like I would when someone in my Year 12 drama class had opened themselves up, divulged something, or exposed vulnerability. Or even if they'd simply nailed a scene or improvisation exercise. But this was not drama class, and this was not an exercise, this was a house with spikes in it.

'Well, you become friends with your parents is how. I meet Dad for coffee some Saturdays up at Miranda Fair. We might go shopping for shaving equipment or buy a bike pump or go to the movies. And we'll talk about our weeks and he'll ask me about school and Courtney and Mum a bit. He doesn't really *listen* that well, my dad, but you know, he rolls up, which is cool. I guess what I'm saying, Mrs Gonzales, is that you develop a relationship with your parents that you somehow can't when you're sharing a roof. And you know, the Sutherland Shire is pretty conservative; it's just *divorce* but still everyone tiptoes around me as if I'm some abuse victim or I've lost my ability to see, when I really haven't suffered at all. I was just relieved that the yelling had stopped, and I could finally get some sleep. And anyway, Mrs G, you can visit me and Courtney in Glebe, stay over even – we're going to have the coolest place!'

Nina's heart lifted up into her neck and eyes, burning the inside of her forehead. She had obviously never considered an empty house. With nothing but the memory of the three *gone people.* One who left her for a rope, the other who left her for horses, and now her daughter, who would leave her for study and fun in the city with her boyfriend. I'd fucked up. Of course Courtney hadn't filled her in on our plans yet, the woman was as frail as quail bones.

'This is a beautiful fruit whip you made me, Mrs Gonzales.' I smiled.

'You're a good kid, Neil.' Nina inched closer, and as she always did after I finished a fruit whip, ran two fingers across my face and said, 'So like Tommy in this light.'

I didn't mind. Whatever helped. But a minute passed like this, and I heard the shower stop, so I thought I should wrap it up.

'Mrs Gonzales?'

Nina shot back to reality, removing her hand from my cheek and quickly transferring her attention to her untouched smoothie. She snorted and gurgled at the drink until it was all sucked down her throat. I watched in awe as she pulverised the drink, noticing her body and mind filling back up as the fruit went swiftly down. She breathed out and spoke with both breasts heaving to the new beat of vitamins A through E. My dick was growing thicker in my Bonds.

'Men don't talk, they just . . . decide on their own.'

I nodded at this horrible, stripping truth. It was fucked, the way this woman had been left here to blend on her own. But as waves of thick afternoon light poured through the window onto Nina's bronze, freckled, forty-four-year-old neck and breasts, there was nothing tragic about her in my mind; she was a ripe goddess one hundred percent and I had a fat dick and I didn't even lean over myself to hide it.

With a clip-clop-clip-clop-clop and a thud, Courtney appeared in the brick proscenium arch of the Gonzales home. Never had she looked so complete, so beautiful. Like she had torn all the teenage poetry off her walls and let herself be the Amazonian grownup God had intended. She wore a black vintage dress with a choking frilly neck. The dress curved tightly around her hips stopping an inch or so above the knee where her awesome leather boots (that we had bought from Paddington Markets) nearly met the hem. She had spent the bathroom session working on her face, colouring her eyes, lashes and lids blue-black, and her lips sienna red. She wanted that Courtney Love/Kate Moss gothic heroin-chic look and she'd achieved it. I, for one, was scared.

'Babe, you look so incredible.' My voice was higher than normal.

'Do I look like Christina Ricci in *The Addams Family*?' Courtney asked in her self-deprecating way. 'Like totally fucking depressive?'

Nina started crying again so I moved over to the sink and put my arms around her. As I stood there holding her in the kitchen, my cock started to grow more, flicking out of my undies and slapping my leg. I turned to look at Courtney, who was shuffling with the contents of her handbag.

I can do this tonight, I thought.

3

Sutherland Shire is otherwise known as 'the birthplace of the nation.' Captain James Cook first sailed into the sandy wasteland of Kurnell in 1770 and thought 'Why not set up here?' For eight days Captain Cook and his scientists and mariners scoured and mapped the area. One of the *Endeavour*'s crew, Forby Sutherland, died on shore, so Captain Cook named the port in his memory – which is pretty depressing if you ask me. Now over two hundred thousand people live in the leafy, sunburnt oasis, which never ceased to amaze me and Courtney. We walked to and from school every day, past the thousand brown-brick houses, up the popular big-lawn streets like Gannons Road, Gunnamatta Road, Burraneer Bay Road and hardly saw anyone! There was the odd old man in lemon shorts watering his driveway, or a skater-boy practising his grinds on the curve of a neighbour's guttering, and, yes, the sporadic passing of white Holden Commodores and orange Mitsubishi Magnas, but really, for a thriving, well-populated, truly historic shire – where the fuck was everyone? Hiding under their couches in fear of terror? Asleep? Or just making sausages mash sausages mash sausages mash?

*

Linking her right index finger with my left pinkie, Courtney led me up Jacaranda Road. We were free as the wind for an entire night – and soon for the term of our natural lives. My mother was working the graveyard shift for the fifth night in a row and Nina was totally cool with Courtney staying over at my empty house. Well, my sister would be there but my sister being there was like no one being there. Nina had even shown support of our impending union with a series of winks and double eyebrow raisings as we left the house arm in arm. In months past, Courtney, me, Stuart and Gordon used to work together constructing stories for our parents, of houses we were *meant to be* staying over at. Sometimes the strategy got way out of hand with everyone allegedly staying over at everyone else's place, so that no one had any place to go and we'd all end up huddled together in a church or a park or an abandoned tunnel, wondering why we went to such efforts to freeze to death away from our inviting beds. The only good thing about staying out all night in the cold (apart from the sense of camaraderie, the freedom to smoke cigarettes, and the sunrise) was that at 6 am McDonald's opened, offering a 'bottomless cup of coffee' for $1.20. We'd all sit there, battered, cold and wired, drinking this horrible black muck and feeling so alive because we had just stayed out all night and not much happened, but no one knew about it. Most of the time we ended up at my place though, cos Mum didn't get home from the hospital till eight and Agatha didn't care what we did; she had no friends of her own so mine added some flavour to her life, even if they were seven years younger than her. I felt bad sometimes for Mum, working hard through the night to provide us with food and shelter, while we sat up giggling and smoking on the deck, and eating all the bread.

My mother the eccentric, at least by Cronulla standards. A buoyant, inquisitive woman, always quoting the *Sydney Morning Herald*. My mother imported hormones from America. She had been menopausal since I could remember, her moods were fully mad, and often resulted in her closing the door on us and sobbing for half a day, or slapping Agatha across the face in the kitchen, or chasing me around the house with a wooden spoon.

Mum was a mess of thoughts, feelings and contradictions, and this became brutally clear the moment you entered our house. There was shit everywhere. Mostly papers and books, accompanied by half-started knitting projects and tapestry adventures, a busted blender turned upside down in the hallway, a box of cutlery from St Vincent de Paul's on the side table, sixteen dresses from an auction, and a collection of allen keys on the counter beside a pincushion and twenty-three used tea bags she was saving for the garden. Dad hated mess. When he came home from a day of driving classes he wanted nothing more than a cold beer in front of the news. The beer was doable, but when Dad sat down there'd either be a candelabra jutting into his behind, or a box of useless jewellery found at a garage sale in Kirrawee taking up half the space. Either way he was never settled. Dad would extract the object from his buttock, and it would begin. Dad calling her a 'failed housewife' from the living room and her taking it all submissively from the kitchen until one too many barbs hit the mark and she snapped, retrieving a frozen popper from the freezer and hurling it at his head.

Then Dad left, and the house got considerably tidier, in case he came over again I assumed, but he never did, he just sat out the front in his instructor car until I went out front to meet him. He had left the clutter behind and nothing could make him go back. Dad once said, 'Lonely people are drawn to clutter because it makes them feel popular.' Perhaps Mum sensed he would leave her one day, so she cluttered up the house in advance.

*

'So irenic,' I said, as we walked past a dozen silent trees and houses, Courtney's lacy black dress sailing softly along in the half-wind.

'Ironic?'

'No, *irenic*, it's all so irenic.'

'What does irenic mean?'

I paused, enjoying the knowledge. 'Peaceful.'

We mooched down Burraneer Bay Road, past Caringbah's local swimming pool and around the back of the Anglican church where a fresh sign for the season shouted *God believes in New Year's resolutions too: Get fit, lose ten kilograms, go to church!*

'Did Mum make you drink another fruit whip?'

I loved talking about Nina and her idiosyncrasies. 'Yeah, pineapple, kiwi, orange and mint again.' I smiled with the corner of my lips.

'You're so good with her.'

'Ah, not really, no. Fruit whips are good for you, right?'

Courtney grinned and kissed my ear, but her smile faded and dipped, twisting her face into its most familiar form: the long shape of despair.

'Do you think Mum will lose it when we tell her about moving to the city?'

'I told her,' I admitted.

'You told her? Shit, Neil . . .'

'She seemed ok with it, really she did – especially when I told her she could come stay with us.'

Courtney stopped on the kerb and took me in her arms.

'I never want to lose you.'

'You don't have to,' I said into one of her little ears.

We walked on, talking about university and all that came with it. Our favourite topic was what clothes we would wear and what hairstyles we would experiment with, for once we left the Shire we could finally become the people we had always wanted to be.

'I want a "Christianity Sucks" t-shirt!' I said loudly.

'"God is Gay".'

'"The Ramones".'

'Who are The Ramones?'

'I don't care, I just want the shirt.'

'Cool,' she said.

'And in the night we will make economical meals in our tall terrace house.'

'That we share with a lesbian and two Asian students at the bottom of Glebe Point Road.'

'Near the markets.'

'We'll drink at the local pubs.' Courtney gestured the guzzling of beer.

'And fuck every night on our futon which we bought for thirty-five bucks from a guy who left his phone number on fingers of paper stuck to the campus noticeboard.'

'Heaven forbid, we will actually fuck, Neil?'

I punched her lightly on the shoulder and she fell off the kerb onto the road.

'You'll see,' I said, winking at her with smooth promise. 'Your mum should talk to someone, Courtney, like an analyst or a priest or something.'

'Not a priest. What the fuck do priests know about real-life problems? All they do is sit in cold rooms drinking light beer and trying not to think about little boys.'

'Well, a therapist then.'

'Yeah, I know, but she won't. She blames therapy ... well Dad blames therapy and drugs for why Tommy did it – and she believes what Dad believes.'

'Parents are so scared.'

'Yeah,' Courtney replied. 'I definitely think we'll be different though, as parents. We'll be much more in touch and aware.'

'Yeah.' I nodded like a cocksure American as we turned down Willarong Road past a young boy reluctantly washing his father's boat. 'Baby boomers got all the cheap real estate and inheritance but their parents couldn't really teach them much about the world. Kind of feel sorry for our parents.'

'Our kids will be so lucky!'

We rounded the last corner to Stuart's house, tummies grumbling and foreheads dotted with nervous sweat. It was a thrilling type of trauma; the final party of our school life, where everything would happen and nothing would be left behind.

'You going to dance with your hands in front of your body?' I asked her, pinching her hips.

Instantly she went to dancing, clicking her fingers to every second beat, as she famously liked to do whenever she was smashed.

'Ha ha!' I said, and she kissed me on the mouth.

'Did Gordon tell you what he got on his TER, bub?' Courtney asked as we descended Grandview Parade.

'No,' I laughed, remembering the brief phone call I'd had with my best mate earlier that day. 'He just mumbled something like "the whole thing is shit".'

'What do you think he was trying to say?'

This was a familiar game only we played in private; me or Courtney would relay one of Gordon's angry, stunted sentences then translate it to the other in grand detail. We saw it not as mockery but as a celebration of our friend's efficient delivery.

'I, Gordon Braithwaite, believe that the Higher School Certificate is not simply a measure of man's intellect, but a measure of something far, far lesser than acumen – that is, "memory retention".

I, Gordon Braithwaite, am a highly intelligent man but I have smoked way too many cones to remember fucking *logarithms* or what year Hitler died or whatever.'

Courtney was giggling so I ploughed on, doing Gordon's low, British speak to perfection. 'The Higher School Certificate is therefore a load of bullshit and I should get full marks because I can suck more bong than any fucker here and I play the drums!'

'Sounds like he got less than fifty.' Courtney bit her bottom lip in concern.

'Yeah, he doesn't want to go to university anyway – wants to make cash.'

'He is totally right though – if that *was* him speaking. The HSC is a ridiculous construct, the whole thing should be wiped out and re-imagined, gearing itself towards the realities of the workplace, not some meaningless political quiz for private school kids – alienating the weak!'

I was not exactly sure about her use of 'alienating the weak' but I loved it when she fired up (her nostrils flaring like a boxer's cheeks after the ninth round); these strong and driven conversations made me feel like a demigod, above the rest of the world in vibe, insight and general coolness. These were the chats of the new generation, and me and my hot girlfriend were at the fucking helm: we would take our brilliant love all the way to university and never ever apologise again!

The university adventure was sealed and locked in beyond doubt or speculation until a friend of mine from *OnStage* (the Year 12 state drama finals), Julien, told me about a university around three and a half hours west of Sydney in a small town south of Orange (weirdly, Orange is the home of the apple). Then he arrived at my door with his mum in a silver Tarago playing the *Hair* soundtrack.

The humble university grounds sat wedged between the chilly, pie-shop-littered town (every country town makes 'the world's best pie') and the iconic, snaking raceway, Mount Panorama. The morning wind whipped our eyes and noses. Julien hugged me as if we had crossed the Tasman in a kayak together without a map.

'Nelll-eeeeee! Look at us goooooo!'

Inside the theatre/media complex, tie-dyed third-year students massaged each other on crash mats, laughing and gesturing five times louder than necessary, stinking fabulously of Drum tobacco, sweet chilli sauce and carpet. Finally, after ten years of being labelled a 'wanker' or an 'arty-farty wanker' or an 'arty-farty wanker faggot' at school, I felt as regular as tasty cheese, shuffling down the corridor, eyes zipping over every inch of the building.

I performed Edmund from *King Lear*, plus my original HSC monologue *Belinda* (better than ever!), though I failed miserably when thrown three sand-filled balls and asked to juggle. I was moved from room to room participating in improvisations, neutral mask workshops, breathing exercises, yoga and ice-breakers. The whole experience was a blur, but on the way home, as Julien's mum pushed the Tarago past gorgeous postage-stamp towns like Oberon, Blackheath, Leura and Springbrook, I couldn't tear my thoughts away from the open vibe and crisp, thrilling air of the campus, and ringing in my ears was the last thing Dick Hindmarsh (the bearded head of theatre) said to me as he packed up the crash mats and left the rehearsal space: 'Don't come here if you want to be an actor, Neil, come here if you want to create! Do you want to make something beautiful, Neil Cronk? I have a feeling you do.'

The big bulging trees that lined the wide streets, and the zestful eyes of the (stinking) students gripped my lungs – making me breathe in short, sharp pockets all the way home. I didn't know what I wanted to do with my creativity, all I knew was that I wanted to do a lot, and this place seemed to embrace that very notion. I couldn't help but feel it was a shame not to look into it further, but I couldn't and I wouldn't. I wouldn't. I'd stay quiet like I always did, like they always told me to.

Years 7 and 8 were a bit of a nightmare for me. I just couldn't find any friends. I mean I wasn't mad searching for them, with a sign on my head saying *Please be my friend I'm a deadset loser*, but it would have been nice. I was friends with Matthew Smith from my maths class for a while. I'd go over to his house on Saturdays and listen to Faith No More and shoot baskets in the drive. But then he (overnight) became friends with David O'Brien and the next thing I knew I had an appointment on the oval after school to fight David and I had never even met the guy, really. I went to the principal and told him about the fight, hoping he would stop it, but he just peered down at me from beneath his bushy grey eyebrows and said, 'There are certain things a man has to go through before he becomes a man.' Which made no sense at all, because a man would not have to go through anything to become one if he was already being referred to as a man.

I unlocked my bike and rode off in the opposite direction from the oval. I knew I was in for it tomorrow, but I didn't care: I was no fighter, especially when said duel was against someone I did not know or hold any ill feeling towards.

The next day at lunch Matthew Smith asked me to play cricket with him and his friends against the big wall. I thought, 'Oh, this is a turnaround', and took the tennis ball in my hand. I strode in to bowl with a relieved disposition, but I never got to roll the arm over, for David O'Brien was in the umpiring position and he slammed a cream bun in my face just as I made the delivery crease. It was a planned move, as everyone broke out in laughter. Especially Matt.

I stood up, wiped the cream off my face, walked over to David and punched him in the nose the way my father had taught me in the living room. The entire school surrounded us, everyone screaming 'Fight! Fight! Fight!' I wondered whether they would all be cheering 'Dance! Dance! Dance!' if David and I had been dancing together.

David got up and stomped towards me, at which point I recalled his position as captain of Sutherland district's rugby union team and wished I could retract my right cross to the nose. He put a three punch on me and I fell to the ground, but I stood up, dizzily, and as he gloated to his friends I thumped him in the neck and again in the face. He fell over into the bubblers, and I swear a few guys were cheering for me now, I could hear my name through the fog of static. I'd shown some sort of masculinity and the masses were appreciative. Then David changed temperatures, holding my jaw in one hand as he delivered several blows to my mouth and eyes with the other. I woke up in the sick bay with Miss Flynn dousing me in Dettol.

Conclusion: I was better off not having friends. So I took to reclusion with fierce commitment, spending recess in the library reading about the Aztecs, and lunchtime in the music room listening to the Christian band rehearsing their dynamic set of hymns and gospels. I grew fond of such tracks as 'Here I Am, Lord', and often found myself humming 'On Eagle's Wings' on my bike ride home. Of course Stuart was in my life, but he dropped in and out like a spider, and then took off to smash someone or root someone or something. Mum worried about me; I even overheard her talking to Dad in the kitchen, asking him if he thought I was gay or possibly even autistic. But Dad just shrugged and said, 'I don't know,' and wandered off for a dump and a shower.

That winter I did think about killing myself, but to tell the truth I couldn't choose a way. Hanging seemed really difficult, drowning just sounded so ugly with your head exploding and all, and I hated the sight of blood so there was no way I could slit my wrists. I also found the whole suicide thing so unoriginal; it seemed everyone in Cronulla was doing it. So I plodded along in my ennui, declaring to myself that to continue on was braver than to feebly give in to the gloom and fuck up those who loved you.

Then Gordon arrived – and it was, I'm not joking, an arrival. One day I was walking through the sea of kids at school in my noble isolation, chewing on a wholegrain sandwich of Vegemite and lettuce, the next day I'm sitting with this British kid, and I'd never felt so good. Is it ok to say you fall in love with friends?

Gordon was my first true mystery and I was drawn to him accordingly. So much of my life in the Shire was known and tangible, until this spotty little British chap landed on its shores, with his restless leg and scared grey eyes. He looked so lost, scrunched up by the bins, flipping a child-sized soccer ball in his hands. Close to invisible he was, though not to me. I saw him across the yard and he saw me, two estranged boys, mislaid in the cruel circus of their age group. I walked over to him like I walked over to Courtney at her brother's funeral, without a thought, just pure instinct, and I was right, I was so right.

I was giggly and alive around him. He was my age but I always felt so much younger. He had done stuff, and endured stuff, lived a million more lives than me. All I had done was write poems, hide from sports carnivals and play music in my room as my parents argued about clutter, whereas Gordon had lived in Wales and London and now here with me in Cronulla. Gordon had moved from town to town his whole life it seemed.

With cool abandon we threw our individual worlds to the side and built our own composite. With his broad shoulders and my broad mind we climbed into each other's lives, hiding nothing and embracing all. When Gordon's dad was riled and smashing up his mum, Carmen, and their house, Gordon would come to mine with his younger brother, Rocky, and stay in the rumpus room for a day or two weeks. We'd watch Bruce Lee movies and eat Vita-Weats. It made me so happy to rescue him from the hell of his house, I almost rejoiced when he called up in a tight whisper asking if he could ride over in twenty. I liked to watch him sleep, it made me feel purposeful and kind, like I imagined a shoehorn would feel, or a home electrician. Even when Gordon slept, his leg shook, he was the epitome of restlessness, so I bought him some drums and we started playing music together in his garage or mine. I wrote lyrics and spoke them low over my simple yet always slightly funky bass lines, as Gordon smashed the skins deftly and with power. Gordon was surprised how easily he took to drumming, and how good he became so quick, whereas I knew he had rhythm and the desire to use it, given the amount of hours I'd sat there watching him tap out paradiddles on his shuddering pink thighs.

'Fuck, that's like thirteen,' Gordon said, counting my first clump of pubes. He already had a veritable ginger map on his area, I'd seen it heaps, wondering when my sprout would arrive. Then, one day, one fine day, I undressed and entered the shower receptacle, swapping places with my father. I began rocking from side to side, like my father had taught me, when I caught sight of my father's face, his typically dead blue eyes glaring madly at my mid-region. I looked down, and things were never the same again.

I don't know what effect I had had, but Gordon grew into a generally sunny bloke. He took to adventures with boundless energy, often snorting laughter out of his nose in uncontrollable bursts and for no apparent reason. He was just overwhelmed, like how a dog moans all crazy when it lands on a beach and feels all the space and water around it. Darkness fell only when we arrived on his lawn, or near his street, where the threat of what lay behind those doors seemed to crush his shoulders and he would walk towards his house like a very cold person, hunkered in and down.

Gordon's father was Peter, and he would often answer the door with blood on his fists and a metal cup full of whisky hanging round his neck from a leather string. Since the war Peter had been haunted by all he had seen, and it manifested in him often mistaking Gordon, Rocky and Carmen for the enemy. When he *wasn't* traumatised and drunk, Gordon's dad was a beautiful singer and wonderful storyteller who could charm the pants off anyone. Gordon loved it when he was like that.

In Year 10 things changed for Gordon and me (in a big way), and I'd confidently put this wholly appreciated shift down to three contributing factors. (1) Our band The White Goods began playing assemblies and selected house parties. (2) Gordon and I had decided, in the spring of 1992, that it was time to start dressing sharp. We spent our Saturdays in the city, trawling Paddington Markets for striped t-shirts and baggy distressed Kepper jeans, and pretty soon the local cattle began to copy our fashion and in this regard we may have been considered 'cool makers.' (3) Stuart came roaring back into my life employing Gordon and me as his official sidekicks, which pretty much ensured our protection and earnt us the sudden and confusing interest of girls.

In 1993 we turned seventeen. That was the year Gordon's dad went missing. One morning he was in the kitchen apologising to Rocky for breaking his train set in yet another flurry of grog rage, the next he was gone, never to be seen or spoken of again. We all waited, in trepidation, for him to return, but he never did. Then one day Carmen ripped open the curtains and the sunlight poured in, we all drank champagne and orange in the kitchen, and I witnessed one of the most glorious acts of nature and liberation as Gordon laughed with all his heart; laughter from his belly expelled out his mouth in large, unshackled guffaws. Gone was the apologetic snorting, and gone was that restless leg.

Soon after this Gordon took to marijuana with gusto. No sooner had he learnt how to suck it than he had financed a double-chamber glass bong, which he treated like the Holy Grail. No matter how ripped he got, every session concluded with Gordon cleaning the shaft with a wire brush, sanitising the cone, then folding the precious mechanism into its terry-towelling swaddling cloth. It was a ritual we came to know and love, and although he was less present and often monosyllabic and dead-looking, Gordon had found a way of accessing the ridiculousness of life and the insideness of music, and he honoured its access-maker. Who was I to take that away from him? I smoked pot for a bit at the start, but then I wrapped proceedings up. It freaked me out, the ultra-awareness and the stadium-sized sound of things in my brain. I already thought about things too much as it was, there was no need to enhance the experience.

Girls came in and out of our lives but the rendezvous were short-lived, for Gordon could not wait to be back in the saddle, one hand on the bong, one arm around me, laughing madly and openly as Stuart told a crazy story or made animal figures out of his cock and balls. The babble was infectious, and the meals disturbing, Stuart convincing all that entered to savour his favourite culinary concoction: English muffins with tomato paste and Vegemite. I had no idea how free we were. That's how free I was.

4

Ron Stone loved washing his boat. Seriously, he washed it twice a week; whether he'd taken it out on the water or not he was always scrubbing away like a madman. Ron designed the garage/boatshed/workshop with this in mind, envisaging long afternoons in the joint, washing his twenty-six-foot speedboat that he had light-heartedly named *The Office*. When I asked Ron why he named the boat this (and let me tell you, asking Ron a question was terrifying, the man was so tall and intimidating and he spoke so infrequently it was like that bit in *Oliver* where Oliver goes up and asks for more food), he told me about 'a bloke in Cairns' who had named his boat *The Office* so that whenever someone called him when he was on the boat, he could always tell the other guy (without lying), 'I'm at *The Office*!' This killed Ron, this was seriously the best thing he had ever heard, and he chortled as he told me. It was an ok joke, I guess.

Inside the Stones' house it got way primal. Moose heads, deer heads and massive fibreglass fish lined the walls of the hall and living room, bolted in and gazing out into the open-plan space; trophies from Ron's hunting efforts of the late eighties and early nineties. Courtney and I both agreed it was way spooky – the surrounding family of creatures bulging out into your own home, especially with the rifle or spear gun that claimed the beasts framed and positioned on the stairwell wall. But we would never voice such opinions in this house. Even though Ron Stone was a reclusive figure, Stuart and the family hailed him Tribal Leader, and his kills were direct proof of his majesty, stealth and fierceness.

Stuart was a different kind of warrior; instead of slaying wild boar in Africa, he preferred to suck piss and shoot magpies from the balcony with his shirt off, and, funnily enough, this was exactly what he was doing when we arrived. Every time I saw Stuart with his shirt off I was reminded of how incomprehensibly long his torso was. It seemed to lift off from his rippling stomach and climb upwards for what seemed like ages before it finally met up with the faraway breast and nipple section. Girls at school were amazed that Courtney was 'just friends' with Stuart. It was historically implausible, for no girl had been to Stuart Stone's house more than once without being dicked, licked or at least finger-blasted by the maniac. And even though Stu was buff as hell, tall and tanned with the chiselled Brad Pitt jaw line, Courtney preferred weedy, weird old me, and I never worried about it. I could tell she didn't take him seriously and this comforted me. Whenever Stone did his swagger or replayed his feats in the sack she burst out laughing and he liked her for it. Courtney was probably the only chick at De La Salle College who thought he was a bit of a knob-shiner.

Bang! From the spacious deck of the waterfront house, Stuart fired his BB gun into the wall of bougainvillea that curved around the back of the house and down to the bay. A magpie fluttered and freaked out, losing a stack of its feathers, wounded, limping through the air.

'Yeah, baby!' Stuart said, opening his one-hundred-and-forty-mile-long arms. 'Joseph and Mary are here! Please do take a seat in my manger for the night, oh virginal ones, and smoke cheerfully on the frankincense bong tube if you will!'

I stepped out onto the balcony, slapping Stuart on the shoulder with a hard, cupped hand. 'Shut up, bitch.' But Stuart continued his performance, setting down the BB gun next to the fibreglass bong and pulling out a bench seat for Courtney. 'My darling Virgin Mary, you look quite *sad* tonight, all in black!'

'*Thank you*, Stuart,' Courtney responded, wry as hell. 'I value your opinion so deeply when it comes to fashion.'

Stuart's eyes blew out and his brain over-fizzed with adrenaline (the steroids had a knack of doing this every hour or so) and before I knew it he had grabbed me by the Adam's apple and slammed me up against the pine pylon, mock-fucking me and choking me with an elbow under the chin.

'This is how you do it, baby, just get into him like this!' Wearing nothing but board shorts and a bandana, Stuart humped away at my floppy, helpless frame, his head to one side, beaming right into Courtney's eyes as he thrusted and foamed like an overheated cattle dog. But Courtney held his raging gaze right through it all. She knew these episodes well and she had developed a set of tools to deal with them. Courtney knew that this was Stuart's way of claiming the space. In a few minutes he would be diluting the whole thing with a string of disclaimers like 'I was just messing with ya! Where's ya fucken sense of humour? Fucken everyone takes shit so seriously – chill!'

As Stuart was reaching mock-orgasm on my poor leg, Gordon finally came out of the backyard toilet (with a copy of *Woman's Day* – he loved reading on the job) and saved me, wrenching the beefcake off his whimpering, art-house friend. Me. Gordon was half Stuart's size but he was a genuine nugget, one of those blokes you can't punch hard enough. Gordon's strength was all karate and life struggle, Stuart's was injected and built, injected and built, injected and built, built and injected. Fertilised by constant looks in the mirror.

Halfway through Year 8 Stuart found himself in his first gymnasium. Student welfare counsellor Shaun Clifford had been assigned Stuart Stone as 'Task Case 1' when Stuart's violent, disruptive and often perverted behaviour with students and teachers had placed him on the brink of his third expulsion in as many years. Then Shaun Clifford stepped in, diagnosed him with 'Restlessness' and 'Obscene Sexual Obsession' and 'Violent Urges', suggesting to the principal that Stuart be allowed to replace science or home economics with a supervised hour in the local gym every second day – under his own personal supervision, of course. Shaun Clifford was a bit of a gym bunny, and believed that a good workout had a calming, almost purging effect on hyper children, as the release of energy and endorphins seemed to satiate the restless, nervous core of the hysteria (or anger, as it often seemed to be in Stuart Stone's case).

Stu loved the joint as soon as he walked in. The hard, weird, greenish-blue metal equipment, the long, tall mirrors and the awesome stack of tough-looking cunts rippling with humps, bumps and tattoos. Within weeks Stu was benching a hundred and fifty kilos and had convinced the management to let him control the stereo. Instead of AC/DC and endless Cold Chisel, Stu was jamming on happy techno, drum and bass, Felix and trance, and sooner than you'd think, the truckies, cops and meatheads were happily pumping iron to the camp, spirited dance anthems. Stu's favourite part was the end of a big session, when he'd stand in a starfish shape in front of his favourite forty-foot mirror and admire the new releases on his long, brown guns, sparkling with sweat.

For the next couple of years Shaun and Stuart set each other challenges, engaging in a friendly yet highly competitive rivalry of toughness and endurance. Eventually, and to Shaun's chagrin, Stuart flew past him into a whole new world of fitness and strength. Not only was Stuart twenty years younger and more nimble, but he had a killer instinct – if he wanted to prove something he would do all it took.

Shaun Clifford had thrown Stuart Stone into the gym to help him calm down and focus, but instead he had given birth to a monster, and a fucking buff monster at that. And, ironically, with all his muscles and self-belief, he no longer needed to bash fuckwits or smash faggots or pick on sluts or remedial teachers, or piss on nips, lebs, wogs or Year 7s to prove his worth, for he *was* 'The Shit' now, and no one could (or would) touch him.

Malaki Stone, Stuart's brother, was four years older than Stuart and Mal liked to remind him (and us) of that as often as possible. He had been working security since Year 10, and was always going on about 'nosing rack', 'hurling muppets out', 'breaking up stinks', and making one hundred percent sure that the 'A Grade flange' was being let in and the 'porky whores' and 'westy driss' were 'barred hard'.

Malaki must have loved his job because he never seemed to break out of it. He wore bouncer-type outfits even when he was at home, and he spoke to you like you were a guest at his club, or at least trying to get in, and Stu idolised him for it. 'Yeah, Mal's working the harder clubs now, and the clientele are punchier and more hardcore, but the rack is straight off the rock and the sluts are A1 Sex Inventions. And the vitamins and sniff are all ticked on the house! Also, get this shit. Sometimes, at fucken Blackmarket, this day club he works at, the owners, right, they pay him to slap on these leather shorts, jump on stage or in the cage or whatever, and be fully whipped by this dominatrix chick, or one of the dancing boys like the faggots there, or just freak out to the trance in front of everyone. In a cage. In leather shorts! How fucken off the chop is that shit!'

Eventually, after six months of relentless begging, Malaki issued a challenge: he and Stuart would wrestle on the front lawn, and if Stuart could pin him down for three seconds, just once in ten rounds, then he could accompany Malaki to Blackmarket the following weekend.

It was invitation-only and the cheerful yet anxious crowd included the wrestlers' mother, Judy Stone, Malaki's girlfriend Ebony, and, of course, Stuart's key support group, me and Gordon.

'Let's go, Stuey!' we cheered, nervously, in our Year 10 sports uniforms, sipping on cans of Swan Light, quietly terrified that Malaki might just rip Stu's limbs off and eat them in the rose garden.

The Stone brothers divested themselves of all but their black Calvin Kleins and stepped down into the earthy colosseum between the front door, the street and Judy's rose garden. They laughed and flexed and stretched, circling each other, shrugging the fear off, scuffing their hooves as if they were bulls before a full-tilt rodeo showdown. Gordon's eyes bulged with excitement, but I was more scared than anything; I had seen Malaki beat a guy up outside Caringbah station one night and it was not fucking pretty. Then Ebony yelled, 'Round one!'

The first five rounds were over before Stuart knew it, Malaki simply using his height and power to barge over Stuart and blast him onto his back. He was like a tractor stomping on a field of silly reeds, following up with two driving knees to the shoulder and armpit, from where he would dribble saliva down onto his brother's face and count back from three to one – 'You're out of there!'

Even Gordon (a lover and participant in martial arts fighting) had lost all hope, shifting to a chair behind Ebony's flowing sarong, embarrassed. Ebony was the opposite; she was loving every moment of the spectacle: two ripped and toned bodies clashing, sweating and springing off each other, rolling and moaning about on the hard, manicured lawn. She twitched and quivered, pulling at the wire of her g-string.

'I'm sorry, little Stu-Stu, you're going to have to do better than that if you want to come play with the big boys in the city!' Malaki said, pushing off his brother and preparing for the next round of front-yard annihilation.

Stuart sat up, spitting blood through a gap in his two front teeth, checking the status of his wobbling, aching jaw. Why was he losing so badly? He had smashed Shaun Clifford in the gym challenge, every chump at school feared him, and even the NRL heavies at Coyotes nightclub thought he was 'proper tough.' Stuart stared up into the golden orb that stung his bloody, cracking lips. Deep down, Mal was a weak piece of shit and Stu knew it. And we knew he knew it, and he knew we knew he knew we knew it too. Gordon thumped me on the shoulder saying 'Watch this now, Nelly.'

Stu scrunched his face in recognition, looking over to the balcony where he caught sight of Ebony and her too-tanned D cups popping out of her bikini top like overripe honeydew melons. Her figure filled Stuart with sweet memories: taking her from behind in Malaki's bed a month ago, sucking on her clit three nights ago in Malaki's shower, and just this morning, while Malaki was at the shops buying protein shakes – giving her the big stick on the rough, burning carpet of Malaki's bedroom floor.

'Round nine! Go, Stuey!' Ebony yelped, lighting a Horizon four-milligram and sucking hard on the thing.

Malaki, eight rounds up and loving it, swept his sweaty blond locks behind his ears and once again bounded towards his blood-soaked brother, assuming the story would play out as it had done thus far. Mal opened his lips to reveal his broad wall of gums as he drove towards Stuart, who stood still like a stalk, hands by his side, as Malaki picked up a bullocking pace. Extending his seemingly telescopic arms and emitting a loud, guttural roar, Malaki gripped Stuart's neck and chest with his massive webbed hands and drew breath to kill with. Stu took one step back and Zen-like spun on his heel, using his brother's rampaging force and speed to turn the both of them around then lift Goliath up off the ground and drive him back into the pylon – smashing his skull against the trestle and holding him there, a foot off the ground, with a thumb and forefinger dug deep into the pulp of Malaki's windpipe.

I couldn't believe what I was seeing, and despite my position as a pacifist, I yearned for Stuart to finish the duel with some more smashing of head. Eat his head or throw him, throw him and then eat his head.

David had flung the thing, and Malaki was no hero. Stu could see it all so clearly now in his brother's beady, fearful eyes. How pathetic that he only lasted three weeks in the police force, quitting after his first call to a domestic. How pathetic it was that Malaki wet his bed until he was fourteen and how he still couldn't even read that well. How paranoid he was, convinced everyone was laughing at him all the time, when, like always, people were thinking about themselves.

The defeat on Mal's face and the magnificently low and fatal choking sound that gurgled from the back of his throat inspired Stuart to lift his brother's skull off the pylon, spin him back around and throw him into the rose garden. But he didn't. A wave of compassion and, in the end, pity rushed over Stuart. He was embarrassed for his older brother, and so he lowered him back onto the grass and kissed him on the forehead.

'Blackmarket, yeah?'

This was two years ago, two insane years where I lost my friend to the underworld, and, when I think about it, lost him forever. Fridays he and Mal would drive in, dressed in puffy black jackets, caps and Lonsdale weightlifting pants. They'd cover a collection of new clubs through till Saturday night, then Sunday mornings launch into Blackmarket, chomp on some biccies, rack up some dust and dance, grinding jaws and making darkness sing until Monday morning. Out of the club and into the light of reality they'd cruise back to one of the boy's pads for a spa and a few drinks, bongs and two or three Rohypnol to take the edge off. Then Tuesday morning Stuart would run ten k along Cronulla Beach, take a forty-five-minute shower, drink a litre of apple and blackcurrant juice and roll up to school with dilated pupils, pasty, blotched skin and chattering teeth – dreaming of being back on the razzle, ripping snow-lines off a model's tits and being held like a baby in the warm arms of the flashing, zapping, buzzing sepulchre. The teachers knew about it, and Ron and Judy were even called to school on occasion, where they were made aware of their son's routine. Absent from Friday, arriving back at school Tuesday with 'crazy big eyes' and 'repetitive jaw movements'. Ron rarely turned up, but Judy did, explaining time and time again in a frustrated drawl that Stuart 'aims to work in the field of nightspot security' and that this was a *necessary* part of his training.

'Does everyone have a drink?' Judy Stone asked, sailing out onto the balcony in high-waisted beige shorts and a tight red Esprit top, verdelho curling and tipping against the round cubes of ice in her smudgy wine glass.

'We're cool, thanks, Mrs Stone,' I said, showing her my beer.

Judy was all set to nod and smile and nod and smile when she caught sight of the BB gun on the table, resting up beside the bong.

'Stuart! Clear your gun away, please!'

As he had done so many times, Gordon politely picked up the BB gun for Stu, and transported it down to its home in the tool shed.

'Stuey! Bong!'

'I'm not going to pack the bong up *now* Mum – we're all about to smoke a fucken cone out of it,' Stuart said, chopping grass in a bowl.

'Alright, alright, don't do your aggressive voice with your mother,' Judy replied, grinning madly at me and Courtney. 'I'm sure Neil and Courtney don't talk to their mothers that way.'

Stu thumbed dope into the cone and lit it, the mull fizzing, blazing, popping then disappearing into the column shaft with a threading *swoosh*.

Judy had this awesome way of ignoring Stuart's bong work, obliviously flicking away at the ice cubes in her glass. 'So how did you two go?'

'Um . . .' Courtney looked to me for direction, so I ceased rolling my cigarette, the Tally-Ho paper hanging off my lip.

'I went ok, Mrs Stone, yeah,' I said.

'Neil got enough to get into where he wants to go,' Courtney added, attempting to quash the topic.

Gordon pulled on the bong too hard and fast, coughing coarsely into the wall.

'You right, pal?' I asked, privately glaring at Courtney.

'Yup,' he said, with a burning cough.

'Fag,' Stuart said, staring down at his nipples.

Gordon and I had left this titanic issue uncovered, but the end was looming. After four and a half years of intense kinship and inseparable day-to-day brothering, it was too much, too much, too too much.

'And you, Courtney?' Judy asked.

'She fucken nailed it, eh?' Stu answered. 'Going to be a lawyer in the city or some shit which will rock when I need someone to get me out of jail.'

'That's precisely why I am going to study law, Mrs Stone – so I can save Stuart from being anally raped in jail by ten large Samoans,' Courtney said.

'Why save him?' she said. 'I'm not asking you to!'

The table fell about in giggles as Gordon recovered, screwing a sweet mix of tobacco and bud into the bronze metal cone, passing it over to Courtney. I could see the indecision on her face. Courtney didn't mind a bong; she went all quiet and funny but she was into it, more than I was. She and Gordon got on well stoned, making toast and laughing at the madness of kitchen appliances. But Courtney had never felt entirely comfortable pulling billies in front of other people, especially grownups. And now, as the sun held off setting, instead shining a garish spotlight on her overdone gothic fashion and thick, morbid black eye make-up, I could see her face shake and burn. I wanted to reach out and take the bong from her grasp, wanted to save her, but at the same time – and look, I know how this will sound – I enjoyed watching her struggle. That feeling of tension and awkwardness was an opiate to me; I didn't need a hit of grass.

'Um, so yeah – probably just do law, Mrs Stone. Thanks.'

Deafening silence reigned as Courtney took a sharp look up at Judy, then back down to her left hand, which by now was poised on the shotty, her right hand cradling the shaft and lighter. For a second it looked as though she might just do it, lift the lighter to the grass and fire it up, but that moment was gone the instant it appeared, and instead she was frozen still, paralysed by the situation. And everyone just sat there watching, including Judy – eyes fixed on Courtney's left hand, waiting.

'It's not a fucken microphone!' Stuart yelled, hitting his neck.

'Or a karaoke machine!' Gordon chimed in. He was ripped, giggling maniacally, eyes like organic cherry tomatoes.

I could almost see her thoughts flitting across her face. If only it had been a joint so she could smoke it. If only Mrs Stone would stop fucking staring at her. If only piss-weak Neil would fucking step in and do something, instead of just sitting there.

'Neil? Do you want this?' Courtney asked, pushing it over as she took a full and necessary gulp of her Stoli and orange pre-mix. Whether it was the situation, or my lack of assistance with bong-hell, she stood up and faced Mrs Judy Stone, breaking the embargo she and I had so firmly put in place today.

'Neil and I are moving in together, Mrs Stone,' she said. 'Looks like we'll both get accepted into university. We're going to live together in Glebe.'

A southerly buster whipped up off the surface of Burraneer Bay, blowing the tops of the trees this way and that in a no-joke, rainless storm that sent us inside. It was a torrid and boiling summer, 1994/95, but Stuart still chopped up a stack of timber and lit the fireplace, setting up a stoners' paradise in the dead-animal museum living room. Gordon on the left flank cradled a cup of VB, Courtney in the middle (who had quickly hit a half-bong when Judy went to the ladies) whispering in my ear whether she should do a wee now or wait until Stuart was done with the fire, and me on the other side of her considering this massive inquiry while sipping Carlton Cold from the bottle; this was the Couch Collective, stunned and stoned and sated, watching (still bare-chested) Stuart crank up the fireplace, sweating like a pig as he carefully stacked the planks. He was skilled. He had *failed* his HSC, but, in this other way, this 'way of the world', this possibly crucial way, he was more adept than all of us, and we marvelled as he stacked and sorted, blowing into the fire which rose before us.

This Violent World was Stuart's favourite film. An Italian-made documentary that filmed people from all over the world who were victims of, privy to or involved in the execution of horrifically violent acts. I'd seen the film a thousand and fifteen million times but still found myself glued to its vivid, way-evil imagery. The first story was about this Nigerian woman who got pregnant to this married guy. This elder tribesman and these younger blokes led her deep into the jungle, stripped her naked and made her climb up a tree and crawl out onto a long branch. First time I saw this I was pissing myself with laughter, I mean it was really funny watching this chick try to climb up this tree in front of everyone. But then it got way dark, the tribesmen bouncing the branch she was perched on, flinging her up into the air. She fell at least twenty feet down, landing gruesomely on the base of her spine and arse. Then the tribesmen made her crawl back up the tree, out onto the branch, where they bounced her off again. Time and time and time again until her vertebrae split, the baby was dead, and she was unconscious, lying in a bed of leaves, leaking blood. Then the tribesmen sang this weird, joyous song which was way fucked up, lit a fire, drank out of a shell, laughed together, and then carried her back into town.

Stuart couldn't believe it; no matter how many times we watched it he'd just sit there with insane eyes, pointing at the screen like it was happening now.

The film went on like this. A family from Hyderabad in India cutting off their tongues with a hacksaw one by one for the equivalent of eight dollars each. Oh, and the young African virgin being chased through the jungle until she couldn't run any further. Exhausted, she collapsed, and was then raped by a pack of twelve-year-old boys as a way of introducing them to sex and confirming them as men. We did our confirmation at Caringbah church, and as weird as that was, being given a sash with some dude's name on it like 'Francis of Assisi', I was way more keen on that shit than the jungle system.

At first Courtney would throw biscuits at the screen and scream at Stuart, slapping him with a hybrid onslaught of Marxist, feminist, Courtney-ist doctrine, but Stuart would just turn to her, chewing on the biscuits she threw, and say: 'This violent world.' And Gordon would nod and grunt into his empty bottle of beer.

The last and most disturbing tale of this VHS was about a Colombian man who, after being caught stealing food for his wife and five children, was sentenced to eat mercury and die in front of his family in a ditch in the town square. A large crowd gathered, including his young wife and these gorgeous kids – like, I don't know if kids become more cute when their dad is about to be slaughtered publicly, but these kids, man, I just wanted to grab them and take them home and tell Mum I'd look after them. The mercury made the guy giggle, which was insane, and Gordon giggled too, which made Courtney scoff, which made Stuart laugh, which made me nervous. The laughter grew as the dude guffawed, barked and screamed his way to death, his face exploding with green foam. His wife did not cry. Seriously, she was way tough. She just watched his body shake and quiver and stop. Then she walked away with the cute children. We had just got up to the bit where the green foam fizzed out of his ears when Ron appeared in the hallway with a sponge and a frown. And then he was gone again.

Courtney could never truly and fully comprehend why it took Stuart Stone so long to get ready. One thing was for certain: it was a lot longer than she ever took. Even tonight she had completed the gothic-chic fashion, hair and make-up package within forty-five minutes. Stuart, meanwhile, had been upstairs for God knows how long, showering, drying and crafting his hair with three different products: mousse, gel and Hold Factor 4 shaping licorice. In his absence and with all the TV and stereo options outlawed by Ron's mute act of political activism in the doorway, none of us had spoken a word for half an hour or so, sinking deep into the mesmerising cinema of the fireplace. Gordon couldn't look at me, and Courtney was too stoned to proffer anything either. So I just sat there, squashed between the two loves of my life, wondering how I could keep this dream alive. Wondering how not to hurt everyone with my future.

5

At 6 pm on Grandview Parade the rain fell light-heartedly on the conifer trees, licking the soft wood and shining up the tilted little road with the help of last light. A man parked his car in the double garage and walked up the stairs to greet his wife, who stood waiting for him with their baby son. A young boy across the road hit a cricket ball which hung from a tree by a thin rope, no doubt dreaming of a big innings tomorrow for the Cronulla–Caringbah Under-12 B team. A girl of no more than thirteen swanned about beneath a sprinkler in her shorts and bikini top, distracting two flabby men allegedly fixing an alternator. A busy housewife darted across the lawn of her brick-veneer home carrying a basket of washing. And two Year 12 graduates climbed the hill, dazed and confused, picking conifer nuts off the pines and flinging them at each other's heads. A rainbow appeared over the top of the trees, capturing the heart of the man, the wife, their baby, the cricketer, the girl, the men, the housewife and the wobbling graduates.

'You got any money?' I asked.

'Not for you,' Gordon replied, flicking a nut at me.

'Mum gave me twenty bucks for the whole night.'

'Your mum's a tight bitch then.'

'Just give us like fifty on tick.'

'Only got fifty on me, dude.'

'Bullshit "only got fifty on me". C'mon!'

'S'all that's on me!'

'What about your cheque account?'

'What about *your* cheque account, bitch?'

'I got $6.28 in my cheque account, bitch, that's why I'm trying to get into yours.'

'What do you want to buy?'

I shrugged, reaching for my Tally-Ho papers.

'You going to pop a pill or you going to pussy out?'

We walked for a bit then stopped walking, waiting at the crest of the hill for Courtney and Stuart. We were all together a while ago, halfway up the hill when the sun shower opened up and Courtney realised she had forgotten her coat and then Stuart, patting at his pockets, realised he had left the Es in his undies drawer.

'You gunna tell me your results?' I asked him.

Gordon kicked at the grass and scrunched his piggish nose, spitting high and flicking his attention to some noise somewhere else in the Shire.

'Just tell me, Gord – what do I care what you got?'

'Why are you asking then, if you don't care?' Gordon snapped back.

'Because you're a dumb cunt,' I joked, reaching for my pouch of tobacco even though I was already puffing on one.

Gordon mock snap-kicked me in the face, stopping his foot just inches away from where the Tally-Ho paper now hung on my big bottom lip – if it was anyone else I would have flinched but this happened so often I could paint the soles of G's shoes from memory.

'Did you talk to Carmen again?'

Gordon shook his head. Carmen would have had him out of school and working three years ago, when he was in Year 9, but Gordon and I had just found each other and there was no way he was doing that. But Carmen needed the money as Peter's disappearance had left her with more debt than compensation, and for a while there Gordon was all set to pull out and go work full-time for someone at something, somewhere in Sutherland.

Gordon's last resort had been to visit the local priest, Father Todd McNealy. Father Todd loved being on the 'students' level', and right away took control of the situation, explaining to Carmen that Gordon was at a *crucial* and *impressionable* age, and therefore needed to stay in school for his own personal development, for his future prosperity in the workplace, his social skills and confidence levels, and also to strengthen his relationship with the one and only Jesus Christ the Lord.

I loved that bit! Gordon thought Jesus was a faggot. 'Why else would a guy wear a dress and spend all this time with twelve men in the woods?' he would say, snorting to himself. But Carmen was not buying a dollar of it. She'd had a bad time with priests and nuns at her boarding school in Melbourne in 1963 and wasn't about to take advice from a man of the cloth.

All that was left was for Gordon to beg, and so he did, and eventually the emotional pleading won out and Gordon could stay on with me and finish his HSC – on one condition: he would somehow bring in four hundred dollars a week. So Gordon got up at quarter past four every morning and started his job as a cleaner, scrubbing phone booths and bus stops until eight thirty, when he would go to school. Then, as soon as the bell rang, he would go to the Franklins' for a few hours, offloading the truck, stacking shelves, cleaning out the fridges and returning the trolleys to their bays. This was the deal and he was cool with it.

'You and Courtney sound like you've got it all worked out – in the city, eh?' Gordon asked, without looking up from his trainers. My skin went hot.

'She was just saying . . .'

'It's cool, man. You gotta get in there and rock out.'

I pushed shag around in the palm of my hand, sculpting a new cigarette.

'Why don't you come in too? Work in the city and live with us or whatever?'

'I'm not part of *Courtney's plan*, dude.'

'Fuck Courtney's plan.' I flipped the shag into the paper and rolled. 'And fuck just doing what Carmen tells you, G. You've worked like six thousand hours a day for years and she just . . .'

'She just what Nelly?'

I took a Zippo out of my pocket but decided not to light up yet. Talking about another guy's mum was dangerous ground, and even though Gordon often shot off about how much of a nightmare she was, how selfish she was sometimes and how he wished she would lose weight and choose better guys, there was still no licence for anyone else to chime in, and I knew this, but still, I cared more about my mate than my own balls, and knew if Gordon stayed here now he would surely be stuck here forever, slowly dying in the suburbs of the Sutherland Shire.

'I don't see why we can't all work it out,' I said, flicking my eyes up at him, my chest vibrating, hands shaking like paper.

Gordon kicked the gutter a few times then spat on the lawn. 'I'm not like you, Cronk, I've got responsibilities 'n' shit.'

'You can't get stuck here, dude. This place, it's like –'

'What am I going to do in the city? Eh? I'm not like you and C, I didn't get marks to go anywhere, I'll just be hangin' round like that tall guy from Ferris Bueller.'

'Who knows, mate?' I said. 'But how exciting is it? We'll be free! Stop thinking of life as some duty you have to other people. What do you want, Gordon? Have you ever asked yourself that? What the fuck do *you* want?'

Gordon just stared at me. 'Do you mean this, Cronk?'

'Of course, man. What the fuck. You're my brother. You fucken . . . you're fucken . . . you gotta come with me, mate. We gotta keep the dream alive.'

'What's Courtney going to say?'

I shrugged. Gordon laughed awkwardly, then pulled a fifty-dollar note out of the inside pocket of his jacket.

'Fifty bucks – but only if you spend it on drugs.'

'Oh, mate, I'll pay you back.'

'Pay me when we get to the city.'

'Are you in? Gordon! Are you in?!'

'If you are.'

We leapt into a hug from quite a distance, meeting with a slap and bang of chests. We held each other hard in that moment, gripping each other's necks and backs with love, meaning and intent. We were a lock of hard promises and there was no turning back.

'Let's go nail this bottle of Southo!' Stuart called out from the base of the street, an umbrella in one hand covering my girlfriend, and in the other a full bottle of Southern Comfort Bourbon. His hair looked fantastically set; even the rain couldn't shift it.

6

There's an awful sense of *duty* involved with being a parent I reckon. I want to be a parent, I really do, and I can fully see myself with daughters, playing in the park, being really attentive, tying up their laces and saving them from out-of-control dogs.

The main thing, in my opinion, that freaks parents out is thinking of things to do all the time. My dad struggled (big time) with this. Saturday would come around and every week without fail he would have to think up something for us to do all day. I had no interest in team sports so he literally had to fill the *whole day* with things, and I never got the feeling it excited him too much. My dad's a decent bloke, but ideas? I'm not sure he has ever had any. So it always ended up with him asking me what I wanted to do. And if I told him the truth, it was to maybe *not* hang out with him, as it always felt like such a hassle for Dad on Saturdays, he was always distracted, reading the paper or stuffing the radio plug in his ear, and making weird and questionable excuses not to get involved in whatever I was doing. Often he wouldn't even turn up, citing some heavy chore Mum needed him to do around the house, but I knew this was crap; Mum was the one who'd suggested we spend some time alone together on Saturdays.

So I suggested we get into fishing. I have no idea why; I'd never fished in my life. The idea came to me when I was cruising round the local area one afternoon and stumbled upon a trail that led down to a little spot called Dolans Bay. The bay was tiny and enclosed and there was this awesome cave that you could sit in and take in the estuary, a place to go and really feel like you were alone. I figured if Dad and I were going to hang out together and he was going to be relatively absent even when he was there, I would find a place I liked and at least get something out of it.

Dad and I spent a lot of time at Dolans Bay, me fishing, him pacing about wishing he was anywhere else. Then one day I told him I was happy to fish on my own on Saturdays if he had other, more *pressing* things to do, and he looked at me, so grateful, then took off up the trail and back to his car where I heard Radio National come on, followed by the engine.

I'm not that into looking at idyllic views, they kind of shit me, like a perfect view makes me feel so broken. Like postcards just make me want to die. I preferred looking at the cracked sides of rocks or some smashed bit of coast or a dead crab in the gloomy water, and Dolans Bay was like that – it really wasn't that spectacular, kind of underwhelming really, which suited me fine, and it reminded me of my dad and me.

One by one I introduced Gordon, then Stuart, then finally Courtney to my secret, excellent spot, and now it was a group meeting place, a sacred place for all of us, which I liked but it kind of shat me too because they always knew where I was. I could always get a new spot, but nowhere else felt like this. Like the perfect pair of jeans, Dolans Bay just sat well. And my cave was our headquarters.

Despite the light rain, I felt like dipping my feet in the water. Courtney was all embarrassed and cute carrying her heels down to where I sat with my jeans rolled up and my shoes off. I had a cigarette going already, the water swirling about my feet, little fish darting psychotically about in the shallows. This would be the last time we all gathered here and it hurt to think this, I couldn't go to the cave just yet.

'Are you ok?' Courtney asked me.

'Yeah, I'm cool, babe – just dipping my feet.'

'Let's get smaaaashed!' Stuart called out, climbing back up the steps to the cave. Gordon followed, waving.

Courtney sat down on the rock beside me, but she didn't dip her feet in, I guess because she was wearing stockings. Instead she sat in a very yoga-ish position, legs folded over one another; she held my face in her hands. 'I love you, Neil,' she said. Clearly the marijuana had won out; she was paranoid I had taken offence to her announcing the Glebe plan, plus she had also spotted Gordon and me in an embrace at the top of Grandview Parade. No doubt her already active little head was buzzing with conspiracy and doubt, and telling me she loved me was a way of restoring order and evacuating all the mess inside. What a drug pot was.

'Awww,' I said, inhaling sweet chemicals into my skull and throat.

'Do you love me too, Neil?' Courtney asked, kissing my nose.

I dumped my dart in a puddle.

'Babe. It's all going to be cool. But are *you* ok?'

She placed her hand on my zipper and squeezed a bit of my cock through the denim.

'Let's go round the bend,' she said, biting my bottom lip.

My heart started beating fast, but I did what I was told. We had to clear a few gaps between rocks but we made it. It wasn't too mossy at this time of year and soon we were on a private jetty just out of sight of the cave. I could hear the boys setting up camp, pouring lids of Southern Comfort and discussing whether there were any dorky, ugly, annoying chicks at school that may just be the most surprising, untold 'fucks of the century', and they had passed them up because they were a bit ugly or annoying but maybe tonight they should give them the stick because they may surprise the fuck out of them with their cock-mastery and technique. This was their main topic of conversation – seriously, they didn't talk about much else – and as I moved around the shoulder of the bay this is what I heard:

Gordon came boldly forward, admitting he had always fancied Sarah Kirkwood. In a 'filthy, doggy style behind the tuckshop kind of way'.

'Kirkwood is a stuck-up land mullet, mate!'

'I dig her,' Gordon claimed.

'Kirkwood? You are a unit, Braithwaite.'

'What about you? What second-rate gear would you stuff?'

'I'd ram that epileptic from Year 11 – what's her name?"

'Kyla Druid? Get fucked!'

'That chick, aside from all the epileptic carry-on, is gagging for pole!'

'Oh Jesus, Mary and Joseph!' Gordon said.

'Remember that fit she had at the swimming carnival?'

'What fit? Which fit? She has a fit every hour!'

'She'll be having a fit on my cock when I take her into the bushes tonight!'

Since I saw Ethan Hawke and Winona Rider at the end of *Reality Bites* I had started kissing really slow and with not that much tongue. It was working well and I could sense Courtney enjoying it more; she never wanted to stop and she moaned louder and from a lower, more woman place. There was no rush in the kiss now, and no need to repeat that scooping motion, our lips were speaking with each other and it hurt, it ached, how true and beautiful it was. She put my hand in between her legs and I feared she was pushing the deed once more.

'We can't do this here,' I said, looking up at the property which the jetty belonged to.

'No one's home,' Courtney said, breathing loud in my ear.

'How can you know that?'

'They would have kicked us off by now.'

'Can we just go back, please? I kind of feel weird . . . and it's raining.' Courtney held my nose between her fingers and peered into me, utter disappointment colliding with rage across her face and eyes.

I stood up, pushing my erection into the seam of my jeans so no one would know. 'I don't want to fuck in front of Dolans Bay anyway.'

Courtney led the way back round the rocks where we met with quite a startling image. There stood the Adonis Stuart Stone, arms and legs akimbo in the mouth of the cave, wielding a half-empty bottle of Southern Comfort, his jeans down by his ankles, underpants around his hips, six-inch tanned penis swinging in the cool evening air.

I went back to the jetty to get my tobacco, and when I returned I noticed Courtney in a state I had never witnessed before. Her body was completely still, though seemingly being propelled forward at the same time, her big green eyes focused on the piece of science up above.

I followed her eyes to where Stuart Stone's marvellous cock swung back and forth like a wrecking ball. Then I returned my gaze to my girlfriend, who was still transfixed. Had she never seen a large penis before? Was she wondering what it would be like to put her little hands around it? Would they fit? If they did fit, would Stuart be happy with them? Would he be happy with what she did to him? Stuart had taken hand jobs from a thousand women aged between thirteen and forty-three; he'd surely laugh in her face at her hopeless technique. The way she clenched and dragged her little ring of fingers up the shaft. And what if she did put her mouth around it? How much would it grow in her face? On her tongue, how would it taste? Would it jab the back of her throat and if so could she take it? And what if she lay down in the cave right now and spread her thighs apart – would it fit? Would she scream?

The cock stopped swinging and Courtney snapped out of her trance, realising that she had been staring at the beast for almost a minute. She dragged her eyes up Stuart's torso, past his t-shirt and up to his neck, chin and eyes. Stuart looked down at her from the cave, no longer in a macho stance, but merely standing there, vulnerable, aware of where she'd been looking, and for how long. Was it curiosity or self-destruction that led her to this moment? She couldn't work it out herself. But as their eyes met for that millisecond, there was the strongest, most foreign, yet palpable attraction ever written in Cronulla history. I read every word of it, and, really, I should have known then.

'Let's get drunk,' I said, lighting a smoke and walking towards my cave.

'Where are you going?' Courtney asked, looking for her shoes and hiding her red face in her hair.

Resting back on the cave walls, Stuart tried to tear his eyes away from Courtney but he couldn't help himself; he was clearly imagining her long pale legs wrapped around his throat as he buried his face in her like she was a laksa. Gordon was propped up on his jacket, watching me hammer into the bottle of brown alcohol.

'Here, babe.' I passed the bottle to my girlfriend, looking down into the orange dust of the cave floor, making sure I held on to the burning pool of booze still hanging at the top of my throat.

So many times I'd employed this method, right here in this cave. Staring down into the floor and counting to twenty, finding the right gaps in my breathing to suck the fluid down and stop it rising back up. I was shit-terrible at drinking hard liquor, I preferred red wine sipped over many hours, to taste the stuff and let it ride into my system, not this whole 'get piss into ya' attitude.

'Remember the time,' I said, finally fucking swallowing the brown hell. 'Remember the time we came here with Daniel Shoes?'

'Yes!' Gordon said. 'And he brought us all that gin!'

'And we went to his house and stole all that jewellery!' Stuart added.

'And Nelly spewed on the carpet!' Gordon said, giggling madly again.

'I had had a bottle of gin to myself,' I argued.

'Shoes loved it! Do you remember what he was like that night?' Stu said.

'I know.' I turned to Courtney. 'This guy, C, he was like such a maudlin, low-key guy, but then we all went to his joint and robbed his parents' house and it was like the first time we ever saw him smile.'

'Shoes, man, Shoes was smashing windows and loading us up with jewellery, laughing his tits off the whole time,' Gordon said.

'Yeah, the dude was a nut job,' Stuart confirmed.

'Then, when we were leaving with bags full of his parents' shit, he calls the cops on himself.' I shook my head in disbelief.

'He's all like "Go! Go! Go! Go!" as he's on the phone to the cops!'

'What happened? Did they come?' Courtney asked, nibbling at the brown bottle of booze with gentle, focused chick-sips.

'Yeah, and he said to the pigs he was held prisoner by these criminals and it was all in the news and everything. He got off and everyone felt sorry for him!'

'About three months later the dude was found dead on his parents' bed.'

'Shit! Oh, ok, that was Daniel Shoes,' Courtney realised.

'Daniel Shoes is Mick's brother,' Stu said.

'Yeah, Daniel knocked himself off the week after Benedict Hawker did,' Gordon said.

'No! Shoes was before Hawker. Luke Dwyer was the week after,' Stu said.

'Luke walked into the water, right?' I asked.

'Yeah, he got done by the cops drink-driving and didn't want to tell his dad so he fucken tied bricks to his feet and walked into Shelley Beach.'

'Hawker jumped off Kurnell cliffs.'

'That's right – down into the rocks there.'

'Which is worse, you reckon?' I said, not thinking.

'Hanging,' Courtney said.

Dolans Bay thumped then went quiet.

7

From the time she was twelve years old, academic achievement and school leadership were integral parts of Sarah Kirkwood's existence. Sarah wanted to make her parents proud, and dreamt of becoming a doctor or perhaps a lawyer, having a beautiful family (a child of each sex) and, most importantly, maintaining a high standing and reputation within the community – perhaps even as a Justice of the Peace! Sarah would be popular outside the church, and even at Payless or Coles on a Saturday, people would call out to her on Cronulla Street: 'Sarah, hellooooo!' But! Sarah launched into study because she genuinely loved it; the teachers at De La Salle College Cronulla had never seen a student like her. Always Prefect, always the first to hand in an essay, always the first to put her hand up, always editor of the yearbook, always organiser of school events and fundraisers – she loved a foundation! If the school could have cloned her they would have.

Her parents rewarded Sarah's indefatigable enthusiasm for school by allowing her half-a-dozen house parties a year. They believed it was essential that Sarah live a balanced life, and unless she let her hair down every now and again this was not going to happen. So every couple of months Sarah Kirkwood's parents threw a do. It was on these nights that Sarah Kirkwood proved to her peers that she was not the straitlaced, stuck-up nerd they had all pinned her as. On the contrary, Sarah was a fucking animal!

Kirkwood's parties were famous for the food, lack of parental supervision and buckets of free booze, but more than this they were famous because Sarah Kirkwood always stole the show, pulling on beer bongs, volunteering herself for numerous Vodka Super Duper Water Squirter championships, and inevitably getting herself so fuck-eyed her dress would end up over her head and at the end of the night some pimple-headed stringbean from 3 unit maths would be dipping himself in her half-unconscious body behind the shed. All the piss would get drunk, the house trashed, and everyone would leave, with Sarah sleeping in the leaf-mulched garden or passed out alone on the kitchen floor. A well-respected train wreck. Then on Monday morning Sarah Kirkwood would stroll into school, impeccably put together with her gloves, hat (tam-o'-shanter) and stockings on, behaving sweetly and studiously, as if none of the weekend's shenanigans ever took place. She was a wonderful anomaly, one I truly respected, as I was well aware that the real reason why her parents allowed two hundred and fifty teenagers over to trample, drink, fight, fuck, spew and wreck the enormous place was because Sarah Kirkwood had no friends.

'Right!' Stuart said, holding up his hand as an indication to halt!

Obedient, we wobble-halted on the kerb across from Sarah Kirkwood's garish mansion, where seventeen- and eighteen-year-olds filed in with painted hair and cases of mixed grogs.

'So there are four pills for Gordon and myself in this baggy here,' Stuart announced, flapping a bag in his palm. 'And four pills in here for Joseph and Mary.' Stuart waved a second bag in our faces.

'Biccies, baby!' Gordon said, licking his hands excitedly.

'Now! They're Mitsubishis, ok? The same ones we had down Lake Conjola ... so don't go too hard too fast!' Stuart warned, pointing at Gordon.

'Ok, ok,' Gordon said, waving these accusations away. Gordon was famous for taking half a pill, then ten minutes later complaining that nothing was happening and taking another half or even a full, then spending the rest of the evening mauled, mute and immoveable on the laundry floor.

'These puppies are strong,' Stuart warned again, issuing the bags.

Courtney snapped a pill in half, a bit of its pink edge falling about in her hand. Everyone looked at it, wondering who would get the extra little bit. Courtney picked her half out of her palm, kissed me on the neck and swallowed her pill, washing it down with a Schweppes Cola we had bought at 7-Eleven. I slammed mine down and the little extra bit. I was nervous as hell, my stomach rumbling and my chest vibrating, but what the hell, it was the end of school, and I was safe in this circle of love.

'Drug-hug!' Gordon called, and we were hugging each other. It felt good to be hugging my friends, seeing Courtney's and Gordon's faces so lit with anticipation. For some reason I couldn't quite match their euphoria. Something was blocking my path. I made the appropriate face but inside, I knew this was the last ride.

'Let's break on through!' Stuart said, pretending to be Val Kilmer pretending to be Jim Morrison pretending to be *nearly there.*

By the gate at the end of the driveway Sarah Kirkwood stood behind a long wooden table holding up a blank netball bib and smiling like a full maniac. Her teeth seemed larger and cleaner than ever and that's saying something. If we were all monsters, Sarah would be the leader and the most feared.

'Helloooooooo! Thank you for coming to my parteeeee!' Sarah said, bouncing from side to side with the bib. 'It is soooooo exciting to have you guys here at Results Party Class of '94!' She was semi-screaming both her tits off.

'Kirkwood, thanks a lot. We're really very excited to be here too,' Stuart said sardonically. 'Gordon is especially excited to see you, aren't you, G-Man? He's been all "Oh, can't wait to see Kirkwood . . . she's so sweet!"'

'You're a fag,' Gordon said, staring down at his Doc Martens. How could he not have seen it coming? 'And ahhhh . . . yeah . . . Hi, Kirkwood.'

'Hi, Gordon. It's really nice to see you as well!' Sarah said, sipping her vodka and orange flirtatiously. 'Now! As it is Results Party Night, it's absolutely compulsory that every Year 12 Class of 1994 graduate writes his or her TER mark on one of these bibs! Ok? Everyone's doing it and it is soooooo funny!' Sarah jumped up and down again, this time showcasing the bib.

'Why?' Courtney asked in the driest of chick-dry tones.

'Because it is just so much fun! Look, here's my one!' And Sarah took away the blank bib she was holding to reveal her own. The bib read 98.7.

'You got 98.7?' Gordon asked. Sarah nodded, winking and flirting as best she knew how, but also like 'How could that've happened? 98.7?'

'No wonder you want to wear a bib,' Courtney said, failing to add that she scored even higher than Kirkwood.

'Yes, yes, I'm sure you did well *too*, Courtney, you're amazing in class. Anyway. Look. Everyone's just *got* to put a bib on and get your number out there and really I mean just don't worry so much about it. Just be honest, I mean who cares what you got, like if I got eighty or even something low like sixty-five I wouldn't care, I'd be proud that I did my best and that maybe I could one day be a real estate agent, or a newsagent, or like my cousin Christina got like fifty-eight and she went and did arts/law, got in the back way. What I'm trying to say is everyone wishes they got more. Even I do! I want to know where I lost my 1.3! I was pretty sure I'd get more like 99.7 but there you are, it's crazy how they mark the tests, and I get scaled down because of the poor standard of the school. But anyway! It's a great conversation starter, I mean just look at the one we're having now!'

'Yeah! Hand me a bib, Kirkwood,' Stuart ordered, picking up a texta.

'Good leadership, Stuart! That's the spirit everyone!' Sarah clapped her hands.

Sarah winked (with both eyes) at Gordon as Stuart drew a big cock and balls on his bib and slinked on through to the party.

'He did really well in biology,' Courtney joked, drawing a pair of tits on her bib. 'And so did I.'

I wrote 'Just enough' on my bib and Gordon wrote 'Stuart Stone is gay' on his. Sarah Kirkwood smiled and grinned and giggled, but I could tell she was dying inside. Again she had tried too hard and failed.

'Dude, it's cool,' I said, comforting Gordon with a scruff of the hair.

'Matthew Updike? Are you serious?!' Gordon bellowed.

'Simmer down, Gord, ok? It's ok, man,' I said.

'The fucker's got a weight problem and he reeks!' Gordon bellowed again.

We hadn't been there two minutes and already there was drama. During Gordon's establishing lap of the party (where he took in everyone's TER bib, scored some chilled cans of ale from the stack of eskies on the grass, and high-fived some of the Jap guys from karate), he spotted his ex-girlfriend, Renee Gulliano, kissing and cuddling up to the rotund and generally unappealing Matthew Updike. Less than two weeks after Gordon and Renee ended their five-month relationship in the car park at Coyotes nightclub in Caringbah, she was already taking other offers.

'Has she not heard of a grieving process? I mean for fuck's sake, I have a heart here! I'm a sensitive guy!'

'Hey hey hey, Daryl Braithwaite, don't go riding off with the horses quite yet. Look to Stuart. Look to Stuart, please,' Stu said.

Stuart took Gordon's pale and pimply face in his hands, consoling and educating at the same time. 'Renee is a bush pig. Remember when we decided to break up with her?' Gordon nodded. 'Yes we do, we broke up with her because she was a bush pig.'

Courtney and I stifled our laughter behind our couple wall.

'She gave no blowjobs, her house smelt like chicken loaf, and bits of her lip fell off when you pashed her. It is a good thing she is with Updike! Look at the two of them. It's a match made in heaven.'

'The guy is in my soccer team!' Gordon fumed.

'He's the goalie, man – enough said!'

That afternoon Sarah Kirkwood had built a little stage and podium between the Australian flagpole and the water feature, and now she was tapping a microphone on it, ready to address her public.

'Hellloooooooo, everyone! Woohoo! Welcome to the Class of '94 Year 12 Results Party!' Sarah jumped up and down as she spoke, evoking a mild din from the one-hundred-and-forty-four-strong crowd of semi-drunk, stoned, cooked, tripping, E-ing, speeding, aerosoled, Amyl-ated teenagers.

'Thank you sooooo much for all getting in the spirit and wearing your bibs! It's such a great conversation starter and let's face it, who cares what you got, as long as you tried your best and continue to follow your dreams.' Sarah jumped up and down again, inspiring even less of a reaction from the crowd.

'Now some of you – and I won't name names, Stuart Stone – thought it would be funny to draw naughty things on your bibs.'

The entire crowd cheered and whooped as Stuart Stone held his cock-and-balls bib up in the air for all to see.

'She's a nice person, Sarah, isn't she? Means well,' Gordon noted to me in his overearnest fashion, and right back at him I nodded support. Sure.

'Soooooooooo!' Sarah swooned, switching the mike to her other hand. 'I just wanted to say that I have had the best time at school with you guys and I hope you have too – with me – and you know where I live so don't be a stranger, feel free to drop in any time and say hi.'

'Will there be free piss?' Stuart yelled, inspiring a loud cheer from the crowd.

'And just have an awesome time tonight. Dance your hearts out and drink as much as you like. I'll be coming round with the beer bongs and Vodka Super Duper Water Squirters so don't be shy! Go crazy! I LOVE YOU, YEAR 12!' Sarah finished with a bang, slipping off the stage and knocking into the flagpole, inspiring the biggest, most enormous cheer of the evening, just as Pearl Jam's 'Animal' came blaring out of the speakers, and everyone threw their arms in the air, moshing and slamming into each other with rough abandon.

'Dude, look.' Stu pointed.

'What? Who? Where?' Gordon asked, looking about.

'The Year 11 epileptic I was talking about is here. Check it.' Through the mosh and mess of sweating, heaving bodies was Kyla Druid, wearing a short skirt and torn Sportsgirl t-shirt, sipping from a West Coast Cooler.

'Jesus – she came up alright,' Gordon conceded.

The evening deepened and dipped as everyone packed off into cliques and corners, merging with those they had formed an alliance with over the past one to thirteen years. If adolescence was a war zone then fashion and music were both protection and artillery, they kept us safe and offered us a position to fire ourselves from.

In the middle of the yard the surfies hung on their girls, drinking warm beer and flicking their peroxide-blond curls and banging skulls to the grungier riffs. Some of the fitter surfer boys had their shirts off, displaying their olive skin, tattoos and pierced nipples. Their girlfriends threw back Subzero spritzers, leathery sunstruck breasts popping out of their Hot Tuna bikini tops. The geeks, dorks and Asians gathered in one corner, drunk for the second time in their lives. On the driveway by the shed the gothics sat in a circle comparing leaves, their minds willingly kidnapped by LSD. Under the eucalyptus tree by the water feature the ravers bounced from side to side in their striped shirts and floppy pants, sucking on Chupa Chups, practising their moves and staying positive. In the lounge room the Samoans passed the footy around, skimming the expensive lamps and chandeliers, fiddling with their cocks as they released the ball. In the kitchen the Italians compared watches, finding coffee in the cupboards and talking about going for a drive. In the front room the fat kids played Commodore 64 and ate nachos, engulfed in puffy beanbags.

By the shed, Matthew Updike appeared to be eating Renee Gulliano's face with every gulp of his fat lips. His elbow yanked her face to his, restricting any movement on her part, and with his right arm he was seemingly digging into her groin, elbow going up then down as if pumping for water. Renee was being manhandled by a novice, mauled by a piped-up young animal. Eight percent of her face and body seemed to be enjoying it, while the other ninety-two percent was hanging on for dear life. It was impossible to tell whether her gasps were cries for help or signs of delight. Updike ploughed on regardless; this was the best night of his life.

'It's like he's trying to pull a small calf out of her,' Stuart commented.

'How could she go there with that fat shit?'

'Walk away, Braithwaite, walk away.'

And they were about to, when a half-cut Sarah Kirkwood and the ever-coquettish Kyla Druid appeared before us wielding two fully loaded Vodka Super Duper Water Squirters.

'Do you guys know Kyla? She's my second cousin!'

'Yeah yeah yeah, we knew that!' Gordon and Stu lied in chorus.

'Aaaaaanyway, we think you guys are pussies and were wondering if you pussies would challenge us to a vodka battle! We may look cute . . .'

Stuart couldn't help but groan in delight, and soon they were all heading over to the south-eastern corner of the lush, over-manicured backyard for a two-on-two vodka duel. I watched them moving away from me – my best mate, my oldest mate, and two girls with bright purple guns – and it felt strangely appropriate.

'Let's go inside,' Courtney said.

In less than seventeen minutes the (Mitsubishi) ecstasy tablet had entered my bloodstream and filled it with serotonin (joy and passion), driving me to piggyback my girlfriend up two flights of white-carpeted stairs, down the hallway, round the corner past the study and onto the floor of Sarah Kirkwood's younger brother Murray's room (he was away at a rugby union camp in the Illawarra). I was in perfect condition to do the deed I was so utterly terrified of. Would I be too quick? Would I hurt her? Was my dick too thin? Would I be bad at it? These thoughts usually crippled my surge but right now all I could think of was flesh. Yes, in my mind Nina was pouring fruit whip on her breasts in the kitchen.

I lay back on the fluffy boyish carpet as Courtney kissed up my torso, lifting my t-shirt over my neck and moaning with the music of the drug.

'You're so beautiful, Nelly. I want you.'

'You're beautiful too.' Nina in her leggings, bending over the cutlery drawer.

'I love your face. And your nose. You have such a cute nose, Nelly.'

'Do you think your mum would approve of what we're about to do?' I asked.

'Why are you asking me that?' Courtney said, handing me an Ansell.

'Just wondering . . .'

Like a man I rolled the condom onto my now sizeable penis. Courtney sat naked and pale before me on Murray Kirkwood's floor; her whole body was waiting for me, open and white. I felt so much for her, but most of all, I just felt sorry for her.

'Do you want me to start on top?' I asked, lifting the teardrop nib of the condom up above my knob to make room for inevitable ejaculation (just as Kim Reynoldson had demonstrated on a Lebanese cucumber eighteen months earlier in the sex education caravan parked on the primary school green patch).

'I want you on top of me, yes. Do that. Neil Cronk, I want you.' Courtney continued to release her elephant-sized feelings. 'I want to be with you forever. And have your babies. And make a home with you.'

'Yeah, me too, C. That's all I want too!' I could say anything on this drug, anything in this moment, fucking anything.

'Fuck me. Make love to me and fuck me,' she pleaded with forced whorishness.

I climbed on top of Courtney, opening her vagina up with my middle three fingers.

'I want you to love me. And live with me. We'll live together,' Courtney moaned as my penis peered over the edges and into the abyss.

'Yes, I want all this too!' I said.

I stuck my dick into Courtney with a swift shove and it fit well; all the warmth engulfed me. Her big green eyes opened up, they were like kiwi fruits, kiwi fruits in Nina's hands in the kitchen. Nina was making me a fruit drink with no pants on. I am fucking Nina from behind as she makes me a drink but then I hear a grunt and a door slam, I turn to see Eric in the doorway, carrying his dead son into the house and me not knowing what to do with my dick in his wife's arse and the fruits whipping green in the glass cylinder are Courtney's eyes.

'Excuse me,' I said, pulling my dick out of her vagina.

Courtney looked at me, gasping, despairing.

'I'm sorry,' I said. 'So pathetic.'

'What the fuck, Neil?' Courtney said, and she looked just so vulnerable, her pale white legs all opened up and just there.

'I can't fucken do it. I'm too wasted.'

'You were doing fine,' she said, tears welling in her eyes.

And then I said it.

'You look desperate,' I said, and I don't know why.

'What?'

'You know.' I gestured to her naked cunt all splayed out on the carpet.

Courtney slapped me hard across the eye cavity, then again across the jaw, and then she grabbed a Darth Vader doll off Murray Kirkwood's desk and began smashing me over the head with it, attempting to crack my skull. I tried to stop the bashing by holding her arms.

'I'm sorry, C! I'm so fucking maggot!'

But this just made it worse, and soon she was on her feet, hurling the contents of the room at me.

Hauling my left boot on, I burst out of Murray Kirkwood's bedroom and staggered down the hall. One of my eyes bled red, the other tears. My ears raged with the vile and hurtful death wishes of Courtney's abuse as I pushed along the banister, past the third bathroom, around the bend to Mr Kirkwood's study and down the three flights of stairs. I was nearly outside, where I would run for my life.

'Nelly!'

Just as I cleared the final steps Sarah Kirkwood and Gordon came bouncing up, hand in hand.

'Are you alright, man?'

'Yep,' I managed, attempting to push past.

'What happened to your eye?' Gordon asked, holding my armpit.

'Do you need some Dettol?' Sarah added, eyes rolling back in her drunken cranium.

'Did you and Courtney . . .? I saw you going upstairs!' Gordon winked.

'Just let me past, man.'

'Dude, it's me!'

'Please, G.'

'Did she hit you?'

'Can you let go of me, please?' I wanted to scream.

'How good are the Es? Have you had another half?'

'I gotta go, Gordon.' I may scream. Let go of my armpit.

'Me and Sarah are going up to Sarah's room.'

'I'm going to show him my awards.'

'Ok – have fun.' I will scream this fucking house down.

'I love you, Nelly.'

Like when Sunday church is finally over and the choir stops singing and the congregation scatters and we're back out on the street away from the Lord . . . I FELT SUCH RELIEF! Ripping myself out of Gordon's grip and pushing past, through the Samoans and over the fat guys in the front room. Through the front door and off the welcome mat, down the front steps and onto the driveway I ran. Down the driveway and over the goths (who were now collecting ants and placing them on their tongues) past a line of couples mauling on the fence. Everything was a blur and a wipe as I made real speed, exiting forever towards the sea. But just as I reached the front lawn I felt an overwhelming need to stop. And look back.

Three flights up, her hair wild and hard and black, was Courtney, my girlfriend of a year and a bit, peering out the window and down the driveway at me. She looked so hurt and so appalled, with just a towel wrapped around her. I stood there, idiotically still, just staring at her. I know I could have changed the shape of that night, and perhaps my life, in that exact moment. With a smile or change in my face. A wave or a shrug of apology. With gesture, with intent, with action. But I didn't. And then she was gone and there was no one in the window, just the haunting dance of the curtain in the faraway sea breeze. The sea breeze . . .

'Oi!'

Across the lawn on the trampoline Kyla and Stuart were entwined like snakes. They looked so relaxed, laughing and kissing beneath the stars. I could not believe the outcomes, Courtney tried to kill me with an iconic children's toy, and here he was tuning an epileptic. Everything, always so easy for him. Perhaps that's it.

'Stu,' I breathed, walking over to the trampoline. 'Stuey.'

Stuart coolly whipped his hands out of Kyla's Sportsgirl t-shirt and rolled over to greet his dishevelled friend.

'Nelly, what's up with your eye?'

'I gotta go, man.'

'Where's Courtney? How's your E?'

I just stood there under the pine tree, gormless.

'Oh your poor baby,' Kyla said, fixing her top and sitting up.

'You guys . . . look . . . I just came over to say I'm off home.'

'No you're fucken not.' Stuart launched off the tramp and onto the grass in a single bound. 'Nelly and Daddy Chops are going for a grownups' chat.'

'Stu, seriously. You stay here with Kyla.'

'Hey! What did I say?'

'Can I come too?' Kyla asked, dismounting the trampoline.

Stuart spun back and took Kyla in his arms. This was my opening, and I took it, launching myself through the hedge and onto the street. Sidestepping a beige Corolla, I bolted for the sea.

8

The waves lifted up, took a breath, a simple intake of air, paused, and then crashed into themselves, coming to nothing, bleeding useless into the pebbly sand.

I stood in and before the ocean, before the great black tarmac of water, and contemplated suicide. I imagined my father arriving at the funeral, seeing my mother crippled with tears and failure, but him not crying. I then imagined not doing it and continuing life, as this sick animal that couldn't even do the simple things like sex a girl. A girl so smart, so funny, so caring, so unique and interesting – now so stung by the cruel words of the young man in her life. I stepped further into the sea, cold water circling round my boots.

'Cronk, you faggot!' The words boomed through the salted air and into my eardrums. I turned around and there he was, Stuart Stone – out of breath but here for me, always there for me.

Stuart and I had been sitting on the shore of North Cronulla Beach for somewhere between five minutes and an hour, I had no idea how long. Stuart hadn't asked me about what happened with

Courtney, he hadn't really asked me anything. We had a bit of a laugh about Gordon getting it on with Kirkwood, and we acknowledged how full-on the Es were, but we did not mention what he had just seen, his oldest friend walking into the sea.

'Kyla seems into it,' I said, watching a lone fisherman drag a bream into shore.

'Yeah, she's fresh.'

'You do her on that trampoline?'

'She'll only let me if I go out with her.'

'Ah.'

'Yeah.'

'So . . .'

'I could vibe with that and say "Yes, I'll go out with you", give her the stick then dump her, but she's only young and I don't want to bring on her epilepsy.'

'Thoughtful.'

The fisherman seemed to be having trouble salvaging the hook from inside the bream's mouth, ripping open its gob with his hands.

'I'm still a virgin,' I confessed.

'I know.'

'How?'

'Well if you weren't one you wouldn't be sitting on North Cronulla Beach in the freezing fucking cold with me.'

'True.'

The fisherman shone his torch right down into the fish, its guts lit up like a paper lantern. Another five minutes or an hour passed by, I don't know, all I knew was I felt good when I was with Stuart. He was massive and mental and, really, we were so wildly different, but I'd never felt so safe and calm with a bloke. I don't even remember when we met, all I knew was I'd known him forever. We'd sat next to each other in Kindergarten, Year 1, Year 2, Year 3 and beyond. When I was nine, in Year 4, I told the class a story about this really loud possum that lived in our roof, and how Dad was always dumping it way out in the nature reserve that backed on to our house, but it always returned. After class Stuart came up to me and said he had a boat, and that his dad would take us and the possum over to South West Arm on the weekend, dump the possum, and me and Dad would never be bothered again.

Saturday came and Ron Stone arrived at our front door. His big car looked even more imposing with a boat attached to it. Stuart launched out of the front seat in just a pair of shorts, pink zinc cream smeared across his nose. He walked towards me with open arms and I never felt so cool, my first ever friend. Dad thanked Ron with a six-pack of Swan Lager, but Ron wouldn't accept it this way, instead he suggested Dad come on the trip with us, and they drink the tinnies there, 'On deck.' Dad went inside, grabbed a hat, a camera and the wire cage with the adventurous possum in it, and off we went on our nautical mission.

The trip was a big hit, and even though the possum *still* made its way back to our roof a month later, despite having to cross lengths of water and land, it inspired a succession of weekend father–son journeys. We even camped out at Bundeena a few nights, and Dad and Ron got on just as well as me and Stuart did. They found a common interest in motor sports, water sports, all sports really, as me and Stuart fished and built stuff, investigated trails and stabbed yabbies' eyes out.

One Easter Dad and Ron bought us our own rowboat to journey off in, and we would, rowing around the reefs while they remained in the big hull, sipping on beers and nibbling on blue cheese, the NRL commentary pushing out the crackling speakers of Dad's battery-powered transistor radio. Often Dad and Ron would tie our dinghy to the big boat and cruise slowly up the harbour, dragging us behind.

The last time we did it Dad and Ron had been up all night playing cards and drinking cognac. They both had 'sore heads' in the morning and weren't speaking much; Dad didn't even finish his scrambled eggs. We were cruising behind the boat, with about forty feet of rope separating us, when Stuart noticed that our dinghy was filling up with water. Stuart thought it was hilarious, so he began whomping and tipping the little rowboat until there was water everywhere, and the thing started to dip.

'We're sinking!' I said.

'Shit.' Stuart looked around. 'Sharks!'

We started screaming, but Dad and Ron couldn't hear us. They had the footy on the radio and were sipping beers in silence, cruising up the harbour, enjoying their hangovers and the absence of their noisy boys.

The dinghy disappeared beneath us into the blue abyss. I began to paddle madly, but my mouth was already full of water, and I couldn't see well. Stuart swam over to me and hoicked me onto his shoulder, ordering me to hold on.

We stayed like this for a while, suspended in the harbour, two twelve-year-old boys dislocated from their fathers, their land, their lives. Stuart's legs kicked furiously beneath us, as he worked his big heart out to keep us both above the water line. He knew I was not a strong swimmer, he knew he had to do this if I was to survive. We screamed a little, but not for long, the boat was too far away, and it seemed a waste of energy.

Dad and Ron were but a speck in the distance by the time they realised we were gone. We heard the horn go and the noise of the roaring engine as it whipped around and stormed towards us. Dad looked pale when they found us, but I didn't know if that was the hangover or the fear of his son drowning. Ron was pissed off, blaming Stuart for sinking the dinghy.

Stuart protested, he said, 'There's a hole in it', but Ron wouldn't take it, he slapped Stuart hard across the face and ordered him to go down into the bowels of the boat and not come out until we were home. I so wanted to slap Ron back; Stuart had saved my life, and if *they* weren't so obsessed with their stupid rugby league game and their drinks they may have remembered they had children tied to the boat and that it was worth checking on them every now and again. But I didn't say anything; I was shivering, incapable of words. I just sat there with a blanket round me, watching my dad spew over the side, and then we were home, and that was the end of our father–son weekends; Dad and Ron never organised much after that, and for this reason neither did me and Stu. We didn't 'fall out', we just drifted into other sections of school/life. It wasn't until later that Stuart came back in to my life as a constant, which was always going to happen, we just needed some time to shrug off the shame.

Now Stuart and I sat together on the beach looking out at the ocean that had nearly taken us both some six years ago. We were bigger now, but still scared.

'Don't stay here, mate,' Stuart said.

'Huh?'

'Go fly, mate. You're the special one. Seriously, just go fly. Fuck Cronulla, it's a fucking hole, mate.'

The black waves crashed hard up the shore, making the fisherman's arduous task more arduous. The drugs and the big friendship bulged in and out of my heart as I sat there next to Stuart in the heavy music of the beach.

'I can't go back to the party,' I said.

'Cool,' Stu said, 'let's go to a *real* party then.'

The braver seagulls ducked and dived in the heavy winds as me and Stuart walked back down the beach past the fisherman and the poor bloody bream, flapping about in the bucket Kyla Druid style.

9

'Stone Family Mechanics' was a household name in the Sutherland Shire. Stuart's great-great-grandfather had passed it down to Ron's grandfather who had passed it down to Ron's dad who had passed it down to Ron. Malaki and Stuart had shown little interest in extending the life of the family business. Ron never felt like much of a mechanic either, but in those days you did what your father told you. Ron ran five workshops in the Shire, and was very popular and respected among the staff and clientele. He had also been known to recruit troubled or retarded kids, offering them a trade and a hard day's work.

The morale and sense of mateship were high across all workshops, and on the last Wednesday of every month all the mechanics would gather at one of the workshops and bond, ordering a dozen pizzas and a few kegs of beer (with a couple of possible 'surprises' thrown in later in the night).

Stuart and Malaki were regulars at these bonding nights, whereas Ron had stopped going years back, declaring himself 'too old to enjoy such nonsense.'

In the office of the Kareela workshop I dragged some glassy speed off the *Yellow Pages* and into my nose, face and brain. The powder cut at my nostrils and eyes but I liked it. I didn't care. I didn't care what happened to me. I would do anything tonight. The dirtier the glassier the weirder the better the further away.

I couldn't quite follow what went next. One minute Stuart was playing cricket with the boys, the next he was drinking out of a hubcap, then he was getting forklifted up into the roof, then he was lining up more glassy brown speed for me to do. Then he had his shirt off and was dancing on top of a Nissan Patrol, pointing at his muscles and kissing them as the boys threw winches and spanners and cans at him and roared with delight. Then it all went fuzzier, and I was standing in a circle with forty-three mechanics aged between fifteen and fifty, all fuck-eyed on booze and gack and pot. Ioannis, the bald-headed Greek chief mechanic, stepped forward.

'G'day, boys,' he said, his gut popping out under his Tahiti singlet.

The entire workshop cheered and hollered, raising their beers and bongs at the undisputed King of the Car-Fixers.

'Special night tonight, as it is the very first Workshop Bonanza of 1995!'

And again the boys hollered, grabbing their cocks or banging spanners onto busted-off door panels. My brain still zapping and my eyesight in sections of there and not there, I looked around for Stuart but there wasn't him.

'So,' Ioannis continued, 'I thought I'd provide something special for my boys to kick off another fine year of car maintenance. Gentleman, please say hello to Larissa the Kisser!'

Loud tacky saxophone filled the workshop as I spun around to see a large, blonde, middle-aged woman appear in the roller-door entrance to Stone Family Mechanics wearing a lacy black g-string and bright red corset, lumps of fat spewing over her g-banger as she wobbled into the circle.

Larissa the Kisser danced around a forty-gallon drum as the boys cheered and leered, grabbing their cocks and hurling beer cans at each other. Ioannis unfurled a rubber mat on the hard concrete floor and before the saxophone song had ended two of the junior mechanics had dumped their load in Larissa and the next guy in the circle was up. My thought system zapped and buzzed, my eyes opened and closed with every beat of the drum, but still I could not make out the direction of the queue nor decipher if there were six, possibly five guys to go until it was my turn.

I had to make a run for it, but every time I did, someone slung me back into the ring. I gave in and stood watching the action in the middle of the circle. A rickety little sixteen-year-old mechanic from the Hurstville workshop hammered away, his tiny white arse shaking and shuddering for less than eight seconds before he came off and was ushered impolitely back to the circle. I thought AC/DC were playing now and people were yelling 'Thunder' but I was not sure. Four or three to go? I tried to get away again but another set of arms made me stay – I was stuck and two to go, one.

I closed my eyes and THUNDER then . . . a single word echoed up my life: 'Go!' Someone or something pushed me in the back, and there I was in the centre of the room. Larissa was on the mat drinking from a bottle of orange juice – she looked really exhausted but she smiled at me nonetheless; a professional. Her forehead was drenched with sweat and there were thumb marks on her neck (well, they were more like bruises).

Larissa curled her fingers and licked her lips and I wondered if she had ever played hockey or if she had goldfish or a family. Did she watch *Sale of the Century*?

'How do you want me?' Larissa asked politely.

I spun away and attempted to run to America but Stuart stood behind me and so did Ioannis and this other prick; they would make me dick this chick before the night was out.

'Give her the stick, Nelly. Get it done, mate,' Stuart said, winking at Larissa like they were wrestling partners arranging a set move.

I turned back to Larissa who was bleeding from her underpants as a cheer emerged and built throughout the workshop. The whole place was calling my name, hands pounding together.

'Come on, special. Come to Larissa.'

I loped over to her. She undid my jeans. I wished the boys would stop chanting so I could focus. My dick was floppy and lifeless and the workshop threw cans at me. I noticed how ugly and pasty they all looked, how like dogs their eyes popped out of their sockets and their gums dripped, and how useless they were at keeping time with a simple clap and chant.

'Here we go! Here we go, little fella!'

Larissa had been wanking me and sucking me for some time now. My eyes were closed; I couldn't watch to know if there was stiffness. She pulled me on top of her and she smelt like white musk, the perfume my sister wore when she went to Northies or even to the dole office. She eased my dick inside her gash which I slid left then right in. I grabbed one of her fifteen breasts and pumped away like a jackhammer. I thought about Courtney and how nice it was when she came over, how I'd answer the door and she would be there in a summer dress. I thought about how well Dad and Courtney got on when we went skiing at Thredbo and how scared she was of the chairlift and how cute she looked in a bib and brace and how much she loved the snow. Courtney said sex should be like falling rain but it was hailing here, sharp black ice. And then it was over and Stuart reefed me out of Larissa and handed me a VB and said, 'Done.'

10

Ioannis dropped me and Stuart at the Red Rooster on Cronulla Street and wished us well. It turned out he was a big reader of books and plays, quizzing me on Shakespeare and Beckett and Henry Miller as we drove south to the beach.

'Nice work tonight, Nelly. I think you went longer than all of the Kirrawee boys put together! Hahahahahaha!'

Ioannis launched into a coughing fit as he drove off, a *Cops R Tops* sticker on the rear fender of his ute next to a pair of Playboy bunny ears.

The wind smelt of salt and vinegar chips. There were a hundred or so kids out the front of the squash courts smoking and pushing energy out and around. Stuart and I watched it all from across the road.

'Bombers,' Stu alerted me.

The squash courts party was organised by Endeavour High kids but all schools inevitably attended. I felt sick as we approached, knowing full well that if there was a pack of Bombers there Stu would end up lashing out at something they said or did. The Bombers were mostly wogs in puffy jackets who spray-painted their 'tags' on walls and listened to rap. They thought they were black and proper gangsters from 'da hood' when really they were just teenagers living in Kirrawee or Menai.

'You have a good time back there, Nelly?' Stu asked me, practically striding towards the venue. Fuck. No way out now.

It worked like chequers in Cronulla. The Bombers would do something one week, like pop one of our footballs with a compass, or call a white chick a slut for wearing a black bra under her sheer white school top, then the white guys would retaliate and the whole thing would build then splinter and fights would break out at train stations and shopping villages all over town. Now school was done, there had been all sorts of promises and threats made about how the two factions were going to end things, and Stuart was always a featured player in the ongoing narrative. Stuart didn't belong to a 'gang.' He wasn't a Waxhead, a Dork, a Raver or a Bomber; he was an independent. But Stuart loathed the fucking Bombers most, because they travelled in groups and picked on the weak. To Stuart, fighting was a personal affair, a beautiful exchange of strength and skill between two opposing forces. Bombers were cowards; they bashed people with bottles, with sticks that had nails coming out the ends, always outnumbering their opponent, often ten to one, and for that reason Cronulla was not their home – at least in Stuart Stone's mind it wasn't.

'S'alright,' I answered.

Stuart slammed me into the traffic light pole, his eyes beaming with speed and steroids and all the things that made him seventeen and Stuart.

'I WANT TO DO SOME DAMAGE TO THESE DAGO CUNTS, OK, MY FRIEND? IF YOU WOULD LIKE TO GET HOME SAFE I SUGGEST YOU WALK AWAY NOW AS I AM ABOUT TO MAKE A MESS – DO YOU HEAR ME?'

'Ok . . . but there's a few of them.'

'There's a few of me,' he replied.

Approaching the kerb Stu was spotted by one of the smaller Bombers, who then called out, 'Here he comes! King of the Convicts!'

Stuart did not even bother with his usual flurry of retorts, such as 'dago cunt' or 'grease ball' or 'immigrant'; he simply launched into the mess of it and somehow, by association, so did I. My face was rammed up against a phone booth. Through the glass I could see Stuart pounding into Daniel De Costa's face with his elbow and kicking Stavros Tsiokas in the gut. I was on the ground when a baseball bat with some spikes in it just swept by my face, but then a long neck of Fosters smashed over my shoulder. I rolled into the gutter, where my jaw was kicked into the kerb – which hurt. Again, like with Larissa, there was noise and there was quiet. There was flesh and blood and there was rain and there was me, and this numb excellent feeling, as another part of my soul was lifted up and taken away. I was crying but I didn't make tears. I just knew I wanted to go. And go and go and go and go. I hated this place. I fucking hated it. No one here had anything to do but harm what they didn't understand.

'Holy fuck! I can see Neil!' I heard Courtney's voice scream.

By now there were about fifty people in the riot.

I was trying to help lovely Seamus Fraser from general studies out of a group-kicking when De Costa's brother Leo busted a knife into my ribs.

Gordon must have seen this, as he arrived within a second or two, launching an array of well-constructed jump-kicks and snap-kicks and force-quick solar-plexus punches to the Bomber's available areas. He broke Leo's jaw with an elbow – I saw it change shape before my eyes.

Gordon then picked me up off the pavement, where my blood was pooling, and dragged my limp body over to a blue Toyota T18.

'Whose car is this?' I asked him as we went.

'Kirkwood's brother's,' he said.

'Fuck! Where's Courtney?' I said, peering out into the muddle of bodies; police sirens growing louder and louder.

'We gotta jet brother,' Gordon said. 'Cops!'

'Where is she?' I said, falling in to the back seat.

'Stu got her. Stu took her in a car. She's safe.'

Like most of the night, everything was bright and then it was gone. I could hear Phil Collins singing the bit before the drum solo in 'Something in the Air Tonight.' I knew which of Gordon's mix tapes this was from, and how it cut out before the end of side A, then flipped over to side B, then finished in less than ten seconds. I could see a Hot Chicken Hero wrapper on the floor and an empty carton of chocolate Moove. I put my hand in my hair and there was glass. I put my hand near my ribs and felt this wet hot feeling like soup – and all I wanted to do was go and go away.

I could not believe all the blood and I could not believe the car was moving, but mostly I could not believe Gordon still had enough space in his brain to perfectly execute the infamous drum solo on the steering wheel as he cranked a U-turn out of there.

No idea. Gordon had no real idea where he was going but he drove on anyway to Bell Biv Devoe's 'Poison.' Up President Avenue, through the five-ways roundabout, past Flower Power, around Sylvania Waters, past Paul's Hamburgers and over Tom Ugly's Bridge towards Rockdale. I spewed some blood and white stuff into the empty Moove carton then rolled a brick-thick cigarette, grinning gratitude through cracked teeth at Gordon in the rear-vision mirror.

'Where's Stu and Courtney, do you reckon?' I asked.

Gordon pulled in to Sans Souci McDonald's for six cheese-burgers, two thickshakes and a stack of napkins. Then we took off back towards Cronulla. It was nearly 5 am. Gordon was driving really fast as 'Why' by Annie Lennox played. She sounded good with the blood and the E – the wavering-ness, the softness, the female cuddle inside this lilting song; warm like breasts on your eyelids. The car went even faster up the incline but then it stopped dead, and Gordon craned around to look at me, patched with bloody napkins, sipping on a thick shake in the back seat.

'Get out, Cronk.'

'What?'

'There's no one on the bridge.' Gordon grinned madly.

The engine was off so we rolled the car to the exact peak on the bridge where the sign exclaimed: WELCOME TO THE SUTHERLAND SHIRE.

Gordon cranked the handbrake and climbed up onto the roof of the T18, hooting and shrieking like a freaked hyena.

'Get up here, Cronk!'

'I've been stabbed!'

'Get up here, the bridge is ours! Captain Cook Bridge!'

I climbed up the tyre and onto the roof, Gordon helping me with the last bit. Soon we were sitting together on top of the car, staring out into Botany Bay where the mariners of this newfound land first sailed in to kill the natives and set up the jails. We were only up there a minute or so before the sun flopped over the edge of the horizon.

'You know what I miss about being a kid?' Gordon said.

'What?' I asked, rolling another fag as best I could with all the pain and wind.

'Being afraid of monsters.'

I nodded, laughing through the smoke that drifted out my nose in perfect plumes.

'When I was eight, I used to be so scared of monsters, man. I'd think they were coming to get me every time it got dark. And they fucken did sometimes, they came in to my room and they got me. But now. Now I know they're not coming. And it really shits me, man.'

The dreams of children never go too far away. Gordon was clearly talking about his dad, I could feel it, see it, he had that face on, the scrunched and punished face reserved for his father the monster. And Peter *was* a monster; he visited in the night, he surprised and fascinated, he terrified in assaulting bursts, shaking the very foundations of the boy. He killed the house of calm and put a scar on top. But still, Gordon missed him. We all missed our dads, in that time, even when they were actually there.

'I know,' I said.

We put our arms around each other as the sun shot swiftly up over Snake Island.

'She really loves you, man,' said Gordon. 'Courtney, I mean.'

'Really?' I said. 'I don't know about that anymore.'

'I didn't tell her,' Gordon said, squeezing my neck. 'But I think she'll be cool, we kinda bonded tonight, she's an awesome girl, it's going to be awesome. Living in the ci-taayyyy!' Gordon beamed, high-fiving.

The Sutherland Shire was dead before me, but there was life beyond the horizon, and I wanted it so badly now. I was *so* in love with my life before tonight and the dreams it had gathered in its wake, but slowly and swiftly, in this collection of hours and moments I lost faith. I was already gone, I was already there, I was already someone else, and I had never felt so anxious. I rubbed Gordon's neck with my thumbs but I could not look at him. I just sucked in a whole pile of smoke, spat sideways and told the truth.

'I fucking hate it here,' I said.

'Huh?' Gordon replied, bewildered.

'Cronulla, the Shire, I fucking *hate* it so much!' I punched the roof of Gordon's car with my fist and the sound rang out. My best friend just stared at my face, then down at my ribs, then back up at my face.

'That's why we're getting out, right?' Gordon asked.

'I gotta go, man,' I said, shaking my head. 'I can't fucking breathe here man! I gotta get out.'

'What are you saying?' Gordon asked, and with such weight.

'The white cars, the beach, the fear, the Christian fucking conservatives, it's hell on earth here, it's small hell, so *small* . . .'

I started crying, and the words, too, fell out in floods, words I would come to regret for the rest of my life, but for some reason could not hold back on this roof, before this bay, beside this man.

'You want somewhere with more street life?'

'It's not just that – it's you, man!' I said. 'I gotta get the fuck away from all of *you* people! Courtney, Stuart, Mum, Agatha, the shops, the charcoal chicken, the fucking acceptance that life is just *this*. It's the fucking *smallness* of mind!'

'And let me guess, you're too *big* for it?'

I nodded, and the arrogance inflamed him. He punched me in the bloody wound beneath my ribs then shoved me off the roof of his car. It hurt in jolts, my face and ribs crashing into the asphalt bridge. I felt faint now, and confused, my vision failing in sections.

'Fuck off then, wonder boy,' Gordon said, crying, looming, above me.

Gordon drove off with a skid, the sound of The Breeders' 'Cannonball' moving away, fading off on that bouncy baseline.

I finally got to my feet, blood pouring out the side of me. I dipped my index finger inside myself, and then licked it. My own blood, it tasted so sweet. The sun was up now and Botany Bay was busy with boats and windsurfers. I heard a truck. I held my arm out. I needed to go to Sutherland Hospital immediately; I was born there after all.

11

The next few weeks were a torturous brand of limbo, waiting for our first-round offers to university, then second- and third-round offers. None of us saw much of each other in this period. Stuart went surfing, fucking and para-sailing in Bali, while Gordon seemed to always be working. I saw him a few times, of course, but it was only brief, on our bikes, at Coyotes for a quick beer, or an even quicker jam in the garage where neither of us quite committed to the repertoire. His restless leg was back, and I knew I was the reason. It took years of love and friendship to stop that thing shaking, then just one crazy night, and it had returned.

While Gordon was ignoring me, I was ignoring Courtney. I knew if I saw her all the feelings would come back and I'd rethink my decision to go, and I knew that wouldn't be right: I *had* to go. But still, she kept calling – even Nina called once or twice to ask me over for a fruit whip – but I never called back. I just nodded at Agatha as she delivered the messages and said, 'yeah, cool, thanks.' And sure, maybe I was a little, or let's call it a lot, embarrassed. And if anything is going to hold a man back, it's that.

So after dozens of unreturned calls Courtney appeared on my front lawn in jeans and a t-shirt, and we walked to McDonald's Caringbah. On the way up Telopea Avenue she picked a rose off a tree and asked me why *I* didn't think to pick it off and give it to her.

'I simply didn't notice the plant,' I said.

She picked the petals off the thing as we walked, leaving a melodramatic trail of broken romance behind us.

We ate Chicken McNuggets in silence then went to see *Cousins* at the Miranda Greater Union, which starred Ted Danson and Isabella Rossellini, it was kind of a stupid and predictable movie, but I liked how everyone was sleeping with everyone. Towards the middle Courtney and I kissed a bit and I tried to finger her but she said she had her period so we just fixed ourselves up and watched the end. On the home we stopped by McDonald's again and got a sundae – I didn't want one but I got one anyway – and we sat out in the children's play area and ate slowly, watching fat kids rock back and forth on plastic dogs.

'How are you?' I asked her.

'Okay,' she said, licking her plastic spoon.

'Good,' I said. I wished we were outside in the adult area so I could smoke, but instead we were here with the kids and it was all about setting 'good examples' and bullshit.

'Why have you been avoiding me?' she said, which was a stupid fucking question, but perhaps the only way in to this.

'Dunno,' I said. 'Didn't realise I was.'

'It was mean, what you said.'

'Yeah, well.'

'You can't just say something like that and then go off and not ever call me or anything, I mean you're an intelligent person Neil, but you're so narcissistic, haven't you ever heard of human decency?'

Haven't you ever heard of fuck off?

'I'm sorry,' I said. 'I felt stupid.'

'*You* felt stupid? I was the one called "desperate" and left there on Murray Kirkwood's bedroom floor completely naked!'

I wanted to laugh.

'Neil? Are you listening to me?' she said, like how Mum would.

'Yeah,' I said.

'Then *what*? Anything to say about that night?'

'If I could have it over again . . . I would do it differently,' I said and left it there. It was true I would have it over and when I had it over I'd stay home and read *The Celestine Prophecies* instead of going out at all.

'It's ok. It's just drugs. And timing . . .'

'We were pretty smashed.'

'The Es were strong,' she said, and it was over, all of it forgiven, well at least on the outside.

'Have you decided?' I asked her, as a blond child spilt his ice-cream cone and went into a psychotic tantrum beneath the slippery slide.

'Decided?' she asked, and she sounded so innocent, all the power was mine and I abused it, never looking at her or colouring my voice – just cold – cold and equivocal.

'University,' I said. 'Where will you go?'

She didn't say anything for a while. She just stared down into her sundae cup painted where the dregs of gone strawberry ripped up the sides. Then she rose and walked over to the entrance gate, popped the dessert in the bin and returned to her position beside me on the steps.

'I'm going to Sydney still,' she said, and in her voice there were tears but the tears had a hand on them, pushing them back behind a gate.

'Where will you live?' I asked.

'At Mum's,' she said, and I scoffed. 'I can't abandon her Neil! My father is going to live in New Zealand with my grandmother, they're separating – Mum and Dad. I have to stay with her or she'll be alone.'

'Ok,' I said, passive as a table.

'Sometimes you have to look after people, and anyway, I can get the train in, it's only forty minutes to Redfern station.'

'Cool, makes sense,' I said, and there was more silence, unless you count that tinny, life-affirming musak.

Six minutes passed and I told her I'd auditioned for the Bachelor of Arts communications – theatre/media course at Charles Sturt University in Bathurst and somehow I had been accepted.

'Why didn't you tell me you'd tried out?' she asked me.

'I never told anyone, didn't think I'd get in.'

'Of course you'd get in,' she said.

'I didn't know.'

'Are you going to go?'

I shrugged. 'The whole place felt magic when I was there.'

She took my hands in hers and rubbed them like they were frozen and she was trying to thaw them out.

'Look at me, Neil.'

I turned towards her for the first time today; her face was flushed and open, she had no make-up on at all except for lipstick, she was not hiding from me, she was asking me to see her.

'How long is the drive to Bathurst?' she asked me.

'Three and a half hours.'

'That's not much!' She smiled.

'It is if you're doing it all the time,' I said.

'Do you think we can handle it?' she said, in a high and bright voice, and all I could think was how right it was to call her desperate.

'No, I want to be free,' I said, and took my hands away, feeling for my pouch of tobacco and looking around at anything but her. I knew I was being childish but still I couldn't stop; it was easier to make things clear to her by being all petulant and aloof.

'It's so hurtful to have you discard me this way, after everything that has happened between us, Neil.'

'Nothing happened,' I said.

'I'm not talking about sex,' she said.

'What are you talking about then?' I said, rolling a cigarette. I didn't care about the future generations, I needed the hit now.

'You hurt me, and you hurt Gordon,' she said.

'Gordon's a big guy, he'll bounce back.'

'Who the fuck have you become? You're like this totally different guy – and in only two weeks!'

I explained it to her. 'In order to grow, we have to unchain ourselves from the past.'

'I didn't realise we were chains.'

I sighed. 'I just need to go and find myself, and I can't do that with the people from my past judging me as I go.'

Courtney could've been anyone she wanted, but instead of reaching out into the great unknown she cowered, the invisible ties of guilt and family hauling her in like a dumb fish.

'You're pathetic,' I said. 'You're all pathetic.'

She stood and said, 'You're up yourself!' and stormed off past the fibreglass statue of Ronald sitting on a bench.

The day I left for Bathurst Gordon came over and we all had some champagne and orange on the front lawn. Me, Agatha, Mum, Gordon, Stuart – even Dad was there, not saying heaps, but he was *there* in shorts and a penguin t-shirt, sipping Fosters out of a can.

I rang Courtney the night before to invite her and Nina answered. Her voice was colder than usual but I could still hear affection in it, something in the way she said 'Mmmm' before 'I'm not sure if she wants to talk to you.'

'She's mad at me still?'

'Yes, she is. You hurt her very deeply Neil.'

'I'm just honest Mrs G,' I said. 'That's who I am now.'

Then she took a deep breath and said something she had clearly been thinking of saying if she was ever presented with the chance.

'Remember to chew what's in your mouth. Where you are going there will be many temptations and many reasons to look over people's shoulders for what else is on offer. But chew what's in your mouth Neil, be where you are and never anywhere else. If you do this, then the rest of them will come your way soon enough.'

I could hear Courtney in the background asking who she was talking to – Nina must have told her it was me because she didn't ask again. Then the call was over and with it that part of my life, in that haunted house, with those stoic women and those insane fruit drinks.

I wasn't expecting gifts but they came at me. Mum bought me a yellow mattress that I could tuck under my arm. She sobbed, handing it over to me in its plastic pop-wrapping. She also bought me a year's worth of underpants and socks, handkerchiefs and lanolin hand cream. Agatha gave me *Journey to Ixtlan* by Carlos Castaneda; she said his teachings had really helped her through her long-term unemployment. Agatha kissed me and I nearly combusted; I could not remember her *ever* kissing me – not once in our eighteen-year tenure – and then she remembered she was coming along with Mum and me on the drive to Bathurst and so she got heaps embarrassed and went inside.

Stuart had bought me some extra-small 'flavoured' condoms and laughed his fucking nut off as I unwrapped them.

Dad handed me a pair of binoculars. He said something about 'looking at things' and then he shut up again, sipping on his Fosters and disappearing behind the shrub.

Then Gordon stepped forward. My heart was racing a million miles an hour. His grey eyes were glassy and his hands were shaking as he handed me a long box, almost as tall as me, wrapped in newspaper. I opened it to find a sword, a long, slender silver sword that had been engraved:

Cronk,
Don't forget us
Gordon and Stuart, 1995

Stuart came forward, a stretched chocolate condom in his hands blown up to resemble a poodle.

'Poodle penis!' he said, hugging me with a set of slaps on the back.

Then Gordon approached me again, holding out the face of the blade. 'Sixteenth-century samurai,' he said.

I hugged him and started crying.

'Take care of Courtney for me, won't you?' I asked Gordon, and he nodded into me, warm tears gathering in the bowl of my collarbone and neck.

'The sword is to protect you,' Gordon whispered, holding me tight as hell. Then we broke apart in a push and I was left with the sword and twelve hundred feelings. Gordon put some sunglasses on and wiped his nose. Stuart punched him in the arm and called him a 'faggot.' I took the sword, held it out like Excalibur, and bowed to my two mates. They bowed back to me, and that was that, we were connected forever.

The last thing I remember about that morning is driving away from that house, the house I grew up in. And Gordon's body diminishing in the rear-vision mirror, his chubby white arms waving at me from the front lawn of my life; he was all I could see. He was all I could feel. He was all I thought about for the entire drive, and then we got to campus.

Part 2

12

Seriously, things are better when you're skinny. T-shirts look more awesome, you can bend over or sit down shirtless in the sun without having to worry about how you're looking, because you're always looking skinny – from every angle. It's truly liberating.

I had been wonderfully skinny for three years now, which was wild considering my diet consisted of beer and sausages, potato wedges and wine, beer and wine, chocolate biscuits, spaghetti bolognese and wine and sausages, and my favourite dish, microwave penne pasticcio from the all-night Coles in South Bathurst. (They had just done up the all-night Coles and I can tell you it was a fucking joke. They put palm trees in it. Palm trees! In a Coles. In the Western Tablelands of New South Wales. What were the intentions behind this? More pineapple sales?)

I looked *especially* thin in the mirror that morning. My weird poking-out ribs and my six-pack. My long brown hair and my goatee. I wish Courtney knew what I was capable of now. With my rhythms and my cock, my thin agile frame, fuck, I could *really* fuck now. I missed that girl mad-style, and when I thought of her it was like being ripped open, whereas Gordon, he could go and get fucked, on so many levels.

Last night, after dress rehearsal, I'd gone to Swanna's house. She and I had been having an affair for three months – since she had started working on my major work. She was practically a virgin when I met her but now she was in tune with nearly all of it. I had broken her in – kind of like what Michael Hutchence did to Kylie Minogue, I guess. Taught the young thing. She loved wax.

It all started when I began the audition process for my major work. Naturally everyone wanted to be a part of it. She came into the studio in a floral dress with a slit up the side, eating from a bag of birdseed, with a *lost look* that could only be described as 'Please help me, third-year man!'

I didn't give her the part, but she was so mesmerising to look at it was impossible not to ruin her life in some way. Tiny and exotic with these dazzling eyes, a curious angel sent from Sri Lanka or God. I had the straightaway stir and quake in my gut and knew that my relationship with Chandra was in jeopardy. Well, maybe that is too strong a word. Chandra and I had lived through a lot in our three years together. A small dalliance with a first year was not going to shake the foundations. At least, that was my justification for firing the starter gun.

I found Swanna in the library later that week, bent over the microfiche absorbed in the bright blue stencils. I told her about this thing called 'intranet' that was kicking off in the computer centre. It was this wild and new way of sharing information across campus. Like sending a letter but the recipient gets it within *seconds.* She explained that she wasn't really an actor but wanted to be involved in my piece as she found my work . . . well I believe she said 'deeply inspiring'. Not to worry, I told her. She said it was meant to be hot this weekend, a rare thing round here. And I said to myself 'tell her about the swimming hole', so the next thing the library knows I'm telling her about the swimming hole called White Rock, out near the Oberon abattoirs.

Was it a Wednesday? We jumped in my Magna and drove out to the humble little lake between two vacated deer farms. It was the world's most peaceful place, except when there were snakes, but even the snakes at White Rock seemed relaxed, slithering about all groovy.

I took off my 'No Jabiluka Mines' t-shirt and my flares and threw myself naked into the green excellent water. Swanna stalled by the car in her singlet and fisherman pants, sheepish.

'Does anyone ever come down here?' she asked.

'Sometimes this dude on his kayak but like, nah.'

She had an *irregularly* hairy bush for her size – it was so bushy it seemed to blend in with the surrounding shrubbery – and her small, dipping breasts housed massive red nipples the size of LPs. Being from Cronulla, I had hardly seen an Indian-looking woman, let alone a beautiful one, and naked, in a lake, before me: Swanna was a swan no doubt. After a nervous, painfully slow submergence into the water she was soon *swanning* about in it. She had no issues with her body or its involvement with the water or all available nature for that matter, and I knew right then the fucking would be good and she would let me take photos of her region – anything in the realm of 'deeply inspiring'.

She splashed about then did graceful things, then spent whole chunks of minutes on her back, floating down the flow so trusting. Akimbo and glorious – there were reasons you met people.

The first time we made love was the second, no, third visit to White Rock. It was clearly her intention to make things move along, as she brought wine and a yoga mat. She laid the mat down by the car and told me about growing up half-Sri Lankan in Australia. How her father, on a business trip to Colombo, had met her mother at a cricket match, fallen instantly in love and brought her back here. Her father was an agricultural scientist and they were married in Canberra, where Swanna lived before uni. Her mother died of breast cancer when Swanna was fourteen, which she admitted she was still not entirely over. Her mother was her best friend and not a day went by where she did not think of her, often wondering what her home town was like, for Swanna had never been to Sri Lanka.

'My father remarried,' she said, her singlet all wet from the swimmers inside it, as she popped open the wine and poured it into teacups. 'But the woman he remarried, Rhonda . . .'

'Rhonda.' I smiled, sipping the cheap chardonnay.

'*Rhonda*.' She smiled back. 'She is a scientist as well, and this, well, I think two scientists together, it makes things very cold and detached in the house. Sometimes I feel like they don't care if I exist or not, they just go on talking about their work as if you're not there, as if you are a lesser thing.'

'What a joke,' I said, my hand in her hair. 'Where is your sister?'

'She . . .' Swanna burped up some wine. 'She moved to America years ago. She's a lesbian and doesn't feel like she can tell Dad, so she took this scholarship with a bank there and her and her girlfriend ran away from it all. You know that feeling?'

'That's why I'm here,' I replied, opening my arms to the countryside. 'Escape the cottonwool comfort of family.'

'Same.' Swanna nodded. 'But I didn't want to be in the city. I wanted to be near the trees and the birds. And a bachelor of arts felt like the perfect degree for an orphaned, confused, half-Asian, twenty-year-old girl.' She laughed.

'Where is your name from? Swanna?' I asked her, my thumb on her eyebrow.

'My mother wanted me to have a Sri Lankan name, but Dad said that would make things hard for me at school in Canberra. So she looked at me, and she said to my dad that I looked neither black nor white, but at the same time I looked *both* black and white.'

'Like a swan,' I said.

'Like a swan,' she confirmed.

She was very tight and the sun was beating down in spears. The orb had such strength in this part of the world, *especially* between noon and 4 pm. But the wine and the comfortable rubber surface and the joy of a new and brilliant connection. Strange . . . never before had I felt so at ease staring into a girl's eyes. Even with Chandra, I couldn't look for too long without all her conditions falling into the act. Courtney, well, I never really got to know, her eyes were so riddled with need and grief I could never even manage the insertion, but Swanna's eyes were somehow harmless, like cardigans. I showed her what it meant to have her own rhythm and she took my confidence and segued into a *whole new* current of her own – one that was always there and we men could never know about, no matter what we read or touched.

'I'm not in Canberra anymore . . .' she whispered, as she went up.

And I knew right at that moment, as the sun shone on her fabulous big bush, that she would definitely be part of the design team for my final show.

13

Chandra didn't wake when I got home from Swanna's place at 3 am. She must have figured the last-night preparations had gone on and on with props and painting and the angling of lights. Little did she know I had been on my way home at 11 pm but I just couldn't get Swanna out of my thoughts. For weeks we had been stealing kisses behind the set and under the seats, backstage and behind the steel mill theatre. Every morning, every noon and every night – out of sight of the actors and the stage manager, we'd crash together, grinding and tearing at each other, then at the slightest suspicion of noise or company we'd bounce away and resume our work, throwing out earnest sentences like 'The pre-show state must be symbolic, ominous even, of what will follow' or 'Where is the OP dress table?'

In the three years I had been at university I had engaged in some seriously deplorable, fabulous, violent, wrong, weird, dangerous, inexplicable acts of multi-sexual feverishness and bondage – I mean the entire theatre/media strand was a breeding ground for bisexual whoring and I was surely its public ambassador, eating sheets of acid and summoning groups of artists to my house for orgies and improvised naked dance sessions. Chandra wholeheartedly approved of such 'experimentation', often chock-a-block herself with a juggler in her mouth, a lighting designer in her pussy, an AD in her arsehole. As long as I didn't get too attached, which I never did. Chandra was a mad bitch, prone to wild artistic fits and hormonal storms during which she would literally try to kill me, but I loved her, and no one had ever tempted me away from her big spiky heart and her bold way of living in the ripe part of the tree.

Until now.

Until this odd little swan with the listening eyes and the broken story put a spell on me. Not a day went by when I did not think of Courtney – her skin, her eyes, her lips, her mind, and the way things ended that January – but every thought of Courtney was always doused in strain. It was intense and shameful to contemplate the girl and what had transpired between us, whereas every thought of Swanna, well, it was like the sun was out. She was freedom and light.

Chandra was snoring, a copy of *The Female Eunuch* on her neck. I put my arms around her and fell asleep, so tired from the twenty-hour day at the theatre and from making love to Swanna once fast and once slow like that Mazzy Star song about falling or whatever. Once in bed I rolled over away from my Feminist and fell asleep instantly.

Chandra elbowed me at 5 am and explained to me where her period sat on the Richter scale of *pain* and straight away I drove down to the twenty-four-hour Coles and bought her a chocolate cake for $11.45. She ate half of it then fell back to sleep. The cake was in her arms as she woke, asking me 'When did you get home?' and 'Why is there cake in the bed?'

'You had bad period pain so I drove down and got you cake.'

'Bullshit.'

'You don't remember?' I asked, spraying myself with Joop.

'You never go and get me cake, you always say *fuck off and have a Panadol* – when do you ever do what I say and get me cake on my period?'

'Last night – heaps of times.'

'You're in a good mood.'

'It's opening night!'

I moved to the door, slinging my satchel over my shoulder.

'Where are you going?' Chandra asked, dipping her long fingers in the cake.

'I have an interview.'

'Who with?'

'Radio.'

'University?'

'No, local. The show is selling out, it's broken out of the college grounds and now the word is out, downtown. General public want a piece of it.'

'WOW!' Chandra exclaimed, about as passive aggressive as one could go. 'You and Julien must be happy with yourselves?'

'There's a boy from the local high school in the show who Julien has his eye on for the wrap party, so yeah, Julien is very happy with himself.'

'Come back to bed,' she moaned.

'I gotta go do this.'

'I'm not well!' Chandra rolled over into the cake.

'Babe, it's opening night – why can't you see –'

'I see! I see! Go go go – don't even kiss me goodbye! I'll just lie here in my puddle of blood and cake and misery – you go do your interview!'

For her major work Chandra had chosen photography, focusing on the relationship between nudes and machines. On paper it sounded great, but on the night it was a series of trucks and dicks.

She knew it. Since the opening a week ago she had spent a lot of time in my bed vomiting and reading Germaine Greer and talking about her period. She was jealous – and why wouldn't she be? Since I had graced the university grounds everything I touched had turned to gold. It had become clear to me that I was a Leader here. I was theatre/media's Che Guevara, although I had never worn a Che t-shirt – but if I had, then I can assure you everyone else would be too one week later. When I got into techno-fire-juggling in first year, so did everyone else. I started building fire sculptures and roaming through the town with a percussion squad – so followed the rest of my course. I coloured my hair purple, pierced my eyebrows and listened to Tricky, involved myself in hectic public orgies – then did they follow with their kerosene, and their L'Oreal Soft Colour, and their flavoured, ribbed and Magnum. One time I walked into the local theatre hang, the Park Hotel, and all the theatre students clapped me. I just stood there by the pool table in my torn-apart and rolled-up stone-wash jeans thinking, Yeah, why not?

But now it was major work time, and everything I had said, dealt, spat, fucked, dreamt or made in three years meant nothing. The final act was tonight and I was only as good as the moment that curtain fell. Tonight was *everything*. My pinnacle work, the work that could allegedly trampoline me to Sydney, to Melbourne, to England, to America even. And no shadow artist on the rag was going to stop the trajectory.

'Your friends called!'

I paused in the doorway pulling on my bluesman hat. 'Who did? Stuart?'

'No – Gordon did. The Gordon guy.'

'What?' I said. 'What'd he want?' My heart started thumping like techno.

'Just confirming time and place.'

'Time and place? Are . . . but they're *not* coming, are they?'

Chandra said nothing. She said less than nothing. She was enjoying having something I wanted so much. Fuck. They were coming to see me and they wanted time and place. Why were they coming? We were no longer friends.

'Did they mention Stuart at all?' I asked, my voice all high up in my throat.

I waited for more information from Chandra but all I received was this: 'OH MY VAGINA HURTS, NELLY! MY VAGINA!'

14

There's something so doomed about things that get off to a great start. The first six months of university – yes, back in 1995 – Gordon came to visit regularly. He loved it, the whole escapade, driving up past Blaxland, Blackheath and the Lithgow zigzag railway, stopping for McDonald's on the way, and then arriving at my place for three days of drugs and music, golf and weird adventures round the town. Stuart came too, on occasion, which was when we first all tried cocaine. The drug had such a reputation that I seriously thought my scalp would blow off and that I would be hooked instantly, then spend months in a chair screaming at the atmosphere, like Scarface or something. Stuart issued me with a 'snow cone' first, peppering a bong with a sprinkling of the off-white crystals. It was wildly underwhelming, and it wasn't until the third or fourth time I did coke that I understood its value, but still, it wasn't my thing. I already talked fast and expressively; I didn't need a line of gack to find myself interesting. If I was to take drugs it had to be mind-altering. I wanted to be transported to the feeling place, where music was richer, the world more tactile, and the imagination within reach of God, or art, or whatever the fuck. Gordon took it more often than me, but even he preferred an E or some MDMA or just beers and strong dope.

As we all kind of expected, Gordon bypassed tertiary education and went straight into the workplace. The bloke Carmen was married to now, Albert, owned a blinds company, and invited Gordon in as a partner. Gordon thrived in the sales department, designing all-new brochures and ad campaigns, and learning the secrets behind running a successful small business. Within weeks he looked the part, wearing suits from Kenrays and scaping his hair all high and tight. Coming up the hill to Bathurst, well, it was a sort of release for Gordon I reckon; an escape from normality into a silly, fictional place full of silly, fictional people where he could kick back and let the mad theatre begin, snorting with laughter, sucking on pipes and pilsners, shaking his head at my weird, wild world. I loved it too. My best friend was still in my life; he wasn't just a sword hung on the wall.

But it all came abruptly to an end, those awesome visits, somewhere between August and October of that first year. Gordon came up late one Friday night, he hadn't even warned me, and when I laid eyes on him his face seemed different, stripped of the usual light and excitement that he exuded every time he arrived. He looked tired and spent. There was a BIG percussion troupe in town, the Bang Bang Brothers, and I was supporting them at the Rafters Bar with my original poetry band, Jack KeroSmack. I was all packed up to go when G arrived forlornly on the doorstep, suggesting we grab a pub meal or something, and failing to elaborate. I was already late for the sound check, I couldn't wait any longer, and so he jumped in the back of the car, work suit on, and accompanied us to the gig. On the ride up to campus he asked me if we could go for a drive to Sofala tomorrow, where they'd filmed *Sirens*. Albert had told him what a unique and fascinating town it was, and only forty minutes away. I had been to Sofala heaps of times, but I didn't tell him this, I just said, 'Yeah, course', and nodded in the rear-vision mirror.

The gig went off, my boys joining their boys on stage for a psycho jam session, the whole of Rafters loose and dancing. Seriously, the fucking roof nearly exploded. There were hula girls and fire dancing, dudes sliding about on computer chairs, and these sick, addictive rhythms accumulating and twisting in that invisible whirlpool between players. No one could resist the magic, except for Gordon, who was propped up on a stool by the bar, sipping on a warm beer and looking bored as fuck. I loved him, but for the first time I wished he hadn't come up. He was making me feel guilty and stupid, when all I was doing was playing the truth of the jam, all I was doing was stretching my sound.

After the gig, the Bang Bang Brothers declared themselves stacked with magic mushrooms, announcing their plan to swing on up Mount Panorama with some instruments and a ton of booze and see where things took us. I packed up my bass and harmonicas, hugged my band and rolled on over to Gordon with the movement order. Gordon stood up as I reached him, his smile puffy with forced politeness, his eyes all cracked and red, nodding, oddly.

'Nice gig, son,' he said, slapping my shoulder.

'You dug it?'

'For sure, man, you're getting good on that thing.'

'Nothing else to do in this town but play,' I said, setting my case down and searching for my fag pouch.

'So what's *the go*, now?' Gordon asked, rubbing his hands together.

'The Brothers want to get loose. Fuck, how amazing are they on the skins?'

'Not bad, yeah. Bit showy . . .' Gordon remarked.

'*Showy?*' I said, raising my brow up.

'Bit much, but yeah, they got rhythm.'

'I'd be showy too if I was them.'

'Yeah,' Gordon said.

There were knots in my stomach now, and I couldn't unravel them with Gordon looking at me all smug like this.

'You want to come up the hill with us? The boys have got mushrooms, we're going to make a fire and go mad,' I said.

'Can't we just go back to yours? Punch a couple of cones, have a chat or some shit?' Gordon asked me, a massive disclosure on his behalf, to admit he needed 'a chat'.

'Man, the Bang Bang Brothers are in town like once a year, and they're psycho for my outfit, like mentioning a possible tour and shit, we gotta go up and get loose with 'em, they're like the most awesome guys, you're going to love them . . . And mushrooms, man, you can get on the skins with them on shrooms!'

'I don't know if I'm up to it,' Gordon said, wiping his tired eyes.

'Fuck, dude.' I looked around. The Bang Bang Brothers were waving to me from the stage door. I turned to Gordon. I knew there was something up, but I resented him for bringing it into my world like this. Perhaps I should've thrown the night away and gone for a cone and a chat with G, but I didn't, I went on with things, so kill me. The Bang Bang Brothers were really wicked guys, although I never heard from them again after that night.

'Alright, let's go then,' Gordon said, and he picked up my bass case and loped over to the Brothers, who stood smoking by the door.

Mount Panorama was home to the annual race week, namely the Bathurst 1000, when forty-five thousand revheads and rapists descended on the tiny town for six days of car racing, partying and chaos. They'd drink all day on the mountain, then come down at night into the town, lifting cars up at the lights, even if there were passengers in them, stripping parked cars of their wheels, and if they were Ford fans they'd destroy the Holdens, and Holden fans would destroy the Fords. Then they'd go looking for a fuck, and if they couldn't find one, which was highly probable due mainly to the ratio of men to women in race week being around a thousand to one, they'd pick a fight. Basically you didn't leave your house in race week. If you were a woman, and you went up on the mountain, you were your own responsibility. There was so much violence and so much rape, the police simply raised their hands and bid you good luck. It was quite a time on that hill.

But for the other fifty-one weeks Mount Panorama was a beautiful place to be, offering the most exquisite view of what I always believed was a gloriously cute city. Flowers grew on the shoulders, men panned for gold in the dam; there was a vineyard even, and a farmyard with alpacas and goats, offering such contrast to the colosseum of war and engines that the world knew it for.

We travelled up in Julien's car. I can't remember what was on the stereo, either something camp or the Red Hot Chili Peppers – that was the extent of his collection. Gordon stared out the window the whole journey, as if he was about to hurl or something, as if he was being sent somewhere ominous.

The mountain was rolling with theatre students when we arrived. There were dozens of bongo drums, some Tibetan peace flags draped between trees, a few forty-gallon drums raging with fire, fire sticks and fire breathers, twirlers and sword jugglers, guitars and a flautist, saxophones and other shit; already Amy Siegfried had her top off, displaying her limbo skills beneath a fluorescent skipping rope.

Julien brewed up the mushrooms in a pot of coffee and we all had a cup. Gordon opted out, settling for a cold beer and a scoob. He said he didn't trust anything that came out of cow shit. I challenged him on this – he still drank milk, which came out of a cow's penis – but he said there's a big difference between a penis and an anus, and besides, it was an udder, not a dick that milk came from. I told him milk was only meant to be consumed by babies anyway, and he said, all churlish and weird, 'Maybe I'm just a big baby then,' and walked off over to the car where he sat down with the door open, drinking from a can of Tooheys New.

The mushrooms arrived in force, taking control of the entire operation, propelling me, Julien and the Bang Bang Brothers onto the grass, where we giggled like girls around the fire. We decided to delve into the woods, and so we all began crawling towards the bright light that speared through the column of thin trees. We crawled and crawled, penetrating the forest with mad faces – I could not look around, and I didn't need to, I could feel the Brothers and Julien behind and around me, as we drilled deeper and deeper into the woods. It seemed like we had been crawling for hours, for miles, until Gordon appeared in front of me with a beer and a girl. He told me to turn around, and so I did, only to realise we were but six or seven metres from where we set out. Gordon shook his head at me, and asked when I was intending to go. I could not mouth the words that made up an answer; all I could do was laugh and dribble.

The initial storm of the magic fungus dropped away, and pretty soon we were all jamming. I couldn't find Gordon anywhere and I had stopped caring. The jam got wild, with dozens of students now naked, some fucking on sleeping bags and cardboard boxes, some groups mauling each other, just a mess of flesh and moaning. I was naked too, dancing on the bonnet of a car with a chain of flowers tied around my dick and balls. Soon there was a procession of naked dancing round the car, and I started pissing on people; they didn't seem to mind. Then Gordon was on the bonnet next to me, he looked fierce, he looked really fierce, and he slapped me even, and took my mouth in his thick fingers and shook it.

'You're a fucken joke,' Gordon said.

'Get your hands off me,' I said, flailing about in his grip.

'Put your pants on and stop pissing on people.'

'Can you please not be grabbing me?' I begged.

'You think you look cool up here?' Gordon asked, whispering at my eyes. 'Because you don't, Neil, you look stupid. You look embarrassing, actually.'

Gordon stepped off the car and walked away towards the edge of the mountain. I looked down at my semi-erect penis dripping with urine, tightly wound with lilies and weeds. I looked up again, but he was gone. I thought about following him, but instead I climbed higher onto the roof and screamed. This was my place, this was my mountain, this was my time, and no hobbit from the old world was going to pop a hole in it.

When I got home Gordon was in the kitchen eating Nutri-Grain in his suit and talking to Chandra, who had stayed home with cramping. It was around 10 am, and so fucking cold in the house. I stood in the doorway to the kitchen, but neither he nor she gave me the time of day. So I muttered something to myself and went off for a shower. The water was glorious on my eyelids and neck, but it stung the thorn cuts on my arms and legs.

When I got out Gordon was gone and Chandra too. There was no note, nothing. So I drank a glass of lemon cordial and went to bed. I fell into a deep well of slumber, dreaming of deer and cigarettes conversing with one another. I woke to a dark and quiet house; I had been asleep all day. I wandered about, looking for human contact – well, for Gordon. Now the drugs were out of my system, the guilt had set in. I finally found Chandra in the den, reading *Birthday Letters*. I asked her what she had been doing and she told me she had been crying. Ted Hughes and Sylvia Plath had had such a powerful love for one another. Were *we* as in love as them? Was love always followed by misery?

I kissed her on the eyelid and she told me that Gordon and she had driven out to Sofala. I asked where he was now, she told me he waited for me to get up and then he left. He had work tomorrow and he didn't like driving in the dark, his eyes were not great. I asked her what they spoke about and she said they didn't speak much at all, but that he looked unhappy.

'Gordon's boring,' Chandra said, kissing me with full tongue. I hated the way she did this; I always believed that tongue should arrive when it was summonsed, not as the first cab off the rank.

'He isn't, he's just different to you.'

'He bought all these weird gifts at the arts and craft shops in Sofala.'

'What did he buy?'

'He bought hand towels for his mother, and an elephant.'

An elephant? He bought a fucking elephant? I shot up and began pacing around the room in tight squares.

'What the fuck are you doing?' Chandra asked, standing up as I moved around her.

'What else did Gordon say today?'

'He just kept saying he wanted to see you, but that you were all fucked up and distracted, pissing on people as they danced around your car.'

'But did he say what he wanted to talk to me about?'

'I don't know anything else!' she screamed.

I grabbed her by the throat and pushed her against the wall. 'Don't fucking withhold anything from me, you cunt!'

Chandra shrieked and gurgled, slapping me hard across the skull and leaving the den. She came back with a post-it note, which she stuck to my chin. Then she left the room again, picking up *Birthday Letters* and snarling at me; her neck was all purple and she was crying straight lines of quick water.

The post-it note was from Gordon. It read:

You're not the only one. G

'And he took the sword, too!' Chandra yelled from the bathroom.

I ran down the hall and there it was: the empty spot on the wall, the lonely hook, the beating heart of my house, gone. Gordon had given it to me as a way of keeping us all connected, and now – well, now he was giving up on me. I couldn't say I blamed him; we had grown into different men. But still, the sword was gone, and I could've sworn he'd driven it right through my chest, because that's how it felt, in that room, on that day.

15

'Why do we always go the route with all the give way signs? If you stay on Rankin Street there are no stoppages at all, just roundabouts, and roundabouts rock!'

Julien was too nervous to drive, so I did it, but that didn't stop the constant commentary and navigation.

'Is Jamie coming to the show?' I asked, changing the subject.

'No, he's working all weekend. Seriously, I have never heard of an ad company that works seven days. It's a fucking joke. This is my major work, do you know what I mean? Key word is "major", and they won't let him go for a single day. It's incredibly traumatic for me.'

Julien was my best friend out here. This made him my outright best friend because I had been here three years and rarely returned to Sydney. I liked being away, and I liked being in a small town where there was nothing to do but live. By nature I was easily distracted, but here, there were no distractions, just utter consumption of my three passions: women, art and drugs. Julien had been my full-time maven in the pursuit of all of the above, until eighteen months earlier, when he met Jamie at a gay march in Blackheath. A kind of 'Reclaim the Streets' type situation, for which our course had prepared a small, mobile, gay-friendly fire sculpture.

Jamie lived in Surry Hills, and since the march Julien had spent four days a week in Sydney, catching the train down Thursday night and returning Monday night, managing to miss only two lectures and two tutorials. I missed him. I missed him a lot. I missed smoking billies in the night and cooking up flavourless pastas and packet curries. Playing UNO and discussing all the hot people on campus. I missed his excellent, non-threatening banter and the way he looked at me – a cool mix of LOVE and TRUST, with a five percent hook of cock and sleaze. He was a fabulous man, and friend, but his work had suffered badly since he found city-based love, so I offered him the title of co-writer and co-director on my show *ME*, which was clearly not called *US*. Julien's main contribution was to get the flyers printed at the post office.

'You know there are people driving from Sydney to see this show, Neil? I checked the list and took some calls at the box office – people know about *our* work and they want to check this shit out.'

'That sounds cool.'

It was a perfect Bathurst day, ten hundred pie shops opening at once and the crisp honest air biting at your eyelids.

'Neil, it's awesome is what it is! You know, Chandra nearly shat her tits when I told her the names of some of the directors and agencies that have RSVP'd, like it's unheard of out here, she is like totally jealous of our talents and successes.'

'Well . . .' I said.

'Nelly-Belly, come on. Seriously, you have to stop ramming that first year.'

'Who?'

'"Who?"! The curry muncher who's always hanging round the theatre with her cunt hanging out her forehead is "who"!'

'Swanna's the designer!'

'Designer of what? Your cock?'

'Our show, Julien. She designed the entire space.'

Julien flicked his butt out the window and humbly dropped down into the centre of his body. 'Wow, she is really talented.'

'Yes, she is,' I said. 'And since when are you Advocate Fidelity?'

'Wow, yeah, okay. But regardless, Nelly Boy, you *have* to tone it down with her mate, because if Chandra found like a g-string in your car or something, or lipstick in the sink, then I would have to make up a story and you *know* I just go completely red and cannot lie. I'm not good on my feet like you are.'

'Thank you, mate. I appreciate your concern.'

'I just can't handle the stress, and like Chandra is a psycho-fanny man. If she found something out like that, and she was in the middle of her period, I swear she would drive a car through the front of our house and I cannot afford the repairs on the car or the house. Like no way.'

We were close now. The pie shops and the throng of townies getting their Saturdays kick-started were behind us. We were on the edge of town on the edge of our tomorrow. I could see the old steel mill ahead of us, that big old beautiful building the council had rented to us for only three hundred and fifty dollars which we had converted into an amazing theatre premises. I could see the word *ME* in enormous print on the street-facing wall, I could see the actors playing Kanga cricket outside, I could see one of the percussionists smoking, and Swanna and her team painting a chair, or was it the coffin? I could see the end of my university career and the beginning of the rest of my adult life. I could see the grassy patch where the actors and I buried a secret under the ground in a box. I could see Dick Hindmarsh, my friend, my mentor and my lecturer, taking notes and chewing tobacco by his motorbike. And now, out of the blue and the cold, I could see Gordon, Stuart and Courtney – all of them together at the after party, shuffling round in fits of discomfort, looking to reconnect all the broken-off stuff. I could see all the beer chilling in the icebox, and the sheets of acid and the girls in my life. I could feel the agents and the directors on my shoulder saying 'we should talk', but mostly I could see myself clearing out of here, down that M4 for the last time, one hand on the wheel, Hendrix playing loud on the stereo. But for now, inside Julien's car, all I could think about were my friends, dressed up and driving, somewhere between Cronulla and me.

16

The last time I'd seen them all was six months ago. It was Gordon's twenty-first birthday and I had been asked to make a speech. I was surprised at the request, considering the amount of time we had spent apart. It was Courtney's doing. She was the one who'd called me and said, 'Will you make a speech, Neil? Please!'

As much as I am a creative person and a left-brain thinker, I hate being late. But with Chandra as my girlfriend we were always late. It took us five hours to drive from Bathurst to Sydney that night, because we *had to* drop in on her mother in Castlecrag, her (bestie!) friend in Castle Cove, and pick up a dress she simply 'had to have' from a friend who owned a boutique in Woollahra. Then we had to drive to Potts Point and wait forty-five minutes for drugs, and then she was hungry, so we had to stop off at Oporto's in Darlinghurst for a Bondi Meal with no chicken (seriously, what is the point of a chicken burger without chicken?). When we arrived at Gordon's party in Wynyard, the speeches were over. Chandra was pretty baked by this point, so she didn't see how much it hurt; I'd prepared something very conservative, funny and sincere, and I never got to say it.

Gordon greeted us but then kept his distance. And as he drank more he drifted further into other patches of people, sharing their snide mockery of me and Chandra, I saw it all. At one point he even commented on my pink leather jacket and I was faced with a wall of guys I went to school with saying 'Pink Jacket! Pink Jacket! Pink Jacket!' over and over again. Yes, my jacket was pink, but why did they have to remind me in the form of a mantra? Chandra wore a smile and a 'hello' around all night, making a big effort with my old friends and first love, but Courtney was sullen and closed, following Gordon round like a maid, or a mouse.

On the dance floor Gordon and I had our best moments. I twirled Carmen to 'New York, New York' and Gordon and I did some shots at the bar, inspiring some old-school rap routines we knew. Busting it to MC Hammer and Vanilla Ice, throwing caterpillar-rolls and revisiting the always potent 'running man' manoeuvre. Two refugee ships desperate to find a common sandbank – something.

'We've not seen you mate,' Gordon said, by the bar, both of us sweating into our beers. 'And then fucken all this time goes past!'

I smiled at him as if to say 'ok,' but he just glared at me like I owed him an apology. The whole night I felt like I should apologise but I didn't know what I had done. I mean, I did, but I didn't. You know how that works?

'I know,' I said. 'It's insane – life, everything.'

'How's uni, mate?' Gordon asked, waving to a set of slouching guys.

'It's amazing, yeah. I'm totally into my work, man, making some really interesting stuff.'

'What're you going to do with it?'

'What?' I asked.

'At the end of the year, what're you going to do after that?'

'Just . . . continue to make art.'

'Who for?'

I felt Gordon snigger. He was waving at someone again, maybe Courtney.

'Yeah, who for? How are you going to make a living out of it?' he asked, beer foam on his pursed lip.

'I will survive, man, don't you worry about me,' I said, winking at my friend, desperately trying to find some of that old ease.

'It's not really a career though, is it? Making fucken . . . art videos and saying poems and shit.'

'It makes me happy.'

'That's what matters.' He barked something under his breath.

'What?' I barked back over my breath.

'I'm just saying, it will be good when you finish the course. Get a look at some perspective on things.'

'Sure, sure, I will see that I do that Gordo.'

'I hope so.' He still had not looked at me.

'How's *your* work going, Gordon?' I switched, nailing the warm end of my beer.

'Yes, very good. Saving money. I'm senior manager of sales now.'

'Wow! You must really love blinds.'

Gordon was looking at me hard. I had to insult him to get him to look at me, and I had insulted him deep. He looked like he might kill me.

'Where's your dad?' I asked. 'Did he call you on your birthday?'

Gordon just glared at me now, his eyes filling with water and rage, and it was at this moment that I knew I had missed something big in his life, and he would never forgive me.

'Are you still living with Carmen?' I asked, handing him fresh ale and a fresher topic.

'Nah, man, I moved out a year ago now.'

'No shit?'

'We've, um ... I've got my own place. I bought a joint on the beach.'

'No way! You bought your own place?'

'Yeah, on Wanda Beach. Last Christmas. I told you.'

'Yes, yes, yes. I just didn't realise you actually bought it.' I punched him lightly on the chest, but it didn't work. It just looked like a shit punch.

'Yeah, it's pretty spesh.' Gordon sucked on his bottom lip.

'Who do you live with? Is it a one bedder?'

Gordon went redder and weirder than he was already.

'You got a girlfriend in there with you, big guy?' I beamed, trying desperately to crack it all open and make it jovial, like it was, like it should be.

'Thanks for coming down, man. Shame we missed ya big speech.'

'Why can't you tell me who you're living with?' I pushed.

'Why does it matter?' Gordon asked, smiling menacingly at me.

'Who is it? Sarah Kirkwood?' That did it.

'It's Courtney, actually, mate. Courtney lives with me.'

Gordon was gulping and grinning now. At me. His face was replenished and not flushed at all. He was like a standing-up reptile in the golden sun.

'We're renovating now, so we're living at Courtney's mum's for a bit, but yeah, should be ready in a month or so, fingers crossed.'

Fuck you, I thought. You fucking thief cunt.

'There she is.' Gordon swung his reptile eyes south-west.

Courtney was out of the bathroom and sailing toward us, stuffing make-up back into her large green bag. Why such big bags? Do horses eat out of these bags?

'You remember Courtney,' Gordon said out loud, his big chest puffing.

It was true. The gloating red stocky Pom had stolen my ex-girlfriend. My first love and still in there. When he came to see me was this what he was holding? Were they all the way back there? Of course they must have been. That explains. They were in each other's realm now and she was an inch taller than him and I could feel Saturdays in bed. Video night and football on television. She knew his chicken nugget dick and he knew her many moods. He knew more than I did. He knew 'pick me up from here and I'll drop you off there.' He knew the kink in her arm and the hair on her birthmark. She knew he lashed out when he was tired, and more when his pride was threatened. She dropped him at kickboxing and she . . . she lived with him too! She cooked in her pyjamas in his kitchen and he made her feel safe like no one else ever had. Gordon Braithwaite was the MAN IN HER LIFE. I was the fool here, I was the silly solipsist, resting on his big fat laurels while the crowd guffawed and their heads rolled off.

'Hi!' Courtney said this to me, but then she turned and kissed Gordon, who squeezed her wrist and let out a small noise of too-big triumph. Then they turned to face me as a couple. I could feel my nose ring getting infected. Gordon's grin had a life of its own now. She looked glorious, even in his arms, though she had lost her fashion sense completely. Gone were the PJ Harvey goth-frocks of seventeen, the edgy torn skirts and customised boy t-shirts. Found was the forlorn garb of conservatism. Just as Gordon would like her. Draped in comfortable, 'feminine' dresses that talked of summer. Gentle pastels and sweet, tactile fabrics. Ribbons in hair and Sportsgirl floral. The unimposing façade. The 'yes, it's ok' look of the Southern Districts.

'That girl you brought with you from Bathurst is a piece of work!' Courtney said, a rare scowl taking over her mouth.

'Her name is Chandra.'

'Right.' Courtney seethed.

'What did she do that was so bad?' I was aggressive back; I hated her clothes.

'She is in there pashing Sarah Kirkwood! Who is blind drunk and cannot stand up. Your friend is mauling her, fingering her in public! Disgusting!'

I laughed out loud. 'She's just having some fun.'

'Isn't she your girlfriend, man?' Gordon asked.

'We kinda got an open thing going,' I said, feeling the immediate need to elaborate. The drugs were in the house now, well and truly. 'Society created these rules and imposed them on us. Society invented "the relationship", but we are choosing to define our own union.'

'Right. Amazing.' Gordon nodded, passive-aggressively.

'She is off her tits on drugs and really I just want her out of here.' Courtney looked at Gordon, looking for solidarity.

'Since when have you been anti-drugs, Courtney?' I asked.

'I haven't had an E since the results party actually. They disgust me, to tell you the truth, Neil.' Courtney made sense in her new clothes.

'Well there's a turnaround,' I said, trying to keep my buzzing face from releasing the news of the two ecstasy tablets I had dumped not forty minutes ago. Courtney wasn't wearing a bra so I could just make out the top half and middle of both her breasts. They looked older, longer and less pale. But still I wanted to reach out and touch them, to put one in my mouth even and show her everything I knew. It wouldn't be like Sarah Kirkwood's party this time. I could take her to a hotel and show her the whole cabaret now. All the weird, wild and unfathomably gentle things I had learnt about the art of pleasuring women.

'I told your slut friend to get a hotel and that Gordon's aunties and his aunties' friends shouldn't have to come in here ... to the *toilet* . . . and see two dykes mauling each other!' Courtney was going full tilt now.

'And then your friend *Chandra* turns to me and calls me "homophobic"! I mean, me? Homophobic? My uncle runs an interior decorating shop in Rockdale.' Courtney took a deep breath. 'Then Sarah Kirkwood passed out in the sink and your fucking slut whore girlfriend starts painting the word "cunt" on the wall with her lipstick, she is a fucking idiot, like if that's the people you choose to hang out with Neil, then . . .'

'Where is she now?' Gordon asked, pushing me aside with his elbow. 'I'll throw the bitch out.' And off he went to throw the bitch out. Then my E kicked in tsunami-style.

'Seriously, Neil,' Courtney said, turning to Gordon's beer.

'Seriously, Neil,' I mocked her, grinning insanely as she sipped.

I reached out and touched Courtney's earlobe, the bit beneath her earlobe, and then the bit where it corners in and goes neck. She quivered in her skin but she did not stop me. Both Es were crashing together like two enormous waves. I want to fuck you, Courtney, and be fucked by you. Let me show you how great I am at sex now. Let me take you from here, let me breathe life back into your clothes, your tits, your cunt, your mind, your soul, your cunt again.

'Take your hands off me, Neil.'

I had one hand on her breast and one finger on her mouth. So much so quick I didn't even see. Everyone watching!

'Take your hands off me!' Courtney screamed, but it was just her and me.

I had called Courtney half-a-dozen times over the separate years. Usually, well mostly, actually, always when I was drunk. Once, when she answered, she was drunk too and we spoke like old and excellent friends. We compared university tales and observations, and she was particularly dry and hilarious as she described some of the more earnest law students she was studying with. Often I called and got Nina. Well, I nearly always got Nina because Courtney was always 'out with friends' and now I knew why. Nina was always so happy to hear from me she would put a reggae album on and pour herself a scotch. I could hear the clink-ice chink away, every time she filled and refilled it. The last time I called I got Courtney and she said, 'You are bad,' and yelled at me for never calling Gordon. I told her I still loved her and she said something horribly clichéd like, 'You've changed, Neil.' I may have said, equally clichéd, 'I just got out of the Shire is all.'

Upside down. Gordon had Chandra by the throat. She was laughing, smeared in lipstick, as he dragged her across the dance floor. The party was torn between looking at me and Courtney, or Gordon and Chandra. Gordon had a great suit on too, may I add. A grey pinstripe number with a mauve shirt and flamboyant vintage tie. He really looked handsome that night, especially when he was dancing – the suit seemed to shimmer. The suit was moving through light. The suit disappeared with Chandra into the elevator shaft.

'Come with me!' Courtney took my hand and led me away from the ogling aunties, grandmothers, uncles and all those peers I used to have Winfield Blues with on the oval. She led me into a dining room that could have easily been a 1940s film set. The chairs were creamy leather, and the chandelier twinkled in a subdued way.

'May I have this dance?' I asked, stepping over a chair onto the floor.

'Neil, you have to go now. There are some stairs at the back of the restaurant. Go now before he comes back.'

Courtney was pushing at my shoulder blades, looking back at the party, which was burning bright with the garrulous many.

I could see what a great lawyer she would be, the split focus and the hard intent – the all-seeing, all-knowing eye.

'Why do I got to leave, sugar tits?' I lifted up my mohair vest and scratched at my torso.

'Neil, please – you're so wasted.'

I sat down and bellowed at her. 'What did I do? What did I do to you people?! What did I do to make you see me like this?'

There was a space in time in which neither of us spoke. Then Courtney started to cry. She wiped her eyes with the sharp of her wrists and then she looked at me like I was a boy she was looking after – after school.

'You went away, over the mountains,' Courtney said. 'And now you sit on that mountain and look down on all of us.'

I stood up and walked towards her. She said, 'No, don't do this,' reeling back at a rate. She was against the wall when I kissed her, my hands between her knees and thighs, before two hands found my ears and a knee dug into my back and I was on the floor and nowhere in this world could I find breath. My pink jacket slid off me as I was lifted up to discover Gordon before me, panting like a psycho husky. He slapped me in the face twice, once with the back of his hand, then Courtney told him to let me go, but he wouldn't, he kept on barking at me, telling me how low I was to cause such a scene, how desperate I was for an audience, how pathetic I was, and finally how weak.

'You got your little prize?' I asked him, smiling.

Gordon headbutted me in the face, and blood dribbled into my mouth. I spat my blood into his open mouth, grinning madly; blood tasted good on drugs. Gordon moved back, and was seemingly about to launch a series of leg-and-arm assaults on my frame when Stuart arrived, dressed in a big puffy jacket and matching puffy MC Hammer pants. He had a bum-bag on his front groin and he just looked so big, like a blown-up, pumped-up version of my old friend from Grandview Parade. He was moving towards us and at the same time bellowing directions at Gordon to halt. Stuart was accompanied by two other enormous guys who were identically dressed, and with them two short Mediterranean women with long legs – one blonde, actually. The girls had a David Jones level worth of make-up on. I could smell it from my place against the wall.

'This is not your deal,' I remember Gordon saying to Stuart.

'Step off, Braithwaite,' Stuart warned, and Gordon did. In stepping off Gordon had conceded two things: that even though he had a brown belt in karate, Stuart was the superior force, and, in an even more savage blow, that I was more important to Stuart than he was. I had gone away to Bathurst, disappeared right up inside my own ego hole, whereas Gordon had stayed here and remained in the friendship, riding Stuart's light and dark, his rage and his arrogance, his chest-beating tales of sex and his brother, mother, father issues. But still, I was Stu's boy. And Gordon knew it, shaking his head at us as we filed down the stairs, the audience looking on.

On the street Stuart lit me a cigarette and we had three laughs before I realised I had left my pink jacket inside. Stuart sent one of his Massive Friends to collect, the one with the head like Steve Roach, while he and I chilled on the corner of Macquarie and whatever streets, smiling and shaking our heads at each other. With some friends it doesn't matter how much time you spend apart, the thing between you stays awake, in waiting.

The buses were loud at this hour. The drivers seemed keen to get home. Sick of the drunken louts from Scruffy Murphy's and the junkies sleeping under the seats in fresh sick.

'What just happened?' I asked, blowing smoke into the city.

Stuart shook his head and kicked bits of asphalt with his Adidas.

'Fuck,' I added, to the nothing zone.

'G loves you man. More than any cunt,' Stuart said, meaning it. I couldn't look at him and I couldn't not look at him.

'When did they get together?' I asked.

'I dunno, man . . . while back.' Stuart stepped on and off the road.

'Fuck. No one told me.'

'I haven't seen a lot of them, eh.'

'What happened? Like, I go away and . . . Aren't there like other chicks Braithwaite can drag into his web? Like fuck. Courtney, man. How did this . . .'

'I don't know what happened. I've been in the city mate.'

Stuart was being uncharacteristically sheepish. Like he didn't want to let on about it. I knew this bloke and the way he went when he hid things.

'What's the fucken deal Stuart?' I asked, the drugs and the night in focus now, making me see and feel the rain I had been left out in.

'Nothing,' Stu said, the worst actor in history.

'Why is everyone hiding shit from me?' I said, smoking at him now.

Stuart shrugged, high up into his neck. Then clapped his hands shut and punched the air a couple of times. He couldn't hide from me and he knew it.

'Fucken tell me man.' I walked over to him.

Then Stuart's Blocker Roach pal came down the steps with my pink jacket. 'Pink Jacket!' he exploded, and I realised we went to school together also.

'Blackmarket!' declared Stuart, ripping the moment away.

I put my pink jacket on and shook my head, recalling who I came with.

'I don't know where my girlfriend is,' I said, looking around Wynyard for her, as if she might just pop out of Hungry Jack's.

'She and Sarah Kirkwood got in a cab.' Stuart snorted, ripping open a packet of Extra and one by one slotting the whole lot in his mouth.

'Here for a good time not a long time,' Stuart said, handing round large yellow tablets to his friends in the car. We were travelling through the city in Stuart's clones' four-wheel drive. I was wedged between the two buxom Mediterranean party girls and I was grateful. I knew I had made something dark back there, and maybe I was *not* the one who had changed and grown up after all. The sloppy artist, the pretentious joy destroyer. The teething, screaming toddler.

Stuart winked at me in the mirror and we dumped, passing round a warm bottle of aloe vera juice to wash the tablet down. Stuart's nose was pecking to the happy-house, warning me of the joys to come, of green lights and corners.

When we arrived at Blackmarket there was a line of people dressed in black. They were all older than me and damaged-looking. Crazy committed to this. Most of them had some kind of leather item attached to their bodies; some had the bottom of their leather pants cut out. Some had bulldogs on chains, dribbling. They all looked worn, drained, with painted white faces. I wondered if they had jobs. Did they work in administration? Or were they in sales? One older man wore a sequined g-string and a leather vest with a heart-shaped burn mark in the middle of his chest and a tattoo on his neck that said *Hatred*. Across the lane there was a set of imposing transvestites and a boy on a chain. One woman had no top on at all, just two Nazi ribbons on her hairy pink nipples.

As we moved past the circus I spotted Malaki, standing at the entrance in a cut-off Lonsdale tank-top, radio ear-pieced up. He made a big open-mouth shape when he saw me. Followed by a warm display of golf applause. And then, like never, Malaki was hugging me, his enormous frame gripping my thin, shaking body. My ear was bent in his chest and it hurt. 'Welcome to hell!' Malaki roared, and a handful of black souls droned 'Yeaaahhhh!' in acknowledgement.

Blackmarket was widely considered a day-club: a nightclub for those who felt the night experience was not near long enough. It specialised in S&M, drug abuse and hardcore techno fantasia. Those who braved the cement steps that led up to the ominous cauldron would more than likely lose days, sometimes weeks, in the place. The windows were blacked out with thick velvet curtains, gaffer-taped to the sills, and no one asked the time. There was no time. Just black. And the human stalls of this market coloured up the inside. Blackmarket. This was where dads' and mums' imaginations stopped, at the foot of these cages.

I was placed in the 'capable hands' of Stuart's bouncy friend Nancy. Nancy was a buzzing small person in a figure-hugging black lycra one-piece effort. She was aged between seventeen and thirty-seven and one could easily imagine her releasing an album of sweet, hooky pop songs. She was sucking a Chupa Chup and smiling up at me. She took my hands and in a high yet surprisingly authoritarian voice said: 'You're with me.'

Through the main auditorium she yanked me. It was just filling up. Early days – it was still night (not 'day'). Past the toilets, where a middle-aged duo were smoking pipes and lightly fondling an Asian man, and up two flights of dusty black steps I followed her pinecone bottom into a room that had a sign on it declaring *Service Room 4*.

Inside was a row of curtain-less showers. A tall man with a chainsaw tattoo on his stomach was showering with no water. He was naked from the waist up, rubbing and scrubbing himself. He nodded and smiled at me as Nancy led me into the corner of the room lined with long rows of lockers. I sat down on a long bench between the rows of lockers and felt the new yellow pill come to life in the back of my eyes.

'I'm doing nursing at uni,' Nancy said in a slight Irish accent, and then expertly assembled some sort of glass pipe, shoving a combination of white, green and brown substances into the golden cone that sat snug inside the glass straw.

Then five men with spray cans and skateboards arrived, slamming over the lockers, creating, with efficient craft, a small cell in which there was no escape. Nancy kept on with her administration; she seemed comfortable with the new punks. Even as they began spray painting the walls with tags like 'skunk' and 'pussy wrestler' and 'dad,' she raised not one of her eyebrows in concern. One of them angled in for a view up her legs, another tried to kiss her on the neck, but she just threw them off with short, sharp Irish sentences and looks of 'this is my world too.' Three of the taller ones, who must have been brothers, lit a spoon. One of the brothers smiled insanely at me through yellow, fucked-up teeth. He said, 'It's ok.' Like Mum did when I was eight and pissed my pants in Target.

Nancy kissed my hair and passed me the machine. I could hear the punk boys laughing. One of them was injecting the other. I sucked on the glass pipe and large static moved up my neck, and with an awful surge of pleasure I threw up on my ankle.

When I looked up, the punk boy with the gruesome teeth was mock-fucking a locker, two others were freestyle rapping about crimes they had committed in Mosman. The room was all air now but the air weighed a lot. Nancy handed me water from a Cottee's cordial bottle.

'You're a cute little thing, you are, you are.'

I was walking now but I had no management. There were other pilots in me, ones I had not yet met.

Down back down there now. Stuart handed me an ICY COLD BEER and took me into the men's toilets. He was setting out some rules for me as he burnt up a spoon full of brown and yellow powder.

'Don't fuck her without a condom. *If it's not on, it's not on*,' he said. 'Enjoy the market but look out for the older guys, they're sick cunts on wrong drugs and they prey on the new young cock. They'll fucken bomb you with Normison and take you home and strap you to their mantelpiece and fuck knows what shape they'll leave your anus, bro.' Stu wrapped a ribbon round his bicep then popped a needle into his arm, pushing down on the butt of the syringe until the compound was inside his body and his brain. I had never seen someone shoot up, and as I sat there watching it, all I could think of was our Year 8 drama project, *Don't Drink the Water* by Woody Allen, where Stuart played the Italian priest, handing out the Eucharist (Minties) to the entire audience. He was very funny in the part and got better each night of the small run.

'There you go!' He grinned, one hundred and forty percent, holding the half-filled syringe out to me.

'Stu,' I said, grinning, already so fucking charged.

'Yeah, man?' It was clear by the way his hands tapped and his eyes darted about the cubicle that he wanted out and into The Action.

'What's become of us?' I asked.

'Don't look down,' Stuart said, placing the syringe in my palm.

Stuart wrapped my arm in the ribbon but I pulled away, dropping the syringe into a puddle of water and piss on the grimy floor.

'Fuck, Cronk, shit!' Stuart said, quickly sweeping up the apparatus and shaking it. 'Fucking drenched in piss, fuck it!'

'I don't like needles,' I told him, but he wasn't looking at me, he was busy drying the thing, tying his muscle up, and emptying the rest of the load into his left arm this time. I told him how I had missed him but he wasn't listening; he was full of the cocktail now. The coke, the speed, the heroin, whatever he had loaded into that thing, it had him, and his eyelids were pulsing, slapping his eyeballs.

'Stuart, what are you doing with needles, man?' I asked.

He shook his head at me and laughed darkly. 'You ever know about those animals?' he asked.

'What animals?'

'The lemmings,' he whispered secretively.

'Oh, yes. I have heard of them,' I said. 'Mammals?'

'They're mammals, but they look like rats. And when they migrate, like from the Arctic every year, they climb up a big cliff and follow the leader right off it!'

'Lemmings can swim,' I said, trying to find him. 'They're good swimmers.'

'They're overcome,' Stuart said. 'With deep-rooted instincts. They want to go, that's why they don't hesitate, just follow each other over.'

'Stuart,' I said, clasping his shoulder. 'What the fuck are you saying here?'

And he just smiled at me.

'Stuart, dude, you're scaring me!'

'There's nothing to be scared of Neil, not anymore.'

And with that he was up and out, Batman-like, disappearing through the doors with a flourish. I slumped down on the ground. I didn't care if I was sitting in piss or whatever. I thought about what Stuart had just told me, asked me. He had asked me to join him and it thrilled me. I don't know why but it did. He wanted me with him, even there. There was theatre in it and there was bravery, but most of all it was about him and me, and our little secret from the world.

Nancy was wearing a laser white g-string and boob tube now and I was dancing with her. My shirt was off and my whole brain was burning with ecstasy and freedom – I felt like there was a collective noun of horses trampling through the caverns of my skull. Nancy and I had obtained serious harmony and rhythm.

'I love your fucking smile!' I screamed into her ear.

'You're fucking cute too!'

'I fucking ... yeah!' I said, grabbing the bit between her eyebrows.

Lathered in sweat and rising too quick to peak, Nancy led me to the chill-out room, a downstairs sanctuary of children's toys and beanbags. We smoked a five-paper joint and she told me about growing up in Cork and I made a joke about 'penetrating' the Ring of Kerry. Then we kissed a bit and I recited the first half of Andrew Marvell's 'The Nymph Complaining for the Death of her Fawn.' I would have done the whole thing but Nancy really wanted to go back. She didn't care much for poetry.

'Come on!' she said. 'You have to see this!'

In our absence the museum of cages had been raised off the ground and was now hanging above our heads. The room was full of people, and most of them were one-quarter clothes and three-quarters flesh, all waiting impatiently for the bongo drummer and the percussionist to let go with the DJ. Was it Nik Fish? Six chubby girls with curly pink wigs danced on speakers holding unlit fire twirlers. This stirred me. I wanted one of those fire twirlers.

'Fire!' I screamed at Nancy. Nancy beamed, chewing her lips.

Then everything in the market went BLACK. And with the blackness came absolute silence. Nancy pinched me, and then six puffy volumes of fire kicked and screamed through the centre of the auditorium. Green light ripped our eyes wider as phat, nasty beats swelled up and landed with another blow of fire from the six chubby demon cherubs.

'Look!' Nancy said, pointing. Was this *Alice in Wonderland*?

The auditorium was jumping now. Everyone facing the front and raving, meeting the furious, mean, fast-footed drum and bass with equal voltages of human yearning. I looked up, choked with pure awe.

In the middle cage, spotlit and godlike, was my friend Stuart, naked but for a string of vine. He was dancing wild and free, tribal black paint across his torso. Like a tiger he launched at the walls of the cage, and then, feline, crept along the perimeter of the space. I caught his eye and he hissed at me, his tongue painted black and red.

'He loves you,' Nancy said. Holding my palm with her thumb.

'He's my oldest friend,' I told her. 'And he is *so* high up!'

'He can almost touch the sky,' she said, in this lilting, haunting tone.

'What do you mean?' I asked her.

She smiled at me, and then kissed my ear with dispassionate nurse comfort. 'We're all on our way, right? Stuart's just the closest to the sky. All the boys who dance the cages, they're all gone now. Corey, James, Benoit, Sebastian, Arrow and Greg. All Stu and Malaki's friends. They all went over.'

'Over where?' I asked.

'Over the edge, Neil.'

'Like the lemmings?' I asked, scared of what her face would do.

My heart sped up as layers of flame danced through the room. I spotted a fire stick leaning up against the speaker and beside it a bottle of kerosene. I needed to do something, to let my friend know that this was not the only way. I needed to tell him the lemmings didn't know what would happen next. I had to show him, make him see my heart.

I poured the kerosene into my mouth, leaving it in a puddle above my throat. I then poured some on the wick and lit it off a small thatch-fire burning behind chubby cherub number three. I pulled the liquid up from the basement of my mouth, massaged it into one shape with my tongue, and shot it up towards Stuart's cage, which was banking now, above me and to the left. The ball nearly reached Stuart's feet, causing him to stare down at me with fresh amazement. Nancy had her hand over her face. I made another. Blew another. Leant back and rocked another ball. I was the Fire Starter, and I had a message for my friend and he was listening. This was not the end, Stuart Stone. This was just the beginning. Don't be afraid. And look what beauty we can make! Then the punk boys from the showers came from behind and tipped kerosene all over me and lit my jeans.

The sky was a purple-orange when I woke up between Nancy and Stuart in the four-wheel drive. They were talking about which bridge was built first, Tom Ugly's or Captain Cook. My chest was charred, I could feel it. When I looked down there was an ice pack on my stomach and some Elastoplasts on my arms. I felt good still, but for a chattering-teeth issue and a migraine on the left side. Nancy looked older in the daylight. But I could tell she would make a really good nurse, if she made it. Stuart had his shirt off and when I looked up from his lap I could see the stitches where they had sucked the oestrogen out of his 'bitch tits.' He stroked my hair and I rested back into him. Good.

The four-wheel drive had excellent shock absorbers, hover-crafting us up over Captain Cook Bridge into the new day. I peeked up and out over Nancy's arms, spotting the *Welcome to the Sutherland Shire* sign.

Sister Nancy asked me if I had a place to stay. Stuart the Hulk intercepted, saying, 'He stays with me.' She said I should stay with her, then Stuart said, 'I give better head.' I laughed and asked to be dropped off at the Woolooware Road roundabout on Burraneer Bay Road. Stuart knew exactly where I was going from there.

When they dropped me on the corner it was 5.30 am and darling Nancy was going on (from her experience) about how I really needed to get to a burns clinic. I said I had been burnt lots of times at university in the fire shows and told her that I'd just score some ointment or pawpaw lotion from the chemist, kissed her hand and walked off towards the Ampol.

The car revved up, holding all of last night's feelings and my friend Stuart. Stuart the life-saver. Stuart the cage-dancer. Stuart the incomparable. I think I saw him French-kissing Nancy as the vehicle went away, but look, that's fine.

I bought an orange Gatorade from the Ampol which sold racist t-shirts like 'Australia = Full', and set off on my journey down Woolooware Road.

'Woolooware' is derived from the Aboriginal word *wooloowa*, meaning *a muddy track*. But that makes little sense, because in Shire terms it is the summit – the holy, and always freshly *cemented*, strip of Mercedes and massive houses. Leading all the way from Port Hacking to Woolooware station, it is a gorgeous, wide, tree-lined cruise of perfect serenity and success. Not many kids from my school lived there, and if they did it was because their parents had inherited or they were lawyers. But lawyers' kids usually got sent away by Year 10 or 11 to boarding schools in the city, like Joeys or Scots; it was rare that a lawyer's kid remained here, for it was widely perceived that if you wanted to get ahead and one day own a place on Woolooware Road, you had to not go to school on Woolooware Road. I went to school on Woolooware Road. Woolooware Road was where all my roads led to over the past forever years and it filled me with a heady mix of joy and terror as I loped down its leaf-laden footpaths.

I had been walking for close to an hour and I was parched, having drained the contents of my Gatorade even before I reached the tennis courts. But I could smell the glorious salt of Port Hacking Bay. I could smell the smoke from backyard incinerators 'burning off', and despite Nancy, despite kerosene, despite my parents' divorce, and despite my burnt face, despite Gatorade, and despite my swirling drug-bogged mind, I climbed the vines that strangled the drainpipe of Courtney's massive family home off Woolooware Road.

I opened the bathroom window and climbed in, using the sink to lever my frame onto the tiles. I was so quiet, not mouse-quiet, but definitely intermediate criminal quiet. I found this charred, weird, rickety pulp in the mirror and straight away recognised it as myself. I couldn't believe it but my wallet was still in my pocket. God bless the wallet. Loyal as a cattle dog. I love my wallet now.

I really needed to take a shit. I rolled down my smoke-mauled jeans and sat on the bliss. The bliss that comes in the form of a Caroma Dalton chair.

'Plonk!' went my long, curling heavy shit and I swear someone heard – someone stirred. How could they not? It was *so* loud. In the first few months of our courtship I always took a shit before I went to Courtney's house, for fear of this exact thing. Fear of the plonk! Wake the neighbours – wake the girl – wake the parents and their marriage – wake the floorboards – wake the ghost of Tommy. I let the concert of my ablution simmer, flushed with the seat down, and used the water I had gathered from washing my hands to stir my hair up into something a little stylish and clean-looking.

I then left the bathroom and tiptoed down the hallway to Courtney's room. It was so quiet in this haunted house, but for the creak of the floorboards beneath my shoes, and the low hum of Gordon's snoring. He only snored when he was drunk. I knew him like an ex-wife. I knew everything about him. About both of them. I was an expert on *them* but at the same time I had no idea how and who they were together, and still could not cope with the notion. Fuck him fucking her. He would sleep deep tonight and she would sleep in sections, twisting and breaking in and out of dream flashes.

I didn't hesitate at the door, I just opened it and yes, he was sleeping smug as a cunt. His pink chest with its ginger hair clustered and rug-like. He was dead asleep, dreaming of Bruce Lee movies, or blinds, or nothing. He looked like a British version of Christ, his arms out wide. Next to Jesus was Courtney. Courtney was awake and she was staring right into my eyes as if she knew I would be standing there. Like she had the train timetable and I was the 6.07 am commuter. She knew I would come for her. She knew how I felt. She knew in her heart nothing had broken us. And that's what I kept on loop in my head as I stood there – the morning after her boyfriend's twenty-first that I had royally fucked.

Clearly I could not stand in her room forever. So we shifted into the hall with her up in a gown waving me to 'go go out go'. I couldn't be upstairs either so we crept downstairs.

Courtney disappeared into the laundry as I rested against the kitchen cupboards. In my first long breath for at least forty-eight hours everything started to drain out of me, including the thrill which had been buoying me so well. I was thinking about myself in a dark fashion and there was evidence abundant. I concluded that stealing into Courtney's house was the worst idea in the world – and that really I should just let people be. Why was I here? And what the hell was I going to do next? I was about to leave the house and run for my life when Courtney appeared in the archway wearing a one-piece fifties swimsuit. She hurled a pair of board shorts at me, and hustled out the door with two red-striped towels. She was not smiling *at all*, but I could tell she was at least looking forward to the feeling of water against her body.

In perfect, loaded silence we ducked and weaved around the wet branches and hanging scrub that decorated the forty-five mossy-stepped bay trail. Courtney led us out on to the rocky clearing. The bright blue sky was beaming, but the sun was holding back.

Courtney leapt off the rocky half-cliff and into the sea. Her body scooped then disappeared in the deep blue beast. She looked good in the water, natural, whereas I was not so mad about big-ocean swimming. I liked the initial burst, the explosive headfuck one received on impact, but after that it was all concern: sharks, boats, drowning, stingrays, seaweed, embarrassment, jelly blubbers, sharks, sharks, sharks.

'What's wrong with your face and body?' Courtney asked, dogpaddling about.

I looked down. My torso was burnt, I had red marks on my arms and I think the front of my scalp was singed. It definitely smelt that way.

'I went out with Stuart,' I said. The first words since I had broken into her house.

'And he branded you with an iron?'

'No,' I laughed, and then thought how to put this. 'Things just got out of hand.'

She bobbed her head and asked no more about it. 'Are you going to come in?' Her hair was stuck to her forehead, making her face the thing that it was. Beautiful and Australian and pure.

'Should I?' I asked.

'If you want to. You look like you need a freshen-up.'

'What's the water like?'

'Wet,' Courtney responded.

Ok then. I took off my jeans as Courtney floated on her back. I saw her peek up at me just as I was slipping off my underpants on one foot. I put the shorts on and approached the edge of the deep blue sea. I stood there for ages, wishing I was already in the mass of water. I kept saying 'now' in my mind but still I could not seem to take that plunge.

'Tommy's favourite shorts,' Courtney said.

I looked down at the shorts. They were too big for me but I liked the design. Hawaiian flowers and a big lightning bolt. Like Tommy.

'They're good ones,' I agreed, but the memory of her brother and his love for the ocean had flattened her spirit.

'I'm getting out now.' She began backstroking over to the rocks.

So I acted. 'Bellybuster!' I launched myself into the air, threw my arms out wide and landed with an agonising slap on the concrete surface of the water.

Courtney was only a few feet away from me when I came up for air and her sadness had turned to rage in those brief moments I had spent under.

'Who the fuck do you think you are?' she asked. 'You ruin Gordon's twenty-first, then you *break into* my house and fucking stand there like a crazy person in the doorway. What're you trying to fucking achieve?'

I had never heard or seen this much fury before – well not since that night in Murray Kirkwood's bedroom.

'Seriously, Neil. You're a fucking child and I think it would be best if you fucked off out of everyone's life. If you fucked off back to your little arts precinct where you're so cool and fucking interesting to yourself.'

'I love you, Courtney,' I said.

There was silence, apart from the distant hum of the Bundeena hydrofoil.

Courtney swam over to the edge and climbed up the rocky steps. She took one of the two towels and started with her hair. Shaking it out then wrapping it up. Once her hair was safely within the twist of the towel, she took the second towel and dried her body from neck to toe. Then she began walking up the stairs away from me.

'Hey, where's my towel?!' I asked, swimming over to the steps.

'You can go fuck yourself!'

I climbed up and out of the ocean and held one arm out to her.

'Don't go. I want to talk to you. Please, Court.' My chest was vibrating.

She unwound one towel from her hair and handed it to me, still damp and pungent with her scalp fragrance. I followed her across the lumpy deck to the point of the cove where the waves bashed and splashed against the rocks and then died, flattening out in a giant, foamy sigh.

'Nature's Panadol,' I said.

'Huh?'

'A dip in the ocean. It's nature's Panadol.'

Two guys with very broad physiques roared past on matching jetskis as ten kids (soon to be adults) swam out to a big blue buoy and back, all in matching Speedos.

'When did you and Gordon . . .?' I asked, leaping the chasm.

Courtney breathed in all the air, then huffed frustration out one nostril and looked up into the sun, her jaw a perfect straight line. I waited. I would not utter another word until she told me what I deserved to know.

'He is very good to us,' she said, and I wondered why, of all the possible answers, she chose that.

'Really?'

'Yeah, he really is.'

'Does she make him fruit whips?' I asked, and she turned to face me. She looked angry, but still so completely divine.

'No, Neil, she doesn't. She doesn't make anything anymore.'

I realised what a vain and stupid question that was.

'You like him?' I asked.

'Maybe I do, Gordon, yes. Maybe I like him because he's a good person,' she said, flicking a shell out to sea.

'I'm a good person,' I said.

'*Are* you, Neil?' she asked, holding my gaze once more.

'I think so,' I said.

'Then why do you abandon your friends?'

'Abandon? I went to university for fuck's sake. Was I meant –'

'I'm not talking about that,' she said, stern and direct.

'Well what are you talking about then?'

'Last year. Gordon was not coping, he was not well, he really needed you, and we all tried to contact you, but you never returned our calls.'

'Wasn't Stuart around?'

'Yeah, sure,' she said. 'As around as Stuart gets.'

'Stuart's always around if you need him. Gordon *knows* that.'

'Stuart's a party boy!' she retorted, with so much disdain.

'He would do *anything* for Gordon.'

'Gordon didn't want Stuart's help.'

'I didn't realise it was so important, I just thought . . .'

'You didn't *realise* how important it was because you were too busy putting tickets on yourself!'

'Get fucked, Courtney,' I said, under my breath, but louder towards the end.

'What did you say?'

I stood up. 'I said get fucked. You can all get fucked. At least I *have* tickets! And d'you know why I do? Because I got the fuck out of the Shire and bought some. That's why, Courtney.'

'Oh. My. God.' She was laughing in my face. 'You think because you took the M4 three and a half hours west to some hippie clubhouse that you are *better* than us? More worldly? More evolved? Clearly the drugs haven't worn off yet, Neil, because back here in this sad little corner of the world that you despise so much, we have been involved in what is commonly known as *real life*, life with *real* things in it, like pain and love and –'

'What happened?' I interjected softly, returning to my seat on the towel by the sea, beside her. 'What happened to Gordon that was so bad?'

Courtney shook her head with hard repeats. She was covered in goose pimples, shivering inside her towel. Then she spoke ever so quietly, her voice lilting and floating in the crisp, clean breeze.

'Gordon's dad had been gone a while, we all thought he was dead. The last we knew was that he was living in the bush somewhere in Victoria, with some other men. Then he just appeared out of nowhere and in quite a volatile state. Especially when he saw that Albert was in the house now, and that Carmen had moved on. So Peter began stalking the house and leaving psychotic messages and like these really weird gifts at the door. This went on for months, and Gordon got so angry, and so quiet, he refused to talk to anyone, he just went around punching the fridge and the car.

He only wanted to talk to you, Neil, but you never called back. He even came up to see you, but he said you were so caught up you didn't even see him there, and so he took the sword and came home. Before that visit, Albert had made him a proposal: the police had failed to find Peter and enforce the AVO, so Albert thought it was time they took matters into their own hands.'

'What did they do?' I asked her.

She took a long breath. 'Peter broke in one more night, he had a gas mask on and was rotten drunk, trying to reef Rocky out of the house – to take him away. Peter said he deserved Rocky, that Carmen could keep everything else. But Albert ... well he and Gordon had a plan, and they executed it.'

'What did they do to him?' I asked her, but she was crying now, tears running down her cheeks in perfect straight lines.

'He won't tell me. He just said "it's done".'

I lifted my hand and placed it in her thick wet hair. She turned her face to me and said 'Neil,' and then we were kissing. I could taste the ocean in her mouth. Her lips were warm and tender; her tongue was curious and cold – like it'd been outside all night. In the kissing we were older now; never had we been this close, this real, or this united by the sea. Her long legs beneath her waist, beneath the towel, and her small, firm breasts behind the Lycra, and I was home again and the noises she made had meaning and desire in them but mostly they were reckless with regret.

'You can keep Tommy's board shorts,' she said and scampered off across the shelf and up into the mossy stairwell.

17

Dick Hindmarsh's beard was longer and bushier and more glorious than ever. He could hide a bike and three small pets in there. And *Ulysses.* Dick had a permanent grin affixed to his face. A rugged survival grin that spoke of good luck but mostly of bad.

He wore brown workers' pants and Asics joggers, a white fashion shirt with a jazz vest spilling curly grey hairs from his big-hearted chest. Every time I saw the man I wanted to cry. I wanted to hold him. I wanted him to know how I was feeling. Because, for the first time in my life, there was a grown man who genuinely invited this exact thing.

Dick was leaning on his motorbike as I approached him from the car, Julien already off inside to check on 'the boy'.

'Who's that bloke?' Dick chuckled.

'Nervous wreck is who this bloke is!' I blurted out as I walked into his man hug. Everyone hugged Dick; this was not reserved for me. Well, that's not entirely true. Julien didn't hug Dick. He'd thought Dick was homophobic ever since Dick had failed him in second-year performance studies. Of course, the reason why Julien failed second-year performance was because he was never there; he was smoking Jamie's pole in Sydney, and no matter how flamboyant he was on the pole, it didn't count as 'performance'.

'All set?' Dick asked, breathing a disturbing blend of International Roast Coffee and Drum tobacco in my face.

'As I'll ever be!' My heart now racing. Standing outside the old steel mill, the enormous *ME* sign bearing down on me and the stagehands and technicians milling about playing hacky sack and rolling up metres of cord; the reality of what I was about to do was setting in. I had bitten off more than I could ever chew. Again!

'Looks great, fella. Had a gander. Swanna's done a bloody great job with the design. And your previews went smooth?'

'Yeah, the performances are stronger than when you last saw it in the rehearsal space; we just have a few concerns about audience mobility for tonight, as apparently there's quite a few people coming.'

'There's buzz! They all want a piece of this one – never seen anything like it, not in my seventeen years of "tending the vine".'

'Dick, I um . . .' That was the thing about endings; they always required some kind of earnest conjuration where the human felt he had to summarise everything lost and found in the past however many months and years in one perfectly constructed, cool yet adequately sentimental speech. 'I'm going to miss ya.'

'Hey!' Dick chortled, blocking me off at the bridge. 'Make some waves. That's how to thank me.'

'Ok, Dicky. But really, mate, you've been amazing.'

'Alright. No need for the big speech. Just knock 'em dead tonight, son. There's top agency people from Sydney coming, a buying lady from England, there's film people, circus people . . . the calls we've had this week – it's all for you, my son. So don't leave anything behind out there. Give it one hundred percent truth. Just stay in your truth, Neilo.'

I nodded nodded nodded. And nodded again. My heart was beating like techno in a gay nightclub.

'Will you be at the party after? Will you please come?' I asked, pressing my hand on his vest.

'The party, yeah . . . nothing like a good party!'

'Dick, I really better get inside – see how Swanna is going with the rig.'

'Yeah, head on inside, mate . . . I just um . . .' Dick's voice cracked in two. 'I got a bit of cancer.'

'Dickie!' I said, my palms on either side of my nostrils.

'I shouldn't be telling you this now.' Dick was sweating. 'I'm not dead yet, don't . . . I shouldn't have told you this now, I just . . . I fucken wanted to say if you ever get *down* – which you will; I truly believe that every artist should be in therapy – I guess what I'm trying to say, son, is that if you ever need help with your spirit, then Prozac is a wonderful drug. I wholeheartedly recommend it to you. I've been taking it since I got the news of the bowel situation, and I don't think I'd have been able to show my face on campus or in the studio if it wasn't for this wonderful drug. Anyway Neil, that's all I'm saying. Prozac is good. Now, 'ave a wonderful show – love ya!'

And with that the wounded grizzly bear, Dick Hindmarsh, was off and away on his big old motorbike with the inconceivably high handlebars.

As I entered the old steel mill Julien ran towards me with a stack of A4 programs and a face full of agony. 'Neil! Massive drama! Are we charging for programs or are we just handing them out? I was thinking of making a donation box, but Swanna doesn't like the idea – *I* like the idea. But you *have* to tell me *now* because there's only four hours until the curtains-up and I'd have to go to Coles and buy some cardboard and hand-craft it. What do you think, Neil? Donation box?!'

'Yeah, buy a letterbox from the hardware and slap a sign on top of it.'

'You're so creative,' Julien said. 'Luke looks so cute in his swimming trunks. Is it bad to fuck a seventeen-year-old?' Julien minced off with the programs, raising his eyebrows coquettishly at Swanna, who was halfway up a ladder with a nail gun – making real progress.

'I'll take you through,' Swanna said, descending the metal steps.

The foyer was *meant* to be playful, reflecting the spirit of childhood, of innocence, of dream life and colour. Swanna had miles of Tibetan peace flags fluttering from wall to wall. The thick wooden pylons stretching up to the ceiling wrapped in pastel balloons, flowers were set in drop-boxes and streamers were bunched together in enormous balls rolling randomly about the polished cement floors. Lollies and rugby league football cards were scattered across the floors as we strolled silently towards the stairway leading to room 2: adolescence.

Room 2 was a barren space of rough edges and white-painted walls. The projectors were all set and ready to fire and Paul, an intense young man with Nana Mouskouri glasses, was behind the sound desk, overexcited about his locked-off, complex soundscape.

'G'day, Pauly!' I yelled, as Swanna and I entered the space.

'Nelly! You got to hear the jams, man. The sound in this room when I launch the bass is off the hook-up!' Paul hugged me. Swanna couldn't help smiling and neither could I; the theatre was indeed a family.

'Will you be round for a sec?' Paul asked.

'Yep,' I answered, winking at Swanna.

'Cool, I'll be back in five then. Mr Moon from Bathurst High

School – Luke's teacher? – he's dropping off some woofers from the school. Free of charge, dude! It's going to be a headfuck, my brother.' Paul beamed and left, wrapping coils of lead around his arm as he went.

This left Swanna and I alone in the space.

'How is Luke feeling?' I asked, circling Swanna.

'He says he can't wait.'

'I'd be terrified if I was him. Performing with all these weird uni students, in front of all these people, and he's still only in Year 11.'

'I think all those feelings make sense in this room,' Swanna said, spinning to catch my eyes behind her shoulder blades.

'I couldn't have done this without you, you know?' I was close enough to kiss her and she knew it. The hairs on her upper lip stood up and her eyes softened, stirring all sorts of things between skull and feet.

'Whatever you say, director.' She led the way out of room 2 and up the stairs to room 3: adulthood. She stood blocking the entrance and staring down at me with dark caution.

'What?' I asked, stopped in my tracks.

'Now it's going to look a bit different from how it was last night, but if you hate it, I can just change it back. Ok?'

'Ok. Can I just see it?'

'Don't get mad – if you hate it.'

'I won't get mad,' I said, pushing past her playfully. 'I don't see what's new.'

Swanna pointed to the bit of wall between the fish tank and the toilet. There were three words made out of fish-food bottles glued to the wall. The three words were, in order, I LOVE YOU.

I turned to face my designer. Her arms were crossed tightly above the large envelope pockets of her male overalls. Her mother was right: she was neither black nor white, her skin fell directly in between the two, it was beyond colour, it simply shone and shone.

'Ok, this is why,' she said. 'The death of the goldfish in this room symbolises empathy. As we discussed, empathy is maturity; when you realise that you are not the only living thing on this planet – you are not the only one who feels pain – then you have grown into a proper adult person.'

'What's that got to do with love?' I asked, moving around the room, wiping some dust off the fish tank and adjusting the glow light taped to the foliage.

'Love is what we are finally capable of,' Swanna said.

'When?' I asked.

'When we have seen death, and left the child in us behind.'

'*Then* . . .' I prompted, moving towards her.

'*Then* we can say the words and mean them.' We were a foot apart. 'When you flush the fish, Paul brings up Pachelbel's Canon and at the same time we make a lighting special on the three words, in the black, then Julien moves the audience out of the space and into room 4: from a great height.'

'Ok . . .' I nodded, beginning to connect with her sentiments.

'Neil? Really? Neil . . .' Her eyes were popping out of their sockets.

'Yes?' I answered, my fingers looping organically into hers.

'Is this it?' she asked, tears welling in her eyes, gripping me tight like the end of the world. I looked back at the three big words. Only my mother, Dick Hindmarsh and Stuart had said them to me. Oh and Courtney, but look at us now.

'Do you mean it?' I asked her.

'Do you?' she responded.

She was the child of a mean father and a dead mother. She was broken and she was strong. She was gracious and she was unerring. She made me believe that I wasn't crazy, and that anything was possible. She first appeared in my lens as the exotic little first-year girl with the hairy bush who I stuck my dick in by the side of the lake. She dissolved into so much more, stealing my heart and overtaking the menstrual photo-artist who lived in my house. In the middle of room 3: adulthood, we kissed with new gravity. Gone was the typical ripping desperation of danger and lust; this was love. We held each other, gentle as insects in the cool of the afternoon delight, and yes, I felt happier than I could remember, and that it would all be ok; and if it wasn't . . . then fuck it.

18

Do people know when you've just made love? I bounded down the stairs, past Paul and his new speakers, through the low cloud of smoking dwarves, past the unicyclists and the dancers, acknowledging Julien's letterbox/donation box and cardboard signage in the foyer, and out the door with a smile bulging off my face. Mum and Agatha and Dad and his new girlfriend would be arriving at the Coachman's Inn right about now, and I could not drive the wagon fast enough to greet them.

I wanted them to see me and be around me, to disprove their suspicions that I was just a strange little boy lost in the clutch of my own delusion and that all the HECS was wasted on fire breathing and juggling classes. I was here and I was *good at it* and I could not wait to hold them and kiss them and tell them I loved them, as they had done three years ago.

The sun was losing all ties with the sky, dipping drowsily out of sight behind the local raceway, also closing down for the day. A group of Aborigines walked along the fence line slugging from a box of Stanley's claret. Ten trucks hammered past, shaking the foundations of the road. I could see the Coachman's Inn insignia from half a mile away and sped up, slipped in front of an oncoming car and twisted into the car park, skidding diagonally into a space reserved for the disabled. I ripped the keys from the ignition, opened the car door and got out, flicked my cigarette into the mush of the motel's lawn, and looked for signs of my loved ones. I heard a screen door bang on its hinges. Agatha was on the veranda of the old hotel in a long black dress. Mum stood behind her in jeans and a brightly coloured jumper, like something from the Jenny Kee winter line.

'Hey!' I bellowed, cantering across the gravel towards them. 'What are you guys doing in this neck of the woods?'

'Hi, Neil,' Agatha replied, smiling cautiously from her position by the door. Mum had floated around in front of her, but neither of them had made any special attempt to express excitement. Quite the opposite. Both of them just stared at me, cold and muted.

'How was the drive?' I asked.

'Hello, gorgeous,' Mum said, meeting me with open arms as I climbed up onto the veranda. 'Come here.'

Mum held me close, stroking my hair and neck with her nails, digging them in with hard affection. She usually let me go right about now, she was not a long cuddler, but today, she was holding me tight for as long as it took. I pushed off and kissed her on the chin.

'Hey, Agatha,' I said. 'I'm so happy you guys are here.'

They continued to stare at me.

'What's the room like?' I asked.

Neither of them answered.

I barrelled past them into the room, opening the blinds to let some light in. Mum's green rippled dress (that we liked to call 'the celery dress') was hung up by the window. Just the sight of their stuff, like Agatha's pink Discman, made me smile. I wanted to climb inside Mum's suitcase and roll around in her belongings. I stood by the bed and stared down into the square case. I was thinking about Dick, and how I would be there for him until he died. I was thinking about Swanna and how, back there in room 2 I would've promised anything, but now she felt a thousand towns away.

'Neil . . .' Mum said, poised in the doorway by my sister. I couldn't breathe, I felt like I was having a heart attack.

'Can't wait for you guys to see the show! I'm so proud of it! I truly reckon it's my best work yet. And all these agents from the city are coming, and like some chick from the UK. You're going to love the design too and the performances, it's cool – the audience are led through the space. Like you don't sit down or anything, it's a moving piece of theatre. It's totally fucking wild!'

'Nelly, sit down,' Mum said.

'Hey, Agatha, have you seen Gordon or Courtney? They're coming too, apparently.'

'I heard they might,' Agatha said, glancing swiftly at Mum.

'Where's Dad?' I asked.

'He's up at The Kelso with his friends,' Mum replied.

'Why isn't he here? We said to meet here. Why don't we all go see him now? Shall we go for a beer now and see him?' I asked urgently, feeling a creamy bead of sweat move down the line of my nose.

'Will you please sit down?' Mum asked, gesturing at the only bed in the room. 'On the bed, Neil, now!'

'Where will Agatha sleep?' I asked, my throat closing up.

'There's a foldout.'

Mum had the most pained look on her face.

'Stuart's coming up!' I announced. 'I spoke to him three days ago – he reckons Malaki might come up too and a friend of ours, Nancy –'

'Stuart . . .' Mum interrupted.

'Can you believe it? Fuck, if Stuart comes I'll definitely be nervous,' I said.

'Stuart's dead,' Agatha sounded proud to know this and not me.

Mum slapped Agatha across the back.

'Well he is!'

'Neil, we have some news. Please . . .' Mum could not have said this softer. I hated her and her patronising face.

'What the fuck did –' I was losing my balance and the walls seemed to be closing in on me. Everything was shaking and pulsating and this feeling, this burning feeling, I knew it – fucking please no.

'Neil, will you please sit down?' Mum asked, but I wouldn't. I was trying to open the window, even though I could see it was bolted shut.

'Sit down on the bed now!' Mum roared, and before I knew it I was sitting on the edge of the bed with my fists clenched.

Mum rubbed her face with her hands and said, 'Ok.' She knelt down before me, peering up at me through her eyelashes, which fluttered as a tear crept along their tightrope and fell onto my knee. I had not been this close to my mother since I was a teenager, and she would read to me in bed. I missed her face, and all the stories it told, the blanket of warmth that fell upon me when I was near it. That's why we lose the handle, I thought, when we veer too far from this face, from this blanket, from this holy storybook.

'Stuart was a beautiful boy,' she said.

How could you make him past tense already? *Was.*

'How'd he do it?' I asked.

Mum let her hair fall over her face.

'Fucking tell me, Mum! How did he do it?' I blared, snot falling.

She was calm still, which killed me. 'Stuart was a very tortured boy. The drugs and the girls and the clubs . . .'

'Tell me how he fucking did it, Mum! I swear!' I warned, gripping her hair in my hands and twisting it down.

'Don't talk . . . let go of my hair please . . .'

'MUM!' I screamed, and then Agatha stood up. Crying black mascara she said to me, 'He shot himself in the head with his father's hunting rifle.'

The world dropped then like a car crash, got slower so that every moment was filled with a million details of tragedy.

'When?' I asked.

'Three nights ago.'

Mum's face was in her lap on the floor, she was humming.

'What time?'

'Neil,' Mum said from beneath her hair. 'This doesn't help you.'

'What fucking *time?*'

'Around a quarter to two in the morning.'

Five minutes after we hung up. I was the last person he spoke to. *Real mate real mate real mate.* He was asking me to save him.

'Why didn't anyone tell me? Why didn't *you* tell me? Why didn't my friends ring and tell me! Why didn't anyone fucking tell me!'

'They wanted to tell you in person.'

'He's been dead three days!' my voice cracked and squealed.

'They wanted to see you first.'

'FUCK OFF!' I screamed, getting up and kicking the bar fridge until the door broke off and I had smashed all the glass inside it. Then I burst from the room, pushed off my stupid sister and down onto the gravel, still screaming up my throat. Stuart Stone is dead and it's my fault.

It was late and I had just returned from the technical rehearsal for *ME* (and Swanna's house). The line was crackling but I could hear him fine. He kept telling me how talented and special I was and how he could not wait to see the show on Saturday. Nancy wanted to come and so did Malaki and Ebony. Who would have thought?

'Can you believe it, Nelly? My brother's coming. Everyone loves you, man. That faggot's never seen a performance piece. Other than Blackmarket! Hahahaha!'

I asked Stuart how he was and he said, 'Filth, everything's wicked,' and he went on again about admiring me, and how good it was partying with me at Blackmarket, especially seeing me blow that huge ball of fire; it was 'symbolic', he said.

'Yeah, wicked night,' I agreed.

'You were on fire.'

'I know. Literally!'

We laughed and filled in more about it.

'Fuck man, you should see Gordon's house now,' Stu said, out of nowhere into the phone.

'Which house?'

'Y'know he bought this massive block of land on Wanda Beach, fucken waterfront and all.'

'How did he afford that?'

'He's making a killing, man. Blinds. And Albert used to be an architect or building guy or whatever, so they did it together, knocked it down then turned it into a duplex so they can all live there.'

'Moving on up,' I said.

'The Australian Dream,' Stuart said, and I could hear him grinning.

'Courtney living there with him too?' I asked.

'Um . . . yeah, think so. They got a pool.'

I wondered what he knew about Gordon and his dad, I wondered if he could tell me what really took place; how much of Courtney's story was actually true, and how much of it was designed to make me feel bad about my behaviour. Surely Gordon and Albert didn't murder the man, surely they just issued a strong warning, surely that kind of thing didn't happen in sweet little Cronulla town.

'I did this real estate course with this homo from L.J. Hooker,' Stuart said, coughing away from the phone.

'No shit?' I said.

'Yeah, the bloke reckons I can start working there if I want. I just got to get this TAFE certificate.'

'How long will that take?'

'Not long, and it's not heaps hard, they said.'

'Cool,' I said, encouraging this rare glimmer of ambition.

'But fuck that, I'm not putting up gay flags and showing losers through houses.'

'Stuart, you'd be awesome at it!' I yelled.

'Why?' Stu asked, serious as all get-out.

'You got charm.'

'Yeah, chicks like me,' Stuart admitted.

'Why don't you give it a bang? See what flies?' I asked.

'I dunno, man . . . Just cruise, I reckon. Party. Got some bouncing work coming up at Tank nightclub. Might go up the Gold Coast. Y'know if you tap a backpacker on the head their panties fall off?'

'But, mate, you've got a gift! You have to use your talent – you have to do something with what's been given to you!'

'What's that, Neil? What's my gift? I can bash up tools and bend blondes over the kitchen table, eat eccies and fucken dance in a cage, like, what the fuck is that? Where is the *gift* in that, mate?'

I had helped Stuart study for the HSC, night after night wandering over to read up on Islam, maths in society, *The Taming of the Shrew*. I put serious hours into getting the big unit up to speed, and it helped me, helping someone else. But still he left the exams as soon as the fifteen-minute buzzer went, exclaiming 'Fuck this for a joke' and throwing his HB pencils at the examiners on the way out of the auditorium.

'You're the gift, Stu. Stuart Stone is the gift. That's why sales –'

'I dunno, man,' Stu interrupted. 'I dunno about that. You're the special one. Everyone knows that. Me, G, Courtney – every cunt. I'm fucken ... I'm *bored* already, Neil. I've fucked the sweetest pussy. Asians, blondes, models, Austrian whores, thirteen-year-olds, whatever. I've been to Spain. I've taken pure MDMA, been to the sickest parties, driven a Ferrari two hundred clicks. I've done it, mate.'

I'd never known Stuart to be a whinger and here he was making that god-awful sound. 'So just give up then, right? You've got this great opportunity with L.J. Hooker and you're just going to throw it in their face and stay on this stupid path to nowhere. Well that's pathetic, Stone.'

Then his voice dipped, went all hollow, and he said, 'You're my real mate, Cronk. You are a *real* mate, you know that?'

'I know mate,' I said, and now *I* felt awkward.

'I could do with a *real* mate right now.'

'I'm seeing you on the weekend – you're coming up, right?'

'Yeah, but I need a mate now eh ...' he said, without a hint of colour or shape in his voice, just this sullen flat line.

'You got mates,' I said, suddenly so sleepy and distracted.

'I've got a million mates, in the green lights and the corners of the bar. But you're my only real mate. I could do with a real mate now eh. Do you know what I mean, Nelly? Sorry, man, had a large one and just took some Rohypnol to get to sleep, but I close my eyes and all I see are faces. I see all these faces but they are not my friends. You don't make friends in the clubs. Just acquaintances with sliding faces.'

'What are you talking about mate?' I asked, peering in to see if Chandra had been woken by the call.

'Nothing, nothing mate,' he said. 'I'm just so fucking bored.'

'Stu . . .'

'Sorry man . . .'

'Stu listen to me . . .'

'I'm being gay; I'm being a faggot . . .'

'Hey . . .'

'You got to get ready for your show . . .'

'Will you listen to me please?' I asked him.

'It's cool man, you got your life going on . . .'

'Stone!'

'You're amazing Cronky, you're an amazing kid.'

'Will you shut the fuck up please?'

'Ok . . . I'm just sayin' . . .'

'You're up here in two days pal, then I'm finished in a week and back in Cronulla – stay with Mum until I sort the next move. I'm going to be just down the road again Stoner!'

'That's wicked . . .' Stu said, his voice getting slower and lower.

'I'll be back in town – the dream-team – just like old times, chase pussy and play golf on the computer at mine. Get wasted and go to Carmen's, eat kebabs or just fucken chill on the beanbags watching *This Violent World.* Whatever man, summer with the boys again!'

'Yeah . . .' he said, with the most cantankerous lethargy.

'Stone? Are you hearing me?'

'Yeaahhhh . . .' he said, nearly gone from here.

'What about L.J. Hooker?' I asked. 'That sounds exciting, Stu. Like an excellent prospect for you.'

Through his nose then from his throat he laughed darkly, kept saying how funny I was, and *real mate real mate real mate,* over and over again and I should have known, but it was all about *ME.*

19

You know when you just can't stop? Driving, smoking, wailing. The Great Western Highway held no cars but mine and the odd trucker on trucker's dust and AC/DC. But, strapped to the sides of the (great) highway were clumps and clusters of walkers, seemingly headed in to town. Where were they all going? Where were any of us fucking going? To hell? To the shops? To prayer? To pasture. I flicked on the windscreen wipers but they did very little. Mainly because the fog of water blocking my vision was not outside the car in the form of rain. It was in my eyes in the form of salted tears. I could not stop screaming because if I stopped screaming that meant it was true. My friend was gone. And my friend was *not* gone. If I continued to drive fast and if I continued to scream and if I continued to smoke, then he was still here. On this planet and approachable. Roaring wagon, my roaring heart. My foot on its throat – distance and bitumen in pain. Past the Kelso Hotel. Past the crumbling silo where the teenagers go to hide. Past the turn off to Sofala. Past Steggles Chicken Industry Headquarters.

Features and creatures of Bathurst whipped by my window undisclosed and wax-figured. Nothing mattered and nothing existed and nothing would. I could twist this wheel and GO towards that wall. I could swing this thing into a truck (HEAD ON). You were everything to me. Come back and I will tell you. Come back and I will teach you. This Violent World – don't leave me here. If you only waited one more day, I was yours again you fucking cunt you fucking impatient scene-stealer – had to do a pre-show before my show. Suicide, you selfish cunt!

And yet here I am without you on this spinning planet of yes and no and maybe. What fuck matter now? What fuck mark indelible? What fuck spent or earnt? What fuck concern?

There was a field approaching. A dark purple field I had never bothered with, the trillion times I'd passed it since 1994, I had never shown it much – I barely remembered it being there, in its sprawling dank. But today, today it reached out and asked of me. Rows of vines and were they wine? Vines dark and expansive and I saw a deer.

'Mummy!' I saw a deer. Deers' heads. Venison – a doe, a deer popped its antlers over the fence and scanned my disposition as I passed. A deer. A female deer? I hauled us over and down the embankment to a skidding stop. I got out on an angle. 'Stuart!' The deer saw me. The deer had had a wagon coming towards it, spinning out of control right at it – careering one could say – and all its deer friends had fucked off and bolted. But this one deer, this special deer – well it had not moved. Special deer remained, its wise old noggin resting on the cut in the fence. Its antlers like sticks reaching out to God, it all looked so make-believe. I said, 'Deer', and it let me touch it. I said, 'Oh dear' and it let me kiss its nose. I never understood why Stuart and I were friends. I never understood why he took such care of me. Ask the deer. There was love in an animal and there were no computers. I said, 'Deer, my friend is gone', but then a townie yelled out to me, 'Better be good – your fucken show!' and I realised all the people walking in to town were on their way to see *ME*. I had wet myself down the side of my blue jeans and I was smoking four cigarettes and I was still screaming and, yes, I kissed that Brave Deer on the nose in the gap in the fence and you tell me, grief, where do we go from here?

Standing at the edge of the Steel Mill forecourt with an open mouth, the smell of piss reminding me of the piss I had pissed on myself.

'Nelly!' Dick yelled, his pink, alcohol-wrenched face beaming hard confusion as he approached me. He had a suit and tie on now, he looked dapper. 'It's five-minute call! Where the hell have you been? Swanna is in tears.'

'Dick ...' I couldn't put the sentence together it was ... not arriving. 'Dick ...?'

'It's alright, son. We all get it. Just take some deep breaths and remind yourself of who you are and what you have achieved over the past few years. You are *meant* to be here, my son.' He patted my back warily, like I might unleash fangs or a cleaver.

'Dick ...' I could not finish the sentence. Tears in my eyes again and yes, I wanted to fucking scream until the roof came off. 'My friend just killed himself,' I said, staring up into his blood-shot eyes.

I could see him lying on his bedroom floor with his brains blown out. I could see his skull in pieces and his brains, his brilliant, neglected and taken-for-granted-by-everyone brains dripping out and I knew right then, before this great man, that I would follow one day soon or sooner.

'Julien? He's inside.' Dick said.

'No, my friend Stu. He was coming to see the show, but he ... he sh-sh- ... shot himself in the head. With a rifle. Just after I spoke to him. I was the last person he spoke to, he spoke to me, and then he . . .'

Dick took me in his arms and soft-bashed my back with his fists, like he was trying to get me to hawk something up – the boy.

'You get a bit of that down your way, don't you, son?' Dick said, now circling my back with the curve of his palm.

'I can't go in there, Dick,' I announced, pushing out of the clinch.

'Ok, ok. Right, then.'

'I can't do the show. I mean, I just . . . even if I could, Dick, even if I *could* do it, I don't know *why* I would do it.'

'Alright. Alright. I'll go tell Swanna to make the announcement. Fuck there's about four hundred people in there. Fuck. Alright. Is there anyone else who can do your parts? Can little Luke do it?'

'Luke doesn't know anything beyond room 2: adolescence.'

'Of course he doesn't.' He sighed. 'I'll go tell them. Fuck.' Dick patted my shoulder and waddled off towards the *ME* sign.

'Am I doing the right thing?' I wondered aloud.

'You want to know what I really think?' Dick said, turning back like he had expected the question. 'I think those who take their lives are selfish little buggers whose one act of theatre ruins everyone else's. Little prick just lacked the balls to get on with the job like we all gotta, so instead of sucking in the deep ones and getting on with it he had to take the darkness out on everyone else!' Dick was dribbling now, enraged. 'You want to look back on this night when you are older and know that your mate with the coward's balls cost you this dream? Then fine, but you're bigger than that. I know you loved him; I am sure you did, son. But this is your dream, not his. Claim it back!'

I slapped Dick in the hair and flesh of his face and then I went to slap him again, harder, but he held my wrist. My eyes were boiling with hot oil and all I wanted to do was run and jump down into the water behind Courtney's house and never come up again. And so, I thought, why not go inside? For in seeking death, I fear no more.

I said this to them: 'I'm sorry, I know I had you all worried.'

The entire cast (minus the dwarves and the unicyclists, who were in the foyer greeting the masses and performing) sat before me on the cold cement floor of room 2: adolescence.

'The past few weeks and months have been so special to me,' I said. 'I've learnt so much from working with you people, and I hope to God you've learnt something from working with me.' I looked up. Luke was nodding, the gaps in his pyjama shorts flailing open. 'I know I scared you all, not turning up till one minute before the lights go up, but I want you to know something . . .' I turned to face the foyer where, through a gap in the wall, I saw Chandra arrive in a pitch black dress only to be greeted by Swanna in a long white dress. Angels and devils. Swanna looked beautiful, her hair swept up off her face allowing her cheekbones to be all that they were; gloriously symmetrical. She looked poised and true in the presence of her adversary. Chandra appeared distracted, forlorn, as if she was attending a funeral. Ours, for instance.

'Why are your pants wet?' one of the second-year dancer girls asked me, wrenching me back into the *reality* of the space.

'It's just sunlight,' I said. Then my stage manager called, 'Beginners, *Me* Company!'

'Come on!' Luke grabbed my arm and hauled me out of the room just as the white squall of audience murdered into the space.

20

Such kindness lives in the hands of the young and free. Luke lifted my shirt up and over my lifeless upper body, dragged my piss-stained pants down, undid my shoes, socks off, then, with the cool and 'done it a million times, love' aplomb of a seamstress, dressed me in my neutral mask and trunks.

We huddled together like kids about to be caught stealing. My breathing was loud and fast – I could not subdue it. Luke, the poor kid, was trying not to look at me like I was in danger, which made me realise I was in danger. I had a ninety-minute show to do, and I was only offstage for the first part, which was rapidly concluding. I could hear the applause of the audience as the unicyclists formed tableaux with the dwarves, and the Tibetan peace flags were set alight – ta-daaaaaah – *voom*!

I was resting against the back of the set flats staring into the caverns of the steel mill walls when Luke appeared in front of me on his haunches. He held my face in his hands and for a moment I thought he was going to kiss me.

'You can tell me,' he said, beaming through the softest skin. TV would love him one day.

'Tell you what, Luke?' I managed.

'What's wrong.' This was afternoon television. Luke, the friendly teenager, concerned by the dark demeanour of the heroic older neighbour whom he looked up to, despite the community's belief that I was 'trouble'.

'My best friend took his life three days ago. I just heard about it.'

'How?' Luke asked, without flinching.

'He shot himself in the head.'

'Yeah,' Luke said, as if he had read about it earlier.

'What do you mean "yeah"?' I asked.

'We had some guys at school do that. One guy did it in his dad's bed. Another guy in the backyard. It's always somewhere visible. Fuck, man, I'm heaps sorry. Suicide is like the fuckedest thing, like fucking *why*? Jesus, am I just raving at you? Neil, I'm *so* sorry! We've got a show to do!'

'It's ok, Luke,' I said, 'I appreciate it.' And I really did.

'I think you're fucking awesome, Neil. Like this has been the most amazing experience for me, meeting you and Julien, you're two really special guys.' And then he kissed me warm and full on the mouth. Yes, this kid would be gay soon, but even more yes, this kid had temporarily lifted me out of my hell and into the spirit of art.

'Let's make waves, huh?' I proffered, rolling up my body to standing. Through the cracks in the flats I could see the crowd. Every inch of the space was full, herds and gatherings of audience towering and shoving at each other on stairwells and through windows and broken inlets to other rooms.

'Showtime!' Luke beamed.

In the centre of the heaving, anxious audience, Gordon had his arm around Courtney. They were staring silently ahead, seemingly oblivious to the wrestle of the throng around them. They looked frightened and I wondered what it was that scared them most about tonight?

*

I have no recollection of anything that happened in the eighty-three minutes that followed my arrival on stage, except that I know the show went smoothly, despite the difficulty Julien and Swanna faced in herding the enormous audience from room to room, and my dad and his drunken friends heckling me from the stairs of room 3.

'He had a fish!' Dad yelled out as I dropped a dead goldfish into the toilet bowl. The whole night, in retrospect, arrived in sections, blurred and skidding, like I barely dreamt it.

Backstage the air was light with kisses and sweaty hugs. Actors, dancers, designers, stage managers, lighting technicians, dwarves, unicyclists, sound artists and collected hangers-on threw off their months of tensions/anxieties/expectations/emotions in warped exultation.

I sat on a busted orange children's chair in the corner of the room. I was not ready to put my suit on, I just wanted to sit here and drink the bottle of beer Paul had given me.

'We did it!' I heard Julien say. 'Seriously! People want to buy this show, Neil, and tour it – and they *loved* my programs!'

I couldn't go out there yet, so I stood and wandered through the cast and crew to the walls and around to the windows behind the green room.

The town was charcoal through the smudge-rubbed window-sills flecked with paint. I lit a cigarette and waited for the engine of my charisma to erupt and says yes, let's go. But it didn't. I was not beautiful or exciting anymore. I was like the town. Charcoal and small and cold in the winter.

Where did my friend go? Was there a place they all gathered, the lost and self-destructive? Was there a room they put them in? Necks burnt with rope or holes in their skulls. Beach-water bloated. I will know this at the end of my conversation with life. I will speak and laugh until my tongue falls out and then I will know this. I will know this because he will tell me when I see him. How will I enter that theatre? With a hole in my head or exploded by sea. Wrists.

Allegedly, it was a 'fabulous thing' when people lingered after a show. It meant the piece had got to them in some way; they wanted to be near it still, even though it was over. To remain here was to hold on, for as long as one could, to the reaching hand of magic.

We entered the buzzing foyer and felt all eyes dart our way. I guess we had moved them from wherever they were before. The farmers and the newsagents, the mechanics and the steel workers, the teachers and the butchers. The landscape gardeners, the bakers and the rapists. If I could move them, I thought, I could move anyone.

'Nelly, my boy!' Dick pushed through the foyer, his ruffled white shirt unbuttoned to the ribs. He was hanging out of himself with pride.

'Hey, Dick,' I said, in my new black suit. Swanna was beside me and I liked this, she knew I needed her but she did not know why or where to from here. Only Luke and Dick knew why I had pissed my pants.

'Oh my boy,' Dick said. 'Come with me! I want to introduce you to some of the talent and theatre agents who've come out to see the show. Rachel, Cliff, Miles, this is the one and only Neil Cronk – creator and star of *ME*!'

Rachel, Cliff and Miles stood in a semicircle clutching their programs. Rachel looked young and hungry for success, while Cliff and Miles almost looked alike, dressed in corduroy everything.

'Hooray!' Cliff said, shaking my hand.

'Bravo,' Miles added.

'Thank you very much,' I said, spinning to include Swanna. 'This is Swanna, she designed the show. It is as much hers as it is mine.'

'Oh, I just painted the walls,' Swanna said.

'Two very big talents.' Dick raised his eyebrows at Rachel.

'We see *so* much theatre,' said Rachel, her voice in such a hurry. 'But nothing like this. I don't even know what I would call it, if I was to explain it to someone.'

'A fucken good night out!' Dick bellowed, guffawing into his beard and then slapping me hard on the back.

'We would be very interested in talking to you if you make it to Sydney.' Cliff held out a business card.

'Are you guys all from the same place?' I asked, scanning the card but not really scanning it at all. Where were my friends? Why was I speaking to the Corduroy Club? I couldn't give a fucken fuck.

'Miles and I are from Piggott and Frost Management in Woollahra. We represent artists. Rachel is a buyer, she buys shows,' Cliff informed me with an elaborate swish of his striped scarf.

'Meaning we can all take a chunk out of you – joking!' Rachel kicked her hips towards me. She was about as sexy as four litres of phlegm.

'I'll make sure I call you guys when I get home,' I said, with the smile of the now-to-be-departing.

'I hope you make it back to Sydney alive. I hear there is a big after party planned. Don't get too carried away!' Miles joked, looking for an invite.

'Oh we like to party us lot!' Dick confirmed.

'Nice to meet you all.' And just like that I walked away.

To breathe salted air would have been nice; to have been swept up onto a yacht and sailed right out of there, sailed all the way to Jamaica without mention of the show or 'the night' would have been a gift from Utopian Travels. But no.

'Hello,' Chandra said, with a small shot of disdain. Despite her avowed feminism, she hated other women, especially talented ones. Swanna could not help bright-shining tonight.

'Hi there,' I said, not kissing her – not anything her.

'Aren't you going to kiss me?' she said, her arms as open as her eyes.

'Sure.' I kissed her with a dry zap on the forehead.

'Congratulations. Both of you,' Chandra said, holding on to my neck.

'Thanks,' said Swanna. 'We're really happy with it.'

Chandra and Swanna and me. A triangle of inevitable hurt. We all felt it, regardless of what we knew or what we hoped for.

'Neil, come with me over here,' Chandra said. 'My friends from the Dark Room want to meet you. They loved the show and they have all these questions.'

'Can we . . . look I gotta meet Mum and Agatha and everyone for dinner – I don't want to mingle. I just want to get the fuck out of here basically, Chan.'

'You can't just *leave*. There's a hundred people who want to eat you! You have to oblige –'

I had had enough of what I was meant to be; I just wanted my mum.

'I don't *have* to fucken oblige shit. I just did a fucking show, I wanna go!'

'But they want to meet you,' Chandra said.

'Fuck's sake, Chandra, I just . . . Can you think of someone else for a second?'

'Fuck you, I *am* thinking about you!'

'There's an exit door through the ladies' toilets. Follow me,' Swanna said.

'Hang on a fucking second,' said Chandra. 'Is *she* coming with us to dinner? I thought it was just family and friends.'

'Swanna is my friend, and my designer.'

'Doesn't she have her *own* friends and family here?' Chandra asked.

'I invited them to come along too,' I replied.

'It's fine, I can meet you later,' Swanna said.

'No, Swanna. You come with us. The car's just outside.' And I led both girls through the toilets and out of there.

21

The Marigold Garden Chinese restaurant was like a brochure of old Asia on steroids and my father loved it. Every time he drove up to see me we would visit 'the Mari.' Dad rarely went anywhere unless he had been 'tipped off' about the place by some important guy he knew. Dad loved being on the inside, he truly loved it. He loved striking up a connection with the waiter or waitress. He aimed high, asking for the chef or manager, but settled for the floor staff, and happily. Rarely did we depart an establishment without Dad exchanging first names with some member of the team. This thrilled him no end and the drive home would consist mostly of Dad reliving some of the great moments shared between him and the staff: the witty banter, the wine knowledge, the small business situation, the food the food the food. Dad would finish the debrief remarking on how they must have really liked him to have shown him that amount of attention. 'Not every Joe Blow gets the treatment!' Dad would say, drunkenly running a red light.

As my love triangle entered the overlit, overdecorated caricature of a Chinese restaurant, Dad had his arms wrapped tightly around the manager's neck. Duc, a forty-four-year-old immigrant from

Shanghai, remembered, or at least made a strong go of pretending to remember, my father, as Dad ruffled his hair and face. Dad had not been to the Mari for nine months, but this was his restaurant still. Dad believed that Chinese restaurants were the best place for a big group, which really confused me when he insisted on taking me there for a one-on-one dinner the previous May. Out of the blue a phone call from a payphone with Dad saying, 'It's Thursday night! I'm in Lithgow! Put some dress pants on – we're going to dinner at the Marigold!'

'What?' I had responded, still reeling from the space cakes Chandra had baked earlier that morning using female buds from Mullumbimby and goat's butter.

'To see ya! I'm here to see ya, son!' Dad yelled in my ear. 'Is there a golf course? I've got me fucken clubs in the boot! Nine holes?'

Mongolian beef, fried rice, san choi bau, sweet and sour pork, lemon chicken, three Singha beers and two bottles of Rosemount shiraz later, we drove back to my place. I set Dad up on the pull-out sofa. I said goodnight, kissed him on the forehead, smoked a fag out the back with my balls freezing off, and then went to sleep, exhausted from the pot, the wine, the food, the challenge. Over dinner we had covered the surface topics, filing through the administration of our lives, but nothing more, nothing to do with how we were both feeling about this thing called living. Why had my father driven all this way merely to say 'hi' and make sure my wagon was running and full of oil and that I had enough warm clothes and wasn't on heroin or gay? My incredulity was validated when he appeared in the doorway of my bedroom at 3 am.

'Neil,' he said. 'Neil?'

I woke up a thousand miles down the deepest well where dreams of huskies and black and white flowers wrestled, and there he was, my father, in yellow underpants and a stained white singlet, staring down at me.

'Dad?' I asked, wiping my eyes and wondering how on earth a flower could choke a big dog like that. Then my father spoke, with the clean timbre of truth and disclosure. I had never heard his voice sound so sweet.

'I'm not entirely ... proud ... of everything I did. And if I had my time again, with your mother, probably would've ... done some things different. Righto.' And then he was gone, and there was just the black rectangle of the doorway.

Chandra woke up and asked me what the fuck had just happened. I told her not to worry and she fell asleep. But she did not snore. The snoring was all my father's. I could hear it all the way from the living room, and I loved it, just lying there listening to it, I loved it so much.

'Are you going to tell me what's going on?' Chandra whispered sharply as we approached the table.

'There they are.' Is there anything more beautiful than the open warmth of a mother's face when she sees you across the room?

'Neil!' she implored.

'I'm so hungry,' I said, and I was not lying. I had literally eaten nothing that day and my body was now having a word to me about it.

My father had booked a large, round table with close to twenty seats, and most of them were filled as we approached. Gordon and Courtney looked snug and smug in the corner near a plant, each gripping a schooner of beer. Seated next to them were my father, who was still standing and clapping, his new girlfriend, and his friend from the Kelso, Brian, who was incredibly fat in the middle but not at all in the face. Julien and his mother were to the left of

Courtney, and beside Gordon were Mum and Agatha. Swanna's dad was there too, but not Rhonda – she was at a conference in Bali or some made-up bullshit. Beside them were three empty chairs. I took the middle seat, with my girlfriend and my designer on either side of me.

I was not capable of this, I couldn't even look up for too long, all I could do was pour beer into my glass from a jug and look down into the menu. I wished the lazy Susan would stop spinning and I wished Stuart was here, talking big and making me laugh, making plans for after, commanding and just . . . being here. Love is in the attendance.

I looked up, caught Gordon's eye, then looked back down again. He knew I knew. He knew I knew he knew and did not tell me. Cunt.

I needed someone to order for me and Swanna was too involved in a conversation with Julien's mum about the musical theatre course in Western Australia. I could not simply ask Chandra to order for me either, it would mean so much in the subtext. The entrees. The prospect of not sharing or sharing. The meats and the vegetables. The rice steamed or fried. The conference would kill me. I was dead already. But still so hungry.

Across the table, over the cutlery and through the amber of the beer trapped inside the glass jugs, I caught my mother's eye. She would bring me food. She had done so for so long. I felt safe looking at my mum. Her calm eyes and her deep wrinkles. She smiled at me and raised her eyebrows, her maternal radar ever active. She knew I needed something and was ardently trying to communicate this with her, without communicating at all. I was one thought away from standing up and going to the kitchen to order direct from Duc when my father shot up, banging his fork against the fat empty beer jug.

'Welcome everyone to the Marigold Garden Chinese Restaurant, good to see you all gathered round the . . . round table, so to speak. People I haven't seen for years – Gordo, Courtney, look forward to sharing beers with you. My daughter, and of course my son and his friends – all of youse.'

A barrage of cutlery and clapping rose up and then collapsed, just like that, as my father fell into the tree with the hawk in it, then found balance with the help of Duc and the Golden Dragon Statue.

'I reckon we could *all* agree tonight was a real beauty bottler of a show. Not your everyday thing that you see every day . . . thing . . . but excellent anyway. Unreal stuff from everyone. Confronting at times, but my son . . . always been bold – even as a kid he was . . . No, it was top-notch . . . stuff. So yep, tuck in to some tucker – have we fucken ordered? Let's drink up; it's all on me. Duc here is going to look after us so don't hold back . . . Alright you lot!' Dad slapped Duc on the back, said, 'You're it, mate, sort us out,' and returned to his seat. Then he poured himself a beer, drank the beer, and went over what he had just said in his head. From the cracked tank of my perception: Julien's mum and my mum were deep in talks about Cheryl Kernot defecting to the Australian Labor Party. 'What's the difference anymore?' Mum asked. 'They're both right wing!'

Gordon and my father were arguing joyously and with vigorous arm movements about the Super League and its effect on rugby league as a code.

Courtney placed her left hand over her beer glass when Gordon went to pour more beer into it. Gordon said 'Come on' and she said 'Let's just take it easy for a bit,' then Gordon said 'It's a Chinese restaurant' and Courtney said 'We have to go out after this,' then Gordon said 'Yeah, to a party!' and my dad said 'Women are all the same' and poured beer into Gordon's glass and ordered another four jugs of VB. Courtney picked at her rice and honey chicken, grinning in the general direction of my chair but not at me. Swanna was busy mingling, introducing herself to Agatha, who, true to form, immediately unleashed a condensed version of her Big Life Plan in Swanna's ear: 'destination weddings', the business partner bitch who left her high and dry, the debt, the court case, and now the horror of living back with Mum in the Shire and her plans to open a star academy for talented kids in Penshurst. Gordon and Dad and Swanna's dad moved to spirits. Dad's new girlfriend said nothing, just sat there smiling at her purse. I considered throwing a dumpling at her open mouth.

I ate everything put in front of me, spinning the lazy Susan for more and more, and drank red wine out of a teacup. I must get to Mongolia one day. Such glorious beef they have. Bursting with product and hurt I got up. The table stopped talking and stared at me.

'Gotta piss,' I said into the silence.

Standing over the circle, piss came out my dick. Then I put my dick back in my pants and opened up the bag of speed I'd bought from one of the dwarves. I unpacked some of the sticky, off-white powder onto the cistern and pressed it with my student discount card. Then I carved it up with the edge of the card and pressed again. The line was

---

that long.

I rolled up a twenty-dollar note and snorted the fucking shit up. The gear was glassy, cutting at the sinews of my nostrils – basically it moved into my face with brazen disregard for the surroundings. I half-spewed some lemon chicken and punched the wall. My fist hurt because I had just punched the wall with it. On the way out of the bathroom I looked in the mirror and in the mirror I saw my reflection. On top of my neck an oval-shaped thing called 'my visage'. Dry lips. Small receding hairline. Long hair like Jesus. Sockets with blue water in them. No meaning. Nothing to say. Floppy skin the colour of camel. Skin for ripping off. Replaceable. Cover your books with it. Ears pink and small. The grand total: a twenty-one-year-old male from Cronulla. I sniffed and the gack fell down the back of my throat.

Hell sat pregnant in my face. Something beautiful had left the building. I was a shell of a man. The scallop of my soul had been sucked out and I couldn't help but think the cliché: I could have saved him.

'Who are you?' Chandra demanded from the corridor, her face red with jilt.

'What . . .?' I managed, barely out of the Little Boys' Room.

'What the fuck is going on with you, Neil? You haven't even kissed me tonight. You won't look at me. You won't even speak! You just sit there staring at that Courtney girl and stuffing your face! What the fuck is going on?' Chandra was roaring now. I'm sure people could hear. I'm sure she wanted them to.

'Nothing,' I said, but something about her earnestness made me laugh. Then more laughter escaped, building and fattening. I was laughing in her face and everything inside me was encouraging more of it.

'Fuck you. You're a pig, do you know that?' Chandra spat.

'Are you enjoying your time at the Marigold Garden Chinese Restaurant?' I asked, guffawing now – pissing myself. 'Please come again!'

Then she slapped me. And slapped me again. In the corridor between the door with the little Chinese boy on it and the door with the little Chinese girl on it.

'My period pain is agonising,' Chandra said in a state of tears and fury. 'And I come here for you. And you ignore me. Just because you think you're the King Shit. Well you're not. That piece of theatre was pretentious and it lacked a through line and I am not the only one who thinks this! So shove that in your pipe and smoke it, Wonder Boy! I'm going home. Have fun with your fucken sluts!' Chandra slapped me again, and then she was gone.

'Stuart's dead,' I said. But it was too late. Just the little Chinese boy and the little Chinese girl on the toilet doors to hear me.

'My dad's gone for a little holiday!' To the dismay of Courtney, Gordon was opening up to my father about his father: a man and a topic he had always been reluctant to acknowledge in daylight. Night after night in Gordon's bed, Courtney would appeal to him, trying to find out what happened, and if not the details just how Gordon felt about it.

'No joke?' Dad said, sipping on his beer.

'Yeah, he's off to the great dugout in the sky,' Gordon said, turning to face the raw surprise of Courtney. 'What?' he exclaimed to her.

I walked over to the table and sat down on my mother's lap. She patted my collar and kissed my cheekbones and whispered in one breath 'Shhhhh . . . it's ok.' It felt good and like I was ten again. If I was ten again I could meet Stuart and I could launch a campaign of life affirmation, starting in 1986 and continuing all the way to this moment.

Agatha said, 'Neil, everyone's looking over,' but I didn't care.

After a while Mum said, 'Son, get up now,' and so I did and the whole table stopped talking and looked up at me, like I was a priest and this was prayer group. I felt how I felt because this is how it feels and we feel what we feel; there is no way around it. So I spoke, quietly and truthfully, about the time Stuart and I went to a birthday party at the Chinese restaurant on Cronulla Street in Cronulla.

'Sarah Kirkwood's sixteenth birthday party and me and Gordon and Stuart were going. We rode our skateboards. When we got there Stuart said try these. Pills. Avils, they were called. Hay fever tablets. You were only meant to take one a day, but Stuart said if you took five you saw things. So we all took ten. Stuart took fifteen. Then we sucked on an aerosol can and went in.

'There was a fat Asian woman singing karaoke in the corner. Sarah Kirkwood's parents were there and they told us, as we walked in, to put our names down for some songs, but make sure we wrote "English" cos if you didn't write "English" then the song would "come up Asian". The table was a lot like this one. Round and full of people. We sat down and Mr Kirkwood let us have a beer each and so we had a beer and felt pretty good, Stuart made some jokes and charmed the aunties and grandmas, as he did.

'Then the Avils kicked in. I went to pick up my chopsticks but there were thousands of them, and if I lifted one up, thousands more would fan out before me, like cascading sticks. Then the waitress had thousands of bees buzzing round her, and the rice had an army of little men in it, waving up at me in workers' helmets. Then, just as I was reaching the point of freak-out, Stuart leant over and asked us if there was a snake coming out of Sarah Kirkwood's ears. We looked over to Sarah Kirkwood and, no joke, a massive python was crawling out her ears! Then another one! Then, when she spoke, a collection of small, oily snakes simply *rushed* out her mouth. The next thing I knew Stuart had lunged across the table and grabbed Sarah Kirkwood's throat. He had a knife and was cutting the snakes up as they exited her mouth and ears and nose.

'Then Gordon yelled, "Stuart! Look at the singer!"

'We looked over at the singer and sure enough she had snakes coming out her top and her ears too! Stuart rushed over and crash-tackled the singer to the ground. Which was when the police were called and we made a run for it. On the way home thousands of silver bins rolled towards us but somehow they all missed. Then we went to Cronulla station and sat in an old broken train until the visions stopped and Stuart said, "Well imagine if those snakes were really there and none of us did anything." Stuart is dead now.'

I stood at the end of the table in the silence. My story was finished and I had nothing more to say. To anyone. So I left the Marigold Garden Chinese Restaurant.

22

Stretching all the way from Peace Park to campus, Rankin Street was notorious for its high-quality pie shops, big houses and indiscriminate rapes. But tonight, tonight it would be privy to a different mix of meat and violence. My show was the last of the shows, confirming the University Calender as officially over. The third years were off into the world. Like Stuart's lemmings, the edge was near.

Across the road from the party Swanna and I sat in my wagon watching the tribes funnel in. She presented me with an orange pill. I didn't think to ask what it was – I merely swallowed it.

'Courtney and Gordon will be looking for pills,' I said.

'They sold me these.'

'Gordon did?' I asked, taken aback.

'Yeah, and some pot,' Swanna said, pouring mull onto a Ventti.

'The guy won't call me to say my friend is dead, he'll forget to do that, but he won't forget to bring some pills up for the party!'

'He didn't know what to do,' Swanna said, all compassionate.

'Is that right?' I replied, lighting a fag.

'He said he didn't want to disturb your show. He knows how much you loved Stuart – he said it would ruin you to hear the news.'

I scoffed; yeah that's the fucking truth.

'He knows how much work you put into your art. He loves you, Neil, you have to know that.'

She kissed me and I'd never hate her. Just him.

Julien fancied himself as a bit of a DJ, and even before we entered the front yard I knew he was behind the wheel of sound because the Red Hot Chili Peppers were dissolving into an anthem of happy techno.

With the newness of drugs and love in our pockets, Swanna and I swanned into the hovel, passing the buoyant welcome of the tie-dyed first years, tunnelling through the tunnel of second-year coolies breaking up tabs from an A5 sheet of acid, by the kitchen where a polite collection of staff members and associated 'modern adults' inserted trays of frozen dumplings into the oven, sipping on soave with a smoke. Like Royce Simmons, I kept my sights down for fear of eye contact slash connection leading to conversation. Reaching the summit of the backyard was relief in bulk. Swanna and I mingled by the tool shed with Gemma and the second-year dancers and their brothers and sisters, passing the joint around, embarking on trivial, brilliant threads of chit-chat that warmly led nowhere. The dancers were thrilled to report back on some of the wilder and weirder responses from tonight's audience, especially those 'morons from Blayney' who 'didn't get it.'

In the bathroom papered with photocopied portraits of Frida Kahlo and John Howard the dartboard, I inhaled a lump of speed which split my brain in two. In four. In eight. In sixteen. In thirty-two. In sixty-four.

When I returned to the backyard there was little or no room to move, both in my thoughts and in the yard. The university had arrived en masse. Regurgitator's master-blasting 'Kung Foo Sing!' jumped out of the speakers and into my brain, kick-starting the kick inside me. I *yearned* to let loose! Let loose with some karate dancing. I advanced my frame and person out the screen door and towards the hopping throb of dancing students but I never quite made it, for by the door was Swanna, talking with Gordon and Courtney. I made an immediate tack to the left but my shirt was in her clutch and I was in the square – just like that.

'Hey, Neil!' Courtney said, her eyes big and pupils dilated with E. I thought this girl was 'drug free' since Results Party. Whatever.

'Hey, Courtney,' I replied, kissing the rosy patch of her cheek. She had left it out for me, as the royals do, offering no path to lip.

'Nelly,' Gordon said. He had a beer in his left hand and another tucked under his arm to allow his right arm to do some shaking. 'Cool show.'

'Yeah,' Courtney agreed. 'Amazing.'

'We really fucking dug it,' Gordon continued.

'Yeah, it was such a feast!' Courtney's eyes did a lap of her sockets. 'Everywhere I looked! I really liked it.'

'What did you like about it?' I asked Courtney, her eyes easier to grapple with than the grey windows beside her.

Courtney took a moment to formulate exactly what it was the show did to her. 'It reminded me of like . . . *Peer Gynt* or something . . . But like a lot more surreal and David-Lynch-fucked-up show. Do you know what I mean? I need some time to sit with it, actually.'

'Yeah man, it was pretty good,' Gordon affirmed, casting a spell of sudden silence over the pleasant review.

'How was the drive up?' I asked, taking the opportunity to finally take in Gordon. He looked beefier than I remembered, standing there beneath the porch light in his puffy North Face jacket.

'The drive?' Gordon mocked.

'Yes, I'm asking you how the drive was.' I straightened my posture in all seriousness. What the fuck was wrong with that for a question?

'The drive?' Gordon asked again, spitting out beer and launching wildly into a fit of hysterics. Swanna and Courtney followed close behind, crying in large, uncontrollable spasms of laughter, holding onto each other for balance. 'We drove in the car!'

'The car went forward!' Courtney added.

These people were clearly demented. I appealed to Swanna but she was way gone too, infected.

'You didn't pogo here?' Swanna asked, like she was the old friend and I was the new friend locked outside the connection room.

'No!' Gordon ran with it. 'We drove!' And they fell about laughing again, guiltily, but then freely once more.

Courtney took my forearm. 'Sorry, Neil, we're just a bit fucked up.'

'I would agree with that,' I said, face like stone.

Their laughter dried up in a flash as I stared down the barrel of G's cruelty. His beady little eyes in gridlock with mine. There was violence in the air between us but no flesh as yet.

'You having a good time?' I asked Gordon, both passive and aggressive.

'Yeah, man. I am having a good time. You?' Gordon replied, coolly.

I stepped towards him thinking yes, I will palm his nose up into his face like Dick Hindmarsh taught me in stage combat, but real this time.

'Neil, don't . . .' Courtney said, only to be moved aside by her big man.

'Don't, babe – I've got this,' Gordon told her, all puffed up.

'Ha!' I did the laughing now. 'Nice to see some good old-fashioned Cronulla gender balance still alive and well. "Step aside, little lady."'

'Don't be a cunt,' Gordon warned me.

'Me? A cunt?'

'Yep,' Gordon said. 'There is one cunt here, and it's not us three.'

'Neil, we're just a bit high is all.' Courtney stood between us, smiling up with overt politeness. 'The drive was really nice. This is such a beautiful town; you guys must feel so blessed to have been able to spend three years here. So pretty and quiet and creative too.' Courtney stopped as the first progression of 'Smells Like Teen Spirit' arrived in four beautiful bars, changing everyone's living thing inside out.

'The town's been good to me,' I said, pushing off G's chest and into the cliché nihilism of the mosh-pit. I thrashed and I burned! 'YEAH YEAH YEAH YEAH!' Then I was picked up and lifted onto the stage where I ran laps for a verse and laps for a chorus, high-fiving Julien and his Luke, then *launching* myself into the air that lived and breathed above the forest of human heads below. I crashed onto the grass, taking skirts and beards and drinks along with me.

Courtney appeared above like the angel she was, I clasped her arms and she pulled me back up from the ground and we danced together ecstatically, blazing joy and power – she was happy and I was happy to be near it.

'I love Swanna, she is so great!' Courtney said, and she meant it.

'I miss him already,' I said.

'I miss him too,' she said, and the scaffolding that time had built fell away. I kissed her on the mouth but then Gordon arrived with a soft warning palm to the throat.

'So so so!' Julien minced across the stage, mic in hand. 'I know Luke and I are like the hottest DJ team this side of Cowra, but it is now my pleasure to welcome the *greatest*-ever karaoke band known to man . . . Ladies and gentleman, please welcome KKK – Karaoke Kool Kats!'

The dense curtain of purple material bought from Lithgow Spotlight that morning was whipped away by the second-year dancers as the KKK band launched into their usual debut-punch of instrumental jive-bunny.

Gordon was shaking his head at me but his hips and feet were grooving along inside it.

'If you need to kiss someone, kiss *me*,' Swanna whispered in my ear. And so I did, with roughness and teeth. Even in this kissing I wanted to make violence on Gordon's head. That small man, that thieving cunt.

'Where will we go?' I asked her, 'when this is all over?'

'You want to go somewhere with me?' she asked, her brown eyes even more dazzling in the moonlight.

'I want to go everywhere with you,' I declared and we kissed again.

'I've never been anywhere, just Canberra and here,' she said.

'Those agents said something about England didn't they?' I asked her.

'Yes, the woman did. And you know what the thing about England is?'

'It's not Bathurst?' I said and she laughed out her perfect mouth.

'It's not Canberra either, yes, but also, you can get this train called the Eurostar, and it goes all through Europe, like down through the rivers and lakes of Sweden to Rome and France. You can get a train from London to Paris, and it takes about two hours . . .'

'Let's go there,' I said.

'It goes through the Chunnel.'

'What's the Chunnel?' I asked her.

'The Chunnel, it's a tunnel to Paris.'

'Let's chunnel to Paris,' I said, 'I love you Swanna.'

'Really?' she asked me, tears in her eyes.

'I loved you from the moment you hit the water.'

'Neil Cronk!' Julien called into the hissing microphone.

From this hard passion – smashed back to reality by the public announcement that I was next on stage.

'What're you going to sing?' Swanna asked, buoyed.

'Fuck, I don't know,' I said, and I didn't.

The crowd parted like the Red Sea for me, as I caught a glimpse of Gordon's confusion. Then I was on stage again and yes it felt good, taking the microphone from Gemma, who had just sung a stirring rendition of 'Nothing Compares 2 U', kissing Julien on the lips and high-fiving Luke. I feigned jumping off the edge of the stage and into the sea below. The crowd laughed and cheered. KKK waited patiently for me to address them. Without a song of choice there was no music here.

Moments went long now. If I moved my eyes too quick in one direction things took a while to render. So I peered tortoise-like through the crowd until I found my man. Gordon was moving out of the mosh-pit, towing Courtney, running away from my attention, running away from things, running away.

'Ladies and gentleman, I have a special treat for you tonight, a song so special I simply cannot sing it alone!'

My voice entered his ears, pulling his neck back in fear and spinning him round in awkward pirouette. We caught eyes, Gordon and me, and so I spoke to him, over the gathering and down into the pores of his face.

'Please welcome to the stage a man who is arguably my best friend, the Eddie to my Charles, the one and the only . . . Gordon Braithwaite!'

Ninety-eight percent of the party had no idea who Gordon Braithwaite was, or Charles and Eddie, but they went nuts anyway, and with the help of Julien's furious pointing from the DJ booth, they kindly attempted to escort my nugget-mate Gordon onto the stage.

But he wouldn't have a bar of it, karaoke-jam terrified him, I could see it so clearly now, all flooding back, he *hated* performing, public speaking – at school he only ever spoke up in modern history because he knew about Hitler's bunker and he knew about propaganda. But this, this was his idea of hell, so I went for the jugular and challenged his manhood, I was in too deep now and this was the only way to spur him on, and I wanted him up here; despite his wholehearted reluctance I wanted him up here so bad.

'Come on, Gordon!' I said into the microphone. 'Don't be a pussy!'

The crowd were intent now, all working together to drag Gordon up onto the stage, which only made him more furious. He would not join me tonight; a million horses could not drag him up for a song. Finally, with a dozen or so sets of hands around his waist and neck, he cracked, and it was revealed to me the extent of his karate training in the past three years. He swung his legs round in a circle, tripping up the second-year dancers, then punched at the arms of the men who held him, one swift jab after another, kicked backwards at those behind him, then rammed a few of the remaining assailants into one another with an incredible twist of his hips – hula violence. The whole crowd was staring at him, and his face was red with rage and embarrassment. Courtney went over to him but he pushed her too and she fell backwards into the screen door.

'Gordon, it's ok,' I said, from the stage, the microphone feeding back.

Gordon wiped his chin and stared at me. The entire party in rapture. 'I don't want to go on the fucking stage!' he yelled, picking up a half-drunk can of beer and hurling it at my head.

I didn't duck; I just stood there and watched it sail past.

Then Gordon was gone, punching and stomping out of there. I dropped the microphone, leapt off the stage and went after him.

23

The wind was behind me and so were the drugs, sending me right down the middle of Rankin Street in the middle of this broken night. I could see Gordon up ahead, chubby forearms pumping up and down like pistons as he crossed Piper Street in front of a storming Woolworths truck. I gasped, it so narrowly missed him, and in the drama lost sight of him, until he appeared in the distance once more, careering off the Rankin Street shoulder, round the Kepple Street corner, seemingly hovering now, like a sturdy vampire out of hell. I leapt up onto the gutter, ducked the branches and pursued him with all my stealth. The huskies and the Rottweilers barked like mad, thrashing at their borders as I turned onto Kepple and discovered him heaving by the 'give way' sign up ahead.

'Oi!' I yelled from the corner, and he arched his neck to see me, standing beneath the lamplight with my arms open. 'It's ok, G!' I said.

Gordon took a deep breath, his North Face jacket sucking up into his neck, and then he took off again, this time on a diagonal, right into the pitch black labyrinth of Machattie Park.

The park was quiet tonight. I could hear the crunch of sticks under my shoes, and the new relationships that formed between the breeze and the trees. I was walking now, no longer chasing, for I knew he was in here, I could feel him. I knew him. I circled the rotunda and pushed out in to the open fernery, where a bikie couple slept in the flaps of each other's leather jackets, whisky bottles tipped over like dead soldiers. The gurgle of the fountain grew louder and I wanted it so, moving beneath the natives where a Circus Oz juggler had hanged herself the year before while out walking her dog. Apparently the dog was crying when they found her, swinging above. Always an audience.

I walked towards the fountain and found him sitting there on the edge of it, hands on his mouth. He was hunched over himself, embarrassed. He looked up at me as I stood before him and I couldn't help but smile – he was my best friend after all, or my brother more like – no matter what went on and where, it would always move between us; this pain, this love, this shambolic swordfight of too much feeling at once.

'Hey,' I said, and so did he as if by mimic.

'Mate, I'm sorry,' he said to me.

'What for?'

'You can't just think . . .' I had never seen Gordon like this, his face bright white and his eyes wide and full. 'We're not all you, you know? We're not all theatre and talking!'

'I'm not asking you to be.'

'There are things we have to do, in our lives.'

'What things?'

He stood up and walked around the place, his hands made their way to his hips, and his shoulders hunkered in, swallowing up his neck. This was the time to say it all.

'You know the things,' he said.

'Why didn't you tell me he was dead?' I asked him. 'Why did you leave it for my mother to say? How could you not let me know? *Me?* It's still me, no matter what has happened.'

'Me,' he said. 'Isn't that a piece of theatre?' He spat onto the grass. 'Isn't that a bunch of people in an old warehouse prancing around?'

I moved in towards him, I did not care if he hit me, I was numb all over, the drugs and the fresh grief and the night the night the night.

'You know I was the last person he spoke to? You know it was me he called just minutes before he pulled the trigger? Did you know that, Gordon?'

Gordon put a flat hand on each of his temples and pushed and pushed in. It was like he was trying to squash his own brain. I moved up to break it, but just as I did he stopped, his hands flinging out to the sides in mad despair. Then he walked right up to me and pointed at my head, issuing the following orders with the most severe whisper.

'Forget him Cronk, forget all about him, he's gone now, don't let him hold you down. Forget about tonight, forget about me, and forget about the dead guy. Just move the fuck on and leave it all behind.'

'Is that what you did?' I asked him, and again he made a fist to punish with. 'It's that easy is it G? Just delete them and go on?'

I thought he would smash me again, finish me once and for all, join me with Stu and the others, but instead he turned and walked out of Machattie Park, stepping up to a jog as he met with the shiny black road.

I wiped away the wet grass and sat down. I thought of following him but he had told me not to, to forget any type of following or remembering, any type of hanging or yearning. So I remained on the bench, rolled a cigarette and thought about Swanna, and all that cool stuff she was saying about London, about Europe, and the train that moved down through it all.

Part 3

24

I wake up and I cannot breathe. My nostrils and my throat are jammed up with nicotine, there's no room for the air to get through. There is a glass of red wine half empty on the table beside me, and three cigarettes lying dead in a Japanese sauce bowl. I have raped my mind with booze again, with even the slightest tilt of the head it's like a bowling ball slides down a table and knocks over all the glassware that is my brain. This is common for me these days; waking up with a chronic, crippling, almost comically hellish hangover. I still can't work out why they call them hangovers, when the sensation I feel is so much more like being *under* something, like a truck, or a dozen Samoans. I will get up soon, take a 500 mg Xanax, drink an Earl Grey and wank. Then I shall have a shower and whack my suit on and do this fucking day. This fucking day.

The rain is loud on my roof though this is not a clear indication of its force. My roof is made of corrugated iron that Gordon and Albert donated to me from a fence they pulled down in Greys Point. Even the lightest sprinkle sounds like an army of Russian drummers are pounding away up there. I lie in bed and I stroke my cock – thinking of Courtney; it is her wedding day today, and I wonder what she is feeling, after all that was said on that beach not hours ago. She is not the marrying type, I know this much, she told me so on our many walks, calls and coffees over the past year. The dress, the day, the dance, the cake, the honeymoon, none of it appealed that much to Courtney. Courtney never had 'the gown fantasy' – she wanted kids, yes, plenty of them, but not marriage. It was embarrassing, she said to me, to stand up in a silly frock in front of all those people and make such silly promises. But Gordon was adamant. 'Marriage,' he said, 'is like screwing a lid to a jar; it fits two things together and makes them one.' The metaphor, like the day, scared her. But she said yes because she knew it was something he needed – he needed to know she was his, and so she gave it over, the great big 'forever.' I knew what she wanted: she wanted to see the world, that's why we saw so much of each other lately, she looked for it in my eyes and my stories. I had seen it, swallowed it and brought it back to her and she reached for it with long and invisible arms.

The rain kept falling on my sensitive roof as I wanked into the doona cover thinking of Courtney's neck and shoulders, a wad of semen dripping down onto my leg, remarkably cold. I had spent so much time alone in this bed the past six months; masturbation had become my best friend. I usually imagined circumstances, of women or girls I had spied down at the pontoon or at the store, but now, with so much practice behind me, I could masturbate thinking of the colour black.

Would she be in the bath now? Or would she shower? I wished I *was* the bath, with its claw feet and porcelain shell. I would be a bath and I would be holding her up. Her flesh would be against mine again, and this time I would not let it go.

My cock flopped about dumbly, stiffening again; fool's gold. I thought about having a bath myself. I hardly ever bathed in the bath at all now, even though I had quite a nice one in the shower recess.

Perhaps it reminded me too much of London, and of Swanna, and of all that hell and loss. No bath could wash the last seven years off, and in a way, well, as ugly as it felt, I liked it on my skin.

No one showered in England, which is not to say they were unhygienic, it was simply a bath culture. Even the gymnasiums had baths. It really threw me when I first got there, I missed standing up and having the hot rays strike my neck from above. And London was even colder than Bathurst; I didn't understand why I had to stand naked on the tiles, freezing, while the bath filled up with lukewarm water. So much puzzled me about the town: why all the men were bald, and why everyone said 'innit?', and why bulldogs were allowed on buses, and how many fried chicken shops there were, and how low the clouds hung, and how big and beautiful the parks were, and how much the people loved their soccer teams but could not wait to blame particular players for everything. But mostly I loved how London-like London was. When Swanna and I took our first black cab into town from the airport she turned to me and said, 'It's so London,' and it was the only thing to say. The cobblestone streets, the red buses, the warm ales in the charming little pubs, it was London, like nowhere else, magical, old, wonderful London, and it was ours to discover.

To move with, Dad gave me three grand and Mum two grand and a lot of underwear. Even then, it was only weeks before we were broke, what with the rental bond and furnishing the place, plus my wisdom tooth became infected the moment we arrived and I didn't have travel insurance. We ate soup most nights and only bought Tesco homebrand products. Swanna took work at the Independent Video Store on Broadway Market and I took a job as dishwasher at an Indian Restaurant on Brick Lane.

It was horrible stuff, and I soon left, landing a job at the Arcola Theatre in Dalston, where I ushered, worked the bar, the box office, and generally ran proceedings when the lights were up. The theatre itself was quaint, housing a blend of new and old works, some bland some bold, and it was there I saw my first Sarah Kane play, and after that, well, the possibilities of theatre were wide open.

Swanna and I spent a lot of time at the Arcola, and because of this moved to a better, cheaper flat just off the Dalston high street. One of the actors, Clive, from the *Faust* that was currently showing, lived in the flat below. We made friends quickly, as the building we now inhabited was basically a commune for actors, musicians and artists. The doors were never locked, we roamed freely, strolling downstairs and upstairs for a beer, or to borrow a CD, smoke a joint or, as it progressed, to engage in orgies. Clive introduced us to a friend of his who owned a series of vacant lots in Stoke Newington, and pretty soon Swanna and I were staging our first production on foreign soil. The piece was not dissimilar to *ME* in style; we took a group of actors and performers and devised a show around the issues in their own lives and the idea of a 'New London' from an outsider's perspective (ie us), then invited an audience to follow them round the space through the experience. What I didn't see coming was the way we would be received. Somehow we ducked the infamous critical slamming of the British press and, perhaps due to our unpretentious theatre-out-of-nothing approach, were elevated to a cultish status we did not entirely deserve.

Swanna and I quickly founded The Scream People, and within six months had private sponsorship and a space of our own. We went about making new work; Swanna took care of all things visual, and her detailed, always tasteful design mesmerised those so accustomed to daggy old British sets and naturalistic designs. Swanna was a taste-maker in her own right and I adored everything that fell out of her heart, her mind, her hands. Those first two years in London dripped with love, we were on top of this new city and we fed off each other, living the work both in and out of the space. Swanna glowed, and I glistened in her light, I cannot remember a moment where she was more than a foot away from me at this time, and if she was, our eyes knew of each other, and our minds conversed regardless.

In our third show as The Scream People I stepped away from performing altogether, much preferring to put the dream together than be at its centre on stage. I liked directing, devising, asking the questions, and there was so much more to see when you stopped concentrating on your own performance. It was a different baring of thought, to face the stage but with my back turned, and strangely I came to love the audience and the art even more this way.

We played the Burdekin with a highly contentious teenage version of Büchner's unfinished play *Woyzeck*, and were then asked to stage a multimedia piece at the National Theatre for their New Vision Festival. And, along with nine other Australians living and working in London at the top of their fields, an invitation to tea with the Queen herself.

We grew together, Swanna and me, and anything was possible when we were looking at each other, when we were engaged, joined. She never feared me or shut down a single notion or speck of thought, and I did nothing but stretch out the vivid plains of her dreamscape, which were so rich with taste, I never met a human with more taste. Even the way she brought out the tea and scones, or how she put her outfits together with her bags, or the way she made the bed; everything was classy, unusual, and when you cast your eyes upon it you felt at home but at the same time you knew you were staring at something you had never seen before. Love with her was a familiar unknown, and we trusted each other in it, we were invincible. The last bath I ever had with Swanna was cold though, and bits of her blood floated about me as red buses passed by our window.

25

And I am not proud of certain things. Tell me a man who is proud of all his movements and I will eat a chair. But what surprised me most, and warmed me deep, was the level of forgiveness and, inevitably, the care that comes with people from the southern suburbs. I was a monster, and I nearly tore them down, addicted to ice and feverish with it, volatile and cruel and wielding trouble, and my friend Gordon, and his stepdad Albert, and numerous mates and blokes from the area chipped in and helped me build my little house on a leaf, overlooking the sea on Bundeena Reserve. They gave me another chance, and I am eternally grateful. It is easy to jump out of the village, move to the cities, and spend your time poking fun at the little places we hail from and their routine ways, but deep down inside you know that's where the real people are, the truly decent souls, and you fight and fight to deny it, until you need them so bad it hurts.

The ferries were too spread out on Sundays and I simply couldn't face the locals anyway. I loved Bundeena and its delicate beaches, the fact that it translates to 'noise like thunder', and the magical sunsets and symphony of wildlife that sends you softly to sleep. The sweetest breeze blows across it, and it's only a hop, step and a jump back to the mainland, but going into town was an effort. Within weeks of living here I knew everyone, and bless their souls I've never met a more twisted, gregarious, and glorious set of people in my life, but at the same time I have never met a chattier bunch. A walk to the shops involved at least four or five lengthy conversations, usually concerning who had just had babies, what famous painters were moving in, and the ins and outs of council planning. Today I could not take the onslaught, so I called my dad and asked him to come pick me up. Let's face it, he was a driving instructor, surely he could manage it.

Dad wasn't really involved in the building of the house on a leaf, which hurt a bit. I thought it would be good for us to spend time together, make something together, and we wouldn't have had to talk that much at all, just hand each other wood, grunt a little, and suck a beer at the end of the day. But his girlfriend had issues with me, especially when she heard of my behaviour while on ice, and how I left a girl in London so soon after a miscarriage. She threatened to take Dad to court and obtain sole custody of their child if he ever saw me again, but lately things had changed, and I'm not so sure why, but lately he's been visiting me, and I've got to know my little half-brother Oscar, and it's nothing short of beautiful. I don't ask Dad how he came to be here, I figure she's loosened her grip, or maybe Dad is lying to her when he sees me, maybe my relationship with my father is covert – ha, ain't that something, to sneak out and see your son as if he's a secret lover!

I placed the kettle on the hob and whipped on the gas. I wiped my eyes and looked out my kitchen window, through the gum leaves to the bay. The local kids were running riot on the shore, which made me smile, if I didn't have this furious cuntfuck of a hangover

I would wander down there and continue the adventure with them. Bundeena had brought me so much since I'd come here. It might seem to my mother and father that I had withdrawn from life and work, 'given up' even, but there was so much happening inside, so much joy in my life, it was just quieter, and slower. I was rebuilding myself out here, a ferry ride from Cronulla, my old school in the distance, and this was the place to do it, with a bottle of Irish, in the mud and trees, with those mad-eyed little black and white bastards who lived this side of the bay.

I was still in my boxer shorts, sipping on the tea and checking my email, when Oscar came blazing through the fly-screen door and into my kitchen, wearing tweed pants, a white button-up shirt and blue vest, with shiny shoes and a hat. The very sight of him running towards me made me want to cry. I cried a lot lately, not sure why exactly; Mum reckoned it was an emotional response to getting off drugs, which had held me numb for so long. I read in the *Good Weekend* the Sunday before an interview with a TV journalist about her happiest moment, and she said it was touching her newborn daughter's skin, and I ended up sobbing uncontrollably for an hour.

Oscar leapt into my arms and demanded we go looking for cicadas. I kissed his blond, heaven-sweating head and looked up at my father, who stood hesitantly in the doorway in trousers and a sports jacket, and I realised, stupidly, and finally, that this was the reason he visited me now: Oscar loved it here. Oscar had the Bundeena in him too. Noise like thunder.

Dad shook his head at the state of my house, bottles and shit everywhere, but he couldn't help smiling as he went. I was alive and he knew it; pickled with grog I was alive.

Dad drove smoothly and slowly, without errors.

'How was that bucks' night a couple of weeks ago?' he asked me.

'Ok,' I said, but I didn't want to talk about it because that would make me think about it.

I thanked Dad for picking me up, and he winked at me. I asked him if his girlfriend was coming to the wedding, and he winked at me again, but cheekier with it. I felt like crying right away; this was the best moment we had shared in so long. To be in on something with another man, to share a sly victory, the easiest of love.

My father scared me, his mere presence in a car, a room, a park. I loved him but I could not reach him, and I had tired of trying. Being away and growing up somewhat had diffused the rage in me, the desire to shake him up, spit in his face, and make him see just how disconnected I felt from him. But with my own failings in the time I had spent as a man, I saw he was not that bad after all. The whole thing of life was so hard to do right.

One night, when I was just younger than a teenager, after my parents had been fighting again, I made my father react to me, I made him jump up.

It was Halloween week at school and everyone was making 'trick or treat' costumes and decorating pumpkins for the big night. I chose to dress myself as one of the zombies out of Michael Jackson's *Thriller* video. It was here I discovered fake blood. My world opened up, I could not believe we were allowed to smear ourselves in the syrupy nectar of death and massacre. I stole bottles of it and brought it home with me, spending hours in front of the mirror applying blood to my lips, ears and forehead, constructing scenarios in my head of having been hacked up, or slashed at, or stabbed in the eyes.

When Mum and Dad were fighting, Dad would often stay out late in the weeks following, coming home full and clumsy in the middle of the night. He'd bypass his own room and come into mine, where I would pretend to be asleep as he told me how much he loved me, breathed the night on me, and then asked me not to tell Mum he was in here. It was at this point Mum would appear in my doorway and ask him to get off the bed and let me be.

One night, upon hearing him enter the house, I opened three of my clothes drawers to differing lengths, and dotted them with blood. I then applied a convincing line of the stuff all the way from my skull down to my ear, and lay down on the carpeted floor, in a swirling pool of purple-red fake blood, and moaned like my skull was opening. Dad walked in, turned the light on, and saw me there on the floor. I opened my eyes, ever so slowly, ever so creepily, and said, 'Daddy, Daddy – help.'

Dad took a step back and bent over in the hall, pulling at the air, and screamed out my mother's name, at which point I stood up and laughed at him, holding a bottle of fake blood. After that show Dad became wary of me, and for the years to come always looked at me with a suspicious eye.

Dad dropped me at Gordon's house where my groomsman suit was. I thanked him again for picking me up and told him I would see him at the wedding in an hour or two. I messed Oscar's hair up and was strolling towards the poolside entrance to the mansion when Dad called to me.

'Son!' he said.

I turned around. 'Yes, Dad?'

'Come 'ere.'

I went over to the driver's side window, which rested at its limit, three-quarters down and on an angle up. There was a large portion of silence and then he broke it with speaking.

'Your mother and me . . . we had a miscarriage too.'

'Ok,' I said, confused as to why he was telling me this now.

'I know it's hard to take.'

'It was a while ago, Dad.'

'Yep, but things hang around, don't they? Not everything goes.'

I nodded, and tapped his hand with my hand, then wandered up to Gordon's place. He was right, my dad; not everything goes away. I felt physically sick every time I thought of Swanna, the pain had not gone anywhere, nor the regret, nor the disgust. I still could not see how or where the weather changed so quickly between us: one minute we were sunny and high on our very own sexual and creative revolution, the next there was death and darkness all around and no way of lifting the clouds up.

26

The orgies ended when I fell through the roof and shattered my right shoulder. Since Glenn and Ivana had moved in above us towards the end of spring, the air moved with sensuality, and everything was heading towards our central areas.

Glenn was twenty-six, Irish, and could well have continued quite successfully as a male model with his chiselled-to-the-fuck jawline and piercing blue eyes. He always seemed to have just the right amount of stubble, and when he smoked or appeared in a hallway through shifting light, James Dean was alive once more, in Hackney Borough. But Glenn was a singer songwriter, wholeheartedly obsessed and plainly influenced by the pop/jazz sensation Serge Gainsbourg; he even wore the same jackets and spoke with that rich velvet relax. Modelling was something Glenn rarely spoke about, so embarrassed by his years in undies on billboards and on catwalks in Milan. He was a muso now, a journeyman only, and fortunately for him (as I have noticed that most models have a passion for either music, acting or photography) Glenn was gifted. He constructed guitar riffs and cruisey little chord progressions that grabbed your attention within bars, pouring his dreamy lyrics over the top of it, creating such a deep, hypnotic groove it was hard to resist shaking your hips or nodding along. Musicians of this time were so swept up with recreating the maudlin, ex-girlfriend folk of Nick Drake and Bob Dylan, it was refreshing to hear a youngster with a sense of swing and sex and playfulness in him. Yes, Glenn had 'style', the elusive thing no man can buy – but boy do we try. I liked being around him, and his girlfriend Ivana, who was clearly Glenn's very own Jane Birkin, adding sweet back-up vocals and gushing moans and sighs where appropriate. They were a famous and highly enchanting stage presence.

Ivana had moved from Serbia when she was sixteen and her English was still very shaky, but she was astoundingly, strikingly beautiful, with her hard eyes and big lips, soft skin and sharp black fringe. She hoped one day to be an actress in 'important cinema'. Many of the women in our circle of artists and actors found Ivana too intense, too earnest and direct, but Swanna and I adored her, and as winter kicked in and London froze up, resembling a perfect place to kill yourself, the four of us hibernated, finding solace and more before the open fire of our living room on Ridley Road.

We never left, and there was no need to, each night was more fun than anywhere outside had to offer, and outside itself was too terrifying a prospect even if there was enticement. We played a highly competitive brand of charades, read out pages from pieces we were working on, drank cheap wine and smoked like chimneys, cooked paella, shepherd's pie, and countless red pasta meals, talking on into the night and early mornings, huddled together in a million coats and blankets, connected by our friendship, our curiosity, and our hands.

One night, it may have been a Saturday, I came home to find Ivana and Swanna running Glenn a bath. They were all semi-naked and had obviously been drinking. I felt very far outside it all, and ached to catch up. I knew Glenn wanted Swanna, it was plain as day, and he had all but asked me through insinuation and looks if he could have her. And he knew I was desperate to fuck Ivana, catching me out on many an occasion gazing up her legs splayed out before me on the blanket, or simply stroking her hair and neck as we lay about watching Tarkovsky.

There was MDMA around that winter, and I had found a pure batch through a friend in Angel. Within an hour we were all high as kites, lingering around the bath which was now heaped with the bubbles of assorted bath products found at the markets by the girls that morning. Funnily enough, Swanna began it all, asking Ivana if she could kiss her in front of us. Ivana did not answer, she simply moved forward into the light of the bathroom moon and they were kissing. In the weeks to come I admired, and envied, the way the girls kissed; there was no chance I could ever kiss Swanna like that, for there was no drive inside it, no carnal need from man to get somewhere beyond it and invade, conquer or fuck, there was just sensuality and pleasure on its own.

I looked beside me to find Glenn with his pants down, jacking off at the sight of the two girls kissing. Ivana raised her singlet over her breasts and Swanna led her into the steaming, overgrown bath. Buoyed by the drugs, we laughed our way through our first foursome, and Glenn and I never crossed paths in the night, shifting cautiously over or under each other's bodies to get to the other girl or part of her. It was challenging, ego-wise, to watch Glenn fucking Swanna from behind, and to see how much she loved it, the feel of another cock, another rhythm, another man, but it was quickly appeased by diving mouth-first into Ivana's shaved and petite quim, closing my eyes and pushing the threat right into her.

The day after our first endeavour we all fell away awkward and Swanna and I made soup in the afternoon, wondering whether they would ever come by again. But we were only halfway through our meal when they knocked on the door in just dressing-gowns, bearing champagne and honey; we were soon on the floor again.

It went on this way for weeks, the girls kissing and licking away at each other in the bath, then all of us getting in and washing each other and laughing at the flesh and the way it rose and changed with touch and stroking, then wrestling to the living room floor or our bed to fuck for hours with music playing and fruit and toys involved. But still Glenn and I manoeuvred around each other. Every now and then I'd feel him bump up against me or a courser hand pass across my thigh, waiting to see if I approved of its question, but I never let him near my balls or dick until, by twisted god or ill nature, the girls began cycling together, and with just their difficult, narrow arses to put things in, demanded we suck each other off before them. I had been here before, at university, and it had not been so bad. I preferred to receive the act, for at least I could close my eyes and dream of a first-year female cultural studies student on all fours, but to have one in your own mouth, well, there was no mistaking what it was. And Glenn's dick was big and uncircumcised with quite a bend in the shaft. Swanna had often remarked how pleasurable the bend was, and it filled me with rage, that it held special powers, but now it just filled me, and as the women clapped and hollered, Glenn blew in my mouth with gusto, and I ran to the kitchen to be sick in the sink. I returned, Glenn cuddling up to the ladies in quiet rejoice, but I would be having none of this victory lap.

'On your fucking knees, Serge, it's your turn.'

The girls howled with laughter as I stood on the bed and fucked Glenn in the mouth, clenching the back of his long neck and cranking myself deep into his gob. But no matter how hard and long I went at him, Glenn just ate the thing and smiled around it, roaring like a lion and clenching my arse with his fingers, pulling me to him and taking my cum and swallowing it with immense pride, then rising up to kiss me on the lips. I ducked his mouth and pushed off the bed, spotting Ivana and her mind piecing all sorts of things together. Her man had taken the violence and the object all too well, and she knew now why he had wanted this all to begin. It was the end of a novel for her, where the beginning finally made sense.

The following night I was drinking in the corner, high off the Valium Glenn had thrown us all, watching Ivana growl Swanna out as Glenn sucked on her tits. It was at that moment I realised I wanted Swanna to be my wife. I wobbled out of the room high as a kite and in the nude. I stumbled onto the glass balcony instead of into the hallway, and I fell three storeys, shattering my shoulder and breaking two ribs. I didn't feel much at the time, so elated was I from the drugs, the epiphany, and the small flight through the air, but the fear rose up in me when I saw Swanna's face above me, so full of love and fear for my life.

We saw very little of Glenn and Ivana after that; my injury seemed to kill all prospect of further liaison. Swanna and I sensed months of discomfort on the stairs, and so we found a cottage in Bethnal Green, streets from the park, and above a brilliant little deli with an internet cafe.

That year we returned to Sydney for the Christmas break. Swanna's father had fallen ill with a stroke and, frankly, we missed everyone a little. Somehow the love and security Swanna and I had found in each other had made us itchy to get home, if only for two weeks, and reconnect with those we used to know and love. It was great being home, and Swanna found Cronulla so amusing; how beautiful it was, and how proud everyone was of it, and how white everyone was too. She couldn't believe what the teenage girls wore though, and how long it took to order something in a shop with the staff taking so long to make a single cappuccino. She helped me rediscover the place and I enjoyed showing off my home, and in doing so letting her in on me and my life, even if I did dress up certain parts to suit my ego. It was a little odd making love in the single bed next to my mother's room, and strange to feel the entire pace of the world slow down, back in Cronulla, where everyone seemed happy, and people took pride in their lawns. It was a family place, and so it felt more than appropriate when we discovered we were pregnant, the morning of New Year's Eve at the GP on Caringbah Road. Even though it wasn't planned and I had absolutely no idea how I would feel or think when it happened, I tell you, I had never felt so happy. It was like I had been dead up until that point, like I had lived without purpose or force and now I was galvanised, now I was in the real stretch of river. I loved Swanna so much in the revelation, and the thought of making a person together made so much sense to me. It was the only thing we had not yet made together, and I knew, like all the other pieces of art and love we had made, this would be the most magic, the most life-changing, and the most true. This was to be our greatest show ever, and it was all for us.

We arrived at Sydney Harbour in the early afternoon, with thousands of other Australians, grabbing the best possible spot for the fireworks. Gordon had suggested we go down there, the four of us, and drink some wine on a rug and watch the light show and 'see the new year in with style.' It was a nightmare finding a park but with the news we had received via a plastic pregnancy stick this morning, the world was a glorious place, and nothing could deter us.

Unlike our friends in London, talking with this couple, with Gordon and Courtney, well it was a two-and-two affair, usually restricted to gender. Gordon handed me a beer and we stood to the side of the rug discussing his business and the infiltration of the Cronulla community by Lebanese people. It was the curse of being the last train station apparently; they all 'got out and had a look around, and who would have fucken thought, they liked it!' Courtney and Swanna lay on the rug eating pineapple and chatting away. I didn't notice it then, as I was doing my best to stay with Gordon's tirade against the fundamentalist Muslim, but Courtney did not ask Swanna a single question. She merely spoke of her own doings: graduating into family law, signing with a firm in Sutherland, renovating the top floor and gutting the bottom floor of their mansion – just rolling on to subject after subject, never coming up for air. Swanna didn't mind though, she was amused by Courtney, she liked her spunk and the obvious big brain, but still she could not work out why she didn't seem the least bit curious about Swanna's own life, and her life with me. I had never seen this in Courtney; vanity and self-interest were not part of her make-up – at least, not the make-up of the girl I once knew. The only conclusion I could draw was that she was nervous, and this made her babble on mindlessly. Swanna looked at me glumly when I said this, as if I had said something stupid, and I knew then she was not entirely comfortable about Courtney and me, as if she sensed there was something still moving there.

Gordon, on the other hand, always kicked off talking about himself, but quickly shifted to friendly interrogation, hounding me for details on The Scream People, life in London, rental prices and such, always placing my achievements and adventures up on a pedestal so much higher than his own, which was silly, because this bloke had made so much from so little. Gordon's blinds company was franchised in Wollongong and Newcastle now. Then he and Albert had begun a little property and construction side project, only to see it prosper into a million-dollar business and growing. They bought big, daggy houses anywhere from Sans Souci to North Cronulla, did them up and sold them in record time, boasting a tidy profit which they then invested in the next house, and the next, with each new project growing in size, splendour and, of course, resale profit. After a few beers Gordon admitted to me that the quality of the work, and the price and standard of the materials, were mostly low, frighteningly low, but no one every complained or noticed, and nothing had fallen apart yet, 'Touch fucken wood!'

Gordon and Courtney seemed genuinely happy, and as the fireworks exploded and the light show began on the bridge, a rainbow of spears shooting out into the universe, I wished the four of us would be friends forever, with adjoining houses decked with barbecues and day beds, tennis on Sundays even, together in love with kids and dogs hurtling and chomping about our feet. Grow old and fabulous in each other's lives, in each other's differences, in each other's in-ground pools. It was a dream and I was having it, my arms in the air and my pregnant girlfriend beside me, smiling widely as all the colours shifted about her gorgeous half-Sri Lankan face and hair.

When we returned to London I received an email from Gordon which said:

N, how was your flight back?
Nice girl that one, keep your dick in your pants.
G-funk

Swanna threw up in tech rehearsals for *The Caretaker*, and Mum flew over to help her out, even though we didn't ask her to. Swanna's dad sent us money, but then he asked for it back a month later; he was spending more and more time at the RSL playing the pokies now that Rhonda had left him for some guy she met at a Planets Conference in Brisbane.

Every morning we woke up I kissed my girlfriend's expanded belly-skin and sang some sort of lullaby to it. I wanted the baby so much I lost all interest in other things. My production of *The Caretaker* was pretty average and quite poorly received, but I didn't give a fuck, where before I would have thrashed and wailed, and written aggressive retorts to the journalist cunt.

Swanna, on the other hand, became even more brilliant as we moved to two and then three months in. She painted madly every day, filled the house with flowers from Columbia Road, baked like a madwoman, and made mixed CDs for the baby with tracks from Air and Chopin, Fleetwood Mac and Moby. We made love with hilarious difficulty, and spent our evenings on the couch dreaming up names and occupations for our child. We were sliding in heaven's slipstream, and it would only get better.

But the sun goes down so early in London, especially in winter, and on 16 March at 4.14 pm it was pretty much pitch-black, which was why nobody saw what happened on Valentine Road, behind the Tesco, when a young black Rude Boy with a hood over his face held a machete to Swanna's hip and threatened to slit her open if she did not hand over her purse and phone. Being Swanna, she attempted to talk him down, but he mistook her long words and clear pronunciation as patronising and racist, so he cut her side, opening up her abdomen, and she fell and lost a gallon of blood to the gutter. And in the blood our first child too, there or at the hospital, on the way, I still do not know. All I know was that it was not there anymore. Not there anymore. Not there at all.

A quarter after midnight before I heard of this. I was in Berlin at the time, checking out the Schaubühnes F.I.N.D. festival, searching for new plays from around the world. An old couple had found her in the gutter, her purse long gone and the Rude Boy too. The old bloke drove her to the hospital and she was 'doing fine' they said to me when I called. But she was far from fucking 'fine', she was never anywhere near fucking fine ever fucking again.

There were no more shows for The Scream People that year, we were on hiatus, as Swanna went on with recovery, walking large parks and seeing small films. She said very little to me, to anyone, the only time she would open up was grocery shopping, where her eyes bloomed and her shoulders straightened as she went at it, furrowed brow, hunting down every last ingredient for the entire week's meals, breakfast, lunch and dinner all the way to Sunday. Her intensity was piercing and somewhat disturbing, but who was I to ask for calm? This was the only place she showed signs of life, even if it did include her fossicking through every branch of broccoli before she found the right one for Thursday's stir fry.

We slept in the same bed but we never touched. The therapist said it would take time, and not to ask too much of her. I fucking knew that, it is called being a decent fucking human being. Fuck's sake, thirty-five quid an hour to tell you not to force a girl who just got stabbed and lost a child.

After a while I started spending less time at home, socialising with some of my old mates from the Arcola, and often came back drunk, which occasionally brought out some loud, boozy snoring. Swanna suggested I sleep in the study on these nights, so I did, on a fold-out couch. I moved into the study soon enough, it was just easier that way, and I felt that was what she wanted.

One night Swanna came in and told me if I needed to be with someone I could see Ivana, she had talked it through with Glenn and they were 'cool with it'. We'd all been there before and she knew I liked sex, and that pretty soon I would do it with someone else anyway, so she might as well be in on it and approving, she said.

So twice a week I rode my bike to the Dalston house on Ridley Road to fuck Ivana. Early on Glenn would ask, so courteously, as if wanting to contribute to the recovery, if he could get 'involved' or 'help', but I just wanted the girl, and he respected this and let us have the afternoons alone. It was good for a while, the agreement, and Swanna seemed genuinely cool with it too, asking a question about it here and there but pretty much leaving me to it. And I enjoyed it, I will admit, Ivana was fucking beautiful and our bodies moved well together, even more so now we were one on one, but she was tiring of how hard and direct I would approach things, and how I never looked at her or kissed her during, so I slowed things up and tried to connect with her, to be intimate and stare into her eyes when we got there together. But then I'd just start crying, convulsing on top of her, so we closed up business and I took to masturbating furiously in the study, or fingering the odd actress in the toilets at Jag Shoes. 'Fingering is not cheating,' Stuart once said.

It was February when Stuart started visiting me in my sleep. He'd appear in a burst of new light, standing on the end of my fold-out bed in a white linen suit and red dancing shoes, smirking ruefully, but then all bashfulness was gone as he peered down at me and said, 'Why do you lie?'

27

The Camellia Gardens seemed so much bigger to me when I was a kid. My nan would take me there on weekends to feed the ducks with half a bag of old bread. It was the deadset highlight of my fucking week and I could not wait to get there and explore. The ponds were like big green oceans and the gum trees soared high above me, and the ducks – there seemed to be thousands of them and all so majestic and dainty as they fluttered and dived, quacking to each other in their own secret language. But now, as Gordon and I hauled out of the car with Albert and Rocky in tow, the place seemed uncomfortably small, with only a scattering of sad-looking ducks lurking in weed by the ponds' perimeters, desperate for a hunk of bread to fall into their small, slimy little oval bed. What magic scale childhood does make of raw adult reality.

We walked under the overgrown palms to the bridge which led to the open green where the matrimonial rose garden lay, and it was at this precise moment it became abundantly clear to me just how fucking hot it was. My back was drenched beneath the blackness of my tuxedo jacket and my scalp dripped with sweat. I turned around to see Gordon's face like a tomato blown up with a foot pump, a V of sweat already forming on his white shirt, which he tugged at, raising his eyebrows at me in fear and exhaustion. Carmen stood waiting for us in an enormous blue and black floral dress with high brown heels, smoking a Dunhill beside the white rose proscenium entranceway to the garden of love and trust. The rose garden was Courtney's church of choice, she no longer believed in Jesus or God, not since the suicide of her brother and the voluntary, pathetic evacuation of her father Eric. She cared not to be married under any such doctrines; she wished only to be surrounded by flowers, and people whom she loved as much as those sweet petals which grew above the pricks and stems.

'Long way from England, isn't it?' Carmen joked, as we hunkered into the shade, Albert kissing his lady on the neck and cheek.

'This is fucken searing,' said Gordon, accepting a handkerchief from Carmen and wiping his sloppy pink mouth with it.

'Just put it off till the afternoon and we can all go to the pub till it cools down,' said Rocky, wielding a cheeky grin. The boy had a point. Rocky was not long off the boat but he seemed firmly on the earth, a far cry from the monosyllabic, disturbed kid we used to know, scuttling into his room to eat tall packets of Doritos and play Commodore 64, Slayer on full bore in the tape player. The navy had saved him, although I was yet to see he and Gordon say a word to each other. Rocky was proud of his brother and you could tell he loved being in attendance, but even at the bucks' night, drunk and high and full of spirit, they still circled each other with wide, sweeping arcs.

'How's Courtney?' I asked Carmen, foot up on the bench by the duck pond where a few dozen guests began to mingle. 'How does she look?'

Carmen's eyes rolled back in her skull then fell forward like bouncing lotto balls, but wider, and rich with amazement and spilled yearning for that time in a woman's life where you stop a room with the way you walk, and where you feel like anything can happen and most likely will if you simply believe it to be true.

'She's just stunning,' Carmen said, grinding her cigarette out on the sole of her Diana Ferrari heel. 'She makes such a beautiful bride.' Carmen started crying, smiling with puffed mouth at her eldest son, who was still battling the oppressive hotness and endless river of sweat that fled down his spine then ran along the lane of his bum crack into his pants, where it pooled and gathered around his thighs.

'I need a fucking bottle of water,' Gordon said, handing the drenched handkerchief back to Carmen then trotting up the pathway towards the teahouse.

I shrugged at Carmen, who seemed bewildered by her son's lack of interest in Courtney's beauty as bride, but then Albert came in and held her, which must have made her understand it was different being a man, on this day, in the heat, and she smiled, then began a lap of welcome to those friends and family who now fell into the green in droves, wiping away the sweat with towels and fanning their faces with booklets.

Rocky and I followed Gordon to the teahouse, which sat innocently beside the gardens' entrance just off President Avenue. Mothers and children were the majority of the clientele, chatting and chirping on the old timber deck which overlooked the twisting trails and creeks below. Rocky hung about on the bottom step, intending to smoke a joint before the ceremony – boy, this kid was relaxed. I told him to save a bit for me, and to wish me luck, for I was 'going in.' He laughed and made some derisory comment about marriage which made me see just how gay he was, and perfectly smug with it.

I stepped inside the men's bathroom to find Gordon naked from the waist up, crouched awkwardly against the wall, desperately forcing his left armpit into the blaring wake of the hand dryer. His shirt was in his other hand, waving in the breeze of a second hand dryer, which he also had going. It was a vision of insanity, weirdness, and sheer balletic flexibility – even though Gordon had stacked on some kilograms since corporate life had taken over, the karate training was still very much alive in the way he had manifested his very own acrobatic Chinese laundry. I took my own jacket off and hung it on a cubicle door, airing my shirt by separating it from my body and blowing down into my chest and gut. I wanted so much to laugh but there was no perspective in my friend's face, he was riddled with big frustration and sheer anxiety.

'Hold this one for me,' Gordon said.

I took up position before the hand dryer, and made sure his shirt was getting a thorough working-over. Gordon's paranoia seemed to fall away as I brought his wet shirt back to drier, crisper life.

'I've always been a sweater,' he said, grinning now, as he swapped armpits beneath the blow and push of air.

'If a man is going to sweat,' I said, 'today is the day for it.'

'It's not that. I'm all over that.'

'You don't look like you are.'

'Why wouldn't I be?'

'No reason, mate.'

'I know what I want. Today I get it,' Gordon said, blunt, somewhat demeaning.

'Good for you,' I acknowledged, nodding smiling nodding.

'Can you ask the chicks at the shop if they have any deodorant? Buy some if they sell any. I stink like a fucking pig,' Gordon said, as it dawned on me: marriage was a type of societal elevation. Gordon had the licence to talk down to me, because I still remained with the paupers of singledom, whereas he was King in wedlock now, and I had much to do and learn from him.

'I'll try,' I said, handing him his near-dry shirt and whipping my jacket back over my shoulder.

I was almost out the door when he said, 'What, you think I should be sweating, Cronk? You think I got something to sweat about, do you?'

I shook my head. You fickle cunt. 'No, mate. It's your day.'

The fat ladies behind the teashop counter laughed loud when I asked them if they had any deodorant. I explained the situation, which induced further hysterics; this was clearly one of the most amazing things that had ever happened in the teashop. I took a seat at the long table by the entrance before the table of brochures and maps, wishing they served beer; I could rape and murder a fucking beer, any beer, even a Tooheys New.

Gordon's bucks' party had kicked off here not two weeks ago. It was Rocky's suggestion to begin proceedings with a tea party, he thought it would be really fun, and despite Gordon's initial reticence, all the blokes loved it, sipping tea and devouring a collection of tasty delights as the chubby women wobbled around us, cleaning up and putting down fresh trays of goodies. Each of the twelve boys at the long table made a semi-erudite speech, and I put it down to the sweetness of the cakes and so too the occasion. Men only joined together on fields or with beer on soiled carpet, yet here we were sipping an old English hot drink for our old English friend, and I'd never seen a group of men more awake and surprised at how possible it was to have fun without smashing people's faces in or downing ten hundred ales. This was sophistication, and all were willing, especially Gordon, who kept whispering in my ear just how great an idea this was, and how he would never forget the tea party at the Camellia Gardens. I told him to tell Rocky this, it was his idea, but I don't think he did, he just kept saying it to me.

The contrast from garden tea party to animal bus was drastic to say the least, as we departed the garden respite and climbed up onto the deck of the musty animal-bus where Albert met us with a tall bottle each of cold beer and a set of rubber tits to wear. Gordon was made to demolish a yard glass of Coopers and a few random shots of green and blue liquid, then was pummelled into the back corner and the words *I Love Cock* were inscribed on his forehead in blue zinc cream. Then AC/DC came blaring through the speakers and we were off on our way to Heathcote, where the skirmish and paint ball fields awaited.

Gordon was hammered before we got to Engadine, which was around the time my face was painted in brown zinc cream, each of us a tribal colour of our own.

'Holy fucken shit, Cronk! You're fucken brown!' Gordon said, lifting me up out of my seat to look at me. 'You look like a nigga!' he spat, swinging a long bottle of Heineken in his hands.

'I am a real brother,' I said, spotting Albert in the corner painting Michael Shoes with bright yellow war paint.

'Gimme a hug, ya cunt,' Gordon said, hugging me.

'It's going to be a good day,' I said, moving back towards my seat.

'You need a beer. Albert, get Neil a beer!' Gordon yelled over four seats of buck hunters. 'You like this bus?' Gordon punched me in the elbow and cackled.

Albert handed me a Heineken and bang, there were six men in the aisle of the bus singing Hunters & Collectors and clinking glasses. The beer was warm but I drank it anyway. I was pathologically hungover, having drunk an entire bottle of Chivas Regal on my own the night before. The only way I would get through this was by saying yes to this day, to my old life, and as a result I stared down at the floor and swallowed. I would drink harder than all of them and I would compete in the animal bus arm-wrestling competition but I am not afraid to say I was scared, this bus was lurching forward, lurching somewhere big and male and broken and I could feel it.

'Mate, the guy is a fucken legend,' Gordon said, as we stalked up the hill on our hands and knees, settling behind a blown-apart silo splattered in shot-out paint.

'Albert?' I asked, panting from thirteen years of solid smoking.

Gordon loaded his gun with pellets and looked at me with utter earnestness. 'Me and Albert have been through a lot together, he turned our whole lives around. I can't thank him enough, seriously.'

It was midday and this was the third 'Warfare'. I was fucking exhausted, and longed to get back to Cronulla, to Bundeena, or just some pub with booze in it. But Gordon wasn't going anywhere, they'd bought seven Warfares and we weren't even halfway. One of the guys was in hospital having done his groin running down a ravine, and I was partly blind in one eye having been splattered with paint every time I popped up. I would be no use in a war, the only thing I could do was protect the art and, you know, linger around sipping tea and wiping down the maps and navigation instruments.

'You know last Thursday me and Albert had a joint colonoscopy,' Gordon said. 'That's how close we are now. The procedure required two days of working up to it, like this whole diet we had to do on the first day and then just fluids the second day, then on Thursday we drink this really strong lemon Picoprep solution which empties your bowel . . . Did you know the human bowel is like forty feet long? And it has explosive tendencies? The drink's fucking disgusting but it's good to get this test, man, we're getting to that age now where heavy stuff like that's a factor. Did you know chickpeas and grilled tomato are the best thing for prostate cancer? If there's a history in your family then get grilling your tomatoes, Neil.'

'I did not know that,' I said.

'Albert's my real dad,' Gordon said. 'I don't even think of my other dad now, he's fucking not my dad, we made sure of that.' Gordon slammed home the gauge and lifted the gun strap over his shoulder. 'I have no love for my old dad, I have a whole lot of love for Albert, but you know what?'

'What?' I asked, somehow giggling now, caught up.

'It doesn't stop me blowing the cunt's nut off.'

And with that Gordon stood up and ran, screaming 'Hasta la vista faggots!' as he blasted away.

I peered over the edge of the busted silo in time to see Gordon hit the ground, surrounded by Albert and Michael Shoes and his brother Rocky, all members of the Red Team, having now officially kidnapped the leader of the Blue Team. I was the only one who could save him, but I simply did not feel like it, and I had failed to buy any more pellets in the gap between Warfares for this very reason. So instead I took off my gun, rolled a cigarette and lay down in the sun, listening to the war cry of the Red Team as they blasted into Gordon's neck and chest. Gordon called out to me for help and I would have ignored it, but in the call was a crack and inside the crack a little boy lost, the little boy I grew up with. Something about the event, the alcohol and the violence had brought this little boy back to me.

'I'm coming for you, G-Funk, don't you worry about that,' I said to myself, hardly believing it. I really had not enjoyed one part of the fucking skirmish day, and I could not comprehend how on earth it was a legal activity. I mean, the bullets really fucking hurt when they hit you, my neck and chin were seriously bruised and the mask fogged up really quickly, which was why I kept lifting it off, which was why I got shot in the eyebrow and partially blinded, and the terrain was littered with dangerous obstacles like broken bins and sharp rocks and razor wire traps which you could hardly see down by your ankles, especially when your goggles were fogged up to the point of nil vision. I was surprised more people did not die out there – not joking. Marriage was such a beautiful gesture, why on earth did we choose to precede the event with this low act of bludgeoning and filth? Women went out on boats and gathered around the engagement ring, talking babies and dresses, sipping chardonnay and enjoying the company of the male stripper. That was civilised, women did it right; men, we had to go to war with paint, we had to rape each other in the dirt before we joined our better half in holy matrimony. Somebody make sense of this for me, please! I'm dying out here. Take me back to the tea garden!

I breathed deep, loading my gun with the four remaining pellets I had managed to save in my top pocket. I had barely shot anyone at all, failed in all my weapons missions – the only thing I had succeeded in was not being caught. Which was mostly due to the fact I had not really participated, preferring to smoke in the bushes until the Warfare was nearly over, then give myself up when we were outnumbered. But this time, well, this time my best friend was squealing in pain, calling my name, and I was so sunburnt, and semi-blind, and fucked off with life and men and love and life and Cronulla and London and art that anger overcame me, and I decided I would shoot some cunt in the neck. I mean, if you can't beat the gang, beat the living fuck out of *one* of the gang, that was what Stuart always said, and look, like most of his brutal poetics, it made good sense.

Through the lightning-edged gap in the silo I could make out Albert's body, leaning over Gordon, his knees on his stepson's shoulders, dripping a long line of saliva inches from my friend's face, to the amusement of the Red Team. I aimed at Albert's fat red neck, and firmed the trigger. A shot rang out and Albert fell back, clutching his throat in excellent agony. One! Rocky then popped out from behind Michael Shoes. He held a beer in one hand and shielded his eyes from the sun with the other in a vain attempt to make out the sniper. Bang! The palm of his hand was now painted; he bent in half like a flip-top phone, dropping his beer and moaning to Jesus. Two! Then Shoes came forward, laughing. Lifting his mask off and grabbing his cock, he said, 'Come out, you pussy, and face me off.'

I thought ok, relit my cigarette, and stood. I walked towards Shoes, who was now pissing in my direction. He saw me and shot his last four bullets, but they flew past my goggles. He had none left so I walked closer and closer to him, his medium-sized cock flailing in the dead air. Three feet away he grinned at me; he knew I didn't have the guts.

'Make my day, Cronk,' Shoes said.

I aimed at his cock and shot at it. I missed, but I got him in the groin, which sent him onto the ground. He then got up, and with rage in his smile he ran at me, cock still flopping about beneath his other rifle. As he lifted his weapon to hit me I shot at his groin again. This time I connected with his penis and he slammed into the scrub, screaming like a baby.

Gordon stood up. He could not believe what I had done, and neither could I. At this frozen time Albert rose and began inching towards Gordon with his gun raised, at which point I yelled out to G, who spun around and blew six bullets into Albert's chest and throat. Gordon then ran over to the Red fort, which up to this point had proved utterly impenetrable, grabbed the Red flag and ran towards me. This was war, this was what they were talking about, strength against strength, force against force, possession and territory, men on the ground, brothers in arms, camaraderie. Gordon leapt on top of me and we came crashing down on the grass, wrestling each other madly, panting like pigs, kissing each other's necks and screaming, 'Blue! Blue! Blue! Blue! Blue!'

Bussed home, showered and changed. Walked to Northies and dropped an ecstasy tablet. Then a different bar called Sting, and the DJ's dropping a cool mix of ironic eighties classics and trip-hop weighted beats. I rested back into the couch talking to Albert's friend Graham about the recession. He was a nice man and I felt good talking to him. I didn't know him at all so there was nothing wrong. Gordon was on the dance floor with Albert. He had taken his jacket off and rolled up his sleeves.

'Neil!' Michael Shoes had blood-red hair and two beers in his grasp. He handed me one of the beers and clinked it with his.

'Sorry I shot you in the dick.' I giggled in the pit of my throat.

'No drama, mate – just lucky you didn't hit anything big!' Shoes exploded with a machine-gun laugh.

'Fucking wild day,' I said, but Shoes didn't respond, he just slugged at his beer once, twice, three times, until it'd hit some spot.

'You knew my brother,' Shoes said. 'Daniel?'

Fuck. 'Yeah . . .' I said. 'Good bloke.'

'Not anymore,' Shoes said.

'No?' I said.

'Well he's fucken dead, isn't he?' And the machine-gun laugh came thundering back into action.

'You never know,' I said. 'You never know where they all are.'

'Yeah, some planet of their own. It's nearly our whole year book.'

'Yeah,' I said. 'Why does everyone do it? So nice down here.'

'You're the thinker,' Shoes said. 'You tell me, mate.'

And I couldn't tell him. I *couldn't* tell him. I couldn't tell him why his brother thought getting done DUI on his first night as a P-plater was enough to walk into the ocean at South Cronulla, I couldn't tell him why Tom hanged himself. I couldn't tell him why Stuart, why my oldest mate, was not sitting here now, why he was missing out on all this, all this war and ecstasy – he would have eaten this up. I couldn't fucking say and it killed me, it fucking killed me, because it was all I wanted to fucking know. It was all I wanted to know in this fucking world: where did the beautiful boys go? Where did the beautiful boys go? Where the hell did they go?

'Remember Shoes?' Gordon bellowed, plonking down on my lap. 'He's workin' in IT! Making a killing, mate. Tell Cronk how much you make, Shoesy!'

Shoes went all shy and I felt for him under this twist of light.

'He doesn't have to say,' I told Gordon.

'Yes he does! You would too if you earnt this kind of coin!'

'I'm doing ok,' Shoes said, cackling into his chest again.

Gordon slotted down between me and Shoes, swinging his arms around both of us. He was fried and he wanted to tell us how much love he had for us.

'Shoes makes like a hundred and eighty an hour. That's like . . . fucken brain surgeon wages,' Gordon stated, spilling bourbon and coke on his shirt.

'I don't know about that,' Shoes said.

'Congratulations, Michael, that's really impressive,' I said, clinking his beer.

'Hookers are on Shoes!' Gordon yelled, looking sunburnt and mad.

'I know a few I can recommend!' Shoes perked up, laughing insanely.

Albert and his friend Graham were outside smoking a joint and it looked nice, when Gordon opened my mouth and threw another pill into me.

'Sluts!' Gordon said, hauling me up off the couch.

Up three sets of rickety stairs we came to a door with a sign that said *French Massage Parlour*.

'That's what's commonly known as a euphemism,' Graham joked.

'A what-emism?' Gordon asked, falling into a wall.

In the waiting room there was a long tank with a Mexican walking fish in it and a Tonka truck. There was an excess of wine-red curtains and a glass counter with a large gold bell on it and a sign beneath saying *Ring Bell if no lady at desk. Thank you please!*

Shoes and Albert had a long conversation with the lady at the desk and pretty soon a succession of younger and older women were lined up in front of us in the reception room. There were six women, and six of us remaining.

'Six brides for six brothers!' Albert yelled.

The manager was a small Asian woman with fake tits and, even in the demure lighting of the 'parlour', it was clear she'd seen some late-night activities.

'There are only three rooms availabullllll, so please one at a time for half an hour or you can take two men and two girrrrrl into room at one time, this very cheaper for you, two men two girrrrrrl, yes?'

'Me and you, Cronk!' Gordon decided, 'and you and her.' He pointed to one Amazonian-type bird with terrible posture, and another shorter girl with brown hair and silver eyelashes, who was almost cute in a damaged kind of a way. The smaller one smiled up at me as she stepped forward out of the line.

'She's bookish!' Gordon said, laughing madly once more. 'Look, Cronk, even found a hooker to suit your type! Hahahaha!'

Inside the room the women inspected our penises and then led us to the shower. Gordon went quieter now, as I felt the second ecstasy tablet rise up and take control in the front of my spirit and brain. We showered together in silence, handing over the cake of soap with jailbird efficiency, this is washing, this is nothing else but washing. The faucet turned off by itself and we grabbed a towel each. I wanted to go home now, but instead I would see this through. This was friendship, this was what we were here for, this was standing by your mate.

'I'm getting married, Neil,' he said to me. *'Married.'*

'I know,' I said. 'I'm going to be there.'

'One woman, for the rest of my life.'

'That's the idea.'

'Just ONE!' He held a single finger up to my nose.

'I get it, man. I get it.'

'Then let's do this thing. Before I sign off for good.'

'Whatever you want, mate,' I said. 'It's your night.'

'Doesn't mean I don't love her!'

'No?' I asked, trying desperately not to provoke the lion.

'You don't know how much I love that girl.'

My bookish friend's name was Kayla, or Kyla, or Kanye, or something. She told me she went to beauty school in Penshurst and just *loved* living near the beach, having originally hailed from Wagga Wagga – it was such a nice change. She stroked my cock as she told me a bit more about her travels, then, as I firmed up in her hand, she rolled a condom onto my penis and asked me what I would like her to do for me in the remaining eighteen minutes.

Across from me Gordon was already pumping away at his big blonde Spiderwoman. He was fucking her from behind when he turned to me and smiled.

'Wonder if Shoes is having trouble? After you shot up his dick!'

Gordon led my gaze down to the bookish girl before me, nodding at her arse as if to say, 'Go on,' nodding harder and faster as he slammed and slapped himself against the Amazonian buttock, which popped up before him like a balloon. He started slapping the woman's thighs, nodding at me and then my girl again, and somehow, under his spell, I flipped my friend from Wagga Wagga around and entered her with ease from the rear. You want me to fuck this chick in the arse, you cunt, then fucken see me do this here on this day.

I was fucking her from behind and I was slapping her thighs now. I built as she reached around and grabbed my arse, pulling me closer to her; she liked it like this it would seem. The drugs were roaring now, I could eat this chick's anus, I could kill her, I could fuck her and then I could kill her after.

'Fucking fuck her,' Gordon said, staring at the space between my cock and the girl's tight, cushion-like arse. 'Fuck her harder, Cronksman!'

'I fucking am fucking her!' I screamed.

'I am watching you! I'm *always* watching you!'

Gordon was literally belting the blonde now when he reached out for me. I took his right hand in my left hand as we continued to fuck the girls from behind over the one bed. He smiled at me as he came in explosive distress, and then he said, 'Yeaaaahhhh,' and fell on top of the blonde, releasing my hand and laughing into her long red back. I would never cum, so I just kept fucking, dragging my nails along her spine until blood emerged in a line.

28

With a touch of her, and just like that, a change came across North Caringbah. How falling in love can turn things upside down in a flash, and make all the dank corners of one's basement burst with gerberas and hope. The heat wore off and a sweet southern breeze swept across the Camellia Gardens the moment she arrived, the moment of The Bride.

I had never seen her stand so tall, as she floated perfectly across the clumsy wooden bridge towards us, connected to her father, who looked frailer than ever, like an industrial-strength straw had sucked the man right out of the man. Her hair was glued to her skull at the front with a complex tapestry of clips and tiny flowers, gratefully releasing itself beneath the ears in a glorious flutter and wave of soft, brown curls which swung in the breeze. Never before, and I mean this, never before had beauty brought with it such an ache inside. I wanted to make like a crane and lift her out of here, but instead I turned to my friend Gordon and smiled like a groomsman.

They had written their own vows, and the crowd delighted in such insubordination. Their modern, gender-balanced declarations were radically new, and they owned the controversy with a simple, confident delivery. She spoke first, whipping the train of her dress behind her and taking the silver microphone in her little hands. The crowd rumbled with adoration for this complete girl, as she repeated after the celebrant her own manifesto of love.

'I, Courtney Gonzales, take you, Gordon Braithwaite, to be my lawful wedded husband. I will do my best to please you, not necessarily honour *or* obey you –' the crowd giggled but for the old folk, who detested the noncompliance '– but always defend and love you with body, heart and soul. Together let us seek peace and tasty, nutritious meals every day, learning from each other and our friends. Thank you for marrying me.'

Gordon repeated these same vows as the majority of the crowd fell about laughing. They had busted open the very notion of marriage vows, but they had done it in the spirit of love, and so no one could prattle for long.

I imagined myself in front of Courtney, saying these things to her, and meaning them. I wondered if I would laugh or cry, but mostly I wondered if she would believe me when I said those things, and a wave of deep sadness passed over me as I wondered if I would ever be in a position where I could say such things to a woman and actually mean them, and for this I envied my friend Gordon, because even in his rough diction and flushed public face there was no doubting the enormity of his love; this was not acting, this was it. All my life I had thought about what on earth 'it' was, and how to get it, and here it was in front of me, the big and beautiful 'it', and I knew right then that it was all there is.

It was at this point in proceedings that Rocky stepped up onto the small vine-wrapped podium, hugged and kissed his brother, hugged and kissed Courtney with an officer's deference, and turned to that beast that was the audience. They were struck quiet, murmurs and quacks all but muted, and I knew it well. This happened a bit in my life, the weird pause that hung dangerous and pregnant the moment before something 'different' or 'unplanned' was about to take place, something that challenged the beige normal we fed on so greedily in the no-alarms and no-surprises white bread status quo.

I looked around at all the frames and faces, women painted in garish blush and rouge, men all hunkered over their booklets waving away flies that were not there, kids clutching high hands dreaming of a pine-lime Splice, all of their mouths agape with threat and ever-ready contempt. Threatened by what this always curious young sailor called Rocky was about to unleash in the vulnerable forum of this day, a day where nothing should go against the order. My heart chugged with warm empathy, for someone else had taken my place, someone else was the devil outsider.

But the crowd had nothing to worry about when Rocky emitted a single, glorious note – his voice had never broken – letting out the most angelic rendition of 'Amazing Grace', which drew tears from every chubby aunty, and hard welling from good and big men with arthritis, jaundice and bowel issues.

The celebrant, a peacock-headed woman with an ice-bitch lilt in her principal's voice, broke the silence that remained long after Rocky's final note, taking the microphone and banging applause into its shaft. She patted the angel-star on the shoulder and led him off the stage. I could kiss him, I thought, later I will tell him this, 'I could kiss you.' The celebrant then ushered Gordon and Courtney towards each other, and spoke gently.

'Gordon and Courtney, on that beautiful note of that beautiful song, I now pronounce you man and wife. You may kiss the bride . . .'

Gordon moved forward and took Courtney's ears in his hands. I waited for her to make her own move, but instead her neck twisted and her eyes drilled right in to mine. There was no crowd in her vision, just me and a message to be sent:

I am getting married now.
I am officially turning away.
I am turning now, and I will never turn back.
You have allowed this.

Gordon stood still and immovable in his place on the podium, smug as Popeye with a mouthful of spinach. He was strong and gloating in it. He had won. Tricked me out and won the only real thing in this town, on this earth, this black-hearted beach. I wanted to scream and say fuck, I wanted to take back all the nights and redraft them with a brighter, braver pen. She was mine and I had let her go. So caught up in the light, so caught up in the fight, so caught up buying tickets for my soul. You fucking fool, Cronk. With your misconstrued dream life and your macheted baby, your stupid, ridiculous house on a leaf. Gordon's house sat firmly on the ground and massive, looming with head room for his mother and her man, for progress and barbecues, love and Courtney, and a stack of kids and poorly behaved poodles splashing about in the temperature-controlled water of the in-ground Blue Haven pool. These were but images and concepts I could only peer at through a long lens, or conjure and mock through theatre. Family and friends, as a notion, were a warped insinuation of a living death, and believing this had led me here, to face a life without it.

And then she moved towards him and up to his level and I was gone forever and the lights were off inside her for me. She took his hair and ears and soul and complications and shortcomings in her hands and said ok, let us go now. Her lips fell open with epic invitation, and I could swear a million hummingbirds flew out of them in curved formation, lusting for pollen and passion and peace, and for the first time in my life I believed. I truly believed she loved him, she had so much love for Gordon, and I realised then, in that moment before they joined their lips in the name of forever, how things were built and bettered with the dance of the everyday. All the tiny things made this mammoth union up, all the times he had picked her up from Sutherland station, made her chicken salad rolls and brought her a Lipton's iced tea, called her about Sunday and fixed Nina's shed door hinge, held her and not fucked her when she was dying with period pain, thought of what she said last night and made something of it the following afternoon, all these unspectacular deposits of love he had made and they were the currency, earning enough to have her see that he was nothing but the right one.

Gordon kissed his bride with unappealing repetitive scoops of the bottom lip and mouth. He kissed like a duck would if powered by Duracell, and I could sense Courtney trying to slow the whole thing down, but to no avail. They stopped kissing as the crowd's holler and high fell away, but then Gordon grabbed her chin and scooped away at it again, which she allowed, with one foot stepping back inside its train to anchor her against the force of her groom. She would take his thin, monotone kisses for all the years to come, for he was her choice, he was the gallant victor, the good option. He would carry her through the night, he would make her happy and safe, and he would love her more than he loved anyone, and this, in the end, was all she wanted, and all that she had asked of me between her legs on a pile of cushions on the living room floor of her parents' house, naked and spent with tawny port and conversation, on the night of their engagement party barely a year before.

29

The dreams came thick and fast that London spring, and then the visitations followed, Stuart arriving on the foot of my bed in the same white suit and dancing shoes, bathed in yellow light and wearing a small, cheeky grin which spoke of how he missed it all, the beach and the easy pussy, the weather and the barbecued chook, shooting magpies and smoking bongs, and of course the time with mates he yearned for most, and this was visible in the corner of his mouth, which cracked inwards with lurking responsibility. The ghost was here for a reason it seemed, and as the visits crept on I became convinced that he would not leave me alone until I had resolved the discontent, or simply returned to Cronulla.

'Neil,' he would say, loosening his tie and hopping off the end of my fold-out home in the study.

'Stuart,' I would say – in my sleep? I had never been one to recall an entire dream; those who could always astounded me and I envied them deeply. All I ever had, when I woke up round eight thirty, was a collection of often despairing images, like me and Agatha eating tinned peaches out of my father's cheeks, or of stabbing a husky on a tennis court.

'Wassup, bro?' Stu said, reclining on the lounge chair wedged between the door and the short IKEA bookshelf.

'Just dreaming,' I would say. 'Is this correct?'

'You are dreaming,' he would reply, condescending. 'When will you start living?'

'Why did *you* stop living?' I asked.

'I told you, bro: here for a good time not a long time.'

'Shut the fuck up with your fucked mantra. It's a fucking stupid excuse and you know it, you fucking coward. Now fuck off out of my study, I want to sleep.'

In a flash, Stuart was hovering above me, vampire-like, peeling my eyelids open with his thumbs. I was far from scared of him. I was always far from scared of him and perhaps that was why he did it. I held his glare until he retreated to his place beside the bookshelf, shaking his head.

'Cheeky boy,' he said. 'Cheeky little Cronky boy.'

'How is heaven?'

'Is that where I am? I thought I was in Bethnal Green, and I can tell you this, from any distance, Bethnal Green is far from fucking heaven!' He doubled over with sick laughter. I hated him when he came, because he wasn't the same, he was always prying and running me down, he didn't let me be like the living Stuart had; he wanted to mould me now.

'Are there girls in heaven?' I asked him, I asked my dead friend.

'Yeah, all these girls are there, but see the chicks are the same, wherever you go in heaven the chicks are just your type. Like, all the chicks in my section are blonde with big tits!'

'Perfect for you,' I said.

'Yes, you would think so, but it gets repetitive, after the same thing a hundred times . . .'

'Ohhhh . . .' I said, getting it a bit.

'Yeah, that's pretty much heaven, mate. It's this gay place where all the things you ever wanted are right there, right everywhere, but it kind of fucken shits you because that's *all* it is, shit that you're into. Makes me think that is what life is about, having shit you don't want and shit you do want together. I'd do anything to bang a *short* chick or even a butch with no tits, but I can't!'

'Haha!' I cried out, heaving with laughter in bed. 'An artist type even?'

'Yes, you faggot. Even one of your intelligent-looking chicks, but I never thought about it when I was alive so that's why all I got is these blonde sluts.'

'Tough work,' I said.

'I know,' he replied, 'but hey, there is hope – this guy I met up with there who killed himself too, he reckons you can swap things if you like, and that gives you variety access.'

'Sounds alright,' I said.

'Yeah, it does. But the thing is, it's dangerous.'

'Variety is?'

'Not variety itself, just the way it's all policed. They get a sense of it. You can be punished. See, they design it for you based on what you wanted in your heart, and if you challenge that too much they take it personally and turn you off.'

'Turn you off?'

'That's it, gone, darkness. The housing people can deploy you to less optimum houses or simply turn you off to the darkness place. Any time they can decide – some of them just do it for kicks sometimes, to Dead they don't like.'

'Fuck.'

'Just like that.'

'Does that scare you, Stuey?'

He sat back in his chair and pondered this, did it scare him, and if so would he admit this to me. 'Yeah, man. That's why I settle for the big-tit blondes. In truth, I hardly even fuck anymore.'

'Why?'

'Well, it is all points.'

'You get awarded points for how good you are?' I laughed.

'No, you faggot, it's not *Sale of the Century*. If you take one of the things you like, say a beer or a surf or a barbecue chook or a gun or a bong or, say, a twenty-one-year-old biking slut, they take credits off your book, and you can only spend a certain amount of credits a week.'

'What do you spend yours on then? If you're not banging sluts anymore?'

Stuart twisted in his chair, awkward now, and in the awkwardness his secret revealed itself.

'You use them to visit me?' I asked, glowing now.

'Visits are expensive, but *you* need the fucking help so I do it.'

'What a guy.'

'Hey, cunt? I haven't had a root or a surf or a beer in months.'

'You can really surf up there?'

'Well *you* couldn't because you're a faggot, but yeah, fuck, man, it's fucked because I can only surf Bells Beach!'

'Why?' I asked.

'Well apparently that was my true dream, which is fucken bullshit – I used to dream about Hawaii and heaps of other sick reefs.'

'Do you know anyone up there? Are any of the other guys that suicided up there?'

'Nah, I never see anyone. Mustn't have given a fuck. Are you going to come up?'

'Me?' I asked, amazed at how he just slipped that in.

'Yeah, OD on meth or something and come stay. I'm pretty sure we'd be housed together.'

'But I like living,' I said.

'Do you?'

'Yes.'

'Is that why you're sleeping in the spare room?'

'We had a bad thing happen, we were pregnant and –'

'I know all the shit.'

'You *knew*?' I asked him, in a rage all of a sudden.

'Yeah, mate. I saw the whole thing.'

I stood up beside the bed and held my fist out in the air. 'Then why didn't you stop the black cunt from stabbing my pregnant girlfriend? Why didn't you help her?'

'Keep your voice down!'

'You fuck off!'

'I can only reach you, Cronk. I can't reach anyone else.'

'Bullshit, how were you watching then?'

'I can watch anyone, but I can only reach you.'

'Fuck off, Patrick Swayze,' I said, returning to bed and burying myself under a pile of pillows.

'What's important to you, Neil?' I heard him say.

'I don't want your help, Stone!' I said, crying now.

'It's ok, Neil. I'm here to listen.'

'Go fuck some tits!'

'Nelly . . .' he said, his eyes all wet with desperation. 'It feels good, mate, when you decide you want out; it's like heroin, and so much more than pussy, when you know you're going to blow your head off. Nothing matters, you're fucken fearless.' He shook his head and smiled at me and for a moment there I could feel the weight fall away and the opiate brilliance of Stuart's nihilism take over – and I liked it, and I wanted to know it more. 'Kill yourself, Nelly, you'll never feel so alive.'

*

I knew things had reached an all-time low when Swanna told me one morning, typically busy as an ant in our kitchen, skidding from one bench to another to stir or clean or scrub or label a container, that she was considering moving to Sri Lanka. I told her she was crazy, and that it was a terrible situation there at present, and suggested that we go to couples therapy in Notting Hill. She said she would be very happy for me to go, but that you have to be a 'proper couple' to go to couples therapy, and we certainly were not that. It occurred to me in this moment that I had abandoned Swanna, I had left this poor girl to suffer on her own. Yes, she had chosen reclusion, she had taken her leave of me, but this, in the language of the broken one, never means you should leave them alone, it means you should persist in asking the recluse to come out into the light, and cop the relentless 'no' on the chin. One day they will come, one day they will choose a hat and walk outside with you, but only if you keep at the door with a quiet, motiveless whisper and an outstretched hand. I had left my post indefinitely, turned right around and leapt straight back into the tangled web of my past, delving deep into dark correspondence with my dead friend Stuart Stone, and Swanna knew it, she knew I was elsewhere.

'Maybe we should try working again,' I suggested. Pour the grief and the pain into our art, stage a wild and honest adaptation of Seneca's *Thyestes*.

She slapped me hard across the cheek and told me I was the sickest person she knew, then she lifted up her top and showed me the scar on her stomach where the machete had gone in.

'Make a fucking play about this!' she said.

Perhaps art was not the solution, but this was our currency, this was how we related from the start; we worked together, that is how we fell in love and how we stayed there. Without work the tyres blew and there was nothing between us to travel on. Months went on without a script, a concept or a rehearsal room floor, she slept in there and I slept out here, reading books and drinking Jameson's from the bottle. We had lost our voice and I was desperate to scream out and make some sense of this.

It was around this time I received a sweet, simple email from Courtney. She had heard through Gordon of our misfortune and emailed me to say she was sorry, and that she was there if I needed her. She said Swanna and I had seemed so 'happy and together' that New Year's Eve down by the harbour, with our 2004 glasses on and our smiles, the fireworks dancing in our eyes, all green and red with tomorrow's hope.

Four minutes after I had read the first sentence of her email I had sent a one-page reply, riddled with spelling mistakes and grammatical errors. I didn't even bother with capital letters, I just pushed it out, like I did in my room the first time I found one of Agatha's *Cleo* magazines lying around; I simply belted it all out and then it was done.

I pressed the 'send' button and a wave of absolute nausea swept over me, I had to get up and go for a walk around Victoria Park, just to deal with the enormous sense of truth and heartache I had released over the Pacific Ocean past Singapore to Cairns, down the coast of Queensland over the army barracks and endless stretch of wasteland to New South Wales, Sydney, Sutherland, then Caringbah, and finally Wanda Beach, up the stairs and into the screen where it would open itself up and out for Courtney's eyes. Of all the people, why had I chosen her to share this trouble with? It seemed perverse, but it felt so right, and so thrilling at the same time. She knew me, that little lawyer girl with the big green eyes and the pale and perfect skin. She knew me well enough to move through this mess with me, and she did, she did so expertly, and with such delicate compassion I was forced to reflect, constantly in the following weeks of communication, just what a complete and brilliant young creature this old friend of mine was, and in doing so began to contemplate a life with her, and to contemplate how and why it had come about that this might never happen.

I told her about the Rude Boy and his blade. I told her about Swanna and her silent departure from me, and our life. About the obsessive cooking ('just like Nina and her fruit whips!') and shopping and the ice-cold stare that went right through me as we wrestled with the kitchen to get our breakfasts done. And then, as the emails went on, and she asked for more and more, I told her about Stuart and his visitations. This, funnily enough, was the part she seized on. It fascinated her, my contact with the dead, and stupidly I did not realise why, I did not see right away that her casual interest was hiding a palpable yearning to establish contact with Tommy, the beautiful brother boy who had truly broken her heart in two.

Dear Neil,

Hey how are you?

So nice to hear back from you!

I'm so sorry to hear of all your sadness. Like I said, you two seemed so happy when we saw you. Did you ever find the guy who did it?

I wish I was there to cook you both a big vege soup!

Things here are pretty okay. Gordon is busy at the construction office in Woolooware two days a week and at the blinds company in Gymea three to four. I hardly ever see him, but he looks so happy with all of it going so well.

I am working, as I think I told you when you were here, and am discovering family law to be more challenging than I had anticipated. It is very intense, and often heartbreaking, which I guess is why no one ever volunteers for it!

The worst cases are the divorces, when it gets to custody especially. It's usually the men who lose out and often their houses are taken from them, and sadly, and too readily I believe, their children. Last month I was representing a woman who was asking for sole custody of her and her husband's daughter, a five-year-old named Clara. We won, which was great as I did the whole case on my own for the first time. But in a way I wish we hadn't won, as the husband, as it turns out, is not quite stable. He spent the following three weeks following me around the Shire, sending me threatening and often quite disturbing text messages, and only a week ago threw a box of weights through our living room window. Gordon being Gordon ran out of the house (in just his Foghorn Leghorn boxer shorts!) and chased the guy down the street. The guy was in his hotted-up Torana, so Gordon didn't quite catch him, but he got close enough to read the licence plates, which served as sufficient evidence to take out an AVO against the man. I haven't been sleeping so well of late, and I guess you could say there are reasons why. See, Neil? Not all is dull in the suburbs! Though I could go without that type of excitement, thank you very much!

You know what's funny? When you started writing to me about the dreams you've been having, and how Stuart is talking to you, well I too had been dreaming a lot, and mostly of you. Not in a dirty way! But you're in my dreams now, last week I dreamt I was in a car and I asked the people in the front if they knew where you lived and they said yes. I asked them to go past your house. I was clearly worried about you. They drove to your house and you came outside and got in the car with us. We didn't say anything in the car, you just looked very cold, so I took your hands and rubbed them, and you smiled, it was really nice.

Dreaming really fascinates me, and I have read a bit about it in the past few years, though Gordon would hate me saying this to you as he thinks it is all rubbish – astrology, dreaming, all of that 'weird shit.' You say Stuart is 'visiting' you, but Neil, have you ever thought about 'projection', that you're actually manifesting Stuart yourself? You are asking him into your dreams because you miss him so much and you want to connect once more and make sense of why he departed so swiftly? I am not trying to undermine what you have been experiencing – you're going through so much, and I don't want to sound in any way patronising or too opinionated – but I have always sensed (from what little I have seen of you in the last six years) that you blame yourself for Stuart's death. That you going off to university and putting on shows, and especially being the last one he spoke to on the phone before he did that horrible thing, that it is somehow your fault. Neil, please know that this is wrong. Stuart decided long before that day, be it consciously or unconsciously, that he was going to take his own life. Nelly, I have so much to say about this, I feel so strongly about it, but I can't write it all out here. I wish I could see you and tell you everything I think, as you know how deep it runs for me, when boys go away who shouldn't. I am still putting it together myself, where I went wrong, and what I could have done to keep Tommy here, but at the end of the day you have to let them go, and know it was not you who led them to it. There is something in them, Neil, a voice or a darkness.

So don't blame yourself. For Swanna, for Stuart, for any of these things. I don't blame you. Gordon doesn't blame you. We just love you. And we love you because we know you and we saw what a beautiful friend you were to him. You were the joy of his life, and I don't think a day went by where Stuart could ever believe that a guy like you would choose to hang out with a guy like him. He was a cocky guy, very arrogant and showy and extroverted, but this was all on the surface, it was all bluster and coolness, and I couldn't help but see through it all to the scared little chap inside, with all his bundles of fear and anger wrapped up and hidden away.

I am so sorry for raving on here – I just feel so deeply about it all, for obvious reasons, and as always, you are in my thoughts.

I look forward to hearing from you, clever one, and all our love to Swanna. I so hope you two can find the light again . . .

Yours,

Courtney.

Oh! PS Neil, the engagement party (yes, you heard it here first) is on 25 September at Mum's house, as apparently we are renovating our place (again!!!!?). I would so much like you to be there, and who knows, a trip home could be the best thing for you. Friends, family, ocean breeze . . .

Emails flowed with obsessive constancy for weeks and days, lifting me out of abject numbness and alcoholism, and into the light again. I had fuel in me; I was loaded once more with something to look forward to, something to think about on the number 8 bus to Bethnal Green, and something to keep me afloat in the house I shared with Swanna and her heaving clouds.

All the footsteps of my daily go-go somehow led to the checking of email. Wherever I was, a percentage of my attention was lost in the flow of them, one eye was always on that screen. On the Tube I would draft my next email in a Moleskine notebook, later typing it onto the computer when Swanna was asleep or out buying turmeric, polenta and haloumi.

And there was *so much* to relay, back and forth between Courtney and me. We had always spoken freely and easily with each other, but this, this frenzy of stories and thoughts and jokes and anecdotes, well email had set us free, it made it even easier to be candid and take risks with each other. She was not the screen, the screen was not her face, her face would never appear and I would never hear her breath in the mouse, and so I wrote with abandon. Limitless honesty and insight jetting out of my skull down my veins into the keyboard and away. I unravelled all the entrails of my fears and movements, my dream-life and my life-life, and she questioned and replied with such detail and compassion I simply could not tell her enough. I fell asleep with sore hands and woke with a million expectations, rushing to take that obligatory piss and then straight to the inbox to see what she had thrown out overnight, and she always had, she never missed a day, she was mad with it too, revealing so much to me in the tennis of it all; the frustrations she endured living so close and constant with her mother; the daily involvement made her feel so 'trapped', but she loved Nina, and she knew she was needed at this time. She spoke of Gordon sparingly, and mostly of how brilliant and stoic he was, and how busy. She loved how proud he was of her, and protective, but sometimes (and I adored such admissions the most) she wished they talked more and about deeper things, and once she even admitted the sex was pretty infrequent and that he often fell asleep when they sat down to watch a DVD, especially if she had chosen the film and it was a foreign drama. This was her brand of admission, always restrained, unlike my flurry of disclosure and mess, but I loved it, and I sailed about the house and the brightening city with abandon, and it wasn't long until Swanna sensed there was something new in my life. I should have known she would go looking, trawl through every email and come to all sorts of conclusions from the space between our lines. She was searching for clues that I was still in love with Courtney, and whether they were literally there or not she found them, and there was no way of convincing her otherwise.

But before this, before things blew up and I was ordered out of there, Stuart ceased visiting me. He made one final appearance, this time without his dancing shoes on. Gone was the usual assuredness that pushed out of his big chest, instead he stood in the doorway with a slouch. He said he was glad I was writing to Courtney, and that finally I was moving in the right direction. Backwards, into life. Then he told me the wildest thing. He told me he had seen Tommy, Courtney's brother, and Tommy had asked him to pass on a set of blessings to give to me to give to her, as he was not allowed; he had been turned off all contact after they discovered him trying to break into Bianca's mind.

For days I deliberated, drinking beer at the Gun on Mare Street and pounding my fists into passing posts, wondering if I should tell her about the connection or not. The word 'Tommy' was enough to bring Courtney down from any high, his death would remain an open wound for the remainder of her life on earth, and I so loved our correspondence and felt so worried this revelation would ruin the whole thing. We were beautiful friends once again, and in the end this was what propelled me to tell her; she believed in the dead, and their role in the lives of the living, and I simply couldn't withhold something of such meaning from her. She was the closest person to me and she had saved me from despair, she deserved all I knew, and when I told her she responded with such poise and calm it occurred to me she knew this was going to happen, and in a way it was why she had been writing to me all along. Besides – and this may sound a little fucked up – my ego roared at the idea of having this in store, of Courtney *needing* me, the super-connector, the people portal. And so I wrote with controlled exaggeration, passing on dreams and conversations Stuart had enjoyed with Tommy that never actually took place. I desperately wanted to give Courtney what she wanted, which was to see and feel her brother again, and so I became him, and it filled me with the most glorious, erotic and satisfying charge.

Tommy spoke through me now; he was my newest and most preferred role. Stuart had simply told me to tell Courtney that

Tommy loved her and missed her lots, whereas I relayed so much more to her, inventing an entire narrative of life for him in heaven. The Bianca quest, his gothic band, his regrets and his desire to spend time with her once more. Boldly, as time wore on and Courtney began to feed off my letters as if her only life source, I insinuated, in the tales, that Tommy was not necessarily sold on Gordon as a life partner for his sister, and that he strongly believed she was bigger than Cronulla, and one day she should break out, and unshackle herself from the burdens of family and career, for there was 'a big world out there,' Tommy said (through me), 'and these duties and burdens such as mum and your marriage will keep you from it girl.'

I ate my breakfast silently at the bench across from Swanna, then caught the bus to Liverpool station and walked across Millennium Bridge to the Tate Modern. I had not been for a year or so and was very excited to see the big, bold building again.

The Tate was quiet on a Tuesday, just some old women and a small school group, so I took longer than usual scanning the new works and the photography, snaking my way up to the Rothko room, my favourite room on earth. Mark Rothko was a deadset genius, so, typically, he had killed himself. He worked mainly with red, which isn't even my favourite colour, but sitting in this small space, surrounded by it, I felt like I was being swallowed up by a giant Shiraz, or by the blood of the gods. Swanna had brought me here the first time. She told me to peer into the maroon and just wait, breathe and wait for them to take hold, and they did – the paintings became red doorways to a deeper red universe, which led to more red and then more deep darker red. There were thousands of layers of red inside a Rothko, and if you trusted him, he would let you see and taste them all. The paintings were brilliant secrets that spoke of a rich darkness in all of us, and I let them have me, on my own in the middle of London.

I was feeling pretty alright, leaving the Tate and wandering along the Thames to Embankment station. London was magical in the summer, business people ripping off their shirts at lunchtime and stretching out their arms, basking in the mere murmur of sunlight on the city. Sitting up there had reminded me of what a girl I had in Swanna. Who else would take you to such a cool place as the Rothko room? Who else would even notice what the reds could do to you if you stared at them long enough? As I hopped on the Tube I wondered if there were quality flowers on sale today. I'd stroll past Columbia Road on the way home and find out. I'd bring her back to life, I knew I could.

I walked in the door carrying a huge bunch of sunflowers and some white roses that were really fucking expensive. The house smelt of dead air and milk and straightaway I knew something was wrong. I heard scratching in the back and followed the sound. In the study was Swanna, dressed in a bra and singlet, sitting at my desk scrolling through a long email I had sent to Courtney a few days before. I held up the flowers. She didn't move, she just stared at me, her eye make-up smudged with wetness.

'Flowers, for you,' I said.

She stood up, wiped her eyes.

'I went to the Rothko room today,' I continued.

She spoke in a hushed voice. 'So I'm this "walking dead person in the house", am I? The crazy girlfriend who shops all day like a fucking psycho, is that me?'

'Swanna, I didn't ask you to read my email . . .'

'Ha! You didn't ask me? Of course you didn't fucking ask me! I'm out there dealing with this little fucking tragedy that happened, trying to keep us healthy, trying to keep my head above water, and you're in here writing to your ex-girlfriend about her dead fucking brother and your fucked-up girlfriend. I mean, who the fuck are you, Neil?'

'Swanna, it's just emails.'

'It's just fuck!'

'I've been having these dreams.'

'You didn't tell me about any dreams. Me!'

'You don't talk!' I screamed.

Swanna took the white roses from me and bit into them. She chewed and swallowed all the petals then ripped into the stems. I pulled a stem out of her mouth and she bit my hand.

'Swanna, come on, this is ridiculous,' I said.

She adopted a coquettish little voice and tilted her head to the side, green mush in her mouth. '"London is so beautiful, Courtney, you'd love it here."'

'I was just trying to let her know there was life outside Cronulla.'

'Life in your fucking trousers?'

'She's stuck in the place, and I care for her.'

'You do or her dead brother does? I can't tell the difference!'

'I can explain all of that . . .'

'You sick fuck.'

'Swanna, I try to connect with you and you just ignore me, so I reached out to a friend. What am I meant to do?'

She pointed at the screen. 'That's not *writing* to someone, that's a whole lot more than writing, that's cheating and manipulating . . . Oh yes, and now I see it all so fucking clearly! I'm the funny little Indian that cheered you up after your friend's suicide, helped you attain your fame and notoriety abroad, and she's the little suburban angel you're going to go home for. She has the hold on your heart, am I wrong? Am I fucking wrong? This was your plan all along.'

She wasn't wrong so I didn't tell her otherwise. I bit into one of the flowers myself then spat the petals onto the ground. I left the house we had found together one rainy Wednesday hand in hand.

When I came home my study was smashed up, the computer in a million pieces with a well-arranged selection of flower petals on top of it. Written on the wall in red texta was:

Some art I left for you.
Swanna

30

Sarah Kirkwood was the first person I saw at the engagement party. I walked in and she was right there before me with a glass of champagne in her hand and a baby in the other.

'Neil Cronk!' she said, kissing me on the cheek. 'Look what the cat dragged in!'

'Yes, the cat just came and got me,' I said, laughing politely.

Her baby smiled up at me and burped and I couldn't help but love the little thing automatically. It was a genuinely cute baby, it didn't look like an old man or a Gremlin, and that's rare in kids younger than one. I wondered what Swanna and my baby would have looked like. I wondered where she was right now. Her phone turned off for the entire week before I left. I had no idea if she would return to the house in Bethnal Green – I didn't even know if she was alive.

'Means he likes you!' Sarah said, handing me her glass. 'Can you hold my bubbles for a second?'

'I'll hold the baby if you like,' I offered, my arms already reaching out.

'Oh, that would be awesome. Do you still smoke?'

'I do,' I said.

We went out front and she rolled one while I held the baby, only just protected from the rain by an overhang of roof. Sarah smoked liked it was Year 12 and we were on the oval again; deep and fast and guilty. The rain was loud on the roof but her baby fell asleep in my arms. Sarah said this was 'not common' and that I must have 'the touch'. Sarah talked about her failed marriage, and how the last three guys she had dated were all gay now; not only had she turned them off herself, she'd turned them off 'the entire gender'! She said she was a drunk there for a while and ended up in the program but found it all a little cultish in the end.

'I really shouldn't be drinking but fuck it. My best friend's engagement!'

'I didn't know you and Courtney were so close,' I said.

'Neither did I till recently. But I love the bitch – she's such a spunk!'

We went inside and Nina took the baby for a while. Sarah and I walked around the party, dodging old classmates and teachers. Sarah was smart and spontaneous, her mind jumping from thought to thought like an electrocuted frog, but the course it took was corrupt, her mind unravelling at a rate of knots then questioning its own patterns constantly.

'I was working at the UN for a while, which was intense. But I gave that up when I had Dylan. Now I'm working for Channel Nine News three days a week and it's really quite whatever, some of the men there are disgusting though I do like television, it killed the radio and it will probably kill me too!'

'What do you do at Channel Nine?' I asked, hoping she would stay near me tonight and ramble on, for the sound of her head dropping thoughts was the best music I'd heard since I saw Radiohead play in Victoria Park with Swanna. And I didn't want to face my old friends alone; I hadn't even really spoken to Courtney or Gordon yet, but I could see them by the pool.

'I help run the news department. It's a long way from the UN but it's here and I'm only part time which is great with Dylan.'

We drank more and followed each other around, bouncing in and out of conversations with uncles and aunties and friends from school. But we did not leave each other's side. If anything, we fed off each other, knocking down the obligatory catch-ups as a team, then happily returning to our own, more fascinating, yet oddly normal connection out front.

'The last time I saw you –' we were smoking again, the rain was hitting her long forehead but she seemed to like it '– you were necking my girlfriend Chandra in the bathroom at Gordon's twenty-first!'

'Nooooooooooooo!' she cooed. 'My lesbian phase!'

I was about to ask Sarah if I could stay the night at her place when Courtney came out and grabbed my elbow.

'Dance with me!' she said, and hauled me inside and away from good old Sarah Kirkwood, the single mother with a son.

'We bought some speed,' Courtney said, directing me up the stairs with her hand on my back. 'You want some?'

I didn't want some at all, I was happy getting drunk and smoking with Sarah Kirkwood. But Courtney was so fired up I bumped a couple of lines off her dresser drawer (adorned with elephants) and felt like dancing too.

'Gordon's being boring because he has to go away on business tomorrow, so you have to get fucked up with me, ok? And stay up all night!'

I hadn't seen Courtney like this for ten years, all scatty and high, talking madly at people and dancing with sharp, rabid movements in front of her friends and relatives, but she did not seem to care, and man, did she let me know how proud and happy she was that I had come, telling everyone in her speech how I had flown in from England especially, and just how important it was for her to have me there. Seriously, she mentioned me more than she did Nina, and nearly more than Gordon – it was kind of embarrassing, with half the people in the room not having a clue who I was. The emails had made us closer than ever, and drugs were spilling this out into the air. I hadn't told her yet that Swanna had discovered our correspondence; I knew this wasn't the time or place. Courtney was so happy at the party, but something told me it wasn't the party itself that made her this happy. She was buoyed by something, and she kept turning to me to acknowledge it; I had lit something in her and she would see it out.

Michael Shoes dealt out more speed in the laundry as the oldies filtered out to their cars and Gordon signed off for bed. Gordon and I had hardly spoken all night but he looked well and proud of his engagement. He told me he would see me in the morning before he left for Kempsey. I said ok, hugged him, and then watched him climb the stairs to Courtney's bedroom, where she would sleep next to him once more – if she got to sleep at all.

'Look what Dad got me!' Courtney screamed, holding a bottle of twenty-five-year-old Grandfather Port in the early morning mist.

'Wowee,' I said, 'that's expensive shit.'

'He told me not to drink it until my twenty-fifth wedding anniversary.'

'Ah,' I said, nodding.

'Let's drink the motherfucker now.' She started ripping the foil off the top.

'Court, are you sure that's a good idea?'

'I fucking love port,' she said, screwing into the cork. 'Don't you?'

We sat out by the pool, smoking and drinking port amid the detritus of the engagement party. The port tasted like cherries and lacquer, it was groovy, and watching Courtney savour it in her mouth amused me no end; she really was a lawyer, with a judge's palate.

'You and Sarah were getting along well?' Courtney noted.

'Yeah,' I said, grinning, 'she's cool.'

Michael Shoes had fallen asleep in his banana lounge, which left just the two of us awake, free to say what we needed to, free to speak of the dead and the living, free to angle in on what the hell was moving here.

'It's funny, isn't it?' she said, her mouth painted red with Penfolds.

'What is, my dear?'

'That we never fucked.'

'Wow, ok,' I said, sitting up.

'We never did, and now we never will.'

'That's the whole idea, isn't it? Of marriage. To *not* fuck anyone else?'

'Are you angry?' she said quietly, and directly.

'Angry?' I asked her.

'That I'm marrying Gordon.'

'No, C,' I said, 'you're not the prize.'

'The prize?' she said, alerted to something here.

'I'm glad you're being looked after properly, I am glad it is him,' I lied.

'It wasn't him,' she said, exhaling smoke out her nostrils. She was wearing a blue chiffon number with a single strap on the right shoulder. The dress ruffled out above her cleavage and dragged diagonally down her long slender back. On anyone else I don't think I would have liked it, but on her, tonight, it looked divine.

'What wasn't him?' I asked, a new brand of headache settling into the side of my skull as the birds announced the first signs of a new day.

'It wasn't Gordon,' she said, slurring her words.

'Wasn't him what? I don't know what you're saying now.'

'Gordon didn't have me first,' she said, and Michael Shoes got up out of his banana lounge and walked inside and out the front door in one swift sequence as if controlled by remote.

'What are you telling me here, Courtney?'

'That night, the night of the results party . . .'

'Yes,' I said, my whole body starting to shake.

'Well I lost you at the squash courts,' she said.

'Yeah?' My voice thinning out to almost nothing.

'I went back to Stuart's house that night,' she said, and his name hung in the air. 'I'm sorry, Neil, but I had to tell you this. I had to say it before I get married.'

I put my twenty-five-year-old port down and stood up in the shock stream. 'You had to tell *me* this before you get married? Why me? I'm not marrying you . . . Jesus, Courtney – you fucked Stuart?'

'Neil, please don't flip out on me,' she said, following me to the pool.

'Fuck!' I said, flicking my cigarette over the fence.

'It just happened,' she said, placing her hand on my back. 'He took me back to his place for a shower, after that awful riot out the front of the squash courts? He said we should wait there until we heard from you guys. But we didn't. So I lay on his bed and watched him inject steroids, we chatted. And then I took my top off and asked him to touch me.'

'No way, and what'd he do?'

'He hesitated, but then I pleaded with him. I said I wanted it over. I asked him for a favour and he obliged me.'

I moved away from her, ducking under vines to get to a spot where she could not reach me.

'*Obliged*. Fucking hell what kind of word is that!'

'Shhhh . . .' she pointed to her mother's room just above us.

'Oh, man,' I said, 'this is way bent.'

'I'm surprised he didn't tell you.'

'Yeah, "Hey Neil, fucked your girlfriend last night!"'

'I thought he might have admitted it to you,' she said. 'Now or then! Now that he comes to you, in your dreams I thought he may have.'

'Who knows if it's even him?' I wanted to hurt her now. 'Maybe Stuart's just a projection, like you said, and everything he told me, of then and now and Tommy . . .'

'Don't you do that.'

'All the shit he said about Tommy is my sick brain making it all up!'

'Don't be cruel, Neil. I know I have hurt you.'

I walked back to the banana lounge and sat. She followed, crouching down and forward before me. Finally she spoke, like a social worker not a lawyer, like a friend not a lover.

'I asked him to do it,' she said. 'I just wanted it done and over.'

'Beautiful,' I said, sardonic as all get out.

'It was,' she said in a whisper, 'it was very beautiful.'

Her hand rested on my neck and I began to cry. Was I crying at how pathetic I was back then? How frigid and scared of such intimacy? Or was I crying over my friend's betrayal? For so long I had tortured myself at the loss of him, only to discover he wasn't the loyal and true mate I thought he was. In the end, I think I was crying because I was beginning to believe that no one was worth loving in this world, that everyone was evil and self-obsessed in their truest hour, and so I cried in the knowledge that I would never let a soul in again, I would go cold from now on in and shut the world out, it was the only option. These were my final tears and the rain was joining me.

'I spoke to him,' she said, 'after we made love on that night.'

'Oh you *made love* now, did you?'

'He said that you and I should be together forever.'

'As he pulled his cock out of your pussy?'

She did not laugh nor miss a beat. 'I asked him why you'd never wanted me enough,' she said, 'I asked him if he knew, if you had ever told him why . . .'

I looked up at her for Stuart's answer, and as I did she stroked my cheek, and her green eyes filled with salted water, swirling about with ten years of concealment and guilt.

'He told me you wanted my mother more than me,' she said.

'He said that?'

'Yeah,' she said, and she started laughing. 'Was it true?'

I couldn't help myself either. I started laughing big and loud and full.

'Yes, it was true,' I said. 'It seemed easier to me, the idea of that.'

'She's upstairs,' she said, and we laughed together as the birds fired up a big song and dance about this brand-new Sunday they were all so fucking proud of.

With the yellow light of reality upon us, Courtney took me by the hand and led me through the kitchen to the living room.

'You can sleep here,' she said. 'I'll get you a blanket from upstairs. Set the cushions up on the floor.'

I did what old Courtney had told me to do. I set the cushions up on the floor behind the couch. The living room of the Gonzales' house was one of those beautiful 'presentation rooms' no one ever entered. They had dinner in here twice a year and most things were covered in plastic. I looked around the room at the glass cabinet filled with Tommy's trophies and further sadness fell upon me. I had never felt so displaced and ugly. What had any of my *wondrous* life come to? The love, the art, the travel. Here I was at twenty-eight, in my ex-girlfriend's house, sleeping behind a couch in a room no one ever entered. I had no place to live, no girlfriend, and no ideas in my Moleskine notebook. All I had was the fresh knowledge that people were pain, and this excluded nobody.

I woke up with her above me, grinding back and forth on my centre, my hand in her hand on the outside of her left breast sliding about on the chiffon. For a moment there I wasn't sure this was truly happening, I was seriously half asleep and dreaming, but I knew it was real when she came down and my lips met hers and the taste of her gums and teeth brought me back to her, and forward, propelled into this passion unknowingly. I peeled the hair back from in front of her eyes but she did not want me to take her in as she moved herself down and around my cock, mocking the act, fucking me with her dress on, hiding on an angle in my neck and face. I parted her hair once more, but again she dived back into my lips and resumed her veiled, fervent kissing of me. When she paused, when she allowed my rhythm to be a player in this, I fell into things as participant mutual, opening my mouth to receive her tongue and teeth, gripping her neck from the back and getting her as close as gravity and flesh would allow, and she made sounds, sharp gasps of horror and joy in harmony as we turned the corners of each other's bodies and found ways to get nearer, and obtusely so. She kissed so differently now, she kissed like a woman, with certainty and intent. She knew what she wanted and how to get herself there, but also, inside this kiss there was punishment; I could feel the self-loathing in every gasp, but still I pushed on, too far gone now to consider my best friend asleep in the room above me. I lifted her out of the blue dress, and she removed my jeans then led my penis out of its home.

'Just fuck me,' she said. 'Please fuck me.'

She fell upon me and I ripped off her underwear, a very thin g-string that would have weighed less than the lid of a pen. She was naked now as I spun her round and placed her on the cushions. She was beneath me as I lined my face up with her face, kicking off my socks; the last of the garments to go. She looked young again, her face all squashed and chubby, riddled with the same fear it spoke of when I got so close those ten, eleven, years ago.

'Do you love me?' she asked, with a catch in her voice.

'Yes,' I said, massaging her clitoris with the tip of my index finger.

'Do you love Swanna more than me?' she asked, and I turned away. 'Do you?'

'Courtney . . .' I said.

'You love her more than me, don't you?' she said, and she held my face in front of hers, begging for this ultimate truth.

'I'm in love with her, yes,' I said to Courtney's big green eyes.

'Are you in love with me?' she asked, through broken breaths, and I knew I could change our lives right then, I could place them together in brilliant controversy, I knew this was the moment, and again, again like every other time before, I faltered at the turn.

'You're getting married,' I said, and that did it. She pushed me off and crawled to her feet. Then she simply walked out of the living room, through the white wooden doors and into the marble foyer with the high ceilings. Sweat glistened on her spine – she was as naked as the night, and the curves of her hips and shoulders danced in the bouncing light of the antique mirror which adorned the wall across from the entrance doorway. She climbed the stairs to Gordon, her eyes set dead ahead. Either not tempted, or too strong, she never looked back.

*

Nina's voice was high in the morning and the sound of the vacuum low. Together they formed a perfect harmonic, which grew louder and louder, infiltrating my dream and then officially waking me from my sleep to reality: *I am naked and Nina is but a few feet away, pushing the vacuum into the living room from the kitchen.* The transition from linoleum to carpet was a relief in audio terms but terrifying in terms of my predicament. I pushed Courtney's chiffon dress under the couch and reached for my jeans, sliding them on just as she appeared above me.

'Oh, hello, Neil!' Nina shouted over the vacuum, peeking down at my semi-nakedness. I spotted the g-string and bra at my feet and quickly plonked a cushion over the top of them as Gordon arrived in the room wielding two tall glasses of effulgent red liquid.

'Berocca, my friend? Gives you back that b-b-bounce!'

Outside the sweetest sea breeze lifted up off the coastal shelf and into my nostrils and soul, cleansing it all, softening it all, placating. Gordon had a coffee now, I was still halfway through my Berocca, smoking a cigarette on the welcome mat in just my jeans. The only other thing I wore was the stink of her perfume on my face and neck and the recent memory of her skin and tongue and mouth and tongue and cunt and tongue and skin on my mouth and hands and hair and face and neck and breasts and skin.

Gordon seemed gallant as the light rain kicked off again, sentimental even, as if nothing could bump him from his spot at the top of the line, and it certainly would not be me, I would hide in the smoke until the car came with my mother in it and a 'yoo-hoo' and a 'let's go' saved me from the bells of hell; please Lord keep Courtney up there in her bed, surrounded by elephants, and please may Nina not find her intimate apparel beneath the couch and cushions. Not while I am here at least, I cannot take one more of Gordon's punches and kicks.

'Courtney and I,' Gordon said to me, like an old bloke looking over his kingdom of wealth and plenty, 'we're so happy you came back for our engagement.'

'Me too.'

'You heard her speech, she just loves having you back from London. She got so worried about you and all, with what happened with Swanna and shit . . .'

'Yeah, she has a big heart, Courtney does.' I waited for him to comment but instead there was silence.

Then, out of the blue, he swung to me, with exultant eyes. 'You know she really loves Elvis?'

'Who does?'

'Courtney!'

'Does she?'

'Yeah! Lately she's been listening to him on her mini-disc player. She loves him, all the old stuff, "Jailhouse Rock" and "All Shook Up", she sings it round the house and at the gym. She even bought me the *Christmas Album* last Christmas which is hilarious . . . *a-ho-ho-ho-whiiiiite . . . Christmaaaassss*.'

'Right, that is funny!' I said, unsure of where this was going.

And then he whispered conspiratorially, 'At the wedding, I'm thinking, you know how there's the wedding dance where the couple just do a really slow one-on-one thing? Well I'm going to mix it up! It's boring and I hate dancing slow, so I'm thinking of coming out in an Elvis suit.'

I waited for him to continue but clearly he was expecting me to jump by this point. 'Ohhhh, right, nice idea,' I said.

'I know, right?' he said, pounding his hands together. 'We do a dance to one of Elvis's pop songs, everyone will lose it!' He slapped me on the bare chest and shook his head at the genius idea.

Then Mum arrived and I drifted back inside to gather my t-shirt and jacket, leaving Gordon to catch up with Mum through the passenger window from his position on the trimmed gutter. When I entered the living room Nina was standing beside the couch holding Courtney's blue dress and tiny underwear. I shrugged pathetically. Nina came over to me, holding the garments in her left hand. Then she kissed me softly on the forehead, ran the back of her right hand down the length of my nose, stopping on the summit of my upper lip, and left the living room, closing the doors to the kitchen behind her.

31

My best friend Gordon has a beer in his hand and he is welcoming arrivals. I am standing beside him taking old ladies' coats and helping prams fit through the doors which usually means a forty-five degree angle is required causing shit to spill out onto the floor which keeps on happening, but I cannot stop it, the hipflask of bourbon I drank at the photo session mixed with the six beers that were on offer in Shoes's esky have gone to my head and balance is absent. The DJ is playing 'Fly Me to the Moon' and the place is glowing, each round table dressed with name cards and daffodils and rows of shining cutlery. Having seen Wanda Surf Club in the daytime I am amazed at the transformation from seedy wooden hall to enchanting dreamland. But when Courtney is in charge, these types of things are entirely possible. The sea is out the big windows and it shimmers appropriately, the moon a three-quarter biscuit from which cool mauve light is made.

'Helloooo,' Sarah says, kissing me on both cheeks. The baby asleep in a pram – I help her wheel it inside to a quiet corner. I had first spotted Sarah at the photo session, stunning in her black ruffled bridesmaid's dress with giant red rose on the left chest area.

Chatting with her as the photographer manipulated all sorts of false and terribly clichéd scenarios, I felt good, and happy she was there to catch my rolling eyes. It was the same brand of goodness I felt now, throwing the fly net over baby Dylan and asking Sarah if she'd 'care for a cham-poo?'

'Does a bear shit in the woods?' she replied, applying lipstick.

I kept checking on Dylan because I wanted to but also because Sarah liked it. Mostly I guzzled champagne and listened to the woman talk, and man could she talk, with a mouth full of tyres she would manage any of Hamlet's soliloquies. We were well into our third glass of Yellowglen and this impressed me further, a girl that could drink properly and quickly. On the dance floor Courtney and Gordon were laughing too hard. Some ugly fuck from my Year 9 PE class was grinding some demented chick who worked at the Woolooware Mobil. 'Moondance' was playing, or some other Van Morrison, I can't be sure, for I am smashed and elsewhere.

'Sorry to hear about Stuart,' Sarah says, a hand on my neck.

'Ah, that was a while back.'

'Still. I'm sorry.'

'Let me fucking kiss you,' I say. Then, with new politeness, 'May I?'

'Tell me what happened, first,' she orders, putting down her flute and focusing.

'To Stuart?' I ask her.

'To you. Tell me all of it.'

'And then I get a kiss?'

'Depends on the story,' and she kissed me on the eyelid.

Bathurst Hospital was a mess. The place was under heavy construction and I couldn't work out where the hell I was meant to be.

It was a post-apocalyptic scene: massacred people in wheelchairs, rubble and bright lights and balloons and staff running for closing lifts.

Gordon didn't come in, he didn't like hospitals, and said he would get some coffee and a paper and meet me back in the car park in an hour. It was kind of him to drive me, I didn't have a licence and the idea of me getting the train offended him, as if trains were jails or places you shouldn't be seen in, transport for the lesser. He had picked me up from the airport, taken me to the beach, and then driven me the three and a half hours to Bathurst. He didn't comment on the state of me, either; my smell, my weight loss, my skin. I was a scaly, jittering, chattering shell of a man and I could feel the concern in his silence. He didn't know the half of it. I planned on being home for a few days only, enough time to see Mum and say my goodbyes to Dick – then I would fly straight back to London and resume taking ice.

When a man is dying he is like a wounded lion, he curls up and whimpers in his fur and no longer resembles the Beast of the Wilderness that he once was. He is still a lion, but there is no fight left in him, and the children of the Beast see him and they know they have to be the Beast now.

'Boy genius!' Dick called from his bed. The room was small with a window looking out over the cranes and trucks. An old Greek man shared the space, but Dick's side held all the cards and flowers.

'Who's this bloke?' I said, approaching. Dick had a 'Comics Out West (COW!) Tour 1991' beanie on, his face was three times its usual size, and his hands were bruised and swollen.

'Ohhhh, my boy,' said Dick, and I hugged him, careful not to tug on any of the many cords stretching out of his bloated, failing form.

'Mate, I didn't bring you anything,' I said. 'I meant to get you some stuff duty free but I clean forgot.'

'Get out, ya cheap bastard!'

I could see how much energy it required of him to make conversation. He was not long to go and it hurt me. I don't think I would have come home for many other people in my life, maybe just my parents and Agatha, maybe Gordon (though Gordon will never die) – but Dick, I had to see him before he departed this sordid stage. I did not receive warning, I simply started to cry, uncontrollably, and the more I tried to hide it the more it flowed out. But it wasn't just Dick, it was the twenty-four hours without meth that had penetrated the numbness and let the feelings through again.

'Sorry, Dick . . . Things have been intense in London.'

'Mate, don't feel bad. All I do is cry,' he said. 'Cry all night and day.'

'He does too,' the Greek man chimed in from across the room.

Dick wanted so much to live. He was fifty-eight going on twenty-one. He had never seen theatre in Japan, or Germany, or even the Blue Man Group in New York, and he and his wife were set on it, and so too were their savings.

'Tell me about London,' Dick said, patting the bed for me to sit.

I sat on the edge of the skinny bed and told him a little about it. Of course he had read the reviews of all my shows and printed out the articles about our work. He was so proud to think his teachings had 'made waves' overseas. I told him about Swanna and the machete, and I told him that I was by no means an angel when it came to love and responsibility.

'I am a wreck,' I told him, and he chortled lovingly. There was nothing but love and acceptance in his soul.

I touched his grizzly beard and he laughed. I didn't tell him that for months now I had been living in an empty house with Swanna, smoking from a crack pipe and not sleeping for weeks at a time. I did not tell him what I do to get this drug, or any of it, how could I? He thought so well of me, he was the only one left.

After the engagement party I flew back to London with purpose. I would give Swanna and me one last chance, for it was painfully clear, on the living room floor with Courtney, that my feelings for Swanna were still abundantly alive and life without her was another mistake for my collection. When I arrived at the Bethnal Green house, wielding Australian flags and a chocolate wombat, Swanna was sitting in the middle of the kitchen with Clive, naked and freebasing, Serge Gainsbourg drifting out from the CD player.

Initially, I resisted, doing my best to get her to a hospital, to a rehab clinic, or somewhere out of here. But she brought me in with soft hands, and built me up a perfect snow cone to ease me into the understanding, and I soon understood, more than I would know, how it felt to feel nothing, and this was exactly where I wanted to be, numb and skating in England with my girl – high above what we had made, and way above what we had lost.

'Son . . .' Dick coughed violently, and I knew I should go and let him rest. His eyes were closing and his lips didn't quite open when he spoke. He sounded drunk. 'Get yourself a martial art. I've been doing tai chi for the cancer, and even though the bastard still won out, tai chi gave me balance and peace of mind for my final moments. This is what we all need . . . the thinking men . . . the artists . . . we need to find a way out of the restlessness and panic into the calm.'

'I'll look into it,' I lied, dreaming of a pipe stacked with meth.

'How is Swanna?' he asked, and I shrugged the subject dead. He nodded, and even though he knew fuck-all, he understood everything. Dick fell asleep at a clumsy angle; his big and beautiful smile collapsing now.

'You're a good dad, Dick,' I said, and I left the ward, pocketing a plastic jar of Endone tablets off Dick's side table.

I didn't own sunglasses and it was frighteningly bright outside the hospital. I could hardly see from the glare. But then I recognised Gordon's blue Lexus.

We drove out of Bathurst without speaking. I put the radio on and it was comforting to hear the Australian accents on Triple M, even the ads were nice. We stopped at Lithgow for petrol and he spotted a pie shop across the road. Gordon loved meat pies so we sat inside and ordered two each. I bit into my first one then went to the bathroom and swallowed two of Dick's Endone tablets.

When I came out Gordon was squinting at me.

'You've lost weight!'

'Oh, man, yeah. Been riding my bike round town.'

'You a junkie, Cronk?'

'No, dude –'

'*Are* you?'

'I'm not a junkie.'

'You look like a junkie. You ate half of one of your pies.'

'I'll eat it later.'

'Don't fucking lie to me, Cronk!'

'I just . . . I've not been eating a lot,' I said. 'We lost a baby.'

'Yes, I know, I know.' Gordon scrunched up his napkin and then threw it at me. 'You saw what drugs did to our other friend, didn't you?'

In the car I asked my friend Gordon if he knew where my father was living now, and if so, could he drive me there. I was not ready to see my mother yet and I figured Dad wouldn't notice what state I was in; he never looked at me for long enough.

The drive to Cronulla was surprisingly fun. Now we had got things out of our system we were free to talk and make the old jokes that worked well. The Endone had kicked in and I felt magic. G-Man dropped me at my father's house and I waved my friend off and thanked him emphatically. He said he would call later that night, 'get some beers.' I would love to have beers with Gordon, and with the sun on my back I decided that it was time to leave the ice alone and maybe hang out here for a bit, freshen things up with salted water and good fruit salads, cold beers, NRL on Fox and normal shit.

My father was still at work, she told me. She was my age and horrible to look at. She was not ugly, she was just severe, and I did not like her one bit. I rarely had such a negative reaction to a person, but she was hard and harried and didn't invite me in. I was not sure what I had done to deserve this from her, so I waited on the front steps for three hours and it was ok, I had a book to read and I was high.

Just as the sun was calling things off my father arrived in his instructor's car, but it was a different one, it said *Cronk/Minetti Driving School* on it. He got out of the car and just stared at me from the kerb as if I was an eleven-foot octopus who'd just loped out of the sea. I opened my arms but he didn't respond, he just stood frozen on the street.

'Son,' Dad said.

'Dad,' I said, and I stood up.

'What are you doing here?'

'I came home for a second. To see some people.'

'Who?' my dad asked, and I wondered why he hadn't come to me yet. A handshake or a hug or even a scruff of the hair.

'Aren't you going to say hello? Haven't seen you in a year,' I said.

'Where ... did you see Loretta?' he asked, keeping his voice down low.

'Some chick answered the door. She wouldn't let me inside.'

'She didn't ask you in?' he winced at what he knew was true.

'What's with the new car? And the new signage?' I pointed at it.

'Oh yeah, we broke off from ABC. Loretta and I have started our own thing; she runs the business from inside the house.'

'Wow, right – so that's that?'

'Look, mate ...' Dad moved up the lawn towards me. 'Loretta's a little funny about things, she –'

'Why are you whispering, Dad?' I asked. He was in front of me now, I could touch him.

'She's not quite ... she isn't ... she's not family-oriented. She just likes things nice and simple,' he said, and I did not know him.

'Are you asking me to leave, Dad?'

'Let's meet up for lunch tomorrow, just the two of us,' Dad suggested. 'She just doesn't like the mess!'

Tears arrived in my eyes. 'Am I "mess"? Is that what I am, Dad?'

He said nothing, just glanced over my shoulder and through the window at the shadow of bitch-woman inside.

'Bye Dad,' I said, and walked away from his new house.

I tried life at my mother's but she wouldn't leave me alone to sleep the days through, she kept on at me about the Black Dog Institute, telling me I was depressed and 'a man can come see you for not a lot of money a visit.' I wanted ice now.

I moved in with Ioannis, one of the mechanics I'd met towards the end of high school. I tracked him down through Malaki, Stuart's brother, who since Stuart's death had gone all clean living, practising yoga on the beach every morning at five and eating wheatgrass and shit. He shook his head when I asked for Ioannis's number, but he gave it to me. For a second there I could see Stuart in his eyes.

My bed was a pink foam mattress beneath the ping-pong table in Ioannis's garage, which was fine because, well, I was not sleeping so much in that time of skating. On top of the bar fridge was a mirror. I was looking in the mirror at my face. My cheekbones pushed out of my skin, my lips were thin and colourless, my eyes were empty and grey, my skin was blotchy, but it was ok, I could pull this off. I wet my hair and moved gel through it. I combed the hair to the side then I tied my tie. I was wearing beige linen pants and matching jacket over a white button-up shirt and a red-checked tie. My shoes were open and I wore no socks. I'd bought the whole outfit from the Vinnies on Beach Street for $15.80.

A week ago Ioannis told me that Gordon called by the mechanic workshop asking for me. He had heard I was living with Ioannis and gave him a letter and Ioannis passed the letter on to me when he got home. We got a whole swag of ice and cooked it, discussing the intricacies of the letter for six days.

Cronk,

Mate, how are you? Where did you go after I dropped you off three weeks ago? I thought we were going to have beers??

Me and the missus are throwing a barbecue at the (newly renovated!) joint on Saturday from 1-ish. We'd love to see you, nothing big, just Mum and Albert and Albert's mate Graham and of course us!

So come along if you're not busy, don't bring anything we've got heaps.

Oh, maybe boardies if you want to swim. We've got an in-ground fucken pool, dude!!!

Righto, hope to see ya!

G.

Ioannis dropped me a couple of blocks from the beach house. I didn't want him to drop me out the front because then they might ask him in, and I didn't want him with me, his face had tattoos on it and everyone knew he ran 'all things drugs' in the Shire. But I didn't want to walk either, as it was 32 degrees and I would surely sweat through my linen suit, undoing all the hard work I had put in that morning.

Ioannis squinted over the wheel; the meth fucked his vision completely. Everything went orange and shook, he said.

'Cronk.'

'Yep,' I said, smoking out the window.

'Do you stay in touch with anyone from your college?'

'Uni?'

'Yeah. From theatre school.'

Ioannis was always asking me about theatre. I appreciated his interest but at the same time I didn't like talking about it. It all led to Swanna and the baby.

'No,' I said.

'What about the lecturer you told me about? The one who loved you?'

'Dick died,' I said.

'Did you go to the funeral?'

Fuck off. 'No.'

'Why not?'

'Because I was in the garage smoking crack with you.'

All the houses that led to Gordon's were either brick or fibro, and most of them had a Southern Cross flag in their windows or on their lawns, hoisted up nice and high to catch the ocean's breeze. Many had boats, or half-fixed cars outside, plenty of apple crates, surfboards and balls lying about like monuments of heroic days.

I could see Gordon's place from the corner. It was impossible not to. The two-storey house was enormous and savage with hard lines and plenty of glass.

I heard familiar chatter, took sixteen deep breaths, swallowed five hundred milligrams of Xanax, and made my way up Gordon's path to Gordon. I should've brought something. Even when people said 'don't bring anything' they still expected you to. I was thinking about walking into town and going to Liquorland or the florist or some joint that sold Darrell Lea when the door opened and Carmen was there, real and alive in her two-piece swimsuit with a golden camisole draped over the top. She had a fruity sun visor on and not-yet-rubbed-in sunscreen on her face and nose. She had lost a tonne of weight but she was still pretty mega, and if I was her, I would have definitely gone with a one-piece and sarong for cover.

'Come in! Welcome to Club Med!' she said, kissing me. 'My, what a fabulous outfit. Gordon, Neil is here! Yoo-hoo!'

'Yeah, I'm going for a *Miami Vice*-type thing, with the linen,' I said, moving through the tiled foyer and out towards the pool. I could see Gordon flipping snags on the barbecue by the ferns. He was wearing short black football shorts and a Hawaiian shirt, a blue terry-towelling hat and shiny silver Ray-Bans. He waved at me with his tongs, sipping on a Crown Lager perched inside a Cronulla Sharks cooler which was shaped like a player and fitted a stubby in it perfectly.

'Haven't you heard of summer?' Gordon asked.

'I thought I'd dress up,' I said. 'It's not every day you get asked to a place like this!' I gestured to the house.

There was no sign of Courtney and I should never have come. All I wanted to do was get back to my mattress in Ioannis's garage and smoke up some meth for lunch, but instead here I was at the family pool party in a suit feeling like something out of the Dada movement: a figure in an incorrect landscape. I hadn't eaten for a long time, I was not sure I could take a sausage or a steak in my mouth, the blood and tissues. Everyone would see this, my inability to do the simple human things, everyone would know, everyone would laugh, by the beach they would mock me, by the beach I would come undone.

Albert was in the pool with a beer. He looked browner than he should be, like someone had smeared shit on him then fixed it with varnish.

'Can I get you a drink, Nelly?' Carmen asked.

'I didn't bring anything,' I said, embarrassed.

'I didn't ask that!' She laughed, tapping her sunglasses back up her nose.

'Beer would be great, thanks, Carmen.'

Carmen had more than embraced her new life, bouncing back up the deck and into the open-plan kitchen with an invisible stack of new dynamite lodged between her wobbling buttocks.

'Come over here, mate,' Gordon said, and I did.

'So, wow, man,' I said as a burning, hot oil sensation passed behind my eyes and down into my throat, locking up my larynx and airway.

'The house?' Gordon asked, mock surprised. 'Yeah, it's not bad, eh?'

'It's fucking massive,' I whispered, unable to talk very loud.

'Ya bring yer togs?' Albert called to me from the deep end.

I shook my head because I was not sure I could reach the deep end with my voice, and also, if they saw me in swimming trunks my body would say too much about it all.

'The view is off chop,' I whispered to Gordon, and it was, Wanda Surf Club directly across the road.

'Yeah, it's fucken heaven, mate. We bought the whole block, knocked down both houses – then Al and Gra built all this from scratch.'

Albert winked at me from the steps. 'We'll make a tidy coin if we ever sell it, I fucken tell ya!' Albert raised his beer at us like the secret was out.

'You want the tour?' Gordon asked me, but he was already off inside, flinging the tongs at Albert.

On my way in Carmen handed me an icy cold bottle of Crown Lager and, even though I didn't favour the Foster's line of drinks, I thought if I could slam down six or seven of these quite quickly, I might be able to stabilise just enough to pull this function off and get back to Ioannis's garage for a pipe before my soul inverted itself.

Norah Jones's 'Come Away with Me' floated through the kitchen, Carmen on backing vocals pumping Paul Newman French Dressing into the IKEA bowl stacked with cos lettuce, spring onions, half an avocado and one punnet of cherry tomatoes. Under instruction, I took my shoes off.

'Kitchen, for the ladies,' Gordon said, leading me down the hall.

I glimpsed the garage, laundry, TV and media room, study, 'possible nursery' and the door to the underground wine cellar and then we were away to level two.

The stairs were soft beneath my feet, thick, almost shagpile carpet stretching up between my toes. Gordon seemed in a rush to have the tour over, weaving in and out of rooms before I got the chance to really see them, although his pride burst when we reached the upstairs bathroom. He paused, resting against the door.

'Look at that shitter! The seat has a foot pedal. And that bath has jets in it, and look, the trimming is all vintage. Courtney had a lot to say about this room, she loves a good bathroom – chicks, y'know?' Gordon raised his eyebrows at me and before I could say 'yeah' he was out of there and across the hall. I lingered in the big green bathroom, staring into the metallic bathtub, wondering what would take place in there. Love making? Dual bubble baths? The washing of little ones? I wished I could lie in it now, in my suit, with no water running.

'Come check the master!' Gordon blasted and I went.

The master bedroom was wide and long with ocean views and a large walk-in wardrobe. Gordon patted the king-size bed with his hand. 'Workbench,' he said, winking at me.

'Yeah, right, workbench, nice one,' I said, imagining.

'Yeah, she likes it. Gets nice light in the morning but doesn't get too hot you can't sleep, if you know what I mean. And wardrobe for all her shoes and shit.'

'Yeah, it's really sweet.'

Gordon knocked on the walls a while, distracted by something, then turned back to me.

'Y'know, Cronk, if you're ever stuck, there's plenty of room.'

'In your bedroom?'

'No, dickrash – in the house.'

'Ahh!' I said, nodding then puffing my lip in gratitude.

'Just say the word, doss at ours.'

'That's nice of you guys. I'm staying at Ioannis's place right now, but it's nice to know you're here if I get stuck.'

'Yeah, man. *Mekasa musaka*, or whatever.'

'Absolutely.'

'Mine is yours.'

'Yep.'

'What is ours is yours, more like.'

I jumped on this. 'Speaking of "ours", where is Courtney?'

Gordon fiddled with the curtain cords, pulling them apart then closing them again with swift, exaggerated movements.

'Oh, she's at work, her fucken boss makes her come in on Saturdays to tidy up the mess he makes. He doesn't even pay her!'

'Woah,' I said, getting the tone just right.

'She reckons it's all part of being new but I reckon it's all part of being exploited because you're a fucken nice girl and your boss is a lazy prick who offloads his shit on you – don't get me started.'

'I won't.'

'Fuck you look skinny, where did your chest go, man?'

I didn't answer. My brain was burning so I was not even sure what I'd heard.

'Downstairs, mate, let's get some food into ya!'

Gordon placed his hands on my shoulders and stared into my eyes. It was intense because I was blinking like a maniac and I could not stop.

'Neil, you're my brother, you know that. We got to get some flesh on those bones. I don't know what you've been doing with yourself but eating certainly ain't it!'

'I'm just controlling my portions,' I lied.

'And I'm just sucking my own dick!' he said, then slapped me on the neck and walked out of the master bedroom with the 'workbench' in it.

'Lunch is served!' Carmen announced, distributing trays of cold meats and antipasti to the too-long table by the sliding doors.

'Get some proper tunes on!' Gordon said, flicking Norah Jones off and replacing it with Powderfinger's *Internationalist*. 'The Finger!'

I moved towards the table as Albert handed me a glass of Jacob's Creek grenache shiraz I did not want. His friend Graham was sipping on a UDL can of bourbon and Coke, smoking and laughing, telling us of his 'massive night' at Coyotes which ended with pizza on the beach and 'one prick nearly drowned trying to swim over to the tits in the dark.'

The table had a white tablecloth on it with small green flowers imprinted every four inches on a diagonal. There were three salads, one of them Paul Newman French, the other a Caesar with chicken, and the third involved beans, pine nuts and feta cheese with balsamic vinaigrette. There was a tray of lamb chops, a tray of enormous steaks cooked medium rare, and a tray of sausages varying in colour, style and fatness. The sausages were accompanied by a stack of cooked onions and garlic. There was a square plate of marinated red capsicum, some pitted olives and zucchini fritters, a bowl of mixed nuts, and an enormous wooden bowl full to the brim with roasted, buttery potatoes and kumara wedges (the new alternative). There were three bottles of wine on the table, two bottles of sauce (HP and Fountain tomato) and a loaf of crusty French bread from the Baker's Delight on Cronulla Street.

There were six chairs at the table. I was seated at the end closest to the pool. The chair across from me must have been for Courtney, because it was empty and there was a glass of sparkling water in front of it, with a slice of lime clipped to the rim. I was the first to be passed every single bowl, plate and tray, and somehow I managed to pick a few things that I might just be able to eat without seeming too ungrateful or peculiar, and without my body protesting.

'If you have pasta, then antipasta, are you still hungry?' asked Albert, unleashing a joke he had surely used before.

Carmen burst out laughing and so did Graham, but Gordon just shook his head and looked over at me, appalled.

'So, Neil, are you working on any projects right now?' Carmen asked me, chewing on a length of marinated capsicum (off the carbs).

And no I was not. I was simply doing drugs in a garage with a Greek man named Ioannis. I should have gone back to London and started work again but the whole town was tainted for me now, for that's where Swanna was, bleeding to death in Bethnal Green, her teeth cracked and yellow and her lips falling off. I was working on not going back at all; I was working on hiding away, and slowly dissolving into the local mist.

'Oh, look, Mrs Braithwaite, I, um . . . I just had a pretty intense few years in London with my company, so I'm just taking it easy right now, kind of chilling, gathering my thoughts in the sun, know what I mean?'

'Oh yes!' Carmen interrupted. 'Gordon told me you were having incredible success in London, he said your work was lauded over there!'

'Neil smashed London,' Gordon said. 'Fucking smashed it.'

'Was it movies?' Albert asked, mauling a long, floppy steak with his hands and teeth.

'Ah, we integrated multimedia sure, but no, the um, the work was essentially theatre, Albert, so live performance,' I went on. 'Kind of performance art but not horrible like a chick chained to a wall screaming for ten hours, more physical theatre and mostly devised, but with some multimedia elements, but then kind of flipping that very notion on its head in a postmodern, kind of anti-theatre context.'

The room fell silent, everyone eating and nodding, proffering nothing, and I wished I was dead in the pool outside, floating upwards.

'How's your mother and Agatha?' Carmen segued.

I hadn't seen Mum since I moved out to Ioannis's. I had disappointed her on so many levels she inevitably offered me an ultimatum, saying I could stay in the house and let a man from the Black Dog Institute come visit me, or move out right away and continue to ruin my own life like a fool. 'So many people need you to get better, Neil, do it for them.'

My mother and father had proved to me that banishment *was* parenting. Father had banished me under orders from the new woman. Mum had banished me because she could not have an unfixable problem in her house, or at least a problem disinterested in repair, which was I.

'Mum's alright,' I said. 'Busy and things.'

'She found a new guy?' asked Carmen.

'No. She just works and looks after everyone else.'

'Graham's single!' Albert said, pointing at his mate who was lighting another Peter Jackson, his meal not yet half eaten.

'And Agatha?' Carmen asked.

'She's dating a DJ, though I think he's only a mobile DJ.'

'Like Moby Disc?' Gordon asked, giggling.

'Yeah, maybe,' I said. 'She likes saying she is "dating a DJ" but I saw his van and it said Moby Disc on it.'

'What does she do now?' asked Carmen, and I wished the questions would stop.

'I don't know,' I said. 'She was doing a small business course at TAFE, but I don't know if she saw it through. She starts a lot of things.'

'You should get her involved with your work,' Albert said. 'Set up a company here, we got a lovely theatre off Cronulla Street – it's on Beach Street isn't it, Carmen? What's it bloody called again?'

'Cronulla Arts Theatre,' Carmen said, proud of her knowledge.

'Yeah,' said Albert. 'You do the arty stuff and she could do the admin.'

'Albert has such great business ideas, you should listen to him,' Carmen nodded.

'Ok then,' I answered, setting down my glass.

'You been to the Cronulla Arts Theatre? I could show you through.'

Gordon shook his head and laughed mockingly at Albert. 'What the fuck, Al? You've never been to Cronulla Arts Theatre in your life!'

'I know one of the blokes that renovated the foyer!' Albert blared.

'You're a fucken goose, Albert,' Gordon said, winking at me. 'Neil's one of the most well-respected theatre guys in the UK and Europe; why would he want to work in that little shitbox?'

'Who wouldn't want to work in Cronulla?' Albert said, shifting his chair to face me.

I pulled out some potato I had been hiding under my tongue. 'What's that, Albert?' I asked, trying to recall the thread of his suggestions over the past four minutes.

'Why wouldn't you want to work in Cronulla? By the look of you, a bit of time here would do you good!' Albert laughed at me, menace building over the bowls and pepper shakers between us.

I knew this feeling, I knew it well. He thought I was belittling him and his town of choice.

'Albert . . .' Carmen warned.

'What've you got against making your entertainment in Cronulla?'

'I didn't say I did . . .'

'Leave him alone, Al,' Gordon chimed in.

'Just answer the question: why wouldn't you want to work here?'

I could hear the waves from across the street and I turned to the window in hope of finding their foaming crests.

'That's where we're having the reception,' Gordon said. 'Wanda Surf Club. Just there, can you believe it?'

I flicked my head back to Albert and held his eyes. What I wanted and what I felt about what I wanted was taking over, and I was exhausted by being here, and holding up this mask to fit the crowd. So I let it fall to the ground and the monster in me rose up and spoke. Fuck you, you dumb, art-less cunt, you don't know me, you don't know me one bit.

'I think my work would be lost on you all, Albert,' I said. 'I'm not sure the audience would connect with it or understand any of the themes or nuances; that's why I don't want to work here.'

'There's the answer, now let's talk about something else,' Carmen said.

'No!' Albert fired up. 'This is just getting interesting. You reckon I wouldn't understand it? Is that what you think?'

'I just don't think Cronulla's my audience.'

'But you're from here?' Albert said.

'It doesn't feel like home to me though. It never has.'

'That's not Cronulla's fault, Cronulla's heaven.'

'I don't want to make art for people who think like that, Albert.'

'What's that fucken mean?'

'Cronulla *looks* like heaven, but it's not,' I said.

Albert leant over the table and leered at me. 'I've seen a lot more in my time than you know about ok, you little arty poofter.'

'Ok!' Graham stood up. 'Let's go have a smoke outside, Albert.'

'Good idea!' said Carmen, starting to clear the plates and bowls.

'But *have* you?' I asked Albert, my eyes never leaving his. 'Or have you just seen what you want to see? Because that's what I see when I come home to Cronulla, a bunch of white people who believe what they want to believe and see only what they want to see – which is more white people who believe what they want to believe and see what they want to see.'

'What about a musical?' Carmen suggested. 'Everyone loves a musical.'

'Mum, fuck,' Gordon said.

'You too smart for us, are you, mate, too worldly?' Albert said.

'I'm just not sure I'm the man for the job,' I said.

'Then get a real job,' Albert whispered.

I stood up and wiped my mouth. Albert simply gazed right through me, half-drunk smugness dripping down his hang-dog, beer-fucked face.

'I'm going to use the toilet now,' I said.

I walked up the stairs and opened the door to Gordon's celebrated bathroom. I sat in the metallic bathtub and retrieved my mobile pipe from the inside pocket of my jacket. Smoking meth requires a temperature that causes the compound to vaporise, so I insert the amphetamine into the cup of my pipe and light it for this. Eventually the meth ghosts and I hit it. Fuck those liberal-voting philistines.

The meth ripped through my skull and neck and everything was erased, all the highs and all the lows, there was just a long and ever-dry plain and I was on it, skating and sliding cleanly through the nothing-land. I lay my head back and gripped the round edges of the tub and it brought me back to her, and that last bath we had together in London. I could think about it safely and easily here, because I could not feel a thing. This here was the only way I could manage retrospect. In the rink I can look back and it doesn't kill me, it doesn't kill me at all.

'This is how it feels,' she told me.

We have been lying in this cold bath for hours. Days maybe. I don't know. Time is no longer a moving thing; it's just treacle, continuous treacle.

'Feels?' I asked her. Her eyes were looser than usual today, too heavy for their sockets. Her cheekbones pushed out past her nose, no longer supported by the scaffolding of flesh. Her hair was thin like raw fettuccine, and half of her face was a scabby mess of pus and scab, the other showed how hollow things had become.

'When we die, we go back to how we were when we were just born,' she said to me. 'We shit in the bath and we are helpless.'

I did not speak. The dripping.

'Neil,' she said, 'what will we name the baby?'

'I don't know,' I said. And then I didn't say anything again. This dripping.

'Is it fair if we call it Courtney?' she said to me with the coyness of a schoolgirl, sliding down a little into the bath, her legs pushing over the ridges and rails of my hips.

'Why would we call it Courtney?' I asked her, connecting with rough logic. She had never let it go, the email stream that she discovered, even though there were no 'incriminating' words or offerings to be found. Swanna still saw it as a huge betrayal, and despite my pleading with her to 'move on,' it was always dormant in her, and it was moments like these, in the still of the night with the water shifting around us, that she would help it up and out into the world once more, to start a fire I guess, or just to let me know how dark it got inside.

'Hello little baaaa-beeeee. Shall we call you Couuuuuuurtney?' she said, her voice squeaking up into the thin cold air.

'What baby?' I asked her. 'What's this baby?'

'Our baby, our new baby.'

'What new baby?'

'Shut up,' she said.

I looked out the window and a red bus passed by with passengers in it. Could they see inside this bathroom of hell, did they wonder what it was like for us, or were they just hungry for dinner and a sit on the couch.

'Courtney,' she asked again. 'Do you like that for a girl?'

I would have answered, but the bath began to change.

'Swanna, what's going on?' I said, red and pink filling the spaces, expanding and deepening in sections of dissolution.

I fucking freaked as Swanna blankly watched the blood exit herself and fill the tub with colour, like grenadine, like any cordial did. She touched it, lifting out a small bit of red congealment, and held it up to me as I pushed back onto the taps.

'I think we are to be punished,' she said to me, as if this was exactly what she expected, as if this was the next bulleting point.

'Swanna, what are you saying? Why is there all this blood?!'

'I think God is killing our children for all the stupid art we have made. He killed our first one, now he is killing this one, then he will kill us.'

I stood up in the bath and looked down at her, once the most calm and gracious girl, at one with nature and free as a bird and brilliant too. Now she looked utterly possessed, her eyes insane, peering up at me as I held onto the shower curtain in fear. Even through the murk of drugs I could see just how far we had gone, and how close to the edge of each other, and death, we both were.

'Bye bye, baby Courtney,' she said to me in her baby voice.

'Courtney's not dead, Swanna, she's not our baby and she's not dead. You need to centre yourself, she's not dead . . .'

'She *lives*!' Swanna laughed maniacally at this. 'Oh, but how silly of me! Ha ha, of course! She lives indeed, she is inside your heart, she always has been, and she treks down your heart into your balls and you blew her out your dick – you shot her right up into my womb this devil girl – this devil girl grows into a little baby Courtney and because little baby Courtney hates her mother Swanna, she kills her from the inside and she –' Swanna dunked her mouth in the bloody bath then spat the red water at me, a line of pinkness dripping down her scabby chin. 'You could have told me but then you never tell me and this is how it feels.'

'Swanna, I don't know what you're talking about, there is *no* demon, and I said sorry, we were reaching out, I thought I had lost you.'

'You killed me,' she said. 'You killed all of us. You and Courtney and your pretty little beach, run away to her, you are with her now – oh you are, under umbrellas in the sun, aren't you? Planning your next quest, to slaughter girls from other towns.'

'Swan, I think I should call a doctor for us now.'

'There is no phone in hell, Neil, you should know that.'

And with that she stood up straight in the bath and, facing me, she held out her hands. I took her hands in mine but I didn't squeeze for they felt so frail.

'Baby, I love you, but you're scaring me,' I said.

'I will go now, to Sri Lanka, I've never been home before,' she said, and climbed out of the bath, dripping blood and water on floor.

'Don't stop me,' she said as she went, and that was the last time I saw Swanna. Another girl walking naked away from me past mirrors across tiles.

The door opened and Courtney was in the bathroom and she had not seen me yet. She went to the toilet and was about to pull her pants down when she noticed me, pipe still smoking, in a linen suit in her new bathtub.

'What the fuck!' she squealed.

'Hey,' I said, waving with my free hand.

Courtney rushed to the door and slammed it shut and locked it.

'You locking me in? Nice,' I said, grinning at her from within my buzz.

'What the fuck are you doing in my bathroom? Are you on drugs?'

'Meth.'

'Fuck, Neil. Gordon will eat your head if he sees you in here with that.'

'Tasty,' I said, and laughed.

She looked down at her skirt with dismay. 'I was about to take a shit right in front of you!'

'I know, right? How fucked up is *that*!' I laughed again and she almost did, but instead she turned stern and pointed to the door all confused now. Why had she locked us in here?

'You have to get out of here now, please.'

'Ok.'

'I can't have you in here.'

'Neil Cronk is exiting the renovated bathroom!'

I stood up and met the meth. It was punchy and big and it made my body quiver with every ripple of breath. Courtney unlocked the door for me and I went to leave but instead I craned my neck towards her and kissed her on the mouth. She kissed me back for 1.8 seconds, her tongue featuring then retreating swiftly into the turtle shell of its fucking conscience. I had my hands tight on her arse and pulled her towards me again but this time she pushed me off into the doorframe and I laughed at the scuffle.

'You kissed me back!'

'Get the fuck out of here, Neil.'

'You get the fuck out of here!'

'Neil, you're on drugs and you are scaring me. Please leave the bathroom, get your things and go home.'

'What home?' I asked, moving towards her. 'What nice big home do I got? What nice big renovator's dream? Bring a paintbrush! Rear lane access! Ocean glimpses!'

'Nelly, it's me,' she said, pathetic with fright.

I was inches from her face, following her round the mega bathroom, smiling sharp and cocksure into her eyes and soul.

'You have a say in the renovations?' I asked, pointing at the tiled walls.

'Neil, I'll fucking scream.'

'Or did Gordon do it all?' I whispered to her mouth.

'Leave,' she said, backed up against the shower, her legs long and languid in the pink tights that extended from the cave of her tartan skirt. 'Leave!'

'I *did* leave!' I screamed. 'You never did! Eh, Cronulla girl? Look at you, in your stupid skirt in your stupid bathroom . . .' I cupped my face in my left hand and reminisced, 'She had so much inside her, that girl I met in high school, that Courtney Gonzales girl with the big green eyes and the curious, brilliant mind. She's all but given in for a house on the beach and a Woolworths shopping card. I asked her to fly with me but she cut her wings off and played it safe in the suburbs, what a pathetic little chicken, what a disappointing waste of a girl.'

'I'm going to scream in ten.' And she started counting down but it did not vanquish me, I was so sad for her.

'You die here, Courtney. Fat and white and bored, you die.'

She was at five with her head turned away.

'You look for this in me,' I said. 'Don't you? You look for elsewhere.'

Four.

She was at three when I said, 'At least Tommy went somewhere else.'

She slapped my face so I grabbed her by the hair and I twisted it in my hands. I held her mouth against the mirror and saliva came out of it.

She screamed and Albert rushed in with Graham. I was carried down the stairs, across the foyer, through the door and onto the lawn, where Albert hurled me onto the path and then kicked me in the middle of my back. I lunged at Albert from the gutter, but he pushed me down again, and then punched me in the neck and my face smacked on the street surface. He was about to kick me again when Gordon came running out and crash-tackled Albert into the car.

'Leave him!' Gordon cried out. 'He's not well.'

'You got that right,' said Albert.

'Come on, Cronk, we're going for a drive.'

'I didn't finish my salad,' I said, crawling under the car.

'There's lots of salad where we're going,' Gordon said. 'Lots.'

32

There was a break in the speeches now, a contentious issue throughout the planning process, of which Courtney and I shared much conversation on our walks around Bundeena and our weekly little meets for coffee and cake. While Courtney thought it a good idea to push through the speeches and simply 'get it done in one fell swoop', Gordon disagreed, citing a much better ploy to split the night up in two parts. Have the MC (Rocky) pump out an intro then bring up the father of the bride (which, due to Eric feeling slightly out of place having only recently returned to their lives from New Zealand, was to be written and spoken by both mother and father of the bride, which was more appropriate, I thought, as Nina was the closest to Courtney after all; she was the reason Courtney had stayed in Cronulla – she was, in my opinion, the reason we were all here tonight, inadvertently, for if she hadn't laid on the Catholic guilt after Tommy's death and Eric's disappearance, and rolled around the house all depressed making fruit whips like a psycho fruit-whip machine, then Courtney could have flown away freely, to find herself, find her place, and possibly find me in this process), then Albert and Shoes were going to do a little bit of character assassination on Gordon for all the men and blokes to relish, and then a forty-five minute break for drinks and dancing, followed up by the best man's speech (how I got that title I had no fucking idea; I nearly killed his fiancée in their renovated bathroom while loaded on crystal meth, nearly fucked her at their engagement party too) then Courtney was to make a speech about Gordon, and Gordon a speech about his wife, his little wife; signed, sealed and delivered in white lace.

Being at a wedding is like being inside a pinball machine; one bounces from trivial conversation to polite conversation to incomprehensible conversation to utterly awkward conversation, ending up somewhere near the corner of the room with a chubby auntie angling for more drinks and a melba toast with smoked salmon and a bit of green something leaf popped on the thing – then WHACK away again.

Flung from corner to corner, beyond all control, I wondered where Sarah Kirkwood had gone. I needed her now so badly – to save me. I hadn't seen her since she went to breastfeed Dylan halfway through Albert and Shoes's compelling tale of Gordon spewing on an old woman in a wheelchair when they were drunk at a Malaysian restaurant in Cockle Bay last April. Michael Shoes and his girlfriend Natalie (senior regional air steward for Virgin Blue) had me surrounded and I couldn't escape for the life of me. Shoes was weighed down with drunkenness and kept repeating himself, which would have been fine if what he was saying was not so reprehensibly earnest. His girlfriend remained quiet the whole way through, she seemed thrilled just to be *with* someone, as if that was enough to get through today, tomorrow, and possibly the rest of her life.

'Cronk, thing is, now you're back here, in the Shire . . .'

'Yep,' I said, moving his wet hand off the back of my neck.

'It's the right place for you. Wanna know why?'

'Tell me,' I said, looking around for Sarah, for Courtney, for someone.

'Shire is about friends and family.'

'Yes,' I agreed, and I did.

'That's what you need right now – see when you go away, when you leave the Sutherland Shire . . .'

'Shoes, buddy . . .'

'Nah, mate, listen!'

'You've said all this!'

'No mate . . .'

'Ok, mate. I'm going to get a drink now.' I tried to duck under his arm and find some free space up the sideline but he had me back in his clutches before I'd even arched my neck.

'No, fucken listen to me, Cronk. Nah, nah, nah, mate, thing is you gotta listen to Shoes now cos he knows, he fucken knows! You go away and get all fucken artsy and shit with drugs and shit overseas, not good for you, mate, and you know why not good?'

'Why not good, Shoes?'

'No friends and family to hold you up. Friends and family, friends and famileeeeeeee.' He blew beer breath in my face and I didn't know how she kissed him on the mouth, which she would do again tonight after a garlic sauce kebab on the way home. 'Friends and family are everyfink – they everyfink! And you can fucken travel to any joint, but you'll never get happy proper cos it's here –' he pounded his chest '– here in the Shire, the fucken Shire, mate, it's all about friends and family!'

'That's beautiful, Shoes, thanks for that, you're so right.'

'And go the mighty Sharks, mate, we got to get to some Sharks games. They're a tough team to follow, mate, forty fruitless years, but serious, come down to Shark Park with me and Nat one night, it's an experience, mate, an experience! Shark Park in the cold and the dark!'

Eventually Michael Shoes required a cigarette to go with his load and he and Natalie made their way outside – to my enormous relief. My brain was pushing against the front of my skull; I needed to put a litre of vodka in it now. Ideally, I would be lying on my bed, drinking from the bottle and listening to the birds of Bundeena, away from people and their need to tell me what I was missing. I was missing the divine reclusion.

I took a tall plastic cup off the drinks table and filled it with vodka, looking around to see if anyone had noticed this, bar staff or civilian, but as far as I could tell I was safe. I didn't really care if they did notice this act of blatant alcoholism, their thoughts of me were already painted with thick black strokes, it was more that I wanted to be alone while I drank it, and for a moment I was. Leaning on the bar I took a deep breath, closed my eyes and swallowed the clean liquid, and for seconds there was the calm I had come to depend on. Then I was tapped on the shoulder and spun around to face Nina and Eric, awkwardly arm in arm, smiling at me with some grotesque plea of desperation, as if I was the one who would make them feel comfortable again, the only one in the room who could take all the spikes away. Sometimes just looking into someone's eyes could be worse than death, when we got this close, when we got this far apart.

'You're looking so well,' Nina said, allowing her eyes to wander up and down the creased black suit that we'd hired from Kenrays on Caringbah Road. 'Don't you think he's looking well, Eric?'

I didn't know why *how we looked* and *how we used to look* needed to be such a featured part of the everyday chatter. I knew how I looked: bloated and red like a pig, like a boozer, like a burst tomato on a stick. I also knew that when I'd landed back here six months ago I was a pale and withering leper, with no flesh on my bones and no life in my eyes and still people said 'you look well'. I also knew that once, when Nina first knew me, I was a beautiful teenager with blue eyes and life abundant in them. I knew I didn't look like that anymore. I knew it well, I had the same access to mirrors that anyone did. Why didn't we just bypass the whole topic of looks and get into the real stuff of conversation? This was what I'd loved about Germany: those people in Berlin had no interest in small talk. If I commented on the weather or their hair they looked at me like I was a gay octopus, but if I asked them about their fathers, or the configuration of stars, or the importance of Heiner Müller towards a new German theatre, their eyes would light up and a truly satisfying conversation would inevitably unfold. Perhaps this was what a fraught history did; it slaughtered the trivial. But then these people around me, well they were also stricken with tragedy and pain. The small talk seemed to act as a helmet against the constant knock of it, a way of disregarding all the bleeding elephants in the room with talk of waves and halfbacks and house prices and 'yeah, no, sounds good'.

'He looks alright,' said Eric in a slow and melancholy drawl that reeked of oblivion, and I loved it: he didn't know, or care to know either.

'Eric and I have bought a property in Robertson, just below Bowral. We're going to call it Tommy's Farm, aren't we, Eric?' said Nina, and she still looked so fucking sexy to me, even with an increase of lines and wrinkles I still imagined bending her over some sort of bench with a blender on it. My love for her was true and full and never had it gone away, never had it even waned. Perhaps that was why over the past six months Courtney only ever visited me in Bundeena. She never wanted me at the new house, never ever suggested I come see Nina at her place, even though I voiced an interest in this in most of our phone dealings.

'You'll have to come visit us,' suggested Eric, and for the first time in my life of exchanges with Courtney's father I felt like this might just happen, Eric and I might just sit on that deck and share a brew and a conversation of sorts, because neither he nor I knew why we were back here, and that was something to share. Then Gordon clutched my shoulder and turned me away from the couple and I was before him once more, ready and obedient.

'Neil,' he said, military commander-like.

'Gordo,' I said back to him, in official attendance.

'Speeches recommence in twenty-five minutes, can we just have a brief chat about the run of things? I need your help.'

He shuffled me off into the chef's quarters where three Asian men lined up an army of chipolatas on floral-rimmed paper plates. Gordon told me to 'distract Courtney for a bit,' as he had something 'special' coming for her in about twenty minutes, just before my speech, and she 'can't get suspicious or it won't work.'

I nodded and told him he could rely on me to distract her, and I sensed it was only me who felt the enormous and ironic resonance of this. He said he knew he could rely on me, he knew this, and on his wedding day by the sea I wondered if and when he would smile. Was this not the happiest day of one's life? It looked tense from my seat in the stands, but who was I, and what did I know about what we should feel and when we should feel it? I was lurching dangerously towards the conclusion that as we aged, we cared less and less about what might happen, and whom it might happen to. We cared much less than we should, but we went about pretending that we cared the fuck out of each other in some vain attempt to obtain a sense of decency, because decency was purpose and purpose was light and without light the ocean said 'come here tonight'.

'You alright, G-Love?' I asked him.

'Yeah, man!' he snapped at me. 'Why the fuck wouldn't I be?'

'No man, it's such a beautiful day,' I said, remembering just how useless and foolish I was and how my words and actions had never caused anything but harm.

'Hey, Nelly,' he said, changing down a key. 'There's one more thing.'

'Yeah, man, anything,' I said.

'Regarding the speech . . .'

'Yes!' I said.

'Just . . . and I want you to say whatever is in your heart about Courtney and me, and about how much we mean to you and what we did *for* you and all, but, well, Albert's a bit worried you might get too creative or – what's the word he used? – "arty" about things, so . . .'

'Mate, you don't need to worry about me,' I said, and he immediately broke into my space with his apologetic hands on my neck.

'It's not me saying it! I feel like a dick saying it – I'm sorry I said it, you say what you *want* to, say whatever the fuck you want.'

'It's only a short speech,' I said, and it was, now that I had decided just to read out the start and the end bits and leave out the middle, the bit where I'd planned to quote from *The Princess Bride* and a bit of *Cyrano de Bergerac*.

'Short and sweet, mate, that's the name of the wedding game.'

'Hopefully not the name of the marriage though,' I said, but he did not laugh because he had not heard me, he was deafened by the sound and power of one man's wedding in his ears.

'Means a lot, you speaking at my wedding, mate. I love you,' Gordon said.

'I love you too, Gordon,' I said, and I did, more than all the sand outside.

'Righto, now go keep Courtney distracted while I prepare *my* show!' Gordon raised his thumbs and disappeared into the kitchen toilets.

I pushed out of the doors and back into the corridor of love-and-marriage to find Sarah Kirkwood standing alone with a packet of Benson & Hedges ultra lights open and flopped out towards me.

'Ciggie?' she said, flicking the bottom of the pack so that one of the darts pushed up in height, suggesting itself like a hand in a classroom of cancer.

'I'd love one,' I said, and we were all set to go outside when Oscar came barrelling towards me in a scream and leapt up onto my waistcoat. I clutched him to me and inhaled the sweet nectar of youth and enthusiasm and I was *feeling* again, feeling something in the manner of hope and it was disturbing, this feeling that life was worth living, and I tried to deny it but his fresh hair and ebullient grin were palpable. His mouth was smeared with dried chocolate and his eyes were razzed with the dance of sugar drinks; he would not sleep for days.

'We're going to run,' said Dad, plucking Oscar from my chest.

'But I'm up next,' I said to him, and like a shot I needed him to stay, I just *needed* him here so badly. Daddy, please don't go again – I'm trapped in the rain, I'm scared of monsters, don't leave me here Daddy.

'Up next what? You singing a song?' he asked with a wink, and I could hear Sarah scoff under her breath at this poor joke.

'No, I'm making a speech,' I said earnestly.

'Neil is the best man,' Sarah said in a reporter's voice, and it sparked my father's fuse, women didn't talk to men like that.

'I've heard him speak before,' Dad said, rocking from side to side.

'It's cool, Dad,' I said.

'Oscar's got to get home to bed; I'll be in the doghouse if I keep him up any longer than this.'

'It's only another fifteen minutes,' I pointed out.

'She's already called ten times, I had to jump through hoops to even get here, son – think of that, why don't you?'

'I should have invited Mum,' I said quietly.

'What?' he said, leaning forward to hear with a scowl.

'Well I had a choice between you and Oscar or Mum and Agatha as my guests, and I brought you because I thought you knew Gordon better, but you're not even staying for my speech, which makes me think I should have invited Mum and Ag,' I said, reaching for a lighter in my pants pocket.

'It's not all about your speeches, Neil. Maybe it's time you realised that.'

'What the fuck?'

'Don't swear around Oscar.'

'I'm not saying it's about my speech, I'm just saying –'

'Sounds like it. Sounds like it to me,' Dad said, crouching down and wiping Oscar's mouth with his shirt as he talked to me, and I can't remember him ever being that close to me when I was young, to my mouth with a wipe or a shirt of hygienic concern.

'I'm going to go outside and smoke,' said Sarah, so polite, and her back is strong and tanned as it moved away down the stairs of the surf club.

'Not a bad sort,' Dad noted.

'Dad, I want you to stay,' I said, turning back to him. 'I want you to be here to listen to what I have to say to Gordon, to my best friend who I built the house with. It's got a bit of you in it too, the speech, and it's funny, it's not weird.'

'Write it down for me, son,' he said.

'Dad, I swear it's not weird.'

'You'll understand one day about sacrifices, you'll understand the real world one day – I hope so anyway. Now go in there and enjoy your friend's wedding, and remember, it's their day not yours, ok?'

And with that he dragged Oscar away, up the grassy hill, underneath the metal handrail and over the road to his instructor's car. I felt gutted, but it sat familiar, a lifetime of exits just when I needed him most. And nothing would change it, not even Oscar with his chubby cheeks and golden spirit could fix this. And as his figure disappeared in the saline mist I allowed myself to give up on him and in doing so lost another chunk of my will to live.

Kirkwood was waiting for me underneath the outdoor shower recess; she pretended she wasn't by checking her phone as I arrived down the concrete stairs.

'Oh, it's you – all good?' she said, pushing off the wall.

'Yeah, I'm cool,' I said. 'I think I lost my lighter though.'

She lit my bent cigarette and I leant on the wall beside her and smoked, sucking in the tar and the ten million chemicals that respected me for who I was.

'That boy loves you,' Sarah said to me, with a teacher's smile.

'Oscar?' I asked, exhaling plumes of smoke and loathing for that man, my dad.

'Yes,' she said. 'He adores you, you're his hero.'

'He's a kid; anyone who is an adult is a hero to a kid.'

'No, he *knows* you,' she said. 'You're one and the same.'

'I hope for his sake you're wrong on that front!' I laughed darkly into the darkness.

She moved closer to me, and I became aware of the precious sweep of freckles that drifted across her squashed nose like a flock of distant birds. She was plain, but she was beautiful in that she knew it.

'You have the same cheeks and eyes; he could be your son,' she said.

'He's alright, that boy, he's pretty alright.'

'And you're beautiful with him, Neil. You're so natural with children, the way you talk to them, you don't patronise them, you just *see* them for who they are and you get on their level. You're going to be a wonderful father one day.'

Time stopped as I considered this, a pram and a barbecue, a baby seat and a trip to the zoo, first day of school, eat your peas, no balls in the house please.

'I'm so fucked up, Kirkwood,' I said, dropping my cigarette and my control too, tears streaming down my cheeks. I could not hold it in anymore; six months of drinking vodka on my own and repressing it all was bursting out of me.

'Hey, hey . . .' she hushed, as she brought me to her and her to me. I couldn't hold her tight enough, I couldn't cry hard enough, I couldn't need her more.

'Don't let me go,' I said, crying into her long neck.

'I won't, I'm here, baby boy,' she replied, gripping me closer, her thumbs in the caverns of my neck, pushing up then down so slow and deep and reassuring.

'I want to be something,' I said to her wet throat. I was buried in her and I would never leave, I would carry on in her normal, capable, compassionate arms. She would save me; she would balance this volcano with sense.

'You can be anything you want to be,' she said to me, her leg moving up and in between mine, alerting my cock and everything that rises.

'Will you help me?' I asked her, and she instantly pushed away from me. Had I stepped too far, misread this entirely? She is but a friend being a friend, and here was I asking for her hand to walk me down this cobbled path. But my paranoia was just that, as she took my face in her hands and stared deep into my eyes, tears welling and wobbling in her own brown globes as she spoke to me in a cracked voice.

'Neil, I'll be anything you want me to be. I love you, and Dylan loves you.'

And I wondered just how she *could* love me, what was this based on: a flirt and a couple of chats at the photo shoot, or was it our shared schooling experience? We'd hardly bonded there. Was this enough for love to rear its head, or was it just the cry of the lonely? Was this the voice of desperation, fearing a life of heated-up Lean Cuisine and unwooded chardonnay in front of the television alone as the baby slept in the nursery?

'We could be family,' she said, and it wasn't a question. 'Do you like me, Neil?'

I kissed her full on the mouth, and she moaned; she had not been touched since the beginnings of Dylan. With every section of hard kissing she pulled away and stared at me, moaning, breathing heavily, making sure it was a physical and actual man that she was kissing, that the face she was holding was not a mirage. My tongue was behind her teeth, I bit her top lip and she squealed, so I crashed into her arse with my left hand.

'We can make a home together,' she said, her hand on my crotch, stroking the length of my burgeoning cock through my trousers. Sex is family, sex is tomorrow, sex is security, sex is contractual, sex is death.

'Kids and a house,' I said, biting her ear, and rubbing my forearm between her thighs.

'You're with me now,' she said, and I kissed her flabby left tit, lifting it out of its strappy home. Her nipple between my teeth, I sucked hard and narrow until she cried out.

'Be gentle,' she said, 'I'm just a little thing.'

You're all sturdy netballers down here reared on baked beans and sausages in a can, don't play coy. I grabbed the front of her neck and forced her back into the shower recess wall, her eyes opened in fright as I scooped my arm down under her hem and further, beneath the tightly wound pantyhose. I found the outskirts of her knickers and they were wet so I slid my hand inside and pressed the top of her clitoris with two fingers – I'm going to fuck you against this wall until the future comes.

'Neil,' she said to me, 'we can't here.'

'We can do anything, Sarah. Isn't that what you said?'

As I pushed my fingers inside her pussy and coiled them up inside her, she rocked back, cracking her head against the brick wall. I tightened my grip on her throat; her windpipe worked hard between my thumb and fingers for breath and this was the magic place, this was the perfect oblivion, this was danger and I didn't care where it went from here.

'Neil, you're choking me,' she said, and for School Prefect I thought she would come up with something less obvious.

'I know,' I said, and I closed my hand tighter around her larynx.

'Neil,' she said, 'you're scaring me!'

'I'm scaring *you*?' I said, and for a second I blacked out then light returned.

Her neck was pungent now, a horrid cocktail of White Musk, baby spew and acrid sweat. I slammed its flimsy flesh back into the wall as the rest of my hand rose up inside her, she tried to scream but my nose and cheek were in her mouth, her legs tightened on my hand and her body froze as she went, quivering like milk, a foot above the ground, neck bent across the shower head, which fell across her crown like a metal fascinator. She looked dumb so I released her.

'Fucking hell, Neil,' she said, pulling herself together and reaching for any available air the sea or wind was willing to proffer.

'It's all good,' I said, and the rain fell like a tissue would fall, soft and wavy in the air, then to the ground without a sound, just as it did last night, when Courtney called me from the hotel and asked me to meet her down by the sea.

33

We were halfway through a Crowded House mega-mix when the Nokia 8210 Gordon had bought for me rang out beneath the folk. Gordon was on acoustic guitar, I was on vocals, and Albert and the rest of the boys were on percussion (saucepan and chopsticks). The groom and his men were all thrown in together, shacking up at Gordon's massive waterfront home, two miles from where the bridal party were gathered at the Rydges hotel in North Cronulla.

Albert had picked me up from the ferry wharf and driven me to Wanda Beach that afternoon, Gordon handing us a cold beer from a bucket full of cold beers the moment we stepped onto the balcony. I had intended to stay the night, as the restaurant we were heading to was across the road and there was no point travelling all the way back to Bundeena, plus the ferry wrapped things up at 10 pm and I had assumed the pre-wedding dinner would kick on till at least the small hours of the big day. Gordon loved a drink, and he loved to drink lots when he was proud, and he had never been more proud. The dinner was good, I had the lamb shanks, though it was the red wines I still remembered, and even though we were fuck-eyed and full as fuck, Albert still ordered six racks of Rib-a-licious ribs on return, which was when my phone rang, a landline number, from around this 9523 part of town.

'Hello,' I said, beneath the second chorus of 'Mean to Me.'

'Neil, it's me – it's C.'

I stepped away from the band, Gordon asking me who it was with his eyebrows. I waved him off with an 'oh just someone' gesture and tripped into the palm with a whisper. 'Courtney . . . wassup?'

'Can you come and see me now, please?' she asked, sniffling.

'What's wrong? Something wrong?' I asked, too pissed to hold the thing.

Gordon had stopped playing guitar and was watching me, intrigued by the way I hid the phone in my hair and neck. Albert was still beating the chopsticks on the pan though, which was annoying, the man had so little rhythm that even Crowded House's 4/4 ballads were a battle.

'Are you ok?' I asked.

'Just come. *And don't tell Gordon*,' she said, hanging up. Like in the American television shows, I stayed on the phone long after the call was over.

'Who fuck dat?' Gordon asked, strumming the first chords of 'Better Be Home Soon.'

'Ahhh, it's just someone from the thing . . .' I said.

'What thing?' Gordon asked.

'The Bundeena thing. Just to do with some . . . *kids* I'm working with.'

'What kids?' Gordon scrunched his fat face.

'You got a coat?' I asked, pointing inside.

'Hey, ya can't go out now – it's fucking belting with rain!'

'And we just ordered the ribs,' Albert added. 'Rib-a-licious!'

Albert kept tapping the saucepan as Gordon strummed the guitar with reckless funk.

I spun around in the kitchen, drunk as I could remember not remembering. I grabbed a North Face puffer jacket off the hook and turned to see Gordon in my face, wielding a beer and staring at me as I zipped up the puff.

'Where you going, Cronk?' he asked, eyes cracked and red.

'Got to do something.'

'Something what? It's the night before my wedding.'

'Yes, exactly. And I've got to go do a thing.'

Gordon shook his head at me, somewhere between pissed off and bewildered. 'What, man? Fucken spill it.'

'I can't tell you.'

'You *are* telling me.' Gordon held me there.

'Can you just let me go?' I pleaded.

'Just tell me where you're going. Albert and me were going to light a joint, get into some jam sessions – eat some ribs. My last night as a single man!'

'I really ... G-Man, I will be back so soon, I just have to do something and it's not important ... I just can't tell you because it's a surprise.' I lied well and he bought it better, chuffed his broken friend was coming good at this special time.

'I love you, Cronky,' he said. 'You know that.'

The ribs man was running from the car as I left, Albert banging on the pan in delight.

I bailed out the back door and into the sleeting rain to see my first-ever girlfriend.

The Rydges was big and there were many parts to it; you took one wrong stairwell you ended up in the staff car park, or the hotel kitchen or just some weird inexplicable bit. It was late and I was afraid of being spotted by the women, so I edged round the hotel foyer into the restaurant, where I ran into all of them enjoying Cosmo's beneath a rotunda. The women all screamed and waved, smoking like fuck.

Nina stood up instantly, concern flitting across her beautiful profile; she knew there was a reason for my presence. I told her, in a whisper, that Courtney had called me. She said Courtney had gone to bed an hour ago. I nodded as she gave me the room card, then I kissed her on the cheek and pretended to leave via the front door, waving to the bridesmaids and associated women-types, then darted behind the reception desk to the elevator.

The bridal suite was on the seventh floor. I slid the card in and opened the door and a warm rush of blood went up then down me. Heart-shaped pillows, white linen, an Arthur Streeton on the wall. Next to the bed were two side tables with matching ornate reading lights. On Courtney's side were her thick-rimmed reading glasses, Marlboro Light cigarettes, a Samsung mobile and a copy of *The Lovely Bones* by Alice Sebold. I snuck further into the room, and there it was. Hanging by the window, before a landscape of chunky, uncompromising rain and waif-thin bolts of yellowy lightning, was Courtney's wedding dress, swinging lightly in the frame of the large window like it had all but gone and hanged itself on its own. I could picture her in it, swaying and smiling like the pale angel she was. I stumbled towards the dress and held it to my face; it smelt like life. I moved my arm up inside the dress as far as it would go. I took out my cock and wanked it, feeling up the inside fabrics and textures of the gown. It didn't take long, there were layers of joy to aid me here; within a minute I let out a deep, primal moan, jacked on the carpet and left the room.

*

The beach roared loud from east to west, and nowhere a human, just black sky, white sand and ghostly, quivering figures in the wind, be they birds or actually wind. Wind making sand dance, or just wind. Every step I took confirmed the dumb drama of the situation. Why had she brought me out here, what game was this? She knew I was cosy with her man, nestled in booze and silliness, with our own kind, with good joy, big and good joy, and so she had to pull me out and make the night here, bring it back to womankind; weddings were all theirs, whether they wanted them or not. In this line of thought I considered returning to Gordon's place and abandoning the SOS altogether, but the memory of her voice on the phone gripped me, the weakness in it, the dislocation; that little-girl-lost sound threw me back down the shore every time I turned towards Elouera. I was all but on my knees, thumping the sand, when I heard my first name thrown out into the wetted air.

I followed the echo of that one strong syllable down the beach towards the rock pool where the sand ends and the esplanade begins. A figure formed fully in view, mingling with nature by the water's edge, yards of brown hair whipping about in the wind, hair that I had held in my hands and smelt. Hair so clean and flowing it would make my adolescent dick hard just seeing it in a scrunchie on Mondays in rollcall.

'Neil,' she said, softly, and the weather turned, like Nirvana did so abrasively from verse to chorus. The ocean was screaming now, cut up into pieces by a new, ungracious wind. And she was right there before me, in her drenched green cardigan that gripped her small breasts like cling wrap. 'Do you think I am doing the right thing?' she asked, tears in the pit of her eye sockets.

'What?' I asked, wiping my eyes to see her clearly.

'Tomorrow,' she said, pulling a length of wet hair from her mouth. The waves ripped, swung and danced behind her.

'What about tomorrow?' I asked. 'You're getting married.'

Her face twisted. 'Yes,' she whispered, as vulnerable as fruit.

'That's it, right?' I asked her, and she nodded. 'You love him,' I said and she did not nod. She did not shake her head either; she just stood there, inches from my frame, staring at my chin.

'I'm just so scared something bad will happen.' She started to cry and I grabbed her and held her against me, I could feel the toughness of her nipples, hardened by wind, against my ribs and I liked it.

'Nothing bad is going to happen,' I said. 'Not with you.'

'How can you know?' she said, pulling away from me, but hanging onto my shirt. She banged her fists against my chest. 'How can you know I won't have a boy and he won't go shoot his head off, or hang himself? How can I know that won't happen to me?'

'Because your son will be strong.'

'Tommy was strong, and he left. He's out there somewhere!'

It hit me, stupid me, why we were down at South Cronulla beach, right across from The Point and Shark Island where Tommy had surfed religiously, famously. She was about to do the biggest thing in her life, and without him.

'Gordon is so strong and you are so brilliant, your children will know themselves so well, things like that will never happen,' I said, and she let go of my shirt, turning away like it was all so ugly she simply could not look at it.

'Do you really think I'm pathetic for staying?'

'Staying where?' I asked.

'In Cronulla. For never travelling or moving to the city.'

'I used to,' I said. 'But now I wonder if I'm stupid for leaving. All I did was make silly shows and destroy a woman from the inside out.'

'You did more than that.'

'I think you're about to do all the things that life is really for, and whether you went overseas or not, this is the best thing.'

'You look down on me, don't you? Because I never left.'

'I could never look down on you, Courtney.'

'I had to stay. I needed to look after Mum.'

'I know that.'

The wind and the sea threw her hair up and with it all she knew.

'Do you think Tommy will come?' she asked me, retreating away to the rocks, all coy now as the storm hummed and simmered.

'To the wedding?' I followed.

'To watch me marry Gordon.' She climbed up onto the shelf, nearly slipping on the mossy rocks.

'He'll be watching,' I said and she laughed darkly, turning on me now.

'As if you fucking know,' she said. 'You just make it all up!'

I hated her suddenly, this game was fucked and boring and I just wanted to go back and eat the fatty ribs Albert had ordered and get more fucking drunk, but instead I followed her up onto the slippery rock shelf.

'You're a fraud,' she said, throwing a rope of seaweed at my legs. She was close to it, the creamy waves rushing up to her knees, pushing her forward and back like a reed.

'I told you everything he told me,' I said.

'Stop with the fucking bullshit, Neil! For one fucking second!'

My heart sank but at the same time I didn't care, I'd lost interest in what people thought of me, I was dead in that way too.

'Did Tommy say *any* of the things you told me?'

I shook my head.

'Did he say those things about Gordon?'

I shook it more.

'Did he speak through Stuart at all?'

I paused, looking down at my purple, shaking hands.

'I felt him there, I swear I did . . .'

She started crying; shaking her white and purple face at me. And then a wave pushed her down onto her front and her hands both split open on the barnacles, drawing out fast blood and one primal scream from deep down within the girl. I crept over to her, lifting off my hooded jumper and wrapping her hands in it, folding and rolling it over. Waves rolled past and through us. She lifted her face and stared at me.

'Come away with me,' she said. 'Let's run. Let's do everything we talked about when we were kids, let's just fuck off out of here and go, the two of us, seriously, let's go now, let's get the bus to anywhere!' She took my neck and gripped it hard. She would go too; I could feel it in the pulsing of her thumb.

'No,' I said, 'I can't do that to G.'

'You can lie to *me* though,' she said, 'about my *brother*.'

'I can't take you away, we're not kids anymore.'

'You are,' she said, 'the same gutless child.'

'Maybe,' I said, and she discarded my hand.

The night enclosed us, the seagulls squawked their discontent. Just let me die here on this beach and you can all eat me alive – Mum and Dad, the birds the teachers the waves the wedding party.

'I can't be here with you anymore,' I said. 'I have to go.'

'You *should* go,' she said, facing the sea again. 'After the wedding you should go away forever, and leave us all alone, don't call, don't write, and just disappear into thin air, please.'

I nodded at the holes in the rocks, then walked on up to Cronulla Street and took a cab to Bundeena. It would cost at least sixty bucks but I did not care about the money, I couldn't go back to Gordon's place, she was written all over me.

34

There was a wedding on and it was my duty to distract the bride. I walked back inside the surf club leaving Kirkwood to fix herself up. The walls were dressed with wooden plaques announcing the loyalty of club members, and framed black and white photographs of lifesavers lined up and reeling rope out to a buoy through their bare hands, chests puffed out, dressed in identical one-piece swimmers, a giant flag waving away in the wind beside – those halcyon days.

As I entered the hall heads turned towards me like clowns at the Easter Show and I wondered where my speech was, I could not feel it in my pocket anymore. Fuck, I'd just wing it: 'They're a beautiful couple, really complement each other, fire and rain, joy to be around, health and happiness, babies and Rottweilers.'

With this in mind I angled towards the drinks table to see my best friend vodka but Courtney was upon me, her hand in my armpit, her face red and flustered, she was in a flap but still, always, delightful.

'Gordon, I mean, Neil, where have you been?'

'Hey?'

'Where is Gordon? They're about to resume speeches and no one has seen him. He hasn't left, has he?'

I wished he had and I could take her away now.

'He wouldn't do a runner would he? We're already married! What's there to be afraid of?'

'Shhh, Courtney.'

'There's only one more song to dance to then the speeches!'

I took her hands in my hands and moved my lips near her ear. 'Well if there's only more song to dance to we better dance to it,' I said, and led her onto the floor without even waiting for her answer. I winked at the DJ who then pressed play on that Green Day song about having the time of your life, and our bodies were against each other, drifting clockwise to the melancholy riff. Her hair smelt like Wella Balsam and modesty as it flicked and feathered my nose and eyelashes. We were dancing now, and there was no one else in the room, it was true.

'Where is he?' she asked me, so quiet but somehow more harsh.

'He's not far,' I said, 'he'll never be too far.'

I prayed this song would never end, though I feared it was less than three minutes.

'And you?' she asked me, calmer now, her body dropping into mine for the purpose of this dance, this stalling waltz.

My eyes were closed and I was listening to her body move within this realm of ours; every shift in hand, every glance of breast on shoulder, every tilt of neck or spill of breath was mine and I would feel it all, as we both did on those glorious walks and wanders of our collapsed youth.

'Me?' I asked her. 'Where will I be?'

'Will you be far?'

'Last night on the beach you made it clear to me . . .'

'I always want you near me,' she said. 'That's what I hate about you.'

'I always want you near me too; even in London I missed you.'

'I missed you every day,' she said, and I believed her, though I could not see her face. I moved my hand up her back and circled her fine spine.

'What is it?' I said. 'What is this thing of ours?'

'Gordon worries about us, you know? He worries I will run away with you one day. That I will just wander off – even with children I'll run to you.'

'Can you see that?' I asked her, and in the perfect dark we spun.

'I love Gordon,' she said to me, in earnest.

'Why?'

'Because he will never break my heart,' she said, and it landed like a seaplane on a millpond, it just slid on in and rested there as truth.

'But is that love?' I said and there was no response, we just danced, spinning and prancing one step two step and back one two.

'I don't know,' she said. 'After Tommy I don't know what anything is.'

'Is Tommy with you now?' I asked her, and her breath faltered.

'How dare you ask me that?'

'Sorry,' I said.

'He is but he isn't, I don't feel him so much anymore, I don't feel *anything*.'

'But love? You said you feel love?'

'I feel disconnected to everything; it's all away from me.'

'Courtney, so do I. I feel completely disconnected from everything, I feel numb, nothing moves me, nothing reacts, nothing's there.'

'I know,' she said. 'I know you do. So do I.'

'Then what are you doing here?' I gripped her to know.

'Neil, don't,' she said, dipping her head.

'Fuck, Courtney!' I said, too loud, and the end of the track was near enough. I pushed her out in front of me and with the light ravaging my eyes I pleaded with her to make one true thing of all of this, one true thing and now.

'How?' I said. 'How can you feel that way and be here now?'

'I think,' she said, with a tear in one eye and a smile in the other, 'I think because I *am* disconnected, I *can* love someone, and *properly*,' she said to me. 'Because I can see them for who they are. We were *too* in love, you and I. Neil, it cannot work for any length of time. It's too much with you.'

'I'm too much?'

'For me, you are, yes, and I am ashamed to say it.'

'So you choose this instead?' I gestured to her dress.

'No,' she said, placing my hand on her stomach. 'I choose this.'

There was a child beneath my hand, and that was why she spoke of it last night by the sea, her fear of 'the kid' becoming like the rest of us failed fellows who were brought up on manicured lawns by idyllic beaches beneath the orb which draped us in golden sunlight – the blessed fellows who chose their own exit before it came to them, the lemming boys who wandered up the cliff and dropped away without a change of expression, blindly fading out in perfect unison, un-keen on what might come to bear on this land, in the mall, in the marriage, in the marketplace. She'd said she'd run away with me too, fucking fickle – you're fickle, you said, 'Let's go away from here,' and I should have done – I saw this now so clearly, I should have taken her hand, her new foetus, her big green eyes, and shown them somewhere else, but I only ever jumped when there was no netting, and I only ever stayed when the parade was on down the road, all I did was wrong here, and that was why I had to go, like how she said last night, 'away from here forever.'

I met her stunned and stunning face with mine and yes, I kissed her full on the mouth. There would be no speech, there would only be what was necessary, and in this world it was 'hello' and 'goodbye'. Her mouth opened up and I pressed into its wetness, my thumbs coasted over those cheekbones for the last time, and the disconnected were connected.

And then the sound of trampling feet emerged from the distance, mixed with the sound of old vinyl, scratchy and suggestive. I raised my head from the shelf of her lacy shoulder to see Gordon, dressed in a bright white Elvis outfit flickering with glitter and mad purple flares, skid out of the corridor and into the main hall. He wore a big black wig and his face was red with performance anxiety as he screeched to a halt a few metres before us and hit the first, ravaging line of the 1956 remake hit 'Hound Dog'.

The bass and drums followed in as the night turned slow before me. Gordon, my best friend, my pathologically shy friend, who had a conniption every time the teacher asked him to come up to the board, who never even sang the anthem out loud in assembly, who would rather fork his eye out than make a speech – was performing 'Hound Dog' in front of a two hundred strong crowd, and I couldn't help but feel it was for me, or against me. His voice was low and I guess it vaguely resembled the man, but still it was a struggle for me to watch him forcing out the rockabilly number with exaggerated choreography and iconic Presley affectations. It was gratuitous – for there was no need to be Elvis tonight, no need to impress her at all with this fat dead guy; you have won her already, my friend, with sheer perseverance and nobility, why the flamboyance? That's the way I tear things down, not you. And my heart sank further to my belly when halfway through the number he noticed the loaded, ripe expressions on my face and Courtney's, our hands still in each other's grasp, and the crowd that circled round us were not laughing, nor were they smiling, but staring open-mouthed at this repulsive controversy that took place when there was love in a triangle.

Gordon stopped and dropped his fake microphone before the guitar solo even took place. He gestured to the DJ to kill the track and there was silence in the room, but for the scraping of a couple of chairs on wood and a run of high coughs. Gordon's shoulders fell down in misery; he shook his head at the floor and I knew it well. Courtney dropped my hands and just stood there next to me, remembering her vows, and the dress she was wearing. He was smiling insanely at me but there was no surprise in his eyes. This was what he had expected. Then he cast his eyes over to Courtney, who whispered, 'Gordy, we were just waiting for you,' but he wouldn't be having this, the King would not fall tonight, or any night, so he hopped up onto the podium and grabbed the authentic microphone, which screamed and squealed in his sweating hands.

'Where do you think you're going?' he asked her and she stopped, turning round to face him. 'Everyone take their seats, please, it's time for part two of the wedding speeches.'

Courtney didn't move.

'Darling, take your seat. Now.'

She looked to me for direction but I looked away, crossing the floor to the drinks table which was crowded with people I knew, may know, didn't know, should have known or never knew I did know – but I would penetrate the forest of all, my need for vodka was beyond human understanding, I would eat their legs to get to it.

'Unchained Melody' came on as Gordon ordered us to find our seats. Kirkwood was with her baby on table 12 by the window but I did not honour her with any brand of look or wave. Was it true I had nearly choked her to death?

'Double vodka please,' I said to the pimply teenage girl behind the drinks table, my head between two women. One of them was Nina, and she turned to me.

'Nelly,' she said. 'Follow *me*.'

I took my drink from the girl and followed Nina into the corner with big reluctance in my steps. I could not take another berating, another moral judgment from the Bible-belted beach believers, and if she offered one I'd show my teeth.

'It's not your fault,' she said to me, 'don't go that way.'

And I was calm and I remembered her, she always looked between things, like a Buddhist she saw the pain behind the anger behind the action.

'What just happened?' I asked her, pulling on clear liquid as if for air.

'You lost,' she said to me, her compassion turning to scorn. 'Most of my girl's heart is made up of you, but you lost . . .'

'What?' I asked. 'How did I lose?'

'Like all men, you show no courage when it counts. You can cry at the football but you cannot handle us.'

'But Nina I'm no good for her – I'm a fucking wreck!'

'And there you go again – you *want* to be a wreck. God has given you the choices and you have thrown them all to the floor because it makes you feel *fucked up* and important, but you're not, Neil, you're just like the rest of us, but weaker.'

I was too hurt to speak. Where had all this come from? I was wearing my groomsman's outfit, I had my best-man speech somewhere, I just wanted to do what was right then go home and drink myself to death, like Jack Kerouac did, except my mother would not be joining me, she didn't believe in the practising dark. I hunkered down into my chest and closed my eyes and immediately the whole world spun in the blackness – all I could make out were these sparkling red lights, which were trying to form a shape, a face – in my head. Whose face was this? Stuart, is that you shaping up in my mind's eye?

'I'm sorry, Neil – that was terrible of me,' Nina said, and I was dragged back into the living land, where people were circling their chairs then sitting. 'We all adore you, Neil. I think I always adored you *too* much – I so wanted you to be my son, especially after Tommy left us. And I've had a few too many, it's all coming out – weddings, hey? They do it to us, *so* much emotion – too much!'

'It's ok, Mrs G, really . . .' I just wanted to go, and go, and go.

'You know our place is your place, always. You need a home-cooked meal, your washing done, or just some company. I know things aren't always easy between yourself and your mother.' She turned right in towards me now, I was the focus of her life and I liked this so much. 'We have two spare rooms now, and Eric and I would love to have you, I mean it,' she said, and I believed her. I could help with the maintenance, and just talk to her in the kitchen. I might even find myself in her bed one day, holding her while she cries, or pouring berry fruit whip all over her tits and sucking it off. I don't hate the idea – I always found it easier, the thought of fucking you, Nina, than the thought of your daughter's profundity, I always wanted to be between your legs. Can we go now, please?

'I love you, Neil, we all do,' she said, kissing me on the side of my mouth. My dick heated up and I wished she would not leave me here.

And then Nina was gone, and my eyes drifted up to the podium, where Gordon had the microphone in one hand and a Carlton Cold in the other, and he was staring at me, along with the rest of them.

'They call him the best man, but I'll let you be the judge of that,'

Gordon said, laughing at his own joke. 'Ladies and gentleman, my weird arty mate, the one and only, oh yes it's the glorious fuck-up himself, Mr Neil Cronk!'

35

After the house on a leaf was built, and my time at the rehabilitation facility ('Serenity in the Shire') was done, I rediscovered the art of fishing.

The past couple of months had reunited Gordon and I in the most glorious way but now the house was done I think we were both worried about how and when we would see each other – boat fishing was the perfect way to maintain the rebirth. Being men, neither of us would ever *say* how much the whole adventure had meant, but we knew it had, sitting there on that decking with a beer: me 'alive and well' with a house made of mud, brick and tin to show for it, a house we had built together on weekend breaks from the facility, adding the finishing touches over the Christmas holidays with the help of Albert, Graham, Shoes and some of the local Bundeena kids. Never had I known the extraordinary depths of man until this season, when Gordon Braithwaite single-handedly got his best friend off meth and into the property market and, inevitably, the water.

*

'Did it say high tide was at five o'clock, or low tide?' Gordon asked me, twisting a six-millimetre line between his fingers. 'Forgot that fucken chart.'

Courtney found it deeply amusing, the way we'd board the tinny at Lilli Pilli wharf and drive the thing twenty-five minutes round the headland all the way to Dolans Bay, parking it a mere ten metres from the rocky shore which still led up to that old cave I'd clung to so dearly in the whirlwind of adolescence – my solace hole, our hideaway. We could have driven, walked down there from the street and thrown a line out from the shelf, but we did it our way because 'boat fishing' was the dream and so it would be fishing from a boat. And the sport was apparently a lot more rewarding in other spots, like South West Arm and Port Hacking Bay, but we liked Dolans, it was ours, and as we hung our lines over the edge of our small vessel, memory and its warmth encased us, whether they were jumping or not we knew we felt lucky.

'Mate, I cannot for the life of me recall. High tide is better for fish, yes?' I asked him, resting back on the motor with an orange hand reel in my lap, its line pressed firmly over my index finger, ready to pick up any sign of action beneath.

Gordon loved our amateur approach to angling, tightening the bream hook onto his line and plucking a prawn from the bait box. 'I think high tide is better, yep – well I fucken hope so!' he said, bellowing laughter into the air, and surely scaring off the one dumb and hungry fish we had a chance with.

The sun bounced around inside and outside the scruffy clouds until twilight came to soothe us all. I opened a bottle of pinot noir and unleashed the cheese platter in celebration of a new arriving mood. It had been an hour since either of us had spoken, and even longer since a fish had appeared in our boat, but this was irrelevant, fishing had nothing to do with the fish, and our time together was not necessarily about talking, it was enough just to be here in the hobby, bobbing around on the wet stuff, together, and alive.

'This is a good wine,' Gordon said. 'Where'd you get on to this one?'

'I got it from the Bundeena Liquorland, it was only eleven bucks,' I told him.

'I didn't think you could get a good pinot under twenty dollars.'

We shook our heads and savoured the wine. It smelt like vomit and tasted like dead ants and strawberries, but something about it kept moving in your mouth long after the liquid was supped.

'You know,' Gordon said, peering up into the dotted spray of housing before us. 'Would not be a bad time to place something in the Dolans area, it's still a well-kept secret. I mean, listen to that Nelly . . .' and we listened. 'It's so quiet. You can't buy that kind of tranquillity in Cronulla no more.'

'It's special, that's for sure,' I said, crunching on a cracker topped with the crumbling and always delightful Mersey Valley vintage cheese.

'You know what we could do?' he said, his eyebrows hitting the roof of his scalp like they always did when he had a grand plan emerging, 'we could do what we did with your joint in Bundeena, buy a chunk of land – I mean, look up there, there's plenty of space – we buy a block and whack a little bungalow on it, two bedroom, fresh-water tank, priceless views. Mate, we could make a go of this, it's so cheap to build that kind of joint, you saw how easy we did your one!'

'Which I will pay you back for,' I added, eyeballing him for agreement.

'Mate, it was the land I spent money on, the rest was kids' play.'

'Yeah, but that's because everyone worked for free.'

'Not for free – for *me*!' Gordon said, winking at me cheekily. 'We need to make some plans, Nelly. You're in good shape now – we need to make a five-year plan. You ever read Richard Branson's book, the guy who created the Virgin brand? It's fucken inspiring, dude! That guy just did it *all* himself, didn't wait around, didn't listen to the negativity, he just stayed positive and got it done.'

'I've never read it,' I said. 'I should, but.'

'Business, travel, family, water views – these are all things we can have.'

'It's exciting,' I said, wishing we could go back to the serenity.

'Did you guys ever talk about it?' Gordon asked me, lowering his tone and scratching at his ginger beard with fresh discomfort.

'Did who?'

And he whispered now, into the bait bucket. 'You and Swanna, you guys ever make a plan for your life? Like a list of goals you wanted to achieve?'

I was taken aback. Never had Gordon addressed something so directly – never had he been *this* interested in the details of my past.

'We were never goal-oriented, no,' I answered, lighting a pre-rolled rollie.

'Right, you just went with it?'

I didn't answer, I just stared out into the stillness.

'Do you miss her?' he asked me, and I wondered who had sent him to ask these things of me. Was he working for 'Serenity in the Shire', had they planted a microphone here? My mother? Courtney?

'You don't have to answer, if it's too hard,' Gordon said. 'I'm just asking because I care about you, man, and if you ever wanted to talk about it . . .'

I smoked for a while and then I turned to him. My eyes were hot and my chest was thumping against its chamber, but I wanted to speak of her, I wanted to bring her back into this realm – this harmless estuary, she would like it here.

'I disappointed her, G,' I said, and a tear tumbled down my face.

'No, you didn't,' he said, refilling our plastic glasses with wine.

'You know what Mum said to me, when I left the last time to resurrect things with Swanna?'

'What'd she say?'

'She said, "Swanna has everything, Neil. She is attractive, she has talent, and you've been very good to her. What about Agatha and me?" She says, "We don't have men in our lives. We could do with a man around. It's very selfish of Swanna to expect you to come running every time there's a problem – what about us women at home?"'

'She didn't say that!' Gordon roared in disbelief.

'She did.'

'Did she know about the stabbing?'

'Yeah, man. She knew. I told her.'

'Wow,' said Gordon. 'If women don't get a man by the time they're forty, they go fucking nuts. Fuck, man, I mean – you guys lost a baby and all.'

'We never really recovered from that one. Aside from the meth and other things, that was what really killed us,' I said.

'It's a pretty full-on thing to happen to a couple, Nell.'

'It wasn't so much that event, I mean that didn't help; it was what happened before and after it. I'd been asked to go to Berlin, to meet people and see some readings, I'd been flown over by the Schaubühne and there were all these investors in Germany, people who wanted to throw money at me to make a work there – a work that could tour Europe maybe. I didn't even think of taking Swanna with me, even though she was my creative partner. She was pregnant and I – I don't know why, for the first time I wanted to go on my own. And when I was there I partied a lot and I started fucking this Swedish ballet dancer, she was young and she was just . . . free and young. I stayed an extra couple of weeks, making up lies to Swanna on the phone about workshops and readings and shit, and meanwhile I'm just taking drugs and partying with this girl. When I heard the news of the stabbing I was in bed, I was on GBH, this sex drug, and I was in bed in Kreuzberg. I never told Swanna any of what I had been up to, but she knew, she knew I didn't want her with me for a reason, she knew I was scared of the life we were about to make and . . .' The tears fell in rows now, but I would tell him all of it because then it would be out of me – no longer just sitting there chewing at my soul night and day. 'She always said that the baby was taken from us because whoever put it there knew we weren't *ready* for it. She said they took one look at me, and one look at her, and they severed all ties.'

'Well that's crazy,' Gordon said, and I got the sense he wished he'd never opened this up. 'That's just a chick being over the top.'

'She was right, man, I only ever liked the *idea* of children and family. When the reality came I ran away, and someone saw this, or her body felt this, and it was gone.'

'That's fucking nonsense, that's perfect fucking nonsense, Cronk, and you know it,' Gordon said, shaking his head adamantly.

'And you know what she said to me, when I finally got to the hospital? I asked her what happened, and she said, "It's gone," and I said, "I'm sorry," and she said . . . she said, "You look relieved". That's what she said to me.'

'Well she was probably under, man, and look, I mean she'd just been through a lot physically, you can expect a woman to lash out in that situation.'

'She's right, mate, I killed the kid – and the next one.'

'You keep on like that I'm going to throw you in the fucking sea!'

'Best thing you could do.'

'Cronk, I'm warning you, stop talking like a faggot, ok?'

'I'm sorry, mate,' I said. 'But you asked about my goals.'

We fished quietly as the moon made its first offering to the night, appearing as a sort of fucked-up white banana that a mouse had chewed a hole in, but on its travels managed to insert a row of forty-watt bulbs inside.

'You know Nina and Courtney worry about you all the time,' Gordon said.

'Oh yeah?'

'How does Nina put it? She says, "I hope he has not taken on any of the suicidal tendencies of his fellow artists or the friends he used to know." '

'She thinks I'm going to follow Stu and Tommy, does she?'

'She worries, but I tell her you don't have the balls.' G grinned.

'Ha ha,' I said. 'Cowardice, my saviour.'

We laughed and drank until the bottle was done and we felt stupid in the dark, catching nothing and shivering. As Gordon pulled the boat away I turned and took in the cave one last time, remembering the image of Stuart Stone standing there with his cock swinging back and forth in the early evening wind, and the way Courtney watched it, hypnotised by all it could be.

36

Wanda Beach was empty as I pushed out past the limit of the club, breathing in the air that hit me like a swinging sheet on a Hills Hoist. Left shoe, right shoe, get you off, then left sock, stumble, right sock off – my feet were in the sand. I flung my arms to the side and let the hefty breeze have me – and you can if you want to, lift me up and encourage my wings, I will go with you, please know that.

Sea mist swept over like a flying circus tent, and we will play beneath it, when he arrives down here and yes I know he will – always there to finish things, there will be playtime, two kids in men's bodies laughing big and bright at each other, love and rage in our eyes, teeth bared and knuckles up I assume. Why change now?

I made my way down to the shoreline which fell away steeply in the end. The water was cold around my ankles. I rolled my pants up to my calves as the remnants of a wave exhaled around me. This felt right, it felt right.

'Oi!' he cried, and it echoed shyly away from me.

I turned around to face the surf club but he was nowhere in sight, the mist had erased all but the venue, which made it seem even more glorified than it already was; 'the wedding.' Where was the rest of the world? I wondered. I knew of a church and a school and many suburbs beyond. I knew Forby Sutherland knew something when he arrived on his boat and saw it for the first time. He wanted to make a life here, a good and honest life. He wanted to stay and live and prosper in the sun. I closed my eyes and smelled the salt – I tried to imagine how it felt to be Forby Sutherland, and I was so close to knowing when Gordon pushed me in the chest and I fell onto the hard, wet sand.

'You fuck,' he said, hovering over me, the devil's Elvis except without the wig now. 'What's that about?'

'What?' I asked him.

'I call on you to make your speech, the *best man* fucking speech, and you take off – what's that bullshit, Cronk?'

I sat up and scrubbed my face and hair roughly with both my hands, like my dad used to do when he got out of the pool or the shower.

'I'm sorry, Gord, I just had to get out of there.' I looked up at him; it wasn't good enough. 'I couldn't hack it any longer.'

'Couldn't hack it? What *can* you hack, Cronk? Can you hack me paying for your fucken drug problems and building you a fucken house? Yes! Can you hack walking up on stage at my wedding and saying a few words? No!' Gordon spat on the sand and walked off a few paces to give his head room to shake in disbelief. 'Unbelievable, why do I bother –'

I stood up and screamed at his back, 'Well if you didn't fucking ridicule me in front of the whole audience maybe I wouldn't have!'

'Ex-fucken-scuse me?'

'You're up there with the microphone to introduce me, and you're saying shit like "Oh, I wouldn't quite call him the *best* man in the room, let you be the judge – hahaha" and "the genuine fuck-up himself" and all the other sly remarks you went on with!'

'They were jokes! What, you're the only one who can tell a joke, are you? You're the only one who can entertain people?'

'You entertained people! You sung a fucking Elvis song!'

'You . . .' Gordon walked towards me, placed the palm of his right hand on my forehead and pushed, but I did not fall; my head bent sharply over my neck but I remained upright, and with enough gravity to evade his follow-up shove. 'You *sabotaged* my Elvis impersonation and you know it too, you little faggot! I do *all* this shit for you – I build you back up again but you've still gotta be the high and mighty Cronk, don't you? Always star of the show . . .'

'It's not the case anymore, Gordon. Maybe it was once, but tonight, all I wanted to do was my duty, and –'

'This is what it is!' Gordon was clapping now, laughing and clapping madly. 'I fucked her first,' he said. 'I fucked her tight little pussy that you never got to fuck!' He clapped more, licking his lips. He ran right up close to me and whispered, so gently, so baleful, 'That's what really hurts, isn't it, Cronk? That I fucked her the first time and I'll fuck her the last time. That's what you can't quite handle?'

I shook my head and beamed it all back, smiling wider than Miranda Westfield – I will let you know it all now, on this beach beneath this busted moon, you will know it all tonight and then it will be yours to wrestle with for the rest of your life. I never wanted to disclose this secret, but if this is what it's always been about then I will meet you there, I will more than meet you there, my friend.

'Stuart took it, mate. Stuart Stone got there first. Long before you ever did.'

Gordon's face twisted and imploded, then his cheeks blew out and his eyes flared. 'Watch what you say, Cronk, I'll fucken do you – no hesitation – if you toy with me on this.'

'That night after the results party, after the gang brawl at Cronulla, you and I on top of your car on Captain Cook Bridge talking about monsters and moving away and shit, well that same night –' I placed my hands on my hips and spoke this right at him, so there was no mistake, no agenda, just the ultimate, unadulterated truth '– Stuart, our best and oldest mate, the loyal Stuart Stone, well that same night, at that exact same moment we were on the car, he was fucking Courtney in his bed.'

'No . . . no . . .'

'Oh yes . . . yes . . .'

'How do you know this?'

'Ask your wife! She told *me* all about it!'

'She didn't!' He was boiling now. 'Stone did *not* fuck her first!'

'Fucked her first he did; opened her up like a peach and did her in his bed and she *loved* it – she fucking loved every second of it and so did he. I mean, of course that's how it went, you dumb cunt – look at us, and look at him!'

Gordon was shaking on his feet, mute, and I'd never seen him capitulate like this before. Was he weeping? I circled him, and proffered more, goading him, enjoying the sight of this man crumbling.

'You thought it was yours, didn't you, G-Love? You thought it was in your hands, the big V, you got it, *claimed* it, won it fair and square! But no, you dumb fuck, you imbecile, you didn't think! Stuart Stone has her virginity, and he took it with him to the grave. Yes, that's right, Gordon Braithwaite Constructions, now it's up there in the heavens! And neither you nor I will ever know how it feels! And he is laughing at us right now, Stone is, he's lookin' down at us and laughing all rubbing his belly like the roaring lion that he is!'

Gordon's face was floppy so I slapped it with the back of my hand, and strangely enough it felt good. I got it now – the hitting of other men. I made a fist with my right hand, thumb poking out the end, and cracked Gordon's skull with it. My knuckles rang out in pain. Gordon's nose was bleeding but he still seemed unaware of the hits, of the world, of anything. He was in shock and if the wind changed he would stay that way forever. I squeezed his lips hard until he looked like a groper.

'I love you, Gordon,' I said, 'but you're an idiot.' I released his face and he fell onto the beach, motionless. I wondered if and when he would break out of this catatonia. 'You made me say it, you dumb fuck. I didn't want to say it!'

And then he looked up at me with a face I will never forget, the face of the boy I met in Year 8, fresh off the boat and seemingly mislaid, except the pimples were gone, replaced by scars covered in stubble – but I could see him and I'm sure he saw me. We had not made an inch of ground in all this time away, we were those small boys still, those brothers of the lost property, together forever.

'Do you think I should have married her then?' he asked me with profound uncertainty, and I saw, for the first time, that she herself never mattered to him, she never mattered at all, she was mere sport, a trophy, a ribbon to pin on his fat chest. And the rage arrived in me, and I would do what's required if I had to, I didn't fucking care for lives no more.

'If you don't know that,' I said, hovering over him, 'if you truly do not know the answer to that question, then take the ring off your finger and hand it to me.'

He didn't respond, he just held my gaze from beneath – half his face smashed with darkness.

'I said hand over that ring, you cunt, and I will take your place at that table beside her.'

He did not move. He did not drop my gaze.

'Hand it fucking over, Gordon!' I screamed and still he was inert, his shivering the only sign of life plus the muffled sound of chattering teeth inside his frothing mouth. I had had enough of him and his null and void, so I reached across and grabbed his ring finger, but with the momentum of my lunge he pulled me down beside him, my head thumping into the sand.

He flipped on top of me now. He was behind me and on top of me, pressing his thighs against my thighs. All I could hear from my place within the sand was a low, guttural groan, like that of a bear. With his knees trapping my knees and his elbows in my armpits he slid his thumbs alongside my skull and pressed into my temples. My skull was soft; it folded in like petals on a wilting rose. My brain was in danger as its encasement collapsed.

'I am the only one,' I heard him mutter through the particles of sand. And it had come to this. All the moments of beauty and friendship and shared struggle to now: your wedding to my first love. Your big greed, your strategy, your never telling me Stuart was gone until you arrived in Bathurst and he'd been dead three days. You *are* afraid of monsters. You were always afraid of the monsters; they never went away for a minute – did they, Gordon Braithwaite?

With his fingers in my scalp, bracing his attack, Gordon's thumbs pressed deeper into my temples. I could feel my brain about to burst out my skull and when I tried to scream I had no amplifier. I lifted my thighs to kick him but he had the back of my legs locked to the shore with his corking knees. He went deeper and deeper now, digging into the centre of my head as he wheezed and moaned in ugly pleasure. Gordon wanted to squeeze the very mind out of my head and onto the sand for the seagulls to devour, that was if the waves didn't drag it back down first. My crazy threat of a brain, he wanted it gone from here once and for all.

'You don't belong here,' he said to me, and then it all started pulsing and strobing then stopped.

In the blackness Stuart's face gradually formed in red sparkling lights, then his body, fully formed, in that same white suit – and it wasn't a lie! I hadn't conjured him! He was curling his finger and mouthing, 'Come with me.' Swanna! Courtney! It was not a projection, it was never fiction, this is death for real! I reached out to touch him but as soon as I did I was sucked out of the afterlife and my mouth was full of sand again.

Everything was sideways: the beach, the clubhouse, the shiny street. Gordon was barely visible in the passing mist, washing his hands under the tap that pushed out of the wall beside the roller door to the garage full of surf skis and life rafts, swimming caps and rope, a red rubber speedboat. Whether there was blood on his Elvis cape I'll never know, all I *did* know was that they were married, and that they would go on to have children – one boy, one girl, no, surely more? And they will live across the road from where I lay my throbbing, broken head. And Gordon will smile in the knowledge.

The wind whipped me up to standing and I wondered if Courtney was curious as to my whereabouts, or if she was merely getting on with her night. She was dancing probably, with her hands out in front of herself, fingers clicking to the every-second beat.

My suit was ripped and there was blood in my saliva. Every breath in my brain punished me with an agonising jolt of pain, as if Gordon had set a tripwire in there, and enclosed it forever. I watched him as he took the wooden steps up to the surf club and he was a hero. The hero returning to his wife – back from the jungle. Gordon, my brother, my best friend, you are my hero and I love you more than you will ever know. Congratulations Elvis.

Slowly, I turned away and the ocean was black and simple before me, like a giant door I could so easily step inside. Yes, I will go through now, please. I took my jacket off and laid it down on the beach, sleeves folded in like it was in the shop. I moved down the bank and back into the short water. It wasn't so cold on my feet anymore; the wind had dropped off, it was almost warm now. I continued walking, wading further into the water. Eventually the wetness gripped the under-skin of my balls but it was ok, not how it usually felt, not so alarming.

The ocean floor gave way and I was up to my chest in it now. I did not bother raising my arms, I just impelled myself further into it, swallowing the occasional section of splash and tide. I could not go any further with my head above the line so I stopped and took my final look around. I was not hesitating, merely savouring the last moments of life, and it felt weirdly euphoric, gazing across the endless skin of the ocean, but in the end it was just dull.

There's something so appalling about living, something so greedy and grotesque. The space we take up, all the noise we make, the air we demand; who are we to think we are entitled to it, who are we to think our sound is pleasant, that we are worthy of breath.

This was bravery, this was clarity, this was sense made. It didn't feel like a lot but it didn't feel like nothing either, it just felt smooth.

I closed my eyes forever. I closed my eyes and counted to three. I counted one. I counted two, and then I counted three.

Ok then. I'll come to you now.

I breathed in and pushed up off the ocean floor, launching way above the surface into the night air like a shuttle, and as I fell my scalp became remarkably cold. I was just about to plunge down into the trapping wetness when a horn tooted out from the distance. I quickly shut my mouth, kicked out my legs and began treading water.

And it is just how I dreamt it.

Way out on the far edge of the horizon I spot an oil tanker. It is sitting there against the wall of the world and it is flashing with red and white light. Is that you Stuart? I ask it to honk its horn again for me but it doesn't. I ask it once more to toot that thing, toot and I might stay a while, but it won't. It's just a long steel boat, nothing else. I hang my head back, kick my legs out in front of me and float a little. Soon I will give way to the currents and rips, let gravity win and slide down into the next place, but for now I am resting in purgatory. The last time I lay on water was all the way back then. At White Rock, in the first days of Swanna. Where are you now? I hope you're full of love and home. Please know that this is not you. Please know that this was always me.

The water is even warmer now as it spills across my torso, my chin and up my nose. I turn my head towards Cronulla and the lights twinkle as if winking at me; there must be people inside those houses and apartments. Courtney, do you agree? There are people about and they're living and thinking and listening to music. Is my mother beneath one of those lights? In the sitting room reading the *Herald* or simply eating salted peanuts and worrying. Mum? I don't even know how I got here. And then I think of Oscar. That buzzing ray of light and openness. What will he say when my body arrives all purple and exploded – what will he do when he gets here himself, and there is no one to tell him that it is ok not to know the way.

I never was a swimmer but I know how to fight. And the sound of water, well I can hear it now. I take a deeper breath, move my arms and feel a little older.

Acknowledgements

To my sisters and my father, for the ongoing support. To my agent and mate Jean Mostyn, for pushing me on when I was calling the bank for a loan so I could pay back the advance. To everyone at Pan Macmillan, especially Emma Rafferty, my editor, thank you for the sharp notes and positive vibes. To the wonderful Alex Craig, my publisher, whose fault this is, I thank you dearly. To Christos Tsiolkas, for your generosity and wisdom. To my mum, who read all the drafts, thanks for your honesty and love, and finally to Jonnie, for sleeping outside churches with me.